ONCE IN, NEVER OUT

"Mahoney doesn't sell his readers short. He keeps the action moving."

—*Chicago Tribune*

"Mahoney . . . knows the drill on conducting a manhunt . . . and he takes us through the crime-scene photos, the morgue visits, the criminal profiling, the computer searches, and all the rest of it with scientific precision and absolute authenticity."

—Marilyn Stasio, *The New York Times Book Review*

"Gripping . . . With absorbing exotic background and richly developed characters, Mahoney . . . delivers an unusual procedural that rises far above the genre norm."

—*Publishers Weekly*

"Succeeds wonderfully . . . A superb effort from an emerging master of the genre."

—*Kirkus Reviews*

"A nonstop roller-coaster ride of a thriller . . . Fast-paced and lean."

—*The Irish Echo*

HIGH PRAISE FOR THE NOVELS OF DAN MAHONEY

THE PROTECTORS

"Mahoney . . . has the procedural elements locked down tight, and in McKenna and Cisco he has created a pair of the most likeable dangerous cops in current crime fiction. The locales—New York City and Spain—are nicely rendered, and the conclusion is both surprising and satisfying."

—*Booklist* (starred review)

"Mahoney is a retired cop who writes his mysteries with colorful style and dramatic flair."

—*Publishers Weekly*

THE TWO CHINATOWNS

"*The Two Chinatowns* has clearly been written by an author with real procedural experience . . . The main virtue of Mr. Mahoney's fine detective story is the strength of the illusion it sustains that things could have happened almost the way they happen in this book."

—Richard Bernstein, *The New York Times Book Daily*

"Mahoney . . . knows the nuts and bolts of a sweeping multi-jurisdictional police operation. He is also able to portray complex, believable characters struggling mightily with their own muddled lives. Fans of William Caunitz, Robert Daley, and Ed McBain will savor this top-drawer procedural."

—Wes Lukowsky, *Booklist*

"A complex plot is no deterrent to enjoyment of Mahoney's ambitious thriller . . . Mahoney's characters are always solid, and this tale is almost a primer on Chinese community dynamics. He pulls no punches and speeds to a perfect ending."

—*Publishers Weekly*

MORE . . .

BLACK AND WHITE

"Mahoney gives compulsive procedural buffs exactly what they crave."

"*Black and White* is as gripping a novel about a police investigation as you can get . . . a top-notch thriller."

"Few authors map the political minefields faced by cops on a high-profile case with more realism than Mahoney . . . a brilliantly twisted plot."

"Exact and fascinating."

"Compelling, graphic."

"Mahoney does a great job of showing us an insider's view of a cop's world."

"Mahoney . . . draws on his 25 years as a cop to provide blow-by-blow description of how homicide detectives do their job."

"Suspenseful . . . graphic details . . . the finale is a shocker."

THE
PROTECTORS

Dan Mahoney

St. Martin's Paperbacks

THE PROTECTORS

Copyright © 2002 by Dan Mahoney.
Excerpt from *Justice* copyright © 2003 by Dan Mahoney.

ISBN: 0-312-98387-5

Printed in the United States of America

St. Martin's Press hardcover edition / August 2002
St. Martin's Paperbacks edition / August 2003

St. Martin's Paperbacks are published by St. Martin's Press, 175 Fifth Avenue, New York, NY 10010.

10 9 8 7 6 5 4 3 2 1

ONE

Although he was actually seventy-six, Henri Picard appeared
to be a sixty-year-old man in excellent condition. He was
tall, had a full head of gray hair cut short, and his posture
and bearing further belied his military training. His suit
jacket was buttoned closed, his tie was square at his neck,
and the creases on his pants were razor-sharp. He stood next
to the armored old Mercedes with his hands clasped behind
his back in a modified position of parade rest.

The butler opened the door, waved to Picard, and held up
two fingers. Picard understood, and nodded. La Tesora, the
treasure, was almost ready to leave, and would be out in two
minutes.

Picard didn't like that. To avoid those damned press photographers, Carmen wanted to get to the church early. She
hoped to be sitting in her pew before they realized that she
had arrived. She hadn't told Picard of her new plan, however,
and she was altering his. Pamplona was an hour away, and
Carmen was attending the eight-o'clock mass. He had arranged for an escort from the Guardia Civil to meet them at
the front gate of the estate at six forty-five. Unless they were
uncommonly conscientious, they wouldn't be there yet.

Picard got behind the wheel, turned off the heat, and then
used the car phone to call the front gate.

The gate guard picked up on the first ring. "Ernesto speaking, sir."

"Are they there?" Picard asked.

"Not yet, but it's early," Ernesto answered. "They've still got twenty minutes."

"They've got two."

"She's ready?"

"Just about. Any traffic?"

"Last car passed half an hour ago. Six-ten."

"Open the gate, and call me if they get here," Picard ordered. He then dialed the desk officer of the Guardia Civil barracks in town.

"Sargento Astuvo, Jaca Barracks. How may I help you?" the sergeant said.

"Good morning, Sergeant. This is Henri Picard. Where are your men?"

"En route, Señor Picard. Is there a problem?"

"Yes, but it's not your fault. We're leaving early. Get them on the radio, please, and find out where they are right now."

"Hold on, señor," the sergeant said. He came back on the line a minute later with the information. "They just passed kilometer marker fifty-three. They'll be there in ten minutes."

Fifteen minutes, unless they're driving like madmen, Picard thought. The estate was near kilometer marker 29, so their escort was still twenty-four kilometers away. The road from town wound through the Pyrenees foothills, and Picard couldn't think of a place along the route where he would drive more than eighty kilometers per hour. "Tell them to slow down. We'll meet them at marker fifty."

"As you say, señor."

At that moment, the butler again opened the front door, and Picard was surprised to see that the normally staid man was smiling ear to ear. Then Carmen appeared in the doorway, and the way she looked and the way she was dressed prompted Picard to smile as well. He thought that one year of black would have been appropriate for the death of her husband, and two years was more than enough. Five years was just too long for a beautiful woman to grieve and shut herself off from the world, and he had told her as much at dinner the day before. Carmen had finally listened to him.

Carmen stopped to kiss the butler on the cheek and shake his hand. After twenty-five years of service, the man still hadn't gotten used to Carmen and her ways. The richest woman in Spain was also the nicest and most gracious woman in Spain, and she considered her staff to be her family. The butler blushed, as Picard had known he would, and bowed awkwardly.

Carmen didn't appear to notice the man's discomfort as she walked down the steps. Picard got out of the car and opened the rear door, but he suspected Carmen wouldn't be getting right in.

He was correct. She stopped and did a slow turn for him so he could inspect her outfit. "Are you happy now, Monsieur Picard?" she asked, smiling.

"Tesora mia, you have made me the happiest old man in the world. I am so glad I have lived to see you so beautiful once again."

"Do you think this green is a little too loud?"

"Not at all, it is perfectly your color. You will turn every head in Pamplona today."

The smile left Carmen's face, and Picard thought for a moment that he had said the wrong thing. Carmen knew that she was beautiful, and she had long since become accustomed to being the center of attention wherever she went. Unfortunately, she had also become painfully shy and self-conscious since Hector's death. Her public appearances were rare, and the compliments she used to accept as obvious truth now made her uncomfortable.

But not this time, Picard was relieved to see. The smile returned to Carmen's face. Then she spread her arms and he hugged her like a child. "Isn't it such a beautiful day?" she asked as he patted her back.

"It is, with you in it. Is this new look just for today, or have you finally decided to live again?"

"I've decided to do whatever you tell me to do, just like

the old days. We will be happy again, God willing."

"For you, God must will it. At least one of his saints is entitled to be happy in her lifetime," Picard said softly, knowing she would protest. He loved Carmen like a daughter, but he had other feelings for her that always made her uncomfortable whenever they surfaced. She was a deeply religious woman, and Picard was certain she was a living saint; therefore he worshipped her, and thought it likely that statues of Carmen would be placed in churches all over Spain soon after her death.

And Carmen did protest his sacrilegious observation, but not at first with words. She pinched his back, and he released her. "Monsieur Picard, you will never change," she said with a pout, and then she stared at his face and again smiled.

I really have become a silly old man, Picard thought, conscious that Carmen noticed the tears forming at the corners of his eyes. She used her scarf to dab at his eyes, and then she kissed him on the cheek and got into the car. "Is Ernesto at the gate this morning?" she asked when Picard put the car in motion.

"Yes."

"I'd like to speak with him."

"Certainly." It took Picard two minutes to reach the front gate of the estate. Ernesto was standing outside the gatehouse, waiting for them with his head bowed. Like Picard, Ernesto also considered Carmen to be a living saint, but there was a difference between the ways they regarded her. Ernesto was built like a bull, and he was tough and fearless, but he was also very religious. For reasons Picard could only guess at, Ernesto never looked directly at Carmen's face.

Picard suspected that Ernesto's attitude bothered Carmen, but she had never mentioned it. He stopped next to Ernesto, and Carmen rolled down her window. Ernesto waited in the manner of the old peons, with his hands held in front of him and his head bowed low. "Good morning, Doña Carmen," he said in a low voice.

"Good morning, Ernesto. Tomorrow is your Graciela's birthday, isn't it?"

"Yes, Doña Carmen. How kind of you to remember. She will be six tomorrow."

"Six already? How time flies," Carmen said. "How is she doing in school?"

"Well. She is making me too proud, I fear."

"Has she many friends?"

"Many."

"Perfect. We must have a party for her tomorrow, if that's all right with you and your wife."

Ernesto appeared shocked at the idea. "A party here?"

"Of course, here. Our house will be a happy place once again, and I think a party for Graciela is a good way to start," Carmen said. Then she reached into her purse, took out an envelope, and gave it to Ernesto. "Please tell Graciela not to be insulted. I had thought she was going to be four, so I made the card for a younger girl."

"You made her a birthday card, Doña Carmen?" Ernesto asked, holding the envelope to his heart.

"I made her many, but I think that one came out the best. Please get together with Monsieur Picard this afternoon and make the arrangements. I want this to be a party she will remember."

"Yes, Doña Carmen. You have honored me and my family."

"As you have always honored me by your loyal service. We'll talk again after you and Monsieur Picard have drawn up a list of things you'll need."

"Yes, Doña Carmen. Thank you, Doña Carmen," Ernesto said, bowing again.

Picard made a left on the two-lane highway leading south toward Jaca, and he was sure of two things. Since Carmen was generous to a fault, Picard knew that besides the card, the envelope also contained thousands of pesetas. He also knew that the birthday card made by Carmen would be revered and passed down for generations in Ernesto's family.

Picard checked the rearview mirror and saw that Carmen had decided on a nap. Ten kilometers behind them were the snow-covered Pyrenees and France, clearly visible on that beautiful spring morning in one of the most scenic parts of Spain. At that altitude, the countryside was sparsely wooded, but they would soon be in a lush pine forest as they descended to Jaca. Ahead lay La Llanura, Spain's great central plain, and Picard could sometimes see it in the distance as he rounded curves in the road. There wasn't a cloud in the sky, and all indications were that the beautiful day was going to get even better.

Carmen deserves this weather on this special day, Picard thought. The village priest from Jaca usually came to the house every day to hear Carmen's confession and hold mass for her in her chapel, but today would be a different sort of mass. It was Palm Sunday, and the renovations to the old Basque cathedral in Pamplona had been completed just in time. Carmen had paid for it all, and was even having the cathedral's dilapidated parochial school renovated in the summer. The work had taken ten months, and Carmen had never once visited the project, so today would be the first time she would see the difference her money had made to the ancient cathedral of the devoutly Catholic Basque people of Pamplona.

Picard checked the rearview mirror again at a straight stretch in the road, and he saw that there was another car about a half kilometer behind him, and getting closer. He didn't like that; the road leading from Jaca to the French border was ordinarily little traveled, and Picard didn't believe in coincidence. He loved the old Mercedes, but knew its limitations. The engine was powerful enough, but the weight of the armor plating made the vehicle difficult to operate at high speed in turns. He increased his speed as much as he dared, but knew the car behind would soon be in position to overtake him if the driver had any skill behind the wheel.

The driver did have skill, and more than Picard expected. There was a straight stretch in the road at the Kilometer 36 marker, and by the time Picard had passed it, the car was only a hundred meters behind him and still closing fast. Picard saw something else he didn't like. The car was a late-model red BMW; although Picard thought the BMW was a fine motoring machine, he had years before grown weary of the people who drove them, and believed that BMW owners, as a class, were the rudest people on the road.

The driver of the car behind did nothing to alter that belief. He flicked his brights repeatedly, indicating that he wanted to pass. The road was winding down the foothills once again, so Picard ignored him. However, he did take one precaution, removing the 9 mm Beretta from his holster and placing it on the seat next to him. He checked his rearview mirror again. The driver of the BMW was still flashing his brights, and Carmen was awake and staring out the back window. Picard could see that the driver was middle-aged, with a mustache and a full head of black hair, and he was wearing a red shirt that matched the color of his car.

"Can you see the plate number?" Picard asked.

"Yes. It's SS nine-one-four-six-two."

Picard didn't like that, either. The "SS" prefix meant the car was registered in San Sebastian, the heart of the Basque Country. The beautiful city was also the power base for the ETA, a terrorist organization that had been blowing up Spanish politicians and murdering members of the Guardia Civil for twenty years in its bid to win independence for the three Spanish provinces that comprised the Basque Country.

Kidnapping was another ETA stock-in-trade tool, and Picard recognized that Carmen was a perfect target. Although they were both Basques—he a French and she a Spanish one—it was generally known that Carmen was the most generous contributor to the peace movement Vascos Contra la Violencia—Basques Against the Violence—an organization that had garnered the support of the majority of Basques in recent years.

Picard had the number of the Jaca Barracks on speed dial, and he called it. Once again, Sergeant Astuvo answered the phone. Picard told him about the BMW, gave him the plate number, along with some terse instructions and a request. He wanted the Guardia Civil team at kilometer marker 50 to proceed to marker 45, he wanted them out of the car and ready for action, and he wanted to know if the BMW was stolen.

"Yes, sir. One moment, please," Astuvo said. It was another minute before he came back on the line. By then, Picard was passing kilometer marker 39. The BMW was right on his tail, and the driver was still flashing his brights. "The car hasn't been reported stolen, and my unit will meet you at marker forty-five."

"Thank you, Sergeant. I hope I'm not creating a tempest in a teapot," Picard said. "In any event, I'm going to stay on the line until I meet your people."

"Yes, sir. Understood."

There was another straight stretch of road between markers 41 and 42, and the BMW tried to pass the Mercedes at that point. Picard decided to let him. He picked up his pistol, slowed down, and got as far right as he could. The driver of the BMW didn't give Picard the slightest glance as he passed. Instead, he concentrated on the road ahead as he accelerated and quickly disappeared from view.

Must be doing more than a hundred kilometers an hour, madness on this road in any car, Picard thought as he let go a sigh of relief. Then he picked up the phone and told Astuvo that the BMW had passed.

"Do you want my men to stop it?" Astuvo asked.

"No. Let the driver kill himself without any official help."

"Let's hope he doesn't. I don't know if I should be telling you this, but I checked that car out a bit more. The owner is a San Sebastian cop."

"Then he's an idiot cop, but there's no need for this to go any further."

"Then it won't go any further," Astuvo said.

Picard ended the call, and came upon the green-and-white Guardia Civil car a moment later. It was parked on the southbound side of the road at the kilometer marker, with the front of the car facing Jaca, and, as Picard had instructed, the team was out of the car.

Picard knew both of the cops, Ricardo Brizuela and Alexander Vargas. Both were seasoned veterans with the Guardia Civil, which meant they had seen more than their share of action while working in the Basque Country years ago. When Spain was ruled by Franco, the Guardia Civil had been one of the principal means he used to oppress the Basques, their language, and their culture. The force had been universally despised by the Basques, and with good reason. However, things had changed for the better since Franco died, and the Guardia Civil had become a kinder, gentler police force that, except for highway patrol duties, had been largely withdrawn from the Basque Provinces.

Picard pulled in front of the police car, and the two officers approached. "Sorry we weren't at the house to meet you, Señor Picard," Brizuela said. "We didn't come on duty until six."

"Nothing to be sorry about. Not your fault," Picard said. "What did you think of that BMW?"

"Got him on radar. Passed us doing ninety-seven kilometers an hour, and he didn't even slow down when he saw our car," Vargas said. "Just gave us a wave and kept going."

"He's not going to last long, and we can't imagine where he could be coming from," Brizuela added. "We called the frontier, and he didn't cross the border this morning."

"Strange," Picard said. "There are very few houses between here and France, and nothing I'd consider a point of interest. Did you hear that he's a San Sebastian cop?"

"Yes, Sergeant Astuvo told us," Vargas said.

The two cops got in their car and followed the Mercedes for another two kilometers. At that point, the road ran steeply downhill. Straight ahead was a stout stone wall that guarded a scenic vista of La Llanura. The road curved to the right to hug the hill, but the BMW hadn't made it. The car had plowed into the stone wall and bounced off so that it blocked the road. The driver's door was open, but the airbag had deployed and he was pressed into his seat, motionless, with his seat belt still on.

Picard stopped the car and inspected the scene twenty yards in front of him. From the looks of the damaged front end of the BMW, he estimated that the car had hit the wall at about sixty kilometers an hour. Since there were no skid marks on the road leading to the point of impact, he immediately suspected a trap at a perfect spot. To the left was a guardrail, and from there the hill dropped precipitously for a hundred meters. To the right were pine trees and boulders, a good spot to hide an ambush party.

Although the man behind the wheel was wearing a red shirt, Picard also suspected that he was not the driver who had passed him. He put the Mercedes in reverse, and looked behind him. The Guardia Civil car was blocking him. Worse, Brizuela and Vargas had just left it, and were walking toward him.

"Get down, Tesora! It's a trap," Picard shouted, an instant before his suspicions were confirmed. A rocket was fired into the Guardia Civil car from someplace on the hill to their right, and the car exploded in a ball of flame. The force of the explosion rocked the Mercedes, and picked up both Brizuela and Vargas and hurled them off the road, Brizuela to the right and Vargas to the left. Brizuela hit a tree and fell motionless to the ground, but Vargas fared worse. He was thrown over the guardrail on the left side of the road, and tumbled down the cliff.

Then the ambushers closed the trap. Armed men left their hiding places in the wooded hill on the right, and they took up positions to block any escape. In front of him, Picard saw three men take cover behind the BMW. Two were armed with AK-47s, and the third had a Soviet-era rocket-propelled grenade launcher aimed at the Mercedes. Picard knew the RPG as a nasty weapon, but was still surprised at how effective it had been against the Guardia Civil car behind him. Incendiary grenade, he figured. Because of the smoke billowing from the burning vehicle, he couldn't see the road behind him, but he was sure that avenue of escape was also blocked by other armed men, at least one of whom would be armed with another RPG. He thought that the armored Mercedes might be able to withstand the blast, but the car would certainly be incapacitated.

Picard examined his options, and found none that

wouldn't risk Carmen's life. It had been a well-planned, well-executed ambush, and it was time to surrender. The only bright spot was that the ambushers were wearing ski masks pulled over their faces, so perhaps they planned to let him live. After all, he was a Basque, he couldn't identify them, and they might think he posed no danger to them. If so, that would be their first mistake, Picard resolved.

There was a danger that the fire would spread to the Mercedes, so he put the car in neutral, let it roll slowly downhill to the BMW as the men in front kept their weapons trained on him. Then he shut off the ignition, opened his window, threw out his gun and the car keys, and turned to face Carmen.

Carmen was on her knees on the backseat, her face pressed to the rear window, staring at Brizuela. "We must help that officer," she said, so calmly that Picard wasn't sure that she realized what was happening.

"I'm sorry, Tesora. If he's not dead already, he soon will be," Picard said. "When that happens, don't watch."

"He's alive. I think I saw his leg move," Carmen said, and then she turned and sat. "Monsieur Picard, we mustn't let them kill him."

Her eyes were wide, but she didn't appear to be afraid.

"Then we'll do what we can, but we only have a moment to talk. They are going to take you, Tesora, and there is nothing I can do about that right now. However, if they let me live, I promise I'll get you back."

Carmen placed her hand on Picard's cheek and held it there. "I know you will, Monsieur Picard, and I'll be strong until then," she said, and then looked out the windshield past Picard. "They're coming. Take care of the families of both those officers until you get me back."

TWO

Detective First Grade Brian McKenna's cell phone in its charger and the phone on his nightstand went off at the same time, and he knew what that meant. Something bad had happened in the city of New York, and his Sunday off was canceled. He had heard Angelita get up an hour earlier to feed the kids, and knew she wouldn't be happy. They had planned to attend the eleven-o'clock Palm Sunday mass with her family at St. Patrick's Cathedral, and then enjoy a family brunch at The Wicked Wolf.

Angelita had also heard both phones, and she appeared in the bedroom doorway to voice her opinion. "Brian, please don't go unless you absolutely have to. It's a family day, and we've been planning this for weeks."

"I'll try" was all he could offer. He answered the cell phone first. It was his best friend, Ray Brunette, but that wasn't good news since Brunette was also the police commissioner. "Hold on, Ray," McKenna said. "I have to tell Dennis that I'll call him right back."

"Don't do that. Talk to him, then call me back."

"Where are you?"

"I'll be in my car in five minutes."

"Are you coming in?"

"Have to."

"Am I?"

"Yeah, you too. Sorry."

McKenna ended the call and picked up the other phone. As expected, it was Inspector Dennis Sheeran, the CO of the Major Case Squad. "Sorry, Brian, but I'm putting out an all-hands," Sheeran said. "The Spanish ambassador to the UN has been kidnapped."

"When and where?"

"About a half hour ago. Outside his apartment building, East Eightieth and Fifth. He was on his way to church with his wife. Three men, as far as we can tell. Killed the chauffeur and the bodyguard, took the ambassador in the car. Left the wife standing on the sidewalk."

"Diplomatic plates?"

"Yeah, '99 black Mercedes with diplomatic plates. They'll probably dump the car first chance they get, so we might have something to work with."

"Was Sunday mass the ambassador's usual routine?"

"Yeah, either the eight- or the nine-o'clock mass."

"This has to be the ETA, you know," McKenna said. "They've been acting up again, blew up a judge in Madrid last week."

"I figure it's them, but that doesn't help us much. I checked with Intelligence Division, and they've got nothing on them in this country."

"Did you check with the FBI?"

"Put a call in to Gene Shields. He's checking, but he hasn't gotten back to me yet."

"Is he also on his way in?"

"Uh-huh. I guess we'll all be meeting at Eightieth and Fifth. How long will it take you to get there?"

"I just got up, so figure about an hour."

"Fine. Could you call Cisco and get him there, too?"

"You got it."

As requested, McKenna next called his partner, Cisco Sanchez, and interrupted his morning exercise routine. Once McKenna gave him the story, Cisco didn't mind. It would be a big case, meaning big press interest, and Cisco loved seeing his name in print. However, he did have one concern. "You realize this is going to be a federal case?"

"I don't think I'll mind taking a backseat on this one," McKenna said. "It's already international, and it's going to get complicated quickly."

"Only if we drag our feet," Cisco said.

McKenna wasn't the least bit surprised at Cisco's take on the matter. Cisco considered himself to be the greatest detective ever, and he never hesitated to proclaim his opinion to all who would listen. That could be annoying at times, but sometimes Cisco solved seemingly impossible cases in a way that made some people reluctantly believe that the confident braggart just might be right.

"I'll stop by the office and get the car and radios," Cisco said. I'll pick you up in front of your building at nine sharp."

McKenna lived in the Village, but Cisco lived on East 16th Street and First Avenue, much closer to the Major Case Squad Office at One Police Plaza. "That would be exceptionally nice of you," he observed.

"Correct. Just for today, His Excellency, Most Exalted Detective First Grade Cisco Sanchez, is prepared to be very nice to all of his students."

"Good-bye, Cisco."

Next, McKenna tried calling Brunette back, but he got the service, meaning Brunette was on his cell phone with someone else. McKenna left a message and went on to his next difficult task. She was in the kitchen, dressing the twins, while his daughter slopped her cereal around the bowl at the kitchen table. "Sorry, baby. Got to go," he told Angelita, and saw immediately that news didn't sit well.

"When will you be home?" she asked, without looking at him.

"Can't say. The Spanish ambassador to the UN was kidnapped, and his chauffeur and bodyguard were killed in the process."

"Terrorists?"

"I'd say so. My first guess would be the ETA."

"Shouldn't this be an FBI case?"

"Probably will be before long, but Dennis wants me and Cisco there now."

"Where's *there*?"

"East Eightieth Street and Fifth Avenue."

"Are Dennis and Ray also going to be there?"

"Yep. Everybody's Sunday is ruined."

Then Angelita finally looked up and gave him his first smile of the day. "Then I guess I don't have too much to complain about, do I?" she asked.

"You do, but thanks for understanding."

"And tolerating," Angelita added.

"And tolerating."

McKenna tried Brunette before getting in the shower, but he got the service again. He took a quick shower, and his cell phone rang as he was drying off. "It's turning into a megillah," Brunette said. "It appears that the Spanish ambassador to France has also been kidnapped."

"From where?"

"His apartment in Paris, last night. Ours is messy, but theirs is worse. Military operation. Killed the concierge and a gendarme on the way in. Then blew the front door, killed a bodyguard, grabbed the ambassador, and killed two gendarmes on the way out. Had between seven and ten people involved in the grab. The gendarmes got one of them, and the bodyguard might have wounded another."

"Is the one they got *alive*?"

"Barely, but not likely to live for long. Shot four times, body hits."

"Any demands yet?"

"Not yet, but it gets worse," Brunette said. "Take a seat, and get yourself ready for some personal bad news."

Personal bad news? How could any of this involve me personally? McKenna wondered, but he did as Brunette suggested. He put the lid down on the bowl and took a seat. "Let's have it."

"They grabbed Carmen de la Cruz this morning, about

one A.M. our time. Professional ambush, killed a Guardia Civil cop, wounded another, and also killed a San Sebastian cop they'd kidnapped last night."

That news *did* hit McKenna hard. He had met Carmen twice, had been to her house in Spain, and had killed her husband to bring a tragic case to an unfortunate and unforeseen end.

Carmen had never blamed McKenna for her husband's death, and she had even shared his anguish over the killing. She had told McKenna that he would always be in her prayers, and that meant a lot to him. Ever since, she had never failed to call every Easter and Christmas, and sometimes for no reason at all.

Complicating matters even further was the fact that Angelita and Carmen had become phone buddies over the years, and Angelita thought Carmen was the most perfect woman ever.

"Are you still there?" Brunette asked.

"I'm here," McKenna said. "Is her kidnapping going to be public knowledge?"

"I imagine so. The Spanish prime minister is going to hold a press conference this morning, and he's sure to get some mileage over the ETA kidnapping the most popular woman in the country."

"I can't imagine why they would take her, but we have to get her back," McKenna said.

"I'm sure they have their reasons, and we'll do whatever has to be done. I just got off the phone with Gene, and he's getting everything he can on the ETA."

McKenna was happy to hear that. Gene Shields was the head of the FBI's New York office, and quite an influential character in federal circles. Everything he could get meant everything that was known anywhere about them. "This is going to be a federal case, isn't it?" he asked.

"Already is."

"What's our official role to be?"

"To do whatever we can to help. We can't let terrorists

get away with kidnapping and murdering in our town, and that's my final word on that subject."

Brunette's final word was always law to McKenna, but it was no longer the kidnapping and murders in New York that were foremost on his mind. He went into the bedroom to get dressed, and found that Angelita was doing the same. He told her what had happened, and that changed her attitude considerably. There were some tears, but it didn't take her long to compose herself and form a strong opinion on what McKenna's role should be. "Get dressed, get to work, and get our Carmen back from those filthy murdering bastards" were *her* final words on the subject.

THREE

McKenna was enjoying the beautiful spring weather when Cisco pulled up in front of his building. "Two Nineteenth Precinct cops just found the Mercedes," Cisco said as soon as McKenna got in. "East Eighty-fourth Street and the East River Drive, parked on a hydrant."

"Where's it being brought to?" McKenna asked.

"I'm waiting to hear," Cisco said, and the answer came a moment later from the radio dispatcher. She instructed Sector 19 Boy to guard the Mercedes and await the arrival of a department tow truck. The car would be towed to the 19th Precinct garage, where it would be processed by the Crime Scene Unit.

"How long do you think it took them to dump the car?" McKenna asked.

"Not long at all," Cisco answered. "Less than a mile from the ambassador's building to the East River Drive. Sunday morning, light traffic, not too many people on the streets. Figure under five minutes. They probably dumped that car before the description on it was even broadcast."

McKenna agreed with Cisco's assessment, but didn't bother telling him so since Cisco automatically assumed that everyone with a brain agreed with everything he said. Then he told Cisco about the kidnappings of Carmen and the Spanish ambassador to France.

Cisco had also been instrumental in the case involving

Carmen's husband, and he had met her after the funeral. His reaction to the news was typical. "Cisco likes Carmen very much, and he doesn't like people who kidnap people he likes."

"Meaning?" McKenna asked, just for fun.

"Meaning whoever has kidnapped Carmen has made a major mistake, and Cisco will make them suffer for their callous stupidity."

"What about the ambassadors? Aren't they important?"

"In an incidental way. It's all the same case."

Knowing that the vicinity of the crime scene would be crowded with police and press vehicles, Cisco parked on East 79th and Madison, two blocks from the Spanish ambassador's apartment building in one of Manhattan's most expensive neighborhoods. Since the kidnapping had occurred only an hour and a half before, the short walk gave McKenna and Cisco an opportunity to gauge the character of the neighborhood on an early Sunday morning.

It was as they expected. Rich people typically sleep late on a Sunday morning, but the people who work for them aren't permitted that luxury. Every doorman in every building they passed on East 79th Street was at his post in front of his building, and there were many limos pulled to the curb, with motors running and the chauffeurs waiting for the boss to wake up and come out to enjoy the day. There were also maids and houseboys walking the bosses' dogs, following their leashed charges and ready to pick up the mess.

To McKenna and Cisco, even that sparse street traffic meant there were witnesses to some part of the crime—either the actual kidnapping and murders, or to the escape. Many of them probably didn't realize they had seen something important, but those witnesses would be found and interviewed.

As soon as McKenna and Cisco turned the corner onto Fifth Avenue, Cisco congratulated himself on his foresight in his choice of parking spot. Fifth Avenue was jammed with double- and triple-parked police and press vehicles, so that southbound civilian traffic was restricted to the far lane running along the Central Park wall. Even so, traffic was still light, but very slow because people had to gawk at the commotion.

On the sidewalk, police lines had been established on both sides of the building, but the civilian crowd there consisted of less than fifty people and they were easy to control. Uniformed cops stood on one side of the barriers, while the curious stood on the other. The public was far outnumbered by the police and reporters.

Cisco stopped for a moment to take in the scene. "What a wonderful day and what a beautiful sight!" he observed. "Thank God we're here to enlighten our subjects and guide them through their tasks."

McKenna knew just what was going through Cisco's mind. Although the rank of detective was not a supervisory rank in the NYPD, Cisco considered all cops, detectives, bosses, and even chiefs to be underlings at his beck and call. Through sheer brass and force of character, Cisco usually got away with that attitude.

"How about it, hotshot?" McKenna said. "Let's not keep your subjects waiting."

Cisco was never one to duck under barriers when he could show off and leap over them, and he did, placing one hand on the top of the wooden barrier and hopping over it in a fluid motion. He did it all the time, and McKenna had told himself a thousand times that he couldn't retire until he saw Cisco fall on his ass in front of his subjects.

Then came the moment that made McKenna's day. One of the young uniformed cops stood in front of Cisco and asked to see his ID. Cisco hated the fact that McKenna was more famous than he was, so McKenna decided to rub it in. "That's all right, officer. He's with me."

"If you say so, Detective McKenna, but he should have his shield out," the young cop replied dutifully.

McKenna didn't think it was exactly the right time to point out that his own shield was still in his pocket, so he grabbed Cisco's arm and pulled him away to avert the explosion.

Cisco had been in a good mood, and he surprised McKenna when he took the incident in stride. "Can you imagine that? That kid must have come on the Job while I was having breakfast this morning" was all he had to say, and then he saw something else to frown about.

McKenna saw it too. Dennis Sheeran was talking to Detective First Grade Joe Walsh from the Crime Scene Unit. It was an animated conversation, and it didn't look friendly. They were the only people directly in front of the apartment building, and their presence there told McKenna that the immediate crime scene had already been searched, photographed, and mapped.

Walsh was an old-timer, but another prima donna with a high and frequently proclaimed opinion of himself, and it galled most who came into contact with him that the opinion was accurate. As he said to all who would listen, he was a consummate expert at processing crime scenes, and he always noticed—and usually correctly interpreted—those small but important details everyone else had missed.

McKenna knew that Walsh was off weekends, so he had also been called in on his day off to lend his expertise to the case. Walsh and Cisco were too much alike to respect each other's talents, so it was going to be a trying day for everyone, and especially Sheeran. The job had to be done, but the tender sensitivities of the two potentates would have to be assuaged to get it done right.

On the ground were the two covered bodies, one at the curb and the other in front of the building door. McKenna could tell from the shape of the covering that the body at the curb was in the fetal position, and he assumed it was the chauffeur. He had been shot, yanked out of the car, and left there by the kidnappers.

The body near the door of the building was stretched out under the blanket, but the covering was not large enough to conceal the pools of blood seeping out at the edges, near the torso and the head. There were no small white chalk circles near either of the bodies, which meant to McKenna that no shell casings had been recovered. He therefore assumed the kidnappers had used revolvers to kill the chauffeur and body-guard, not automatics which eject the spent shells.

Sheeran saw McKenna looking at him, and he appeared to be happy to leave Walsh. He nodded toward the front of the building, so McKenna left Cisco standing there while he went to talk to the boss. He knew that Cisco wouldn't mind, since the two of them always worked crime scenes from different approaches. McKenna preferred to hear all everyone else knew about what had happened before walking through the crime. Not Cisco. He preferred to examine the scene first and form his initial opinion as to what had happened, free from the biases of any witnesses who described what they thought they had seen.

Sheeran led McKenna into the lobby, and McKenna noticed that he hadn't taken the time to shave before coming in. Then McKenna saw something he had missed from out-side. There was a bullet hole in the glass of the front door, about six feet up. He looked around the large marble-paneled lobby. Two brass-doored elevators were at the far end, and there was an unattended concierge desk on the left. It took McKenna a moment to find the spot where the bullet had hit on the marble panel between the two elevators. He stood at the spot, lined his eye on the hole in the glass door, and found that he was looking at the top wall running along Central Park on the other side of Fifth Avenue. "I'm assuming we've got the round?"

"We got it," Sheeran said. "Seven point six-two NATO round, armor-piercing. Went right through the bodyguard's head and through the glass, but the marble stopped it."

"Will it do us any good?"

"Don't think so. Too deformed."

"Is the concierge a witness?" McKenna asked.

"Yeah, he's at the Nineteenth with the doorman."

"Has Ray been here yet?"

"Both him and Shields. They left to go take a look at the

car a couple of minutes ago, and then they're going to the Nineteenth Precinct."

"How is this investigation gonna work?"

"We're doing the preliminaries, and then it goes to the Joint Terrorism Task Force for investigation."

That made sense to McKenna. The Joint Terrorism Task Force was comprised of FBI and ATF agents, NYC detectives, and state troopers, but the unit was under federal control. It was a good mix, and they had always operated effectively in the past—most notably, after both World Trade Center bombings. "How about evidence?"

"We collect it, the FBI processes it."

"Is that what has Joe Walsh cranky?"

"Exactly. He thinks everything he finds belongs to him. Not exactly a team player, but he's already done some good work here."

"Hate to say it, but he always will. How about press?"

"Everything comes from the FBI, which is another thing that's galling Walsh."

"It's not going to make Cisco too happy, either," McKenna observed. "When he does something good, he wants immediate credit for it in the pages before the advertisements."

"Which is something you're going to have to help me out with. No secret calls from either of them to any of their reporter pals, and then I really owe you."

"Talk to them hard, and then I'll do what I can. Now, what do we know or surmise so far?"

"Well-planned operation, ruthlessly executed," Sheeran said. "The chauffeur is in the car, waiting right out front. Number One kidnapper is on the scene, walking a dog. Number Two is out of sight, around the corner on Eightieth Street. Number Three is in the park, behind the wall with a high-powered rifle. Seven forty-five the ambassador, his wife, and the bodyguard come out."

"Doorman?" McKenna asked.

"Just opened the door to let them out, but he's on the scene for the whole thing."

"Good witness?"

"Not bad. You're going to find that the bad witness is the wife. Very shaken up, so I think it's gonna be your job to get her to tell us something that makes sense."

"Fine," McKenna said. "Go on."

"First one to get it is the chauffeur. Number One drops the leash, pulls a gun, and runs to the car while Number Two runs from around the corner, also with a gun. Number One shoots the chauffeur in the head, but the bodyguard was good and in action. He was trying to get his gun out and push the ambassador back inside at the same time. Didn't make it. Shot from the park hit him in the back of the head, just about took his face off. As he's falling, Number One gives him another three rounds in the back for good measure."

"And what's Number Two doing?"

"Having a problem. I think he was the one who was supposed to take out the bodyguard, but the doorman and the ambassador's wife got in his way. She started screaming, and the doorman tried pulling her away, toward Eightieth Street. The ambassador made it inside and the elevator was right there, open. He went in, but didn't press any buttons. Just stood there."

"Because his wife was still outside?"

"Presumably, and then the ambassador asked the concierge if they had his wife. The concierge can see the action outside, and he gives the ambassador a bad answer: 'Not yet.' Then he tells the ambassador to push a button and get away. No good."

"He's not leaving without his wife? Pretty brave man, I'd say," McKenna observed.

"Yeah. Brave, but stupid, and the kidnappers knew just what to do. Number Two conks the doorman on the head with his gun, then covers him while Number One runs over and puts his gun in the wife's ear. Drags her over to the front of the building to show the ambassador what he's got."

"And he gives up?"

"Just raises his hands and walks outside. Number One releases the wife, opens the back door of the Mercedes, and the ambassador gets in like it's his everyday ride. Number One then yanks the chauffeur out and gets behind the wheel while Number Two covers the ambassador. Number Three hops the park wall, takes a spill, and drops his scope-mounted rifle. Picks it up, runs across Fifth Avenue, and he gets in the front. The ambassador moves over, Number Two gets in, and then we get into the dog nonsense."

"What was the dog doing while all the shooting was going on?"

"That's the strange thing. The dog took off toward Seventy-ninth when they were shooting up the bodyguard, but then she stopped, sat down, and watched the whole thing."

"She?"

"The doorman saw her pee in the street before the ambassador came out. It's a female golden retriever. After they were all in the Mercedes, she came up and jumped on the driver's door."

"They were gonna leave the dog?"

"Probably, but they didn't. The driver got out, opened the back door, and the dog jumped in, right across Number Two, and landed on top of the ambassador. Then they took off, moderate rate of speed. Stopped like good citizens for the red light at Seventy-eighth and Fifth, and then they're off again. Last seen southbound on Fifth."

"Any vehicles behind them?"

"You thinking a backup vehicle?" Sheeran asked.

"I'm thinking they had lots of backup, just in case anything went wrong on them—just like in France. They were gonna get the ambassador today, no matter what—or die trying," McKenna said. "Going further, I'd say one of their backup vehicles was a van."

"To put the ambassador in when they switched cars?"

"Uh-huh."

"You might be right on the money. There was a white van behind them at the light—old, American make. The doorman didn't see where it came from, but it passed him right after they pulled off in the ambassador's car. There was also another car in front of the ambassador's car at the light on East Seventy-eighth. Three cars waiting for the light in a row, with no other traffic."

"Here's another reason we know there are more than the three who grabbed him. How would they know the ambassador goes to the eight- or nine-o'clock mass every Sunday?"

"Surveillance."

"Which means a lot of hanging around in front of the building for however long it takes them to get the ambassador's routine down," McKenna said. "I'd say we're talking weeks."

"I was thinking the same thing," Sheeran said.

"Now I'll tell you a few things you probably know, but didn't mention."

"Go on."

"About seven-forty the bodyguard comes out, looks around, and sees everything is clear. Then he calls the chauffeur, and the chauffeur pulls up a minute or two later. That's when the bodyguard goes up to get the ambassador."

"True, but how'd you know that?"

"Because you said he was good, and it sounds to me like he was. But when he goes back in, that's the signal for the bad guys to jump on the set. They couldn't have been hanging around before that, because the bodyguard or the doorman would have seen them."

"Yeah. So?"

"That means that Number Four was there from the beginning to put everybody in place. That'll probably be the boss, the one who set this whole thing up."

"What makes you say that?" Sheeran asked.

"Because that's the way I would do it if I were running this kidnapping. I couldn't be right on the set to watch the action, and I sure couldn't take part in it because my picture is hanging in every post office in Spain. Eventually, I'd be identified for sure."

"The police there have the whole ETA leadership identified?"

"Every one. I always make a point of talking to the local

cops when I travel, and the Guardia Civil tells me that those who aren't in jail are fugitives."

"How about the three who did the grab? Will the Guardia Civil have pictures on them?"

"Maybe, but I don't think so. Were they all young?"

"Twenties."

"Recent cadre, I'd bet. This is a hot one, and they can't risk any of them being identified. But the boss would still want to supply direction as it was going down. Any of the witnesses see any radios on that crew?"

"No."

"Long hair?"

"Long enough to cover their ears," Sheeran said. "I guess they could've had radio receivers tucked in their ears under that hair."

"How were they dressed?"

"All the same. Black pants, and green shirts. You know the kind, those shirts with all the pockets they wear up in Spanish Harlem."

"Like the jacket from an old leisure suit—square bottom, worn outside the pants, good for covering a gun in the summertime?"

"That's what it sounded like to me from the doorman's description."

"Didn't he tell you it was a guayabera?"

"Maybe, but I've got no ear for Spanish."

"So they were all dressed alike. Look alike?"

"Same hairdo, same height and weight, same mustache. We had to go through the story with the doorman and the concierge three times before we knew who was doing what."

"Who's *we?*"

"Tommy McKenna and I."

Tommy was in the Manhattan North Homicide Squad, and the 19th Precinct was in Manhattan North. McKenna had only worked with Tommy once before, but that case had worked out well. In contrast to Cisco and Walsh, Tommy was never a prima donna, and he would be the last one to brag that he was the best homicide detective the NYPD had—but he was, and everybody knew it. "What's Tommy doing now?"

"Canvassing this building with his team, door-to-door. I figured he's the one to do it, because rich people never like to get involved by admitting they saw anything."

"If any of them saw anything, Tommy will get it out of them—and before they even realize they're telling him. Who else do we have here?"

"Got the Seventeenth and the Nineteenth Squads canvassing the buildings on each side of this one, but that's just the beginning. When the rest of our squad and the feds get here, we'll have enough manpower to question everyone for blocks."

"No feds here yet?"

"Just three. Shields broke them up, has one with our people in each of the buildings to lend that good old federal presence to this."

"Besides the wife, the doorman, and the concierge, what have we got in the way of witnesses so far?"

"Sparse. Got a professional dog walker. She was walking four dogs near the wall across the street, but on the other side of Eightieth Street. Heard the shot when they whacked the chauffeur, but didn't see it. Then she saw the guy with the rifle on the wall, and she dropped the dogs and ran like hell when he shot the bodyguard. She put the first call in to nine-one-one from her cell phone, and was outside looking for one of her dogs when the first unit got here."

"Is she also at the Nineteenth?"

"Yes, with the dogs, and very unhappy. She has more dogs to walk, and she says they won't wait for their nature calls."

"Any other calls to nine-one-one?"

"Two. Second call came from the concierge, third came from a pay phone on East Eighty-first and Fifth. Spanish accent, wouldn't identify himself, so we've got at least one witness we don't know about."

"Any others?"

"Not yet."

"Evidence?"

"Walsh got here just fifteen minutes before you did, but he's already got a few things everyone else missed. He started with the dog piss, blotted some up."

"The dog piss?" McKenna asked.

"That's what I said, but he's right when you hear him tell it. We ever find that dog, we can prove it was the one here through DNA testing. Find it in the company of a Basque terrorist, and we've got him."

"What else?"

"Possibility of fingerprints from Numbers One and Two. Both held the ambassador's wife around the waist, and she was dressed her best. Nice two-piece yellow outfit, and the skirt had a belt with a—"

"A brass buckle!" McKenna said.

"Right. Walsh went up and got it from her, hit it with his magnifying glass, and said he might be able to get some prints from it."

"If he says *might*, that means he can."

"He goes further than that. He says he might be able to get some prints from it, but he's sure nobody in the FBI lab could. Calls them a bunch of college-trained amateurs with good press agents."

"Sounds like something he would say. How are you gonna handle it?"

"I'm going to have to talk to Shields first, but I'd rather have Walsh go for the prints on it. Only problem with that is, if he gets a good lift, I'm gonna have to listen to him talk about it for the next five years."

"At least," McKenna agreed. "When am I gonna get to talk to the wife?"

"Not sure yet. That's up to Shields, but I think it'll probably happen when he lines up a federal presence to be with you while you question her."

"Is she going to the Nineteenth?"

"I'd say no. She's upstairs with her doctor and the deputy ambassador. I don't think she features going to either the Nineteenth Precinct or Federal Plaza."

That's fine, I can talk to her just as well upstairs, Mc-Kenna thought, and then he looked outside. The morgue wagon had arrived, and the attendants were standing out front, waiting for permission to pick up the bodies. "Let's walk through it," he said, and Sheeran followed him outside.

There was no sign of Cisco, but Walsh was sitting on a park bench next to the wall across the street, wearing that smug I'm-so-great smile McKenna knew so well. Walsh had found something else, McKenna knew, and he was waiting for his public to showcase his miraculous find.

Later, McKenna decided. This first. He took a deep breath, then bent down and pulled the blanket off the body-guard. It was a photo opportunity that none of the press photographers at the barriers missed.

The man was lying facedown, with his head turned toward McKenna. The high-velocity armor-piercing round had exited at the bridge of his nose, and both eyeballs were distended and hanging from their sockets. He was tall, and had been well-built before most of the blood in his torso seeped onto the sidewalk. "What's his name?"

"Jorge Dominguez," Sheeran answered.

"Spanish national?"

"They both are. Thirty-four years old, he's been here with the ambassador for two years."

"Guardia Civil?"

"Officially on leave of absence while they were serving in this assignment, but they're both Guardia Civil. He's a sergeant, the chauffeur's a corporal."

"Family?"

"I don't know," Sheeran admitted.

I'll find out, McKenna vowed as he fixed Dominguez's distorted face into his memory. In murder investigations, he always did, and the picture of Dominguez devoid of life when he should still be alive would keep him going whenever prospects in the investigation looked bleak. Finding the killer was the last debt the government owed to the victim, and McKenna believed it should always be paid.

McKenna replaced the blanket on Dominguez, and went

on to the chauffeur. He was lying curled up on his left side, and the bullet that had entered his brain as he sat behind the wheel hadn't exited. Death had surprised him; his eyes were wide open, but his face showed no pain.

Sheeran knew the drill by then. "Roberto Hernandez, thirty-one, been assigned here four years. Sorry, don't know about his family, either."

Hernandez's jacket was open, and McKenna could see the empty shoulder holster, and knew that the pistol had been removed during the official search of the body.

McKenna took a long last look at Hernandez's face, replaced the blanket, and stood up. "Whatever the politics, there's no right reason for this," he said, more to himself than to Sheeran.

But Sheeran had heard. "We'll make them pay," he answered.

Can we? McKenna wondered. Not much to go on, so far. Then he saw that Walsh had stood up and was waiting for him across the street. There was still no sign of Cisco.

Walsh was still smiling smugly when McKenna reached him. He was a big man in his late fifties, sixty pounds overweight, with a full mane of curly gray hair that belied his age. As usual, Walsh looked unkempt, wearing a checkered sports coat, baggy pants with no sign of a crease, unshined brown shoes, his top shirt button open and his tie at half-mast. It was a look McKenna didn't like in a detective, but in Walsh's case he made an exception. Walsh left no stone unturned at a crime scene, and he didn't mind getting dirty as he did his job.

"What have you got?" McKenna asked.

"Maybe some prints from the guy with the rifle," Walsh said, then reached into his coat pocket and removed a small clear-plastic evidence bag. There was a shiny new quarter in it, one of the commemorative series coins.

"Where did you find it?"

"Under this bench," Walsh said. "When he jumped over with the rifle, he landed hard and went down to his knees.

Must have kept his change in the bottom shirt pocket, and this one fell out."

"I don't know, Joe. No way of proving that quarter came from him. Anybody could have dropped it."

"Oh, yeah? Well, how about this one?" Walsh asked. He again reached into his pocket for another clear evidence bag, and this one contained a Spanish one-hundred-peseta coin. "Spanish terrorists kidnapping the Spanish ambassador, and here I've got a Spanish coin found two feet from where one of the terrorists fell. Think maybe you could make a case out of this one?"

"You think you'll be able to get prints off it?"

"If there are prints on either of them, and I'm allowed to process them, then sure I'll get them," Walsh stated. "Maybe you should tell Sheeran that."

God! This man is insufferable, but he's probably right, McKenna thought. "I'll tell him."

"You might also remind him that there's no such thing as a perfect crime once Joe Walsh shows up on the scene."

"Why don't you tell him that yourself?" McKenna asked.

"Already did, of course. Many times."

McKenna was certain of that. "You have any idea where Cisco is?" he asked.

"In the park."

"Doing what?"

"Lord knows."

McKenna was happy to leave Walsh. Using the bench as a ladder, he hopped over the wall into Central Park, but saw no sign of Cisco. However, he did find the place where Number Three had hidden while awaiting the signal to go into action. The area was wooded, and dead leaves were matted down at a spot four feet from the wall. McKenna searched the ground near it, and it took only a few seconds to find the ejected 7.62 mm shell. He was about to pick it up when he again heard from Walsh. "Don't pick the shell casing up. I'll get it later."

"You knew about it?" McKenna asked.

"Yeah, Cisco told me. There's an unfiltered cigarette butt

in the leaves behind you. Leave that there, too."

McKenna looked behind him and saw the half-smoked, dry, unfiltered butt on the ground. "Why don't you just come get them?"

"I told you, I'll get it later," Walsh said, and McKenna understood. Cisco had found the shell casing and the butt, and had told Walsh about them, but Walsh didn't know whether or not he could make it over the wall. If he couldn't, he wasn't going to let Cisco see him fail.

There was still no sign of Cisco, so McKenna walked through the woods to the road that circles the interior of the park. It was closed to vehicular traffic on weekends, and there were kids on skateboards taking advantage of the smooth asphalt roadway. The road sloped up at the point McKenna exited the woods, and it was there that he saw Cisco, standing at the top of the hill, surrounded by kids.

Cisco saw McKenna at the bottom of the hill. "Watch this, Brian," he yelled down, and then he performed one of those Cisco-feats that always amazed McKenna. First, he buttoned his coat. Then he did a handstand on a skateboard one of the kids was holding for him, and he came down the hill on it, zigzagging in sharp turns back and forth on the roadway by shifting his weight on his hands.

All the kids on the top of the hill hooted and applauded Cisco, and two of them followed him down riding piggyback on one skateboard. They managed to make every turn Cisco made, and stopped behind him when he reached McKenna.

Cisco put his feet on the ground and stood up in one fluid motion. Then he put his foot under the skateboard and snapped it into his hands.

"How long you been practicing that stunt?" McKenna had to ask.

"Believe it or not, first time I ever tried it."

McKenna did believe. He considered himself to be in excellent shape for fifty, running three marathons a year and working out whenever he could, but he knew that he had never in his life been in the shape Cisco was in. "Not bad, for a beginner, Cisco."

"Not bad?" the bigger of the two kids asked, protesting. "Our man Cisco is awesome."

"Yeah," the smaller one agreed. "Awesome."

McKenna took a moment to measure Cisco's two new ardent fans. He guessed that the older one was ten, and the younger one eight. Both were dressed skater-style in sneakers, long-sleeved T-shirts, and baggy jeans that hung low to expose their patterned boxer drawers.

"This is my pal, Brian," Cisco told the boys in Spanish. "He tries hard to be just like me, so he's a pretty good guy. Do me a favor, and say something nice to him in Spanish."

"Does he speak Spanish?" the younger one asked, also in Spanish.

"Sure he does. Try him out. Be polite, and then tell him something about yourselves."

"I am Gabriel, and this is my brother Steven," the older one said. "We're very pleased to meet you."

McKenna recognized the lisping accent peculiar to central Spain, and he suspected that Cisco, despite all outward appearances, might actually have been working on the case in his own way. "And I am Brian McKenna. I'm very pleased to meet two of Cisco's other deputies," McKenna replied in Spanish. "Are you guys from Madrid?"

"Used to be. Now we're from the Bronx."

"From the Bronx? You came all the way down here just to skateboard?"

"Every Sunday. Our mom works on Sundays, so our dad brings us to his job."

"Tell him where your father works," Cisco said.

"He's a doorman at a building over there," Gabriel said, pointing toward Fifth Avenue.

McKenna was ready to take a guess. "Is the building at Eighty-first and Fifth?"

"Yeah, that's it. Nine twenty Fifth Avenue."

"Now tell him about all the bird-watchers," Cisco instructed.

"The Basques?"

"Yeah, tell him about the Basques."

"They've been here every Sunday for a while, watching all the birds around here with binoculars."

"Where did they hang out?"

"They were always in the woods over there," Gabriel said, again pointing toward Fifth Avenue.

"How many of them were there?" McKenna asked.

"I don't know. Sometimes maybe five, sometimes more."

"Were they here this morning?"

"Yeah, but not too many. Just the lady and two others."

"The lady?"

"Yeah. She was the teacher, or the leader, or something. She always tells the other ones where to go to find the birds."

"She's very pretty, and very nice," Steven added.

"What makes her so nice?"

"Because she gave us twenty dollars this morning to go buy breakfast and ice cream."

"And did you?"

"No, we weren't hungry. We made believe we were going to buy breakfast, but we just went and hung out at the fountain for a while."

"Do you still have that twenty dollars?"

"No, he's got it," Steven said, nodding to Cisco. "Good deal for us. Gave us thirty dollars for a twenty-dollar bill."

Might not be such a bad deal for Cisco, either, McKenna thought. "Were there any other kids here when she gave you the money?"

"No, too early. Just us," Steven said.

"Yeah, way too early," Gabriel agreed. "There was just us and the Basques."

"How do you know they were Basques?" McKenna asked.

"Because they had a big bird book with lots of pictures, and we saw it was in Spanish," Gabriel said. "We asked her about it, and she said they were a bird-watching club from Spain."

"She told you that in Spanish?"

"Yeah, but she had some kind of an accent."

"Maybe Basque accent?" McKenna asked.

"No, not Basque. They sound like us when they speak

Spanish," Steven explained. "We asked her about the book in Spanish, and she told us in Spanish."

"Then one of the others talked to her in Basque, and she told him to shut up in Basque," Gabriel added.

"How do you know that? Do you guys speak Basque?"

"No, but our grandmother does. She used to tell us to shut up in Basque all the time."

"Not all the time," Steven said, correcting his brother. "Not when Papa was home."

"Your father doesn't like your grandmother?" McKenna asked.

"He doesn't like any Basques," Gabriel replied. "Says they think they're so great, but all they really are is bomb-throwers and murderers."

"So your grandmother who speaks Basque is your mother's mother?" McKenna surmised.

"Uh-huh."

"Did you ever tell your father about the Basques in the park?" McKenna asked.

"No," Gabriel said.

"Why not?"

"He'd tell us to stay away from them. He says they're always trouble."

"Did you ever understand anything else the Basques said when they were talking to each other?"

"No, but we know one of their names," Gabriel said proudly.

"What is it?"

"Elodi."

"Elodi? Is that a Basque name?"

"Uh-huh. We once had a Basque boy in school named Elodi, so it must be. Sometimes they have funny names."

"In school in Madrid?"

"Uh-huh."

"And how do you know one's name was Elodi?"

"Because that's what the lady called him last week when she was yelling at him over something. She said *stupid,* too, in Basque when she was yelling at him."

"Is that another word your grandmother taught you?"

"Uh-huh, but she doesn't call us that."

"Who does she call stupid?" McKenna asked, already knowing the answer.

"Papa!" both boys replied at once.

"I see," McKenna said. "Do you boys know what happened on Fifth Avenue this morning?"

"Sure," Gabriel answered. "Some people got killed."

"Were you around here when it happened?"

"No, we were at the fountain."

"So how do you know?"

The two boys looked at each other, but didn't answer. Instead, Cisco did. "Their father always tells them they should stay away from trouble. If they see a bunch of police cars at one spot, they should go the other way."

"So you guys went across Fifth Avenue to have a look when you got back from the fountain?" McKenna asked.

"Yeah, but only for a minute," Gabriel said.

"Does your father know?"

"We didn't see him see us, but maybe."

"What makes you think *maybe?*"

"Because we heard him calling us right after we got back into the park."

"But you didn't answer?"

"No way."

"What time are you supposed to meet him?"

"Twelve o'clock. He gets us lunch, and we eat in the basement."

McKenna had many more questions he wanted to ask the boys, but he thought it had already gone on too long. To avoid any legal problems if the case ever made it to court, he wanted a parent present before he grilled them on details.

Cisco was thinking the same way. "How about this? We have to talk to your father anyway, so why don't we all meet at his building for lunch?" he asked.

"Are you gonna tell him we went to see the bodies?" Steven asked.

"Of course not, but I think you guys should do that. Don't

forget, you two are going to be very important in this case. He's gonna find out, sooner or later."

"Then we'll tell him later," Gabriel said.

"Yeah, later," Steven chimed in.

FOUR

Joe Walsh had gotten into the park somehow, and he had already picked up the butt and the shell casing by the time McKenna and Cisco met him there.

"Anything good?" McKenna asked.

"Like I told you, it depends on who's processing it," Walsh replied.

"Suppose it were you?"

"Then it would be excellent. The butt's a Gauloise. French brand, also common in Spain."

"You were able to tell that already?"

"Of course. I noticed the tobacco is darker than the stuff used in American cigarettes, and it also has a distinctive aroma. A Gauloise, and I'd stake my reputation on that."

"Did you also happen to notice that 'Gauloise' is printed right on the butt, you fat windbag?" Cisco asked.

"I think I might've noticed that," Walsh admitted.

McKenna hadn't seen it, so he assumed the brand name had been on the side of the butt facing the ground. "So could you get prints from it?"

"If anybody can," Walsh replied. "Then you can give it to the FBI to process it for DNA in the saliva."

"And the shell casing?"

"Clear ejector marks. Our Ballistics could process it as well as the FBI."

"You ready for another mission, one that will involve some theatrics?" McKenna asked.

"My specialty. What do you want me to do?"

"There's a pay phone at the corner of East Eighty-first and Fifth, maybe a few of them. I want you to dust all the receivers, and make a show of it when you take a few lifts."

"Who's the show for?"

"A doorman at one of the buildings on the corner. I think he might be a witness to the kidnapping, and I want to have some leverage on him before we talk to him."

"He made a nine-one-one call?"

"If it's him, he did. Spanish accent, refused to identify himself."

"Okay, I'll impress him."

"I've got a mission for you, too," Cisco said.

McKenna braced himself for some pointed Cisco sarcasm, but Cisco really did have a mission for Walsh. He took a folded handkerchief from his pocket and gave it to Walsh. Walsh opened the handkerchief to reveal the bonanza, a crisp twenty-dollar bill folded in half.

"Nice," Walsh said. "I'd bet this bill came from an ATM not too long ago. Whose prints do you think are on it?"

"The leader of the kidnap team and a couple of kids. I'll give you elimination prints on the kids later."

Walsh folded the handkerchief, put it in his pocket, and focused on McKenna. "You better talk hard to Sheeran, because I want this job."

"I already told you, I will. But if I can do it, you better not screw him by whispering to your press pals."

"Until when?"

"Until the case is over."

"Wait a minute," Cisco said. "Are you saying there's that tight a lid on this case?"

"Everything to the press has to come from the feds," McKenna explained. "That's the rule, and Dennis was real clear on that."

"So we get no credit while they grab the glory?"

"I'm hoping it doesn't work out that way."

"Then you better take a good look at their track record,"
Cisco said, then hopped over the wall. McKenna followed,
leaving Walsh in the park to make his own way out. A quick
look told them that the crime scene had been wrapped up;
the bodies had been removed, the barriers were gone, and so
were all the uniformed cops and reporters. The only visible
police vehicles remaining were Joe Walsh's Crime Scene
Unit van and a row of double-parked unmarked cars that
stretched for two blocks. McKenna could see FBI vehicle
identification plates on the dashboard of many of them, so
he knew the feds had arrived in force and were conducting
canvasses in the buildings with the help of detectives from
the Nineteenth Squad, the Seventeenth Squad, and the Homicide Squad.

A building maintenance man was hosing the sidewalk,
washing away the last vestiges of blood. At street level, at
least, Fifth Avenue had been returned to its rich residents.

Then they saw Tommy Bara come out of the ambassador's building. Bara was an old-time, well-respected FBI
boss well-known to both McKenna and Cisco. His square
jaw and his Don't-try-me attitude made him look like a tough
guy, and he was. McKenna knew that Cisco had gotten on
Bara's nerves during a case they had all worked together,
and that could be a problem since Bara had recently been
promoted to head the Joint Terrorism Task Force.

It was bad. Bara greeted McKenna cordially, and Cisco
perfunctorily. If Cisco noticed, he didn't seem to mind.

"Are we working for you now?" McKenna asked.

"Probably just for today," Bara replied. "Shields and Brunette have worked it out, and this is gonna be a totally federal
case once the smoke clears."

So we're out after today? McKenna thought, and he recognized that the problem was Cisco. He also recognized that
Bara didn't have the weight to shut him out of the case if he
really wanted to stay in. Cisco, maybe, but not him—not the
famous detective who was also the good pal of Ray Brunette,
Gene Shields, and many reporters.

So what next? McKenna asked himself. Call in some

chips to stay on the case, and maybe leave my partner in order to do it? No, that's not the way to operate, he decided. Let's wait a day and see what happens. "Where's Inspector Sheeran?"

"At the station house with Tommy McKenna and a couple of witnesses he found."

"Good witnesses?"

"Fair. A maid and the mistress of the house, twelfth-floor facing Fifth. The maid was watering the plants at the window, and she saw the guy lying behind the wall. When she saw him stand up and put the rifle on the wall, she called her boss over. She arrived just in time to see and hear the shot. Saw the shooter hop the wall a few seconds later with his rifle, take a fall, then get up and run across Fifth Avenue."

"They couldn't see what was happening in front of the building?"

"No. Too high, and the windows were closed. Climate-controlled central air and heating, never a need to open a window in the apartments in this building."

"But they heard the shot?"

"Heard a bunch of them. When they saw the rifle, they were geared to hear a shot. You know how sound travels up and intensifies in Manhattan."

McKenna did. A mildly annoying backfire at street level could sound like a bomb going off to those rich folks on the high floors. "So they didn't see the getaway?"

"No."

"Or the white van?"

"If they did, they took no notice. They say no."

"How about action in the park?"

"What kind of action?" Bara asked.

"The team leader, probably directing the whole scenario from the woods," McKenna said, then told Bara what he and Cisco had learned from Gabriel and Steven. He also told him about the coins, the twenty-dollar bill, the Gauloise butt, and the spent cartridge shell. Throughout the account, Cisco appeared to be totally disinterested.

"So there's a woman running their operation?" Bara asked.

"Yeah, and it shouldn't be too hard for the Guardia Civil to attach a name to her," McKenna said. "How many female terrorists are high up enough in the ETA to run an operation this big?"

"Not too many, I suppose," Bara said. "You guys did good."

"I did nothing," McKenna said. "Cisco found the boys, and he's the one who got the info."

"Okay, then *you* did good," Bara said to Cisco, but he didn't appear happy saying it.

"What did you expect?" Cisco asked indignantly. "Naturally, the best detective does the best work."

"And the best detective would be you?"

"The very best, ever."

"I see you haven't changed much, Cisco," Bara commented. "Still as difficult as ever."

"Everyone knows the best never come easy," Cisco retorted.

McKenna thought it was time to change the subject before things got out of hand. "What do you want us to do, Tommy?" he asked.

"You and I are gonna go up to interview the ambassador's wife. The deputy ambassador is still with her, so we might as well hear what he has to say while we're at it."

"Fine. Has anybody else been up to talk to them?"

"Just a little chitchat when I went up to arrange the interview. Nice people."

"And me, Tommy? What do you want me to do while you're hobnobbing with the dignitaries?" Cisco asked.

"Take a break, and give us all a rest."

As McKenna had expected, the ambassador's apartment was large and luxurious, a corner unit on the tenth floor that offered a nice view of Central Park as well as a peek of the East River at the end of East 80th Street. The door was answered by a uniformed maid, and they were shown into the living room.

The ambassador's wife was seated on the sofa with the deputy ambassador when Bara and McKenna were announced by the maid, and both rose to greet them. Bara made the introductions.

Señora Diana Clavero was an elegant woman in her sixties, tall and thin, and she exuded charm. She did none of the things older women sometimes do to disguise their age; her hair was shiny gray with streaks of black, she wore little makeup, her nails were painted with a clear coat, and her yellow jacket and dress were tasteful and demure. However, despite a bandage covering her right ear, she possessed an ageless beauty that made McKenna guess she could have been a fashion model in her younger days.

There was nothing fashionable about Juan Diego Ibarretxe that morning. Like Sheeran, the news of the kidnapping must have pulled him out of bed in a hurry. He was unshaven, dressed in jeans, a polo shirt, a blue sports jacket, and wore penny loafers without socks. He appeared to be in his early forties—young for his position, McKenna thought—but his eyes glowed with interest and intelligence in a friendly face. Like Señora Clavero, he was also tall and thin.

McKenna immediately got the impression that Ibarretxe was a nice guy, someone with whom he could easily deal.

"Is there any news on my husband?" Señora Clavero asked.

"Sorry, nothing yet," Bara said. "Has your government received any demands yet?"

The señora deferred to Ibarretxe for the answer. "None that I'm aware of, and I just got off the phone with Madrid. Please sit down and make yourselves comfortable," he said, indicating a sofa across from the sofa where they had been seated.

They all sat down, and then the señora asked if she could offer them coffee or tea. Both declined, and McKenna took out his notepad and pen, ready to begin.

"Before we start, Detective McKenna, I hope you don't

mind my telling you how happy it makes me that you're assigned to my husband's kidnapping," the señora said. "I followed the Hector de la Cruz case with great interest, and so did many others in my country."

McKenna looked to Bara, but Bara suddenly seemed to be at a loss for words. He nodded to McKenna to give the señora the news. "Actually, señora, I'm not assigned to this case. I'm a city cop, and the kidnapping of a diplomat gives the FBI primary jurisdiction. I'm just helping out until they get all their people and resources in place."

"And then?"

"And then I go back to working my other cases."

It was apparent to both McKenna and Bara that news didn't sit well with the señora, and she had just one word to say. "Pity."

"I assure you, señora, we'll have our best people working to find your husband and get him back," Bara said, but Señora Clavero said nothing.

The silence was becoming uncomfortable, and McKenna decided it was up to him to get matters back on track. "I'm assuming Ibarretxe is a Basque name," he noted, merely as a way of breaking the ice.

"Yes, it is. When it comes to names, most of our tongue twisters are Basque," Ibarretxe said, smiling. "I don't know if being Basque would make me a suspect in your eyes, but let me take the time to take myself off your list."

"You're not on our list, I assure you," McKenna said.

"If that's true, then please consider this just background information. I am a career diplomat with fifteen years of service and a top security clearance. I was raised in the Basque Country, but I have absolutely no sympathy now for the ETA and its methods. More than that, like the vast majority of Basques, I think that the present arrangement the Spanish government has with the Basque provincial governments is fair and equitable."

"You said you have no sympathy *now* for the ETA," McKenna observed. "Does that mean you once supported them?"

"Years ago, most Basques did. You see, we were on the losing side in our civil war in '39, and Franco was not a forgiving man. He repressed our culture, made our language illegal, and overtaxed us while intentionally keeping the Basque provinces poor and underdeveloped. The central government was universally despised by us."

"And the situation now?" Bara asked.

"The time for fighting is over. The three Basque provinces are an autonomous region, the schools are run in the Basque language, and the central government has invested heavily in our infrastructure so that the Basque Country might now be the most prosperous region in Spain."

"Then why are they still fighting?" Bara asked.

"The ETA *says* they're still fighting to unite all Basques into an independent Basque homeland, which means uniting the three Spanish provinces in the Basque country with the four French Basque departments—but nobody takes that idea seriously any longer. You see, the Spanish Basques have always been Basque first and Spanish second, but the French Basques are another story altogether. They've never been repressed by the Paris government, so they've always been French first and foremost, and Basque second. They have no desire to secede."

"Does the ETA usually operate in France as well?"

"Not usually, but they cross the Pyrenees to use the French Basque region as a safe haven whenever things get too hot for them in Spain. At times, they are allied with Iparretarrak, the French Basque separatist organization."

"Is Iparretarrak also a terrorist organization?" McKenna asked.

"Through and through. Pull the same types of crimes as the ETA on a smaller scale—bombings, assassinations, and kidnappings. However, they enjoy very little support from the French Basques, so up till now they've been pretty ineffective."

"*Up till now?* Does that mean you think they pulled off the kidnapping of your ambassador in Paris?" Bara asked.

"No. I'd bet that the people who took our ambassador

were ETA, but I'd also bet that they received logistical support from Iparretarrak."

"Logistical support?"

"Weapons and explosives, and surely the location where they're holding our ambassador right now is one of their safe houses."

"I still don't get it," Bara said. "If it's generally agreed that this independent Basque homeland will never happen, and neither the ETA nor Iparretarrak have much support among the Basques, then why are they still fighting?"

"Nobody seems to know why Iparretarrak is still fighting. As for the ETA, many people believe they're now fighting for themselves, not the Basque people. They collect an unofficial tax from most merchants and factories in the Basque country, and that's still going on."

"Extortion?" McKenna asked.

"Basically, but what it means is that the ETA is still well-funded. What they're principally fighting for is amnesty and prison locations. The government is holding over five hundred convicted ETA terrorists in prisons all over the country, including in the Canary Islands. The ETA wants them all moved to a prison in the Basque Country while they negotiate the amnesty issue."

"Any chance of that happening?"

"Not that I've heard. The government is refusing to budge, and the ETA's position has only lukewarm support from the Basque people. Don't forget, they call themselves freedom fighters, but those in jail have been convicted of murders, bombings, kidnappings, and bank robberies. Now that the reasons for the fight have basically been resolved, many Basques aren't anxious to have those people loose and walking about in the Basque Country."

"Would your government be prepared to negotiate with them now to secure the release of the hostages they're holding?" Bara asked.

"I don't know," Ibarretxe admitted. "They certainly managed to enhance their position. Holding two ambassadors and Carmen de la Cruz will give them leverage and all the world media attention they never seemed to be able to get before, so negotiations can't be ruled out."

"God, let's hope not," the señora added, saying it in a way that gave McKenna the impression she was deeply in love with her husband.

"Why do you think they kidnapped Carmen de la Cruz?" Bara asked.

"La Tesora? I think that was a grave mistake on their part, but they've become cannibalistic lately," Ibarretxe stated. "Many of the people they've kidnapped in the past couple of years were Basques—either politicians or other people in the public eye who have opposed their cause. Although she never publicly admitted it, it's generally known that Carmen was a major contributor to Vascos Contra la Violencía, the Basque peace movement."

"Do you think they'd kill her if the government doesn't give in to them?"

"Kill La Tesora? I don't think so," Ibarretxe said. "If they even threatened to do that, they'd be finished."

"Is she that popular in Spain?" Bara asked.

"I think 'popular' is the wrong word to describe how our people feel about Carmen. Spain is a very religious country—the most Catholic country in the world—and Carmen is *revered* there. Some actually believe she's a living saint, so murdering her would be like murdering Mother Teresa. It's unthinkable."

"Then why did they take her?"

"To deprive the rest of the country. Think of it like stealing the *Mona Lisa* from the Louvre. The thieves would never harm the painting, but they'd be depriving the French of one of their fondest national treasures."

"So the Spanish people will be very anxious to get her back?" Bara asked.

It was the señora who answered. "They'll probably be more anxious about getting her back than getting their two ambassadors back, and that's not good for me."

"Do you have any more details on her kidnapping?" McKenna asked.

"None, but I've requested that I be sent everything known about it as soon as it becomes available," Ibarretxe answered.

"How about the Paris kidnapping?"

"Same answer. I've already told your police commissioner everything I know right now, but I'll soon know everything that's known about it."

"Which brings us to another point," Bara said. "I propose that there be a free and constant exchange of information between the FBI, the French police, and the Spanish police on all three cases."

"Very sensible, and my government has already authorized me to propose just that. They have also arranged a similar accommodation with the French."

"We have almost nothing on the ETA, so we'll also need everything you have on them."

"You'll have it, and soon. Copies of all our police and intelligence files on them are being made as we speak, and a plane has been chartered to bring the files here. Should be arriving at JFK sometime tonight, and I'm authorized to offer more. Colonel Segovia of the Guardia Civil knows more about the ETA than anybody else we have. He's in Paris right now, but if you like, he could be here sometime within the next few days."

"That's a good idea, and we accept," Bara said.

"Good. What's next on your agenda?"

"Basically, I'd like to hear Señora Clavero describe what happened this morning in her own words, and then answer whatever questions I might have."

"I can do that," the señora said, and she recited the story as best she could remember. Her eyes misted when she told about the murders of her chauffeur and her husband's bodyguard, and McKenna liked her more for that. She also gave credit to the brave actions of the doorman, but she was able to add nothing that McKenna didn't already know, and he took few notes. Then it was time to get into details. "Is your ear hurting you?" he asked.

"Not really, but it looks a mess. Swollen, and pretty bloody right after it happened."

"Were you hurt when they stuck the gun in your ear?"

"I guess that's when it happened, but I didn't feel it at the time."

"Do you know what kind of gun it was?"

"Small revolver. They both had small revolvers, but I certainly couldn't tell you the type."

"Would you be able to recognize any of those men if you saw them again?" he asked.

"The man who killed Roberto, definitely. The man who was with him, probably. The man with the rifle, I don't know."

"Had you ever seen them hanging around before this morning?"

"No, and if they had been there before, I wouldn't have seen them anyway. Thanks to Jorge, we always entered and left the building in a big hurry."

"Excuse me," Bara said. "Who's Jorge?"

McKenna was surprised at the question, and it meant to him that Bara hadn't yet had time to review the case thoroughly. "Jorge Dominguez, the bodyguard. Apparently he was pretty good," he explained, and then returned his attention to the señora. "Was there anything distinctive about any of them, as far as you can remember?"

"I think one of them was wearing a wig. His hair didn't look right to me."

"Which one was that? The man who killed Roberto, or the other one?"

"The other one, the one who hit our doorman with the gun."

"Were you able to see if they had any radio receivers in their ears?"

"Radio receivers?"

"They would look like hearing aids."

She closed her eyes to think about it. "I really couldn't say," she answered after a few moments. "I don't remember seeing their ears, their hair was too long."

"Did any of them speak during the kidnapping?"

"I've already thought about this, and I'm certain just two

things were said. The one who first grabbed me said in Spanish, 'Stop screaming, puta, or I'll kill you.' "

"What does puta mean?" Bara asked.

"Spanish for 'prostitute,' " McKenna answered, and then returned his attention to the señora. "And what else was said?"

"The one who shot Roberto said something in Basque to the dog when he let it into the car, and then he said the dog's name. The dog is called Duquesa."

"That's 'Duchess' in English," McKenna said for Bara's benefit.

"Is this important?" the señora asked.

"Could be," McKenna said. "Did the dog look healthy?"

"Healthy and happy."

"And it had a leash and collar on, right?"

"Yes. Just before he shot Roberto, he dropped the leash and let the dog go. It was a yellow cloth leash."

"And the collar?"

"Yellow, too, I think."

"This is a lot to ask, but did you notice whether or not there was a dog license hanging from the collar?"

Once again, the señora closed her eyes as she tried to visualize the scene. McKenna could see that it was painful for her as she relived it again, but she appeared apologetic when she opened her eyes. "Sorry. I think I remember a license hanging from its collar, but I'm not certain," she said, shaking her head slowly as tears formed in her eyes. "When the dog jumped on the car door, I was staring at Roberto and Jorge lying on the ground. They were like family to us, and you saw what they did to them?"

"I saw. Horrible, and certainly not something easy to forget," McKenna said. He couldn't think of another question, so he turned to Bara. With a nod of his head, Bara indicated that it was time to go. They stood up and thanked the señora and Ibarretxe for their time.

"You'll keep us informed of any progress you make?" the señora asked, but the question was directed at McKenna, not Bara.

"And me as well. Call me anytime, day or night," Ibarretxe said. Then he took out his wallet and handed McKenna
his card.

Sorry, Tommy. Looks like the ambassador's wife and the
deputy ambassador aren't buying into me getting shut out of
this case, McKenna thought, hoping he was successful at
suppressing the smirk that rose to his lips. He said nothing,
and waited for Bara to answer.

Bara did. "We'll keep you both fully informed."

Ibarretxe showed them out, and they were at the door
when a thought hit McKenna. "Mr. Ibarretxe, the señora classified Dominguez as a very suspicious kind of guy," he said.
"Would you agree with that?"

"Totally. He could be a real bother sometimes, saw threats
to the ambassador everywhere."

"Was he required to file reports on a daily basis?"

"Monthly basis, standard embassy form that didn't quite
fit his job. It's designed for reporting hours worked, expenses, or anything unusual that happened during the
month."

"It didn't fit his job because he was always working, and
he had no expenses?" McKenna guessed.

"Exactly. He was getting premium pay for his position,
and couldn't put in for overtime. As for expenses, he had an
embassy credit card to pay for those."

"So what did he put in his reports?"

"His constant suspicions, and an equally constant, very
neatly written stream of suggestions to improve the ambassador's security."

"Did any of his prior suspicions ever amount to anything?"

"No, and neither did the overwhelming majority of his
suggestions. I know that on more than one occasion, the ambassador asked him to tone it down," Ibarretxe said, and then
showed an embarrassed smile. "A few times, I also asked
Jorge to tone it down. Turns out he was right the whole
time."

"What made him like that—so suspicious of everyone and

everything?" McKenna asked, and thought he already knew the answer.

He did. "Served too long in the Basque Country when times were really hot for the Guardia Civil," Ibarretxe said. "I understand that he had amassed quite an impressive array of medals before taking on this position."

"We've got to see his room," McKenna said.

"His report for this month?"

"Exactly. Let's see if he was paranoid, or just plain good."

Ibarretxe went back into the living room to relay McKenna's request to the señora. He was back with her moments later, and she appeared to be distressed over the idea. "Are you sure this is necessary?" she asked. "We always respected Jorge's privacy, and I haven't been in his room since he came here."

"Can't say for sure that it's necessary," McKenna replied. "It's just a hunch I've got, and sometimes my hunches work out."

"They frequently work out," Bara added, giving McKenna his first hint that Bara didn't think it was such a bad idea. "Besides, the time for worrying about Jorge's privacy is over. He's dead."

"I suppose you're right," she said, then led them back through the living room and down a long hall to Jorge's room. She opened the door, flicked the light switch on the wall, and inspected the room from the doorway. Satisfied, she stood aside to let them in.

"Small, but certainly neat enough," Ibarretxe said, and the comment told McKenna that Ibarretxe had money or came from money. McKenna estimated that the *small* bedroom was about twice the size of his own bedroom in the Village. There were a double bed, two dressers, an entertainment center, a desk, and a sitting area with two sofas and a coffee table between them. Heavy drapes covered the two windows.

Despite all the furniture, the room was large enough to accommodate it all tastefully. The kitchenette and dining area were in a wide hallway between the main room and the bathroom. It looked like a model apartment ready for showing, and the only personal adornment was a family photo on one of the dressers showing Dominguez, his stout wife, and two children in a studio setting.

Thinking the desk was the place to start, McKenna opened the center drawer and immediately found what he was looking for. On one side of the drawer was a pad of the blank embassy reports Ibarretxe had described, and on the other side, a lined legal pad. The pages on the top half of the pad were covered with Dominguez's neat, precise handwriting.

McKenna picked up the pad and began leafing through it.

"What is it?" Bara asked.

"We would call it a daily activity report," McKenna replied as he continued browsing through the pages. "Every day starts with 'Time on Duty: Seven A.M.,' and then he goes on to report everything he did during the day that had anything at all to do with his job." He flipped to the last page, and smiled.

"What does it say?" Ibarretxe asked.

"It says that Jorge Dominguez was a lot sharper than anybody gave him credit for."

"Meaning?"

"Does *ornitólogo* mean 'bird-watcher' in Spanish?"

"Yes, but what does that have to do with anything?"

"To get the ambassador's schedule down, the team that kidnapped him spent weeks in the park, posing as bird-watchers while they surveilled this building. Jorge's last entry in his notes was at seven-thirty this morning, and it says that *los ornitólogos han vuelto al parque otra vez. Hay solo tres esta mañana, la mujer y dos hombres.*"

"*Ay, caramba!*" Ibarretxe exclaimed. "A very sharp man. I only wish I would have told him so while he was still alive."

"Would you two mind filling in the gringo?" Bara asked.

"Sorry, boss," McKenna said. "Jorge's last entry this morning was: 'The bird-watchers have returned to the park again. Only three this time, the woman and two men.' "

"No description?"

"Not this morning," McKenna said, and then leafed back

through the pages. "Same entry last Sunday, same time, but he writes it was the woman and six men. Short and sweet, still no descriptions on them."

"Where was he watching them, from up here or the street?" Bara asked, and all turned to the señora.

"It must have been from the windows," she said, pointing to the drapes. "He had a good view of the park from them, and he never left his room before seven-thirty."

Bara went to one of the windows and pulled the drapes back a bit. "This is it," he said. "The trees are just starting to fill out, so in another few weeks he wouldn't have been able to see anyone on the ground in the park."

"Do those notes help you?" Ibarretxe asked.

"Not without a solid description. Just tells us what we already know," McKenna replied, and then he went back a few more pages in Jorge's notes. "Same thing the Sunday before last. The woman and six men, no descriptions. That was the first Sunday of the month, the day after he started keeping notes for this month's report."

"Then let's see if we can find his notes from last month," Bara suggested. "Maybe he wrote their descriptions there."

"His notes aren't what we should be looking for at this point," McKenna said. "The boys Cisco found are sharp. They were at ground level with the bad guys every Sunday, so they could give us a better description on them than we'll find in any notes Jorge made from up here."

"So what *should* we be looking for?" Bara asked.

"His camera and photo album. Jorge was a very precise guy. The reason he didn't bother writing down all their descriptions is because he didn't need to. He took their pictures."

"He does have two cameras, and he used them all the time," the señora said. "One in the car, and one he kept someplace up here. He took pictures of anybody who looked suspicious to him, and that covered quite a few people."

"Did one of them have a telephoto lens?"

"The one he kept up here did."

"So you knew he was photographing people from the windows here?" McKenna asked.

"That I didn't know. What I do know is that he would run out of here all hours of the day or night to take a photo of anyone who was hanging around the building."

"If he was up here, how would he know if there was anybody hanging around outside? Did he spend all his time at the windows?"

"No, the doormen would call him."

"Did he pay them?"

"I don't know."

"There's never been anything on his expense reports about paying doormen," Ibarretxe said. "However, we are quite generous to the staff here at Christmastime."

"We are?" the señora asked, and the question told McKenna two things: One was that she didn't know the way things were done in New York, and the other, that the luxurious apartment was supplied to them by the Spanish government, all expenses paid.

"Used to be three thousand for the building staff, but Jorge insisted we raise it to four thousand every year," Ibarretxe said. "I believe we did so last year."

"Nice number," McKenna said. "Let's find the camera and photos."

Finding the photos proved to be the easy part. The two thick photo albums were in the bottom desk drawer. One album contained photos taken around the building. They were all shots of people taken from a distance, and then a head shot of the same person with the zoom lens. The other contained photos taken around town, one photo to a subject. Very few of the subjects in the photos looked suspicious to McKenna, but he conceded to himself that the bird watchers probably wouldn't have aroused much suspicion in him either.

Unfortunately, the photos turned out to be useless; under each photo, Jorge had written the date and location where it had been taken, and the last photo in the albums was dated March 20. The search resumed for the camera, but it wasn't in any of the dresser drawers or in the closet.

"This is crazy," Bara said. "It's got to be here, but why would he hide it?"

"I don't know," McKenna replied, looking around the room. Then he thought he had it. "It's not hidden, it's in the place he wants it if he needs it in a hurry," he said. He pulled back the drapes of one window. Not there, but it was on the wide windowsill behind the drapes of the other window, right next to a pair of quality high-power binoculars. The camera was a good one, a Nikon with a 300 mm telephoto lens attached.

McKenna picked up the camera and examined it. "Roll of thirty-six, and he's shot twenty-eight," he announced. He put the camera to his eye and adjusted the zoom lens to focus on one of the skateboarders standing on the park roadway. It was Gabriel, and he filled the lens.

"Can you see those people in the park clearly?" the señora asked.

"Señora, if our luck holds, your Jorge has given us great pictures of the people who murdered him and kidnapped your husband."

FIVE

Bara had a lot on his mind, and it didn't take him long to speak his piece. "Brian, that was a hell of a job you just did," he said as soon as they got on the elevator. "You know I'd love having you stay on this case."

"But?" McKenna said, prodding Bara on.

"Cisco. He has a tough time following directions when they don't exactly coincide with the way he thinks things should be done."

"I know he ran you ragged and tried your patience on that last case," McKenna conceded.

"That he did."

"But there's no escaping the fact that he still did good and managed to close the case."

"It turned out okay. We got our man, and both the Bureau and the NYPD wound up looking very good."

"So everybody was happy except you."

The elevator doors opened. They stepped out into the lobby, but Bara wasn't done. "Forget me, for the moment," he insisted. "Let's talk about this case. There's already police agencies from three countries involved. To solve it, we're going to need a team effort—and that isn't Cisco."

"Only with team players who don't realize that he's almost as good as he thinks he is, and sometimes just as good. He'd add a lot to this case, once people got used to his ways."

"And you're used to his ways?"

"He drives me nuts sometimes, but just as often he makes me laugh. We're a team."

"An inseparable team?"

"If I had a choice, I wouldn't go without him. I want to work this case, but so does Cisco."

"Sure he does. He smells headlines and glory, another chance for him to dance center stage in the spotlight."

"And show off some pretty good police work while he's at it," McKenna countered. "That'll happen, but that's not why he wants this case. He wants it for the same reason I want it."

"Carmen?"

"Yeah, Carmen. Like me, he knows her, respects her, and loves her in a certain way. Remember, it isn't often in this game that you get the chance to help out somebody you actually know and like."

"Then you should both keep this in mind. There will be plenty of international police cooperation on this case, but we're only actually working the New York angle. Freeing Carmen will be up to the Guardia Civil."

"I know that, but all three cases are intertwined. We catch the people who took the ambassador, and then we squeeze them—maybe even turn them—and we might be in a good position to help the Spanish police get her back."

"I hope you don't mean physically help them."

"That would be nice," McKenna said, "but that's not what I mean. They're sending us intelligence information on the ETA. We do our jobs right, and we'll be sending quite a bit of information back to them."

"Give me some time to think about it," Bara asked.

"Can't do that, Tommy. He's already contributed too much to cut him out. Can we be candid for a moment?"

"Sure, but I already know what you're gonna say: I'm the boss, but you've got the weight."

"True, but that's not what I was going to say. I was gonna ask what you think Juan Diego Ibarretxe is doing right now."

"Talking on the phone with somebody high up in the State

Department, making an official diplomatic request that you be assigned to this case," Bara said. "Hell, with the heat that's already on, he might even be talking to the secretary of state himself."

"Right. So without calling in any chips, I'm in anyway. And if I make some noise about bringing Cisco along, then what?"

"He's in, too. I see what you're getting at," Bara said. "Okay. You've got a deal."

"Good. Next issue: How long will it take you to have that film developed?"

"On a Sunday? I don't know," Bara said. "I don't think we can get it done commercially today, and our photo section doesn't work Sundays."

"Neither does ours."

"I guess I'll have to call one of our photo technicians in, but I don't know how long it will take."

"Why bother?" McKenna asked. "Do you know Joe Walsh?"

"That blowhard? Know him well enough to despise him."

"Do you know him well enough to know that he's a great amateur photographer, and that he develops all his own pictures in the photo lab he's got set up in his basement?"

"Maybe I don't despise him all that much," Bara said. "Where does he live?"

"Park Slope, Brooklyn. With no traffic, about a half hour from here."

"Would he do us that favor?"

"He'd do me that favor, if there was something in it for him that only you could arrange," McKenna said. "Should arrange, I might add, because he's the best crime technician in the business. He's done pretty good today, finding things anyone else might've missed."

"Like what?"

"It was him that found the coins."

"You didn't mention it was him that found them."

"Because I knew we'd have to talk about it. Walsh still

has them, along with the twenty-dollar bill, the butt, the spent cartridge case, and the señora's belt buckle."

"Then I'll get them from him," Bara said. "This is a federal case, and we're the ones who are going to be processing the evidence."

"We're talking fingerprint evidence here, and nobody can lift prints like Walsh can," McKenna stated.

"We've got some pretty good people, you know. Nationally renowned."

"Nobody as good as Walsh, and this is the most important case to come along in some time. Use him, and you can rest assured you'll get good lifts on any remotely usable prints that are on those things."

"Brian, do you have any pals who aren't complete egotistical pains in the ass?"

"Yes, but they aren't the best at what they do. Cisco and Walsh are."

"If I let Walsh do it, can you keep him from tooting his own horn in the press about it?"

"Yes, at least until this case is over."

"Then that's fine, I guess. Once the case is over, anything he has to say will only make the back pages."

"Thanks, Tommy. Let's go give them the news."

"How's this. I don't feel like talking to Walsh, so you give him the news and the rules."

"Fine."

Bara took the camera from around his neck and gave it to McKenna.

Walsh's Crime Scene Unit van had been moved to the corner of East 81st Street and Fifth Avenue. A black building maintenance worker was manning the door at 920 Fifth Avenue, so McKenna guessed that Cisco was using his "break" to grill the boys' father. There were two pay phones side-by-side on the East 81st Street side of the building.

They found Walsh behind the wheel of his van, working on the *Sunday Times* crossword puzzle. Bara waited in front of the building while McKenna talked to him.

"How'd you do with the phones?" McKenna asked.

"Perfect. Lifted some prints while the doorman watched, real interested. Then Cisco talked to him. The dope denied making the call, said he never used that pay phone. Then Cisco told him we had his voice on tape from his nine-one-one call, so it would be better for him if he 'fessed up. Confused the guy, but he still denied making the call. Next, Cisco told him we probably had his prints from the phone."

"And that did it?"

"No. This guy really didn't want to talk, so Cisco gave him that big-time federal threat."

"Lying to us isn't a crime, but lying to the FBI is?" McKenna guessed.

"That's the one. Cisco told the guy he could be back with a fed in two minutes so he could tell his lies again. That might've done it, because the guy started blabbing."

"What did he say?"

"Don't know. They went into Spanish at that point, and then Cisco took him to the maintenance office in the building to interview him."

"And they're still in there?"

"Uh-huh."

"Then Cisco is busy and doing good. Are you ready for a few very important missions that will keep you pretty busy for a while?"

"Very important missions? Of course. That's what I do," Walsh said.

"We need all the evidence you have dusted by the best."

"Including the brass buckle?"

"Uh-huh."

"Then it will be. Who specifically is *we?*"

"Tommy, Cisco, me, and the other members of the Joint Terrorism Task Force."

"Are you and Cisco making the move?"

"Only until this case is over."

"Good thinking. The feds are a glory-hogging bunch who never give us credit when credit is due, but it tickles me to learn they've finally come to their senses," Walsh said. "Did you get them to actually admit that Joe Walsh is the best crime scene man in the country?"

"In so many words, but here's the deal. You still can't tell your reporter pals how good you're making us all look until the case is over."

Walsh appeared physically hurt by that rule. "No matter how good I do?"

"No matter. It's the same Sheeran Rule he gave you this morning, doubly reinforced. If you can promise me that you'll play by that rule, I've got an even bigger mission for you."

"Tough one for me, but you've got my promise. Let's have it."

McKenna gave him the camera. "There's twenty-eight pictures in there that we need developed in a hurry by an expert."

"You got one. Pictures of what?"

"We're hoping pictures of the kidnappers while they were acting as bird-watchers in the park."

"How'd you get this camera?"

"I'll tell you, but we don't have time to talk right now. Bring me the pictures, and you get the whole story."

"How many prints, what size, and where do you want them delivered?"

"As many as you can, in whatever size you think best, and delivered to the Nineteenth Precinct as soon as possible."

"Say no more." Walsh put on his seat belt, and a moment later he was speeding down Fifth Avenue, roof lights flashing and siren blaring.

"Looks like you really wound him up," Bara said as McKenna rejoined him. "Did he understand the gag rule?"

"He understood, and you won't be reading any of his exploits in the press until this case is resolved."

"I hope so. Where's Cisco?"

"In this building behind us, talking to the doorman."

"Another witness?"

"Made one of the nine-one-one calls this morning, and he's the father of the kids we found in the park. Reluctant at first, but Cisco and Walsh fixed that. Cisco's had him in there for a while, so I'm guessing he's got a lot to tell. You wanna go in and find them?"

"No," Bara said. "For me, inviting Cisco aboard will be a personally unpleasant chore. I'd rather wait as long as possible before doing it."

"All right. Then why don't we talk about the dog while we're waiting?"

"I'll listen to your thoughts."

"Okay. First, let's make a few assumptions. Let's assume that this whole kidnapping team is from Spain."

"Fine."

"And they arrived here some weeks ago, at least, with the express purpose of planning the ambassador's kidnapping on this specific date, and then pulling it off."

"Another good assumption," Bara said. "It had to be today, because they wanted all three kidnappings to take place on the same date. Big surprise for the Spanish government."

"So we're looking for some recent arrivals who somehow acquired a female golden retriever named Duchess. Now, here's a tough one. Let's assume the dog has a license."

"That *is* a tough one. Señora Clavero said she wasn't sure whether or not the dog had a license."

"I know, but we'll know more after we talk to her doorman. In any event, the dog knows and likes Number One, the driver. That means he's had the dog for a while, probably since this kidnapping was in the planning stage. They decided they needed a dog for their plan, and they got that one. The question is: Where did they get it from?"

"Could be anyplace. The ASPCA, a pet shop, a friend, or maybe they found it in the street."

"Let's go through them, one by one. If it's the ASPCA, they require that you produce some kind of ID, get a license for the animal, and that license has got to be mailed to the address on your ID."

"Tedious job, going through all the ASPCA records for a golden retriever adopted in the last month, but not a hard job. I guess it has to be done," Bara said.

"Maybe, but I don't think it's the ASPCA. This group wouldn't want to show any kind of ID to get the dog, and I think we can discount pet shops as well. They usually sell puppies, and Duchess isn't a puppy."

"So where does that leave us? Got it from a friend, or found it on the street?"

"If they just borrowed the dog for the job, I think you can discount the friend angle. They were going to leave it on the set, and how would they explain that to whoever? And what friend would want his dog associated with a kidnapping of this magnitude, anyway—even if he gave them the dog?"

"I see. If this friend gave them the dog for the job, he would have to know what they were planning. So you're saying it's most likely they found the dog on the street?"

"Or stole it. If that happened, there's a good chance that there's a police record on the theft somewhere."

"Easy enough to find out. So if we find out Duchess was stolen, where does that leave us?"

"Maybe with a neighborhood where they're staying right now, a place to start looking if everything else we're doing right now doesn't work out."

Bara looked at his watch. "Eleven-thirty. Considering that the kidnapping happened less than four hours ago, I'd say that we're pretty far along in this investigation already."

"We've been lucky so far," McKenna said. "If it slows down, we're going to be spending a lot of time looking for people seen walking a golden retriever named Duchess."

"I don't think it will come to that," Bara said.

"Let's hope not, but it might."

They spent a few minutes in silence, and then Cisco came out of the building alone.

"Where's the doorman?" McKenna asked.

"Downstairs, changing."

"Is he done for the day?"

"He is now. I talked to the building manager for him. Our favorite doorman is taking the rest of the day off, and probably the rest of the week off. He's going to call his wife, then we're going to take him and the boys out for a nice lunch."

"You got a lot from him?" Bara asked.

"Enough to make him a material witness. The government's going to be paying to stash him and his family in a good hotel."

"Does he know that?"

"Know it? Had to promise him that before he'd talk at length. Also had to promise him that they'd all be under guard until we rounded up all the desperadoes involved, and that still wasn't enough to get him really talking."

"You didn't promise to pay him for the information, did you?" Bara asked.

"No, I simply told him that the ETA had also kidnapped Carmen de la Cruz. He's a religious man and a real fan of hers, and that pissed him off good and proper. When I told him that telling me everything he knows might help us get her back, he was ready to talk and talk and talk."

"What'd you get?"

"The rest of the story, and a few bonuses. Plate number on the van, and he had a partial plate on the other backup car. It's an old Lincoln Town Car, late eighties or early nineties. Made a few calls, and now I've got both plate numbers they had on those vehicles this morning. Both sets were stolen from the Macy's parking garage in Queens last night."

"They only stole the plates?"

"Uh-huh. The plates were all they needed."

"Then that doesn't help us much," Bara noted. "Those plates are off those cars by now."

"But it does tell us that the vehicles they used probably aren't stolen," Cisco countered. "If they were stolen, why would they bother to put stolen plates on top of stolen plates? They would just dump the van and the Town Car when they were done with the job."

"I agree," McKenna said. "They've still got the van and the Town Car, and probably legally own them."

"And we're going to find out who at least one of them is and where he lives, because Cisco has much more to tell.

Our doorman watched that Lincoln get a parking ticket two weeks ago, right over there," Cisco added, pointing across Fifth Avenue.

"Start at the beginning," Bara said.

Cisco did. The doorman, Juan Santos, worked every Sunday from 6 A.M. to 2 P.M., and his wife worked Sundays for a Midtown office cleaning firm. As the boys had said, they stayed with him on Sunday, usually playing in the park while he was at work. Then they all met at Santos's building at 2 P.M. for the ride home to the Bronx.

Two Sundays ago Santos had first noticed the van and the Town Car. The drivers had pulled up across Fifth Avenue from his building, and six or seven people had gotten out. Santos hadn't paid much attention to them the first Sunday, but he had noticed that one of the passengers was a very pretty woman with long black hair. A few members of the group had binoculars and cameras, and they all hopped the wall and disappeared into the park. Since that section of Fifth Avenue along the park was a No Parking zone, the drivers remained with the van and the Town Car. The group emerged from the park a couple of hours later, got back in the van and the Town Car, and all left.

Santos's curiosity had been aroused when the group returned the next Sunday at about 7 A.M. and repeated the procedure, leaving the two drivers in the cars. The Town Car was parked behind the van, and the Town Car driver got into the van to chat with the driver while they were waiting.

Santos was inside at about eight o'clock, talking with the concierge, but he kept his eye on the door and saw a radio car pull up behind the Town Car. The driver of the radio car was writing a parking ticket for the Town Car, so he went outside and yelled to the men in the van, telling them that the Town Car was getting a ticket.

The men in the van had then done something Santos had thought strange at the time. He had figured that the driver of the Town Car would get out of the van and try to talk the cop out of the ticket, but he didn't. The van just pulled away, the cop put the ticket on the windshield of the Town Car, and then the radio car drove off.

The van returned a few minutes later, and the driver parked it in the same spot. The Town Car driver left the van, took the parking ticket off the windshield, put it in his pocket, and waited in the Town Car until the group returned.

Today, Santos half-expected them to return again, and they did—again at 7 A.M.—but this time they had the dog with them. Only the woman and two others hopped the wall into the park, and one of them was wearing black pants, a green guayabera shirt, and carrying a gym bag. Two men and the dog walked south on Fifth Avenue, and they were also dressed in green guayabera shirts and black pants. Santos lost sight of them when they crossed Fifth Avenue and walked down East 79th Street.

At least four men remained with the van and the Town Car. Santos saw two sitting in the Town Car, and two sitting in the front seats of the van. He had no idea what the group was doing, but his curiosity was definitely aroused.

Around seven-thirty, Santos noticed that one of the men in the guayabera shirts—the one without the dog—was standing on East 80th Street, just off the corner of Fifth Avenue. Santos looked down Fifth Avenue, and saw the one with the dog standing near the corner of East 79th Street. Santos was watching them when the concierge came out to tell him he was going downstairs to use the men's room.

Santos returned his attention to the van and the Town Car when he saw that the drivers in each had started their engines and were talking on radios. He had the feeling then that something was going to happen, but he didn't know what. He watched the Town Car pull out, go south on Fifth Avenue, and he stepped into the street to get the plate number as it was leaving. He got it, and he saw the Town Car double-park on the other side of East 79th Street. The two men got out of the Town Car, and were looking north on Fifth Avenue. Santos thought they were looking at him, and then he noticed the two men in the van were definitely looking at him.

Whatever was going to happen, Santos felt it would be something bad. He turned around, walked into the building, and wrote down the Town Car's plate number. He then looked outside, and saw that the men in the van had shifted their attention to the dog walker with the four dogs. She was on the other side of Fifth Avenue and had just walked past the van, but she didn't appear to be paying any attention to them.

Santos was just about to call the police from the concierge desk when he heard the shots outside, and then a woman screaming. He looked outside and saw the dog walker run past without the dogs. The man in the passenger's seat in the van was looking down Fifth Avenue, but the driver was looking through the building door at Santos. The woman had stopped screaming.

At that point, calling the police seemed like a bad idea to Santos. Less than a minute later, the van pulled slowly from the curb. Santos went outside to get the plate number, but only managed to get the last three digits, 145. He saw the van stop for a red light a few blocks down Fifth Avenue, and he was pretty sure it was behind the Town Car and another car. When the light changed, the three cars continued south down Fifth Avenue, and he saw that they all turned left in a line someplace around East 74th Street.

Santos then ran down Fifth Avenue to see what had happened. The doorman from the ambassador's building was holding the ambassador's wife, and she appeared to be in shock. The two bodies were on the ground, and he recognized Jorge Dominguez. He didn't know the chauffeur, but he surmised he was the Spanish ambassador dead on the sidewalk.

At that moment, Santos realized who the people were he had been watching for three Sundays in a row; for the first time, the ETA was operating in the United States. He walked back up Fifth Avenue, passed his building, and called 911 from the pay phone. He reported the two murders, but panicked when the 911 operator asked for his name. Having lived most of his life in Spain, he knew that the ETA dealt harshly with witnesses against them. He hung up, and decided not to mention another word about the killers to anyone.

After he had finished interviewing Santos, Cisco had called the NYPD Alarm Board and gave them the Town Car's plate. As he had expected, they told him there was an alarm on the plates, and they had been stolen the night before from a car in the Macy's parking garage in Queens.

Next, Cisco had called the 115th Precinct, the precinct that covers the Queens Macy's store. He asked the clerk at the complaint desk if any other license plates had been reported stolen in the Macy's garage last night. There were; commercial license plates bearing the number GX-109145 had also been stolen from a van in the Macy's garage, so Cisco had the plate number that had been on their van when the ETA kidnapped the ambassador.

"So the woman and two others went into the park," Bara said when Cisco had finished his account. "We know that the one in the green shirt has the rifle in the gym bag, and he leaves in the ambassador's car—with the rifle, but without the gym bag. Also in the gym bag had to be radios so the woman and the other guy could direct the operation."

"Figure some extra firepower, too, just in case anything went wrong on them," Cisco said. "According to Santos, the bag was bulky."

"All right, but does Santos say that he never saw the woman and the other one get back in the van or the Town Car?"

"Never saw them again once they entered the park, so those two didn't make the escape with the rest of the crew. Might've just walked out of the park and hailed a taxi, but we can't be sure. Those two are the only loose ends in Santos's story."

"No matter. Cisco, you did real good," Bara said. "So good, in fact, that I'm hoping you'll consider an offer."

"Cisco is prepared to consider."

"I'm hoping you'll accept an assignment to the Joint Terrorism Task Force to continue working this case."

"A very sensible offer, Mr. Bara, but Cisco must first consult his loyal assistant."

"I already told him, Cisco," McKenna said. "If you go, I'll go."

"Then it is decided. Mr. Bara, Cisco will lend his extensive expertise to your unit until he brings all these lowlife, murdering, filthy foreign scoundrels to justice."

"There's also a small problem here, Cisco," McKenna said. "I promised Tommy that you'd get off your high horse, that you wouldn't annoy him at all, and that you'd work hard at getting along with all the mere mortals in his unit."

"You did?"

"Yes."

"Brian, you're taking all the fun out of this job. Are you saying that you want me to be just like you?"

"I guess that's one way of looking at it."

"All right. I guess I can be boring for a while, if it's absolutely necessary," Cisco said, then turned to Bara. "Tommy, I accept your terms, and I won't be giving you any problems."

"Very glad to hear it," Bara said, and the two men shook on the deal.

"So I'm in for the duration, but would you mind answering a few questions for me?" Cisco asked.

"Not at all. Go ahead."

"Would you agree that it shouldn't take cops like us too long to wrap up this New York crew?"

"We're doing good, so far."

"Very good, maybe?"

"Okay, it appears that we're doing very good," Bara conceded.

"Then please tell me that we're in this until we get Carmen back."

"Cisco, you know I can't do that," Bara said, shaking his head. "We'll do our job in New York, which means getting the ambassador back and arresting those responsible for his kidnapping."

"And that's it? We get the ambassador back, and it's case closed?"

"Basically. If we develop information along the way that helps the Spanish police locate Carmen, so much the better. But keep in mind that the ambassador is our mission, not Carmen."

"Cisco doesn't like that answer."

SIX

Bara decided that Cisco would reinterview Santos and the boys in the presence of one of his agents over lunch. They would then be brought to the 19th Precinct to view the photos Dominguez had taken, and they would ultimately wind up at the U.S. Attorney's office to sign a statement.

Bara also found a way to save the government some money. The FBI maintained a safe house for witnesses near New Paltz, New York, fifty miles north of the city line, and the Santos family would be staying there. He arranged the security detail for them, and that detail included agents to drive the boys back and forth to their school in the Bronx.

Bara then drove McKenna to the 19th Precinct station house, and they saw that all the reporters who had been in front of the ambassador's building were camped outside, awaiting developments.

The precinct CO's office had been commandeered by Brunette, and he was there with Shields when Bara and McKenna entered. Brunette was seated at the CO's desk, writing on a pad, and Shields was pacing.

McKenna had the feeling they were interrupting something. "What'cha doing?" he asked.

"Putting together a press release so we can get rid of that crew outside," Brunette answered.

"Who's going to give it?"

"We'll decide that now." Brunette took a quarter from his

pocket and flipped it in the air. "Call it," he said to Shields.

"Heads."

It was heads. "I guess Gene is giving the statement," Brunette said.

"Not so. I won, and that gives me my choice," Shields countered. "I think that photogenic police commissioner the press loves is the one who should be giving it."

McKenna thought Shields was right, but didn't say so. Brunette was a tall and handsome black-haired man, and he was always ready with a quick comeback to any difficult question they might ask. He was also the most popular police commissioner in recent memory—and very fair with the press—so most reporters took pains to portray him in a good light. Shields had headed the FBI's New York office for ten years, and he was a well-respected figure around town, but he was nowhere near as photogenic as Brunette, and he didn't enjoy quite the same positive relationship Brunette had with the press.

"Okay, I lose," Brunette said. "I'll be the one talking to them today, but it's you from then on. Your case, your press conferences."

"Deal," Shields said, then turned to Bara. "Give Ray some good news to tell them, please."

"Probably can't tell them much of it, but there is good news," Bara said, and then he filled in Brunette and Shields on the developments in the case. Both appeared content with the progress. When he finished his report, Bara officially requested that McKenna and Cisco be transferred to the Joint Terrorism Task Force. That request was immediately approved by Brunette and Shields, but Shields did have one question on Joe Walsh's role in the case. It was a question both McKenna and Bara had anticipated. "Both Sheeran and Brian have given him the rules, and Walsh agreed to abide by them," Bara said. "Nothing to the press from him until the case is over, and I'm fairly confident that's the way it's gonna be."

"Just to be sure, I'll also have a chat with him," Brunette said, but his mind was elsewhere. He called the desk officer and told him he wanted a copy of the parking ticket that was issued to a Lincoln Town Car on Fifth Avenue at about 8 A.M. the Sunday before. He also wanted all DMV information available on the owner.

"Anything good been happening on this end of the investigation?" McKenna asked after the desk officer left on his mission.

"The dog walker was interviewed, and she's gone now," Shields said. "Not much help, the only one she said she would recognize if she saw him again was the shooter in the park. The ambassador's doorman is a much better witness, and quite a guy. Even though he got bonked on the head, he says he could ID all three if he saw them again."

"Who interviewed him?" McKenna asked.

"Tommy McKenna."

"Did he happen to ask him if the dog had a license hanging from its collar?"

"He did, and the dog *did* have metal tags hanging from its collar," Brunette replied. "Maybe a license, maybe just a name tag."

McKenna wasn't surprised that his namesake had thought to ask the question. In most cases, once Tommy had finished an interview, there wasn't anything left to be asked. "How did he do with the two witnesses he found in the ambassador's building?" he asked.

"They both say that they might be able to recognize the shooter in the park if they saw him again, but they didn't see any of the action in front of the building."

"Are they still here?" McKenna asked.

"I believe so."

"Did they mention seeing the Basque woman and the other one in the park?"

"No, but Tommy wouldn't know to ask them about them," Brunette said. "He didn't know that the action was being directed from the park by her."

"Then, for once, Tommy has to give them a few more questions. I'm hoping they noticed the Basque woman and her pal. If so, maybe they can give us an indication on where they went after the action. How about the Mercedes?"

"My lab people are still going over it," Shields said. "The kidnappers must've wiped the car down when they dumped it, because we've got no prints from the door handles, the rearview mirror, or the steering wheel. Some prints from the dashboard and windows, but I expect we'll find those belong to either the chauffeur, the bodyguard, the ambassador, or his wife."

"Dog hairs?"

"Plenty from the backseat, so they figure the dog must be shedding. Long gold hairs."

"Where's Tommy now?"

"Upstairs in the squad room," Brunette said.

"If you don't need me for anything right now, I'm gonna go up and tell Tommy about the people in the park," McKenna said to Bara.

"Go ahead."

McKenna found Tommy in the 19th Detective Squad office, enjoying a cup of coffee with the doorman, who was wearing a bandage turban on his head. "Good to see you, brother," Tommy said when he saw McKenna. "Glad you're working this case."

Although they were in no way related, McKenna appreciated the "brother" designation from Tommy, since it was well-known throughout the Detective Bureau that only detectives Tommy thought to be hard-working and very competent were entitled to be called "brother" by him.

"Are you going to be staying on it?" McKenna asked.

"Ray asked me if I wanted to, but I declined. Getting too close to retirement, and this case might stretch out in the courts for years once you get them."

Tommy had thirty-five years on the job, and had been talking retirement for years, but McKenna had always figured it wouldn't happen anytime soon. Although Tommy had never said so, McKenna knew that he loved being recognized by many as the best homicide detective in the city. But Tommy might be serious this time, McKenna thought, because he didn't want in on a big case that would involve many court appearances once the kidnappers were caught. Retired cops don't get paid to go to court on their old cases, but they must always answer the subpoena to appear.

Tommy then introduced McKenna to José Gomez, the ambassador's doorman. McKenna told Gomez that he admired his dedication and courage during the kidnapping, but Tommy went further than that. He told Gomez that he was going to put him in for the mayor's heroism award, and Gomez was obviously pleased to hear it.

"Do you have any further questions for Mr. Gomez?" Tommy asked McKenna.

"Not one, but we're going to need him in about an hour to look at some pictures."

"Pictures?" Tommy asked.

"I'll explain in a minute," McKenna answered, then turned to Gomez. "Why don't you go out and get a bite to eat for an hour or so?"

"You said pictures. Do you mean pictures of the killers?" Gomez asked.

"If we're lucky."

Gomez left, and McKenna then brought Tommy up-to-date on the case. Tommy saw the problem at once. "Looks like I have to ask Sandra and Daniela a few more questions about those two in the park," he said.

"Are they still here?"

"Went out to pick up breakfast. They should be back in a few minutes."

"Which one's the maid?"

"Daniela. Nice lady, and very cooperative."

"And Sandra?"

"Sandra Bullmore. Old money, very refined, initially reluctant to be involved. Said her friends would think her foolish once they found out she had volunteered a statement to the police."

"How did you change her?"

"At first I tried civic duty, but that didn't work. Then I used the class struggle angle on her, and she was on board. A member of her high social class had been kidnapped and his servants murdered by violent low-class reactionaries. We can't have that, can we?"

"Snooty?"

"At first, but now we're pals. She's led a sheltered life, and she now recognizes that this is the most excitement she's ever had."

McKenna made himself a cup of coffee, and he and Tommy made small talk until Sandra and Daniela returned five minutes later. Daniela was carrying a bag from Henry Pool's, one of the city's most exclusive delicatessens.

Sandra was a brunette in her fifties, slightly overweight, and she was attired in a gray pantsuit, with a string of pearls around her neck. Her maid was Hispanic, also in her fifties, also slightly overweight, and she wore a black uniform with a white apron.

Tommy introduced McKenna, and then told them he would have a few more questions. He also told them that he wanted to show them some pictures, but that the pictures wouldn't be delivered to the station house for another hour.

The ladies didn't seem to mind the wait, and then Tommy was solicitous enough to ask if they would rather eat before the short interview. It turned out to be a tough question, and they talked it over for a minute before deciding that breakfast could wait. Despite the obvious employer-employee relationship, McKenna got the impression that Sandra and Daniela were friends.

"Who wants to be first?" Tommy asked.

"If you like, I'll go first, ma'am," Daniela said to Sandra.

"Not necessary, dear. You went first the last time," Sandra replied. "Why don't you have your coffee and enjoy your Danish while I get this chore out of the way?"

"I don't mind being first."

"And neither do I. I'm first, and that's that."

"Yes, ma'am, but if it takes too long, I'm going to finish my Danish and then eat yours."

"You do that, bitch, and you'll have to make lunch for a week," Sandra said evenly, shocking both the McKennas.

"Suit yourself, cow," Daniela replied, apparently unconcerned. "I don't mind making lunch, but you can be sure I'll be spitting in your soup for a week."

The two women glared at each other while the McKennas remained shocked and speechless. Tommy was the first to recover. "I see you ladies have decided to really let your hair down today," he observed.

Sandra and Daniela ignored him and continued glaring at each other. Sandra was the first to break. She could contain herself no longer, and burst out laughing. Daniela followed suit, and the two ladies hugged each other and slapped each other on the back.

"I see," McKenna said. "You girls played a little joke on us."

"Yes, we did," Sandra said. "Was it a good one?"

"A real side-splitter. Where did you dig that routine up?"

"We invented it ourselves about ten years ago," Daniela said proudly. "Everyone we know has already seen it, and we don't get to use it too much anymore."

"How long have you two been friends?"

"Friends? Whatever gave you that idea?" Sandra asked, smiling. "I hate her. She's lazy, she's slovenly, and you already know she's very disrespectful. I wind up doing most of the work myself."

"And I hate her more than she hates me," Daniela proclaimed. "She's cheap and fussy, and she eats all the pimientos out of the olives."

Only in New York can wackos like Sandra and Daniela hide out among us, usually unnoticed, McKenna thought. "I see," he said, then turned to Tommy. "So these are your two prize witnesses? Could you honestly believe anything either of these two ladies ever told you?"

"Not anymore," Tommy replied.

"Wait a minute! We were telling the truth about that man in the park," Sandra protested.

"Yes, every single word," Daniela added. "We wouldn't lie about a thing like that. There was nothing funny about it."

"We know that. Brian was just kidding. We're both ready

to believe anything else you might be able to remember," Tommy said. "However, you have to promise to be good, or we'll send you home without asking any more questions or letting you see the pictures."

"Okay, we'll be good," Daniela said.

"And very serious as well," Sandra added.

"Wonderful!" Tommy said. "Sandra, you're first."

Sandra was a model of decorum as she followed the McKennas into a small interview room off the main squad office. She took the seat indicated by Tommy, and the McKennas sat across the table from her.

"Okay. We're at your apartment window again, Sandra, right after Daniela called you over," Tommy said. "Close your eyes, think for a minute, and then tell me what you see."

Sandra did as she was told, and took the full minute to bring the scene back to her mind. "Like I said before, I see the man in the park. He's wearing a green shirt, and he has a rifle on the Central Park wall. It looks like he's getting ready to shoot."

"Okay, Sandra. Keep your eyes closed, but forget about that man. Look deeper into the park, toward the road. Are there any other people there?"

"Yes."

"How many?"

"One, a man."

"What's he doing?"

"Just standing there, but I know what happens next."

"We'll get to that in a moment. Does the man have anything in his hands?"

"I don't see anything."

"Is there anything on the ground close to the man?"

"I don't see that either right now, but I know there must be."

"What do you know must be there?"

"A green bag, like a large carry-on bag."

"You saw him with that?"

"Yes, later. After all the shooting and screaming. I'm trying, but I don't see him now. I'm not looking at him, I'm looking at the man with the rifle. But I do see him again later."

"Was there anyone with him then?"

"A woman."

"Can you describe her?"

"Young, I think. Long black hair, and she's wearing a very long skirt. It's brown, or beige."

"Young? Can you be more specific?"

"Maybe thirty, but I can't be sure. She was too far away."

"What do they do then?" Tommy asked.

"They walk away."

"Together?"

"Yes, they're together."

"Which way do they walk?"

"Left."

"On the road inside the park?"

"Yes, on the road."

"Left? So that would be south."

"Yes, south."

"Does it look to you like they're in a hurry?"

"No."

"Does that strike you as strange now?"

"I didn't think about it before, but I guess so."

"Why is it strange?"

"Because there were just a lot of shots very close to them, and that poor ambassador's wife had done a lot of screaming. They're not excited, and it looks like they don't care."

"Open your eyes, Sandra, and take a bow," Tommy said.

"I did good?"

"You did great. I hope Daniela does as well as you did."

"Don't tell her I said this, but she'll do better. She was at the window longer, and she notices everything about people."

"Why do you think that is?"

"Because she's very picky. She remembers every little thing that's wrong with someone. If somebody's clothes don't match exactly, she remembers."

"How about faces? Does she remember them?"

"Especially faces. One time we had a delivery boy who brought groceries to the apartment, and he had a tiny pimple on his nose. You know, he was going through that stage."

"An acne pimple?"

"Yes, acne, but not a bad case. I never even noticed it. That was five years ago, and he's certainly no longer a boy, but she still calls him the boy with the pimple on his nose."

"Then I can't wait to hear what she's got to say."

Daniela was just finishing her Danish when McKenna brought Sandra out. "Was it hard?" Daniela asked her.

"Very hard. You won't be any help at all."

"We'll see about that," Daniela replied.

In the interview room, McKenna directed Daniela to the seat her boss had just vacated.

"How did Sandra do?" Daniela asked.

"Very well," Tommy replied. "She told us what we needed to know."

Tommy knew his subjects, and didn't use the same close-your-eyes style he had used with Sandra. His questions for Daniela were clear cut and concise, but he asked her to think about each one for a few seconds before answering.

"When you were looking out the window this morning, did you see anybody else in the park besides the shooter in the green shirt?" Tommy asked.

"The apartment is pretty high up, so I saw many people," Daniela answered at once, disregarding Tommy's instructions.

Tommy didn't take any notice. "I'm talking about pretty close to the shooter," he said.

"Close to the shooter? Yes, in the park, but closer to the road than to the man with the rifle."

"How many people?"

"One at first, a man. After the shooting, I saw him and a woman."

"Did the man have anything with him?"

"A green piece of luggage."

"Where was it?"

"At first, it was on the ground next to a tree. After the shooting, the woman put something in it, and the man carried it when they walked to the road."

"Did you see what she put in the bag?"

"Something that looked like a rectangular black box, and there was a strap attached to it. She had it around her neck, took it off, and put it in the bag."

"Could it have been a radio like the police have?"

"I was gonna say that. It could have been a radio."

"When did you first see the woman?"

"After the shooting stopped."

"Where did she come from?"

"From behind a tree, right next to where the man was standing. The tree near the green bag."

"Did you think she was hiding?"

"I'm sure of it."

"Why do you think she was hiding?"

"Because she was peeing. That's why she went behind the tree—to pee where nobody could see her."

"She was peeing?" Tommy asked incredulously. "What makes you say that?"

"Because she was wearing a very long skirt. When she came out from behind the tree, she had it pulled up to her belly button. I could see the top of her boots, and I even saw her panties. White, very tiny panties, the kind you men like. She pulled the skirt down and straightened herself out before she put the radio in the bag."

"She was wearing boots?" McKenna asked.

"Yes, very high brown boots. The type you see prostitutes wear sometimes, they came up way past her knees."

"Lace-up boots?"

"Yes, lace-up, with lots of buckles. Very tacky, I think, and they certainly didn't go with the rest of her outfit. If you didn't see the boots, if you didn't see the panties, and if you didn't know she had just peed in the park with a man standing right there, you might think she was a nice girl."

"What else was she wearing?"

"Long skirt, beige-and-brown-checked. Wide brown belt,

big brass buckle. Long-sleeve brown sweater, vee-neck."

"Can you describe her?"

"I can't say how tall she was, but she was almost as tall as the man. Long black hair, maybe thirty years old, nice figure. Big bust, but not too big, and long legs. Very pretty face, I think."

"Was her hair straight or curly?"

"Wavy."

"What makes you think she was pretty? Could you see her face?"

"Not too clearly, we were too far away. But she walks like a woman who knows she's pretty. You know what I mean, a confident walk, like she's used to everybody looking at her."

"Did the man and the woman leave the park together?"

"I don't know if they left the park, but they must've left the area. They walked together to that road inside the park, and they made a left."

"Were they in a hurry?"

"No, they walked like they didn't have a care in the world."

"Would you think they were lovers?"

"No, unless the man was her sex slave. I got the impression that she was in charge."

"What gave you that impression?"

"When they were leaving the woods, she pointed at the bag on the ground, and then she just turned and started walking. He picked the bag up real quick, and had to run with it a bit to catch up with her."

"Let's get back to the tree," McKenna said. "Was it a big tree?"

"Big enough to hide her behind it."

"How wide would you say it was?"

"Fatter than me, but not as fat as Sandra."

That was a pretty precise measurement, McKenna thought. He figured that both Sandra and Daniela were about the same height and weight, and that they might even wear the same dress size. He looked to Tommy, and saw that he was puzzled, but he had no further questions.

"Am I done?" Daniela asked.

"Yes, we don't have any more questions for you," Tommy said. "Thank you very much."

"Did I do good?"

"Great, but you left us with some questions that we have to answer."

"I have a question. Did I do better than Sandra?"

"I'm not saying," Tommy replied, so Daniela looked to McKenna.

"Me neither," McKenna said. "Let's just say you both did great."

"You can say that if you want, but I'm gonna say that I did better."

"Suit yourself," Tommy said. "Why don't you go outside and finish your coffee with Sandra? We'll be with you in a minute or two."

"Peeing while the shooting's going on?" Tommy commented as soon as Daniela left the room. "What do you make of that?"

"Nothing. It was the obvious assumption for Daniela to make after what she saw, but the woman wasn't peeing," McKenna answered.

"Then what was she doing with her skirt pulled up to her navel?"

"Climbing down the tree, but the ladies didn't see that because she was climbing down the side opposite them. She was up the tree with her radio and a perfect view of the ambassador's building, directing the kidnapping. When it's over, she climbs down and they calmly split."

"So that's the deal with the high boots under a long skirt? She pulls up the skirt, and climbs up," Tommy said, and then stopped himself for a moment. "You know what it was she had on the boots?"

"Not just buckles, like Daniela thought she saw," McKenna replied. "She was wearing that spiked leg apparatus linemen wear to climb poles. She had them strapped to the boots, and they were brown to match the boots, but she didn't want to be seen in the park taking them on and off. Time-consuming job, I imagine."

"Right, and good planning on her part," Tommy said. "If something goes wrong on them, she doesn't want to be seen wearing them. That's the reason for the long skirt."

"You know what else it tells us?" McKenna asked.

"That you're going to be looking for a smart, pretty, careful Basque knockout who also is very athletic. Nice combo if she weren't a political fanatic who's surrounded herself with a bunch of stone-cold killers. Good luck, and I'll catch the rest of the story day-by-day on the evening news as you plod along."

SEVEN

By the time McKenna returned to the CO's office, Brunette and Shields had the DMV printouts on the 1989 silver Lincoln Town Car, and much more. "Looks like we have some answers to your questions on the dog," Brunette announced.

"Stolen?" McKenna asked.

"March fifth, from a backyard in Corona, Queens. The owner had the dog tied up there. Dog gone, rope cut."

"Licensed?"

"Yep. Collar around the neck with the license and name— Duchess."

"So there's a good chance they've got a place somewhere in Queens," McKenna reasoned.

"They do, but we don't know how much that helps us," Shields said. He took the pile of printouts off the desk and passed them to McKenna. "Let's see what you think."

McKenna took a seat and read while Brunette and Shields waited and watched him with undisguised interest.

The Town Car had been registered in the upstate town of Catskill by Antonio Ramirez on March 12, a month before. March 12 was the same day he also registered his other vehicle, a 1990 white Ford van. Ramirez had a valid insurance policy with Colonial Penn for both vehicles, and the effective date of the policy was March 9. The address Ramirez had listed when he registered the vehicles was a post office box in Tannersville, a small town about thirty miles west of Cat-skill.

Ramirez had obtained his driver's license on March 7, five days before he had registered the vehicles, and he had done it the hard way, taking the DMV test for his learner's permit on February 8, and passing his road test on March 1. The address listed on both his license and his learner's permit was 91-02 Denman Street, Apartment 3A, in Corona, Queens.

Although Ramirez had only had his license for a month and a half, he had already earned his first speeding ticket during a run of bad luck. At 5:30 A.M. on the morning of April 6—the same day his Lincoln had been issued the park-ing ticket on Fifth Avenue—he had been stopped by the state police on the New York State Thruway and awarded his ticket for doing seventy-two in a sixty-five-miles-per-hour zone.

McKenna studied the printouts for a few more minutes. The last item was a blown-up fax of Ramirez's license, and he committed the face to memory. Nothing remarkable about that face, he thought, and then he placed the papers on the desk without comment—but with a big smile.

"You got the deal, Brian?" Brunette asked.

"I think so. Do you?"

It was Shields who answered. "Yeah, we humbly think that we're just as smart and just as good as you are."

"It's got to work that way," McKenna said, still smiling. "If the big chiefs don't think they're just as smart or smarter than the Indians, the whole system falls apart."

"Very true," Shields said. "Orders issued by the chiefs without confidence aren't diligently followed by the Indians. The chiefs have to have a ninety-something-percent track record to keep their confidence up and the system running."

McKenna had played this game with Brunette many times, and he knew just what Brunette and Shields were do-ing. It was to be a brainstorming session, and he decided to play along. "And how do the chiefs keep their confidence up?"

"Simple," Shields said. "This is how it's done by wise chiefs . . ."

"People like yourselves, for instance?"

"Yes, by wise chiefs just like us. When confronted with an important puzzle, they put their heads together, reach a conclusion, and decide on a tentative course of action. Then they find themselves an unusually discreet, smart, and talented Indian—someone like yourself, for instance—and they show him the puzzle. If this special Indian comes to the same conclusion they did, and he recommends the same course of action they're contemplating, then the orders are issued and the plan goes forward with confidence."

"Sensible," McKenna said. "But what happens if this Indian doesn't reach the same conclusions they did?"

"They never tell him. Chiefs can't be wrong and the Indians right, but they do reexamine their own conclusions, looking for holes. If they find the holes, then they modify the conclusions, alter the plan, present it as their own, and implement it."

"And if everything goes right?"

"They never mention the Indian, and they take full credit."

McKenna smiled, knowing that was the way it worked in some big circles—but never with chiefs like Brunette and Shields. However, he liked the game, and was still playing. "And if something goes wrong?"

"Blame the stupid Indian, of course."

"Of course. And how do they first present this puzzle to the Indian? Do they tell him it's a test to see how smart he is, and that they already have the answers?"

"That's right. So let's see how smart you are."

"I'm game, but tell me something first," McKenna said. "What are we doing with this information now?"

"How do you know we're doing anything with it?"

"Because Tommy Bara should be sitting in on this session, helping you two give me the test. He's not, so I assume you've already given him a mission."

"Very good," Shields said. "For starters, Tommy Bara and most of the Indians in your new unit will be very busy for the rest of the day and, I imagine, most of tomorrow. He already got to the postmaster in Tannersville and found out that Ramirez had listed his Queens apartment when he rented the post office box."

"When did he rent the box?"

"March seventh," Shields replied.

"Figures. Five days before he gets the Town Car and the van, and a week after passing his road test. Ramirez is their advance man, the guy with all the valid ID who sets up everything they needed to pull off their kidnapping."

"Maybe, and now here's the first question for you," Shields said. "Why did he rent the box?"

"The obvious reason—to get mail at a place they figured we'd never find out about. But we got lucky. If it wasn't for that parking ticket, maybe we never would have found out about the box."

"What kind of mail?"

"Besides instructions from Spain, the regular kind of mail. Letters from home. We've got seven ETA people here that we know about, and they've been here for at least three weeks. Presumably at least some of them have family, and they need a way to communicate with them."

"So the families would know about the box?"

"No. The families send their letters to an ETA drop in Spain. Whoever's manning that drop forwards the letters to the box in Tannersville."

"But why Tannersville?"

"Because it's near their base camp, the place where they're holding the ambassador right now," McKenna said. "Do you know the area?"

"I didn't, but I know something about it now. Ray told me that you and him rented a ski house near there for two seasons back in the eighties."

"Did he tell you how we paid for our season rentals?"

"I told him," Brunette said. "Cash, the only thing the owner would accept."

"That's right. Only cash," McKenna said. "People buy those houses as money-making vacation properties they can enjoy. Beautiful area in the Catskill Mountains, only a hundred thirty miles from town, straight up the Thruway. Right between two nice ski areas, but there's something for all seasons. Lakes, camping, hiking trails, horseback riding, you name it. The owners use the houses when they can, but they're always for rent."

"Got how that works," Shields said. "They take the mortgage off their taxes, and put the cash in their pockets without declaring it as income."

"That's how they do it," McKenna said. "The usual deal is that someone rents the house for three months, cash in advance, with a big security deposit. As long as the renter has ID and looks halfway legitimate, he's in."

"And you think that's what Ramirez did?"

"That's what the guy calling himself Ramirez did. 'Antonio Ramirez' is a carefully constructed identity, created just for this job," McKenna said. "As Ramirez, he rented the perfect hideout—big house in the woods with plenty of room for the rest of the team, no nosy neighbors, large transient population so the gang isn't noticed, and no paper trail leading people like us to them."

"What about the Queens address?" Shields asked.

"Waste of time; nobody's there," McKenna said, and then he noticed that Brunette was nodding and smiling.

So Ray agrees with me, McKenna thought, and he must have told Shields as much. Let's have some fun. "Is that what you have Bara doing, Gene? Wasting time and manpower to run down that Queens apartment?"

"You're not alone in that opinion," Shields said. "Tommy also thinks it's a waste of time, but he also knows it still has to be done."

"It does, but how much time he wastes depends on how it's done. Do you have him getting court orders for the Con Edison and telephone company records on the Queens apartment?"

"That's right," Shields said defensively, and both McKenna and Brunette knew why. Since the chiefs of security for the phone companies and utility companies in New York

City were all NYPD retired bosses, Brunette knew that Mc-Kenna could get all the information necessary in an hour. If it worked out that he might need the information for trial purposes, he could then waste the time getting the court orders to make his evidence legally palatable.

However, both men knew that might be the NYPD way when time was short, but it was never the federal way. With a shared smile, Brunette and McKenna decided it would be done Shields's way, without negative comment.

"Okay, Bara will get the court orders for the phone company and for Con Ed, directing them to provide the billing information for their customer at the apartment," McKenna said. "He'll get the records indicating that someone calling himself Antonio Ramirez lives there and pays his bills, but it will take an intensive surveillance to establish that he's really not there anymore—and hasn't been since he got his driver's license."

"Why not?"

"Because he doesn't need the apartment after he got his license. That's when the rest of the crew arrived, and that's when he moved them in upstate."

"Maybe it's not a total waste of time," Shields said. "Maybe he made some phone calls to Spain from the Queens apartment."

"Maybe, if this gang isn't as smart and careful as we're giving them credit for."

"So you'd be surprised if he did?"

"Very," McKenna replied. "The ETA has been pulling kidnappings for more than thirty years. They've got over five hundred of their people in jail in Spain, so maybe they had to learn the hard way how to do it right."

"I agree," Brunette said, ignoring the rules of the game for a moment. "These three kidnappings are the biggest stunt they've ever pulled, so the plan was checked and double-checked to get it right. That means no stupid mistakes like phone calls to a traceable number in Spain."

"Let's say for the moment that we agree on that," Shields said, then returned his attention to McKenna. "Why do you think he got that Queens apartment in the first place? Just to get his driver's license?"

"That's right, because he needed more than his bogus passport in his Antonio Ramirez name to register the vehicles he'd need. He needed a driver's license. To get that, he needed a phone bill and a utility bill to show DMV in order to establish state residence."

"So what kind of ID did he use to rent the apartment? Just his passport?"

"And whatever else their forger cooked up for him. Not too important, because he probably paid cash in advance for the place, and I bet it's a dive."

"Why didn't they just have their forger cook him up a driver's license?"

"Spanish forger with no experience in our driver's licenses? Too risky. They knew they'd have the kidnapped ambassador and plenty of armed people in the van at some point, and they didn't want a shoot-out with the police if they got stopped on their way back to Tannersville. So they asked themselves: If it had to be a license good enough to pass police inspection, why not spend a little time and money to get a real one? After all, according to Ibarretxe, they're well-funded."

"Sounds plausible," Shields said, but one look at Brunette told McKenna that he was right in line with their conclusions. "How am I doing on my test?" he asked.

"Not bad, so far," Shields said. "But you don't get your final score until you tell us what your plan would be."

McKenna wanted to get that part right, so he took a few minutes to think it over. Just when he thought he had the answers, his cell phone rang. "I'm on my way back with your photos," Joe Walsh said.

"How'd we do with them?" McKenna asked.

"You'll like them. Twenty-eight nice shots of seven bird-watchers, and one of them's a real beauty."

"The woman?"

"She could make the cover of the *Terrorist Times* any time she wanted."

"Are the photos good enough for identification?"

"Even if you're blind in one eye and can't see too good with the other. Good photographer, good camera, and a great developer, so you've got good pictures."

"Thanks, Joe. Looking forward to seeing you," McKenna said, and ended the call. He then relayed the information to Brunette and Shields, and began his plan. "It's a pretty simple one, but it will require a lot of manpower. There are about ten small towns in the resort area centered around Tannersville that fit the bill, meaning towns with lots of rental houses so that this group won't be conspicuous. You have to relocate whoever's working this case to someplace near there."

"According to you, that would be a lot of people," Shields said. "It would probably be best to rent a motel."

"A motel close enough to the resort area, but far enough away to keep the locals from getting nosy. We know they use the Thruway to come down to town, so one on Route Thirty-two near the Thruway exit would be best."

"Are there many motels there?"

"Plenty, and this is the off season. You could get a good deal if you rent the whole place."

"And then?"

"Tedious police work. We'll have their pictures, and we know their cars, so part of the team stakes out the post office, gas stations, supermarkets, the Thruway entrance, and any place else they'd be likely to go."

"And if any of these people show up?"

"They have to be followed back to their house, and that will be difficult on those back roads. They'll be on guard, and looking for a tail, so we'll need some equipment ready to go."

"Locating transmitters?"

"If they leave the car for a few minutes, that would be the way to go."

"And the rest of the unit? What would they be doing?"

"Cruising the back roads in inconspicuous vehicles, looking for a house with the van or the Town Car parked outside—and maybe a golden retriever someplace in the yard. That's a lot of back roads, but it still shouldn't take that long to find them."

"What about garages? Do many of the houses have them up there?"

"No, and those that do usually place them off limits to the tenants as part of the agreement. The owners like to store their own stuff in there."

"So how long do you think it will take to find them?"

"A week, at the most."

"And when we do?" Shields asked.

"To capture them without getting the ambassador killed? Sorry, Gene. That's another puzzle calling for another plan. How'd I do with this one?"

Shields looked to Brunette, and got a nod and a smile in return. "Pretty good," Brunette said.

"Pretty good? Meaning?" McKenna asked.

"Meaning I think we're ready to proceed with our plan with a high degree of confidence," Shields announced.

Walsh entered the precinct CO's office with a flourish, holding the stack of five-by-seven photos in a way that reminded McKenna of Moses holding the Ten Commandments. He had made three copies of each of the twenty-eight photos, and he awarded Brunette, Shields, and McKenna a set apiece.

Brunette thanked Walsh, and then dismissed him with the message that he wanted to talk to him later. However, Walsh was a difficult man to dismiss. "Am I in trouble?" he asked.

"No, Joe, you're still in good graces," Brunette said. "I just want to make sure you stay that way."

"Don't worry, Commissioner. Not a word to the press until it's over, and that's a promise."

"Okay, Joe. I believe. How long will it take you to get the lifts off all our treasures?"

"Hours, but I'll have them sometime this afternoon—if I'm permitted to get to the lab right now without enduring another lecture."

"Enough said. Get back to work."

Walsh left, and the three men sifted through the photos.

McKenna thought the photos *were* good, maybe even as good as Walsh thought they were. By the change in the clothes worn by the subjects, he could tell that Dominguez had taken two shots of each of the seven bird-watchers on the two Sundays before. And Walsh was right about Dominguez; he had been quite a photographer, capturing each bird watcher in a full-length shot and a head shot on each date. On both dates, all but the woman had either a camera or a pair of binoculars around their necks. All the men were in their twenties or thirties, and McKenna studied their photos until he was certain he would know any of them if he saw them.

As for the woman, there was no need for McKenna to study her photo; she had a stunning face that was easy to remember, and maybe hard to forget. He looked closely for flaws, and could find only one. There was a small space between her front teeth, and he wondered why she had never had it corrected. Maybe she didn't want to be perfect, he thought, just another unflawed beauty fit for the covers of *Elle* or *Glamour*. On second thought, McKenna thought that small gap enhanced her appearance, giving her an aura of innocence, and that caused him to wonder what had happened in her life to turn such a delightful-looking woman into a cold-blooded killer.

McKenna stacked the photos, and found Brunette and Shields watching him. "Pretty, isn't she?" Brunette asked.

"I'll know her if I see her again," McKenna replied.

"Looks like she's in great shape, too, wouldn't you say?" Shields asked.

McKenna realized that he hadn't even got past her face to study her figure, but he didn't want to admit that. "Sure. Looks very athletic, just like we figured."

"Nice photos, but I don't think we'll be able to use them today and still keep ourselves free from court worries after we get this crew," Shields said.

"I agree, if we're still thinking about showing our witnesses photo arrays today," Brunette added.

As good as the photos were, McKenna knew Brunette and Shields were right. According to court-mandated procedure, witnesses must be shown a photo of the subject in a folder that also contains photos of five other persons not connected to the crime being investigated. These five others must be of the same general age as the subject, the same race, and also must have the same general hair characteristics.

Usually, that was not a problem. Every detective squad has pictures of hundreds of people to put in their photo arrays with their suspect. However, in this case, McKenna realized there was a monumental problem. The photos of the subject and the fillers all had to be the same size, shot from the same angle, and with the same background. Since the filler photos maintained by detective squads were all three-by-five shots, and since none of them were shot from the tenth floor with the park as a background, the witnesses waiting to identify the killers couldn't do it today. "So now what?" McKenna asked.

"We could have somebody shoot our fillers from the ambassador's apartment tomorrow, but it would be a problem," Shields said. "Unfortunately, we're not going to get that many people in the park to pose with cameras or binoculars around their necks, so we'd be taking pictures of our people for the filler photos—and we're going to be needing everybody we've got upstate tomorrow."

"Then let's not worry about dotting every *i* and crossing every *t*," McKenna suggested. "We know that three of the people in these photos were the people who actually grabbed the ambassador, and that's all that's important. Let's get them all, and sort out which one did what later."

"The director's not gonna like that," Shields said. "He's a stickler for proper investigative procedure."

"Nobody argues with success," McKenna countered. "Once we get them, you can tell him you decided to go for the Best Evidence Rule. When it comes to identifications, the courts have always preferred lineups to photo arrays. We catch them, put them in lineups, and have the witnesses tell us then who did what in front of the building."

"All right. We'll do it your way, and kill two birds with one stone," Shields said. "Bara promised to keep Ibarretxe informed on any progress we make, and the director just told me to make sure we do just that. Give him a call, and then go fill him in."

"You want me to tell him everything we're doing?"

"That's not what *I'd* want you to do, but I've got a boss, too. In this case, we're going to have to take many political considerations into account as we do the job."

McKenna called Ibarretxe, and was given an appointment to see him at 4 P.M. at the Spanish Embassy. Ibarretxe said that he expected to have the full details on the kidnapping of the ambassador in Paris and Carmen's kidnapping by then, which suited McKenna just fine. However, it did leave him with almost three hours to kill. He took his set of photos and the DMV printouts and went up to the Detective Squad office. He decided to use his downtime to stay abreast on his paperwork. He used NYPD forms to type his reports on the interview of Ibarretxe and Señora Clavero, the discovery of Dominguez's camera, and the receipt of the developed photos from Joe Walsh. They were short reports, and he was just putting the finishing touches on the last one when Cisco came into the squad office.

"Did you get any more from the boys and their father?" McKenna asked.

"Nothing significant. What have you been doing here?" Cisco asked, and McKenna told him. After Cisco studied the DMV printouts, McKenna was glad that Cisco arrived at the same conclusion he had: the whole gang was upstate, and Bara was wasting his time in Queens.

Next, Cisco thumbed through the photos, and he stopped at the woman's. "This gorgeous creature is the enemy?" he asked, holding up the head shot.

"That's her."

"Then we're really moving up in class, amigo. I can't wait to meet her."

EIGHT

The Spanish Embassy was located at East 48th Street and First Avenue, close to the United Nations, and McKenna arrived right on time at 4 P.M. One of Ibarretxe's aides was waiting for him in the lobby, and she escorted him past two security checkpoints to Ibarretxe's office. Ibarretxe was waiting at the door to his office. He greeted McKenna, brought him in, and dismissed the aide.

Ibarretxe had a large office, appointed with enough luxury in the way of furniture and paintings to give McKenna an indication that being Spain's deputy ambassador to the United Nations was a big job. Ibarretxe had taken the time to shave and change his clothes, and he was wearing a formal pinstripe suit. Since the embassy was on a Sunday schedule, and McKenna had seen nobody else there except for the aide and the four security people, he assumed that the deputy ambassador had taken the trouble to change solely for their meeting.

Ibarretxe sat at his desk, and McKenna sat in a comfortable leather chair facing him. "Have they issued any demands yet?" McKenna asked.

"A couple of hours ago, by fax to *El País*. Madrid newspaper. No return number on the top of the fax, so it was untraceable."

"What are they demanding?"

"A little less than was expected. All ETA prisoners are to

be transferred to a prison in the Basque country. All sentences are to be commuted to five years. Those that have already served five years are to be freed."

"No mention of negotiations?"

"None."

"Any timetable or threats to execute the hostages?"

"None, but there is something we expected. The communiqué explicitly stated that under no circumstances would La Tesora be harmed."

"La Tesora?"

"Common nickname for Carmen. The Treasure."

"So they're just as smart as you thought they were," McKenna observed.

"Hard to say. They might just be reacting to events, because there certainly have been some unusual happenings since our people learned they took La Tesora."

"Your people? Do you mean the Basques or the Spanish?"

"The Basques. Euskal Herritarrok is the political arm of the ETA, and it has offices in all the major Basque cities. Mobs formed outside their office in San Sebastian this afternoon. Orderly demonstration at first, with everyone chanting, 'Return the Treasure,' but the demonstration got out of hand and turned into a mob. They ransacked the building, and then burned it. Two hours later, the same thing happened at the Euskal Herritarrok offices in Bilbao."

"Euskal Herritarrok functions as a political party?"

"Yes. Before today, it was the second most powerful party in the Basque Country. The Basque Nationalist Party is fairly moderate and controls all three provincial governments in the Basque Country, but the mayor of Bilbao is associated with Euskal Herritarrok."

"What were the police doing while the mob was ransacking and burning?"

"They watched while the mob cheered, and so did the firefighters. They kept a stream of water on the adjoining buildings, but they let Euskal Herritarrok's offices burn to the ground."

"I hope you don't think this question is out of line, but is there any chance this whole thing was orchestrated by the Madrid government?"

"In the Basque Country? Never. There aren't enough Spaniards living in the Basque Country to form mobs of that size, and the mob was chanting in Basque. Less than one percent of Spaniards speak the language."

"What was the mayor of Bilbao doing while all this was going on?"

"The sensible thing. He stood with the cops and watched the building burn to the ground. Then he made a speech denouncing the kidnapping of La Tesora and demanding her immediate return. Wild applause, so he went even further. Announced he was quitting Euskal Herritarrok and joining the Basque Nationalist Party."

"So I guess Euskal Herritarrok is finished."

"I think the ETA is finished. Without support in the Basque Country, they can't operate."

"Then why did they take her?"

"Madrid thinks it's their last hurrah, and the ETA planned it that way," Ibarretxe said. "The government will be under intense pressure to negotiate Carmen's return, and the ETA gets what it wants—the eventual release of their people before the organization fades out of existence."

"And then peace?"

"Presumably. The prisoners are the ETA's last achievable reason to exist."

The idea made McKenna smile. Let's see how good we're doing here, he decided, and he passed Ibarretxe the head shot of the woman.

McKenna had expected Ibarretxe to recognize her immediately, but he just studied the photo without comment, then passed it back. "Very pretty. Where does she fit into this?"

"She's the leader of the team that kidnapped your ambassador. You don't recognize her?"

"Sorry, no. Should I be able to?"

"I guess I was expecting you could. I'd figured that the leader of this group would be a famous ETA fugitive."

"Maybe she is now, but I'm not aware of it. I haven't been home in a year, so I'm really not up-to-date."

"So there's someone in the Guardia Civil who could identify her from this picture."

"Colonel Segovia will do it, if anyone can. He'll be here tomorrow morning."

"Good. Can you give me the details of the other kidnappings now?"

"Suppose I show you? I have all the police reports on the cases. They're in Spanish and French, of course, but I'd be happy to translate the French for you."

"I speak French," McKenna said.

Ibarretxe showed no surprise, and McKenna figured that, like most Europeans, Ibarretxe expected that an educated person would naturally be proficient in a number of languages.

McKenna had long since become accustomed to reading the reports prepared by other police agencies, and over the years he had found that they all followed the same general format. On top were the reports from the Paris police. The kidnapping there had begun at 4:15 A.M., when two armed men wearing ski masks hijacked a newspaper delivery truck and kidnapped the driver in the Arrondissement 4 area of central Paris. The driver was tied, blindfolded, and gagged in the back of the truck, but he believed they stopped somewhere near the Boulevard Ste. Michelle to pick up another two or three men.

The police were unable to uncover any witnesses to the initial stage of the assault on the ambassador's building, but they were able to surmise what had happened. At about 4:30 A.M., the newspaper delivery truck pulled up in front of the building and one of the terrorists shot and killed the gendarme standing guard in front. It was assumed that the shooter used the ruse of delivering papers to the building to get close to the gendarme, because a tied stack of newspapers was found next to his body.

The concierge was on the phone with his wife when the gunmen entered, and it was assumed that the gunmen feared he was warning the ambassador or calling the police. He was shot dead, two shots to the head. His wife heard the shots through the phone, and called the police. Many police units were dispatched to the scene, but by that time the killers were outside the ambassador's apartment. They attached Goma Two plastic explosive charges to the door, and blew it in.

The ambassador's bodyguard, a sergeant in the Guardia Civil, must have heard the shots downstairs, because he was up and ready for company. He had taken cover behind a couch in the living room, and he had his pistol in his hand. However, he wasn't ready when the door blew in. The door hit the couch, knocking the sergeant over. He managed to get one shot off, and he apparently hit one of the terrorists before being killed by a burst of fire from an automatic weapon. There was a pool of blood found near the front door, and one ejected shell from the sergeant's pistol was found near his body. No slug was found, so the police assumed that it was still lodged somewhere in the body of one of the terrorists.

The ambassador and his wife had been awakened by the noise of the explosion and the gunfire and, according to the wife, they immediately knew it was the ETA. Four men wearing ski masks entered the bedroom, three armed with automatic weapons, and one with a pistol. They bound the ambassador's wrists with duct tape, but didn't harm his wife. They led him downstairs, and the wife called the police to inform them that the ambassador had been kidnapped. This information was relayed to the responding units.

The first two-man unit arrived at the intersection just north of the ambassador's building at four thirty-nine, and the car was hit by a rocket fired from an unknown location. Both gendarmes were killed. The second unit arrived from the opposite direction one minute later, just as the ambassador was being led from the building by four men. At the other end of the block, they saw the burning wreckage of the first unit.

The driver stopped the car just as the back door of the newspaper delivery truck was opened. A man inside unleashed a long burst of automatic fire. The two gendarmes ducked under the dashboard and weren't injured, but their car's engine had been disabled by the gunfire.

From somewhere behind them—the gendarmes couldn't identify the source—a man using a loudspeaker ordered them in Spanish-accented French to remain in the car, or they would be killed. The gendarmes realized that they were outnumbered and heavily outgunned, so they complied. They tried to use their radio to warn other units of the danger. They found that their frequency was being jammed and they couldn't transmit.

A third police unit arrived from the same direction as the first unit, just as the newspaper delivery truck was pulling away from the curb. They stopped at the intersection near the wreckage of the first unit, got out, and took cover behind their car. Then they saw two men on the side street to their right, around the corner from the ambassador's building. One was armed with an automatic weapon of some sort, and the other had a rocket launcher pointed in their direction. He fired the rocket, but missed their car, and the rocket hit a building behind the gendarmes. As the newspaper delivery truck approached them, a man leaned out the passenger's side and fired a burst of automatic fire into the front of the police car, and that engine was also disabled.

As the truck passed them, it made a left at the intersection, and the gendarmes fired a total of eleven rounds at the man standing in the passenger's side of the truck. They hit him four times, and he fell from the truck. The truck continued down the block, stopped to pick up the man with the rocket launcher while the other one sprayed bullets at the gendarmes. The gendarmes remained behind their car and weren't hit. The shooter also got into the truck, and it took off.

At 4:50 A.M. the abandoned truck was secretly found by another unit in an alley about a kilometer from the ambassador's building. The newspaper delivery driver was found in the back, blindfolded, gagged, bound hand and foot, but otherwise unharmed. The area was canvassed, but no witnesses were found. The ETA had made a clean getaway.

The next fifteen reports certified that the French police

had done as much work on their case as the NYPD had on the New York kidnapping, but they didn't have much to show for their efforts. As he read the reports documenting all the procedural steps taken in their investigation, McKenna was able to guess the reasons for the lack of progress. There were no good witnesses, Paris being a city of small buildings when compared with Manhattan; although the assault had occurred in the heart of town, there were no doormen to witness it. It is also a city that is not as heavily policed as New York, so there were far fewer units available to respond on an early Sunday morning than there would have been in New York.

As far as McKenna could tell from the reports, the Paris police had been plagued by bad luck and thwarted by the excellent, well-executed ETA plan; their ETA prisoner had died in the hospital without regaining consciousness. His fingerprints had been checked in France and submitted to the Guardia Civil, but neither country had a record on him; he remained unidentified. Since the ETA killers had worn ski masks throughout the assault, the few witnesses the police had been able to find hadn't helped them at all.

However, the reports gave McKenna cause for concern, and a few things to think about. The ballistics and lab reports indicated that the ETA had used Eastern-bloc weapons: AK-47 assault rifles, Makarov 9 mm automatic pistols, RPG-7 rocket launchers—all older weapons, but still highly effective. But the factor that disturbed him the most was that the ETA had jammed their radio frequency. That meant they had to be monitoring the police radio, and it was reasonable to assume they were doing the same thing in New York. McKenna realized that when the time came to close in on them upstate, steps would have to be taken to maintain radio security.

McKenna placed the French reports on Ibarretxe's desk, and went on to the Spanish reports.

Henri Picard was found at the scene of the ambush, along with Officers Brizuela and Vargas of the Guardia Civil, and Sergeant Rafael Gujas of the San Sebastian Police. Brizuela was alive, but severely injured, having sustained a fractured skull and a shattered shoulder when he was thrown into the woods by the explosion that had destroyed his car. Vargas and Gujas were both dead. Vargas had died as a result of massive injuries sustained when he was thrown off the road and down a cliff after the Soviet-era RPG-7 rocket had hit his car, and it took two hours to recover his body.

Gujas's body was behind the wheel of his BMW, and he had been killed by a single 9 mm shot to the heart from a Makarov pistol. According to the pathologist's report, he had been murdered at about 2 A.M., four and a half hours before the ambush. Blood matching his found on the front passenger's seat and console of his car indicated that he had been shot as he sat behind the wheel of his car.

Picard proved to be an excellent witness. He stated that ten men had taken part, all of them wearing ski masks; seven were armed with AK-47s, two with RPG-7 rocket launchers, and the leader—a short, stout man with a husky voice—only with a Makarov pistol.

After Picard had been asked at gunpoint to exit Carmen's Mercedes, the leader descended from the woods and stopped with his pistol in his hand over the prone and unconscious Brizuela. He then bent down to administer the customary coup de grâce used by the ETA when dealing with Guardia Civil prisoners—a bullet in the brain.

Picard, although covered by many guns, yelled for the leader to stop and he began walking toward him. Amazingly, Picard was permitted to proceed, and the leader hesitated.

That was when Carmen had sprung into action. She bolted from the backseat of her car and ran past Picard to Brizuela. Although many of the ETA fighters could have stopped her, none dared to do so. Carmen threw herself on top of Brizuela and begged the leader for his life. While the leader considered her entreaties, Carmen went even further. If Brizuela was allowed to live, she would cooperate fully with her captors, offer them no resistance, and she promised she would never identify them to anyone.

Those promises saved Brizuela's life. The leader put his

pistol in his belt, then ordered two of his men to go for the vans. The men ran down the road and returned minutes later with two delivery vans from a San Sebastian package service. The drivers made a U-turn on the narrow road and parked the vans in front of the overturned BMW while Picard noted the address of the company emblazoned on the doors, as well as the plate numbers. Then Carmen was asked by the leader to get into the back of one of the vans, and she did so. Apparently, her promises were believed, because she was neither blindfolded nor restrained in any way.

Carmen's Mercedes was then disabled by two of the ETA fighters while Picard watched. They cracked the battery, pulled the ignition coil wire, and flattened all the tires. Before the ambush team left in the two vans with Carmen, headed downhill toward Jaca, they took Picard's pistol, his car keys, and the receiver from the car phone. He was left standing in the roadway, unharmed.

At 8:45 A.M., about two hours after Carmen was taken, the two stolen delivery vans used by her kidnappers were found abandoned on a back road ten kilometers north of Pamplona. As for Sergeant Gujas, his movements the night before were easily traced, up to a point. He had finished working a 4 P.M.-to-midnight tour on Saturday night, and had then visited one of his usual haunts, a San Sebastian bar in the old part of town. According to the bartender, an attractive young blonde he had never seen before engaged Gujas in conversation at the bar. Gujas didn't know the woman, because he had asked the bartender who she was. Then Gujas had bought a plate of tapas and a bottle of wine, and he and the unknown blonde had sat at a rear table for an hour, eating, drinking, and apparently enjoying themselves immensely.

The last time Gujas was seen alive was when he left the bar in the company of the blonde at about 1:45 A.M. Gujas had been single, and had a reputation as a ladies' man, so the bartender had assumed that Gujas had gotten lucky again.

That was as far as the Guardia Civil had gotten in their investigation, except for one point. Picard's description of the leader of the ambush team caused the investigators to believe that he was Raoul Marey, a fugitive French Basque who was thought to be part of the ETA leadership. The government had authorized a reward of fifty million pesetas for information leading to his arrest, and that offer, along with Marey's picture, was being broadcast on the government-owned TV stations hourly.

The last couple of reports in the packet concerned Henri Picard, and they aroused McKenna's curiosity.

After Picard had been interviewed by investigators at the scene of the ambush, he was asked to accompany them to the Guardia Civil barracks in Jaca to sign his typed statement. He had refused, telling the investigators he would visit the barracks that afternoon to be formally interviewed. He was then driven back to Carmen's estate, and that had been his last contact with the police. Picard had disappeared.

Other members of Carmen's household staff had then been interviewed, and they reported that, after returning from the ambush, Picard had made a few phone calls, and then packed a few suitcases. He was gone less than an hour after arriving, driving his old Renault.

The investigators checked with officials at the frontier, and were told that Picard had crossed into France at 11:15 A.M. Although he was not suspected of any complicity in Carmen's kidnapping, the Guardia Civil had asked the assistance of the French police in locating him.

The report on the request for French assistance in locating Picard contained a few additional requests that McKenna found highly unusual. If located, Picard was not to be detained, nor were his movements to be restricted in any way. The Guardia Civil went on to request that a full covert surveillance be placed upon Picard, but if it appeared he became aware of the surveillance, it was to be immediately discontinued.

McKenna knew Picard, and couldn't imagine the reasons behind the strange requests. As far as he knew, Picard was a loyal bodyguard, friend, and confidant to Carmen, and he had been for many years. Picard seemed to be devoted to her, she trusted him implicitly, and Carmen was not a fool when it came to assessing people, their characters, and their motives. Therefore Picard could be trusted, and McKenna thought the Guardia Civil's investigators should know that.

McKenna put the Guardia Civil reports on top of the French police's reports on Ibarretxe's desk, then gave him an inquiring look.

"Not satisfied?" Ibarretxe asked.

"Somewhat satisfied. Everything that should be done has been done, even if the results aren't encouraging," McKenna replied. "However, I must admit the last of the Guardia Civil's reports has left me very curious."

"Monsieur Picard?"

"Uh-huh. The Guardia Civil is very interested in knowing what he's doing, but it seems they're also very anxious not to step on his toes."

"Do you know why?"

"No."

"I believe you've met Monsieur Picard, haven't you?"

"Yes, once."

"At Carmen's house?"

"Yes."

"And what was your impression of him?"

"At the time, he was acting as her butler—and her body-guard, I guess. He's an impressive guy—military bearing, intuitive, totally devoted to Carmen."

"Her butler, you say?" Ibarretxe commented, chuckling. "Care to add to that?"

"All right. The devotion angle is a two-way street. He's devoted to her, but it appeared to me that she's just as devoted to him. She leans on him, and he protects her."

"Very perceptive, Detective McKenna, because that is how Monsieur Picard is known in Spain. El Protector, the person who keeps La Tesora safe."

"El Protector? If I were a bodyguard, I don't think I'd mind carrying that title around," McKenna observed.

"Me neither, but Monsieur Picard is much more than that.

I guess you're not aware that he's also one of the most powerful men in Spain?"

"No, I'm not. How'd that happen?"

"You, in part," Ibarretxe said. "After you killed Hector, Carmen went to pieces. Another tragedy in a tragic life, and she's always been considered fragile. So she shut herself away, but she realized she still had many business responsibilities that had to be fulfilled. Carmen is on the board of directors of most major Spanish corporations, and it was Monsieur Picard who fulfilled those responsibilities for her. He possesses her complete power of attorney."

"He runs her businesses?"

"In a way, probably better than she ever could herself. You see, Carmen has always had this disturbing proclivity to give away all her money. After Hector died, she was going to do just that. Fortunately, Monsieur Picard is a gifted visionary and he convinced her there was a better way to be generous. If she gave all her money away, some people would benefit, of course, but then she would have no more to give and it would be over. He convinced her that the way to be truly generous was to keep making more money and keep on giving."

"And that happened?"

"On a wide scale. All the workers and managers in her businesses were given raises, and nobody is ever fired. Some managers, of necessity, must be demoted from time to time, but they still retain their salaries. The effect was electric. Productivity and profits went way up, sick time and other absences went way down, and workers soon began sewing patches on their uniforms—*"Propriedad de la Tesora"*— "Property of the Treasure," and they wear them proudly. Now Carmen gives away money to every worthy cause she can find, Picard keeps acquiring more businesses—just a rumor that he's looking at a new business will cause its stock to shoot up—and backwater Spain is on its way to becoming one of the most prosperous countries in Europe."

"Where did Picard gain the expertise to pull all that off?"

McKenna asked. "Apparently the Guardia Civil knows quite a bit about him. I imagine there's an extensive Picard dossier hidden somewhere."

"I'm sure."

"Well?"

"Please understand that I only received those reports a few hours ago. After I read them, my curiosity was also aroused, so I called Madrid and asked for the dossier, if it exists," Ibarretxe explained, and he appeared to be embarrassed as he did so.

"And? What did they tell you?"

"Basically, to mind my own business."

"That was a very abrupt reply, wouldn't you say?"

"Never received one quite like it, and I'm not new to this," Ibarretxe said, and then changed the subject. "How have you been doing on the case here?"

"Fortunately for us, I'd say better than your police and the French police. Unfortunately, I didn't know how the co-operation protocol was to work. They've sent us all their reports on their investigations, and I didn't bring any of ours with me to send to them."

"But you will?"

"I'll have to check with Mr. Bara first, but I don't foresee a problem. I'm sure I'll be dropping off all our reports some-time tonight."

"That's perfectly acceptable. In the meantime, why don't you tell me what's been done?"

It didn't take long for McKenna to relay to Ibarretxe all the points in the investigation he didn't already know. However, McKenna had noticed that the French and Spanish po-lice hadn't forwarded any reports on their future plans in their investigations, and he decided to follow suit until he talked the matter over with Bara. Ibarretxe received all the facts, but not the conclusions drawn from them. McKenna didn't mention that the Joint Terrorism Task Force would soon be moving upstate, where he hoped to bring the Amer-ican end of the affair to a successful conclusion.

If Ibarretxe deduced that McKenna knew more than he was telling, he didn't show it by asking any leading questions. An experienced man skilled in the ways of diplomacy, McKenna decided.

NINE

Both McKenna and Cisco were off the next day, and they figured it would be their last day off for a long time. However, there were many federal issues to be addressed, so McKenna called Shields at home early the next morning and arranged to meet him for breakfast at the E.J. Eatery, a restaurant in the Village close to McKenna's apartment. Shields didn't mind, because he said he had a few things he wanted to discuss with McKenna. McKenna got there before Shields, selected a booth in the rear, and had coffee and orange juice waiting when Shields arrived at eight-thirty.

"Can't stay long. Got a busy day shaping up," Shields said as he sat down. "Just an English muffin for me."

"Any headaches for you?"

"A few, but they're being resolved," Shields said, then explained that the Guardia Civil's files on the ETA had arrived. Naturally, the reports were all in Spanish, and there were 211 cartons of files to be translated. If this was to be done quickly, the task was way beyond the capabilities of the FBI's New York office, so Shields had enlisted Brunette's help.

Brunette had complied. Thirty Spanish-speaking detectives were to be temporarily assigned to the Joint Terrorism Task Force until the chore was completed, and they would have plenty of room to operate. The unit had already begun the move upstate, and their office at 26 Federal Plaza would

be used by the detectives translating the files. As McKenna
had suggested, Shields had rented a motel at the Thruway
exit, eighteen miles from Tannersville. As far as the motel
management knew, their new good fortune and high occupancy rate was due to a survey of road conditions on the
Thruway being conducted by a large field team from the
Interstate Highway Commission.

That settled, McKenna waited for Shields to bring up the
matter he wanted to discuss with him. Shields wasted no
time. "Do you know when this Colonel Segovia is getting
in?" he asked.

"No, but according to Ibarretxe, it should be sometime
today."

"I got another call from the director last night. Segovia's
well thought of by the Spanish government, and is in line to
eventually take over the Guardia Civil. The director wants
him handled with kid gloves, and Segovia wants to meet you
as soon as he gets in."

"He knows that I'm just a detective, not the guy in charge,
doesn't he?" McKenna asked.

Shields smiled. "He knows that, and maybe he knows
better."

"So my day off is canceled?"

"Sorry, yeah. Give Ibarretxe a call, find out when Segovia's getting in, and meet him at the airport. I'll arrange to
have a car for you, so stop by the office and pick it up."

"What about Cisco?"

"I don't know if I want to subject Segovia to him at this
point," Shields said.

"Don't worry about him. I'm meeting him for lunch at
The Wicked Wolf. I was gonna try to tone him down a bit,
but it seems he's already done that on his own."

"Then take another reading on him over lunch. If he's
prepared to be polite and deferential with Segovia, take him
along."

McKenna picked up the newspapers on the way home, and
then called Ibarretxe. Segovia was arriving at JFK on the Air

France flight from Paris at 7 P.M. McKenna and Cisco would be there to meet him.

As expected, the *Times* coverage on all three kidnappings was extensive, but McKenna didn't learn anything he didn't already know. He next went to his computer and read the online edition of the Paris newspaper, *Le Monde*. There were no surprises for him there, either.

The surprises were in the online edition of the Madrid newspaper, *El País*. Spain was in turmoil; the coverage on the New York and Paris kidnappings was extensive, but it was the kidnapping of Carmen de la Cruz that dominated the headlines and most of the succeeding pages. The cardinal of Madrid had called for massive demonstrations on Tuesday in Madrid's Plaza del Sol, and in the central plazas of all of Spain's cities to protest her kidnapping and call for peace in the Basque Country.

But not everyone's mind was on peace. Besides the looting and burning of Euskal Herritarrok's offices in San Sebastian and Bilbao, there were other reports of violence coming from the Basque Country. The tortured body of one prominent ETA fugitive had been found lynched in a garage outside Pamplona, the body of another had been dumped on the steps of the San Sebastian city hall, and there had been a wave of other kidnappings reported. The wife of Colqui Guarlzadi, a reported leader of the ETA who was serving a life sentence in Redondo Prison in the Canary Islands, was taken from her home in San Sebastian by three masked armed men on Sunday evening, and the parents of Ducho Herriguandi, another ETA leader serving a life sentence at the prison in Cádiz, were missing from their farm outside Jaca. *El País* reported that the family car was still in front of the farmhouse, and there were signs of a struggle in the Herriguandi living room. The paper said that it was thought the GAL was responsible for the kidnappings.

McKenna didn't know what the GAL was, but apparently everyone in Spain did because the newspaper offered no description or history of the organization. However, the GAL came up again in the editorial pages, and the editors urged the Spanish government to appoint a special magistrate with broad powers to investigate the kidnappings and murders in the Spanish Basque Country. If it appeared there was a chance that the GAL was behind the crimes, the editors urged the government to acknowledge the possibility and take steps to bring those responsible to justice.

McKenna decided that he had to know exactly what the GAL was, and it was the Yahoo! España search engine that provided the answers. Over five hundred members of the Guardia Civil had been assassinated by the ETA since 1968, and the cops in the Guardia Civil, and especially its leadership, didn't take that lying down. Retribution was their response, and the GAL—the Spanish acronym for Anti-Terrorist Liberation Groups—was secretly formed to hunt down and assassinate suspected ETA members in their safe havens in the Spanish and French Basque countries. The GAL was thought to be composed of members of the Guardia Civil and agents of the Spanish intelligence service, as well as hired assassins, and it was generally acknowledged to be a state-sponsored death squad.

For years, the GAL had successfully pursued its mission, thereby enraging the Basque press and people, but receiving little notice and no condemnation from the Spanish press. Then they bungled three assassinations, killing the wrong man in one, and murdering two other suspected ETA terrorists in France who, it was later found, had no connection at all to the ETA. Spanish public opinion and the Spanish press then swung strongly against the GAL. An investigation was launched, and it was learned that the GAL was financed by secret funds from the Interior Ministry.

Arrests, trials, and convictions followed. Among those sent to jail for ten-year terms were the interior minister and the chief of the Guardia Civil, but nobody talked and it was believed that the organization remained intact—but basically inert. The pace of the assassinations of ETA members in the Spanish and French Basque countries dropped dramatically, with only two occurring in the past seven years.

McKenna took some time to assess the information he had just absorbed, and he concluded that the editors were right in being alarmed. The GAL was a revenge-driven, die-hard organization that maintained a code of silence, even under intense pressure. Since ETA support in the Basque Country was becoming scarce to nonexistent since Carmen's kidnapping, the GAL leadership might have decided that the timing was perfect to settle old scores and wipe out the ETA once and for all.

McKenna's conclusion was buttressed when he received a call from Ibarretxe. Segovia had been called back to Madrid for "consultations," and he would not be arriving at JFK at seven on the Air France flight. He would still be coming to New York, but Ibarretxe didn't know when.

"Do you think the subject of these consultations might be the very recent kidnappings and murders in the Basque Country?" McKenna asked.

Ibarretxe took a while to answer. "Very good, Detective McKenna. I see that you've managed to stay informed," he said. "It might be why he was recalled to Madrid, but I couldn't say for sure."

"You can't say for sure, but what do you think?"

"I think that's it."

"Is there any chance that he's connected to the GAL?"

"The GAL?" Ibarretxe said, and then took another few moments before answering. "Detective McKenna, I take it back. You've managed to make yourself *very well* informed, and you've stumbled across our dirty little national secret."

"Thank you, but the question remains. Is there a chance Segovia's connected?"

"In my opinion, no. I don't think Colonel Segovia would ever be involved with the GAL, and I think you'll reach the same conclusion yourself after you meet him."

"Do you think the GAL is responsible for the murders and kidnappings yesterday and last night?"

"What else is there to think? Apparently, they're back in business."

The Wicked Wolf was a law enforcement hangout, and a good part of the clientele consisted of cops, detectives, NYPD bosses, FBI agents, and other federal law enforcement folks who mingled freely there with ADAs, assistant U.S. attorneys, and even the bane of all their lives—defense attorneys. Since more could be learned there than anywhere else on any crime story in the news, most of the town's more astute reporters were also regular customers.

Officiating behind the bar, and maintaining decorum while enforcing all his unofficial rules with a mere grimace of disapproval to the offender, was Chipmunk, one of New York's most famous bartenders. McKenna had known Chip for over twenty-five years, since his drinking days as a young cop in the Street Crime Unit. He no longer drank, but he still came in to see Chip a few times a month, and since the food at The Wicked Wolf was good, he frequently brought Angelita along for dinner.

With Chip at the bar, a drink there before lunch was mandatory—but first the news. "Hear you two have been assigned to the Joint Terrorism Task Force," Chip said.

"For a while," McKenna replied. "Who told you?"

"Tommy Bara was in last night. Also indicated you folks would be leaving town for a while."

"True, maybe a week. He have anything else to say?"

"Just what you'd expect. Moaned a bit about . . ." Chip said, and nodded toward Cisco.

"He'll get over it after I make him look good again" was Cisco's reply.

Before heading to a table for lunch, a Chipmunk tradition had to be observed. He poured a drink of something clear and potent for himself, then gave McKenna a nonalcoholic O'Doul's beer. Cisco wanted a gin and tonic, so after making it Chipmunk led them in his toast to all soldiers killed in battle, all airmen downed, and all sailors lost at sea. A waitress then seated them at their table, and Cisco ordered another round of drinks.

McKenna filled Cisco in on his meetings with Ibarretxe and Shields, and told him about Colonel Segovia's cancellation. Then Cisco surprised his partner. "Have you been paying attention to what's been going on in Spain?"

"Yeah, I have," McKenna replied. "ETA people have been kidnapped and murdered in the last couple of days, and there's some kind of political crisis brewing over there."

"Some kind of political crisis? Seems pretty bad to me. Have you heard what happened near Pau last night?"

"Where's Pau?" McKenna asked, realizing that Cisco had set him up.

"City in southern France. Basque Country. It just came over the wires about an hour ago," Cisco said. "Do you know what the GAL is?"

"Uh-huh. What about them?"

"At least six armed men attacked a farmhouse near Pau last night. Reputed to be an ETA safe house, big shoot-out. It was over by the time the gendarmes got there, but there were two bodies left on the scene. One was identified as a French Basque fugitive, connected to an organization called Iparretarrak. The other was a Spanish ETA fugitive."

"Any prisoners or witnesses?" McKenna asked.

"One, another ETA fugitive wanted in Spain. He was wounded in the gunfight and left by his comrades, but it looks like he'll survive."

McKenna needed a moment to digest the implications of that information, but not Cisco. "What's bad for them is good for us," he stated. "We're the good guys—and everybody knows it. We don't assassinate nobody, and we never will." Then he surprised McKenna again when he reached across the table and grabbed his hand. "First we get the people who murdered Hernandez and Dominguez, and we free the ambassador while we're at it. Gives us credibility in the Spanish press, and then we squeeze those murdering bastards for everything they know on their pals in Spain and France."

Their drinks arrived, and Cisco proposed the toast. "And when we know what we need to know, we go over there and get Carmen back."

Both men raised their glasses, then downed their drinks.

. . .

McKenna was in a taxi, on his way home from The Wicked Wolf, when his cell phone rang. "We know who their leader here is," Brunette said. "Judi Manfreddo, known in terrorist circles as Bombi. She's thought to be responsible for three bombings and three other assassinations in the eighties."

"Where'd you get this from?" McKenna asked. "The Guardia Civil?"

"No. We sent them her photo and the two lifts Walsh got off that twenty-dollar bill, but we haven't heard back from them yet."

"Then what makes us so smart right now?"

"Joe Walsh, and some old-fashioned police work. After he took the lifts off the bill, he visited the Intelligence Division. Went through their WANTED posters, the ones the European cops send us. She wasn't in any of the recent ones, but he kept digging until he found her. She's had some plastic surgery since that old WANTED photo, but she never was what you'd call a bad-looking girl."

"How do we know it's her for sure? Fingerprints?"

"Yeah, the WANTED poster came with her fingerprint file at the bottom. Turns out Walsh had lifted the prints from her right thumb and index finger from that twenty."

"So why didn't the Guardia Civil get back to us with that info? If Walsh identified her so fast, they must know who she is."

"Maybe not. Bombi's Italian, not their usual ETA cadre. Used to be with the Red Brigade when they were going nuts in Italy, but she hasn't been heard from in years."

"Italian? So what's she doing with the ETA, in charge and running their operation in New York?"

"I've given it some thought, but I'll leave it to you to form your own conclusions."

"Am I gonna get the Italian police file on her?"

"Eventually, I guess."

"Does Shields know about this yet?"

"He's my next call," Brunette said. "I'll leave it to him

to tell the Guardia Civil, probably after he extracts a promise from them."

"No publicity?"

"That's the concession I'd ask for if I were him."

Good thinking, McKenna thought, and Shields will see it that way. Why should we alert Bombi that we know who she is, and know her role in this? Better to let her think everything's just fine before we take her and her people.

"Got some more news, minor points," Brunette said. "Walsh also got good lifts off Señora Clavero's belt buckle and the hundred-peseta coin he found."

"And the Guardia Civil wasn't able to identify anyone from those prints?"

"Not yet."

"Not important. We'll do that for them, too."

TEN

The job involved dawn-to-dusk driving, three days of slowly searching the highways and byways of Tannersville and the surrounding villages for the silver Lincoln Town Car and the white Ford van. The approaches to every village and hamlet within ten miles of Tannersville were also staked out on a twenty-four-hour basis. So far, with eighty agents and cops assigned, it had been a bust.

Realizing how fast word travels in small towns, Bara wanted to keep the massive police presence in that neck of the woods as inconspicuous as possible. Therefore, he had established some rules that affected the pace of the investigation and the lifestyles of his people. None of the area's many real estate agents had been contacted with inquiries concerning persons renting houses in March, and all of the area's bars and restaurants were off limits to his people. Breakfast was taken in a luncheonette near their motel at the Saugerties Thruway exit, eighteen miles from Tannersville. Lunch was sandwiches on the road, purchased from the same luncheonette. Except for those agents and cops assigned to the road stakeouts through the night, they were all free to eat dinner at the restaurant of their choice in the small town of Saugerties after the nightly progress and strategy session in Bara's suite.

Bara had also briefly considered using helicopters to help

search for the Town Car and the Ford van, but had ruled that option out. When the ETA hideout was found, he wanted to take them by surprise. He was certain that increased air activity in the area would be noticed by the ETA, and would make them suspicious and nervous. Since all the roads could be blocked in a matter of minutes, they weren't going anywhere, but they were holding the ambassador as a bargaining chip and Bara wanted to avoid a standoff. It would take longer to perform the search at ground level, but that was the way it would be done.

Since it was known that the ETA had monitored and jammed police communications during the Paris kidnapping, Bara had taken precautions to ensure secure communications between all his units in Tannersville. All Joint Terrorism Task Force radio transmissions were automatically scrambled at the source, and could be heard only by units with the correct deciphering chip installed in their radios.

The search wasn't a tough assignment, but it involved long days and a few sleepless nights for everyone involved. The cops and agents were away from their families, the tours of duty were fourteen hours, and there were no days off. What kept morale up and everyone going strong was the knowledge that their quarry was close by, or had been; the used car lot where the Town Car and Ford van had been purchased had been located in Tannersville.

The salesman who had sold the vehicles was the only local resident who had been interviewed so far, and he had been kept unaware of the focus of the investigation. He had been shown Ramirez's driver's-license photo, and he had confirmed that Ramirez was the buyer. Ramirez had visited the car lot three times; once to buy the vehicles on March 11, paying cash, and twice the next day to pick them up one at a time after the salesman had them registered in Ramirez's name.

According to the salesman, Ramirez had always arrived alone and on foot. He had offered to follow Ramirez home and bring him back to the lot after he had picked up the first vehicle, but Ramirez had refused the offer. He said he liked walking, and the salesman had left it at that.

What particularly interested Bara was the elapsed time between the pickup of the first and second vehicle by Ramirez. About four hours, according to the salesman, which prompted some calculations from Bara; if Ramirez walked at three miles an hour, the ETA hideout was within twelve miles of the used car lot.

The golden retriever was chained to a doghouse behind the house off a rural dirt road, about six miles from Tannersville. There was a pickup truck in the driveway and lights were on in the house. McKenna had been the one to spot the dog, and he followed the procedure Bara had implemented for identifying golden retrievers. He dropped Cisco off in the woods next to the house and then called for backup. Eight agents arrived within minutes, and their cars were ferried out of sight. The reinforcements were also deployed in the woods around the house.

The dog knew they were there, and followed their moves with some interest, standing attentively with its ears erect and tail wagging. However, there was one thing everyone in the Joint Terrorism Task Force could attest to by then: golden retrievers were great pets, but terrible watchdogs. The dog didn't make a sound, and neither had any of the other eight golden retrievers identified in the past three days.

Since McKenna had spotted the dog, by Bara's rules the unpleasant chore fell to Cisco. One hour after nightfall, he left his spot in the woods and approached the dog with his gun in one hand and a Baggie in the other. He petted the dog, then searched the ground around the doghouse until he found what he was looking for. He picked up the dog feces with the Baggie, and the collection part of the operation was over.

Ten minutes later, McKenna and Cisco were on their way to the lab in Kingston, forty miles away, to drop off the feces for DNA comparison against the dog urine collected by

Walsh after the kidnapping. The FBI had contracted for the lab's services on a twenty-four-hour basis, and the results would be obtained by morning. Until then, a two-man surveillance would be maintained on the house.

After dinner late that night, McKenna and Cisco were in McKenna's room, when Bara knocked at the door. "Just got a message from Mr. Shields," he announced. "You're to call Ibarretxe immediately."

Ibarretxe had McKenna's cell number, so McKenna was momentarily surprised that the deputy ambassador had bothered to go through channels to get the message through. Something important was up, he realized, so important that Ibarretxe had made the request official. "Am I to call him at home, or at the embassy?"

"At the embassy," Bara replied.

McKenna realized that Ibarretxe was working late, and he also realized that Bara wasn't leaving until the call had been made. Ibarretxe picked up on the first ring, and got right down to business. "Are you alone?" he asked.

"No. Why?"

"Because I have a sensitive issue to discuss. I received a call from Monsieur Picard today. He'll be arriving tomorrow, and he wants to meet with you at your earliest convenience."

"Where is Picard arriving from?"

"I don't know. Apparently, the Guardia Civil and the French police haven't been able to locate him."

"Where does he want to meet?"

"Wherever you like."

"What's your government's position on this meeting?"

"I can't imagine how the interior minister or the minister for foreign affairs feel about it, but I'm instructed to facilitate Monsieur Picard's wishes in every way possible."

"What's your take on the reasons behind those instructions, if you don't mind my asking?"

"That Monsieur Picard is a man of extraordinary influence, even more than I'd imagined."

"I'll have to talk to my boss about this before I can give you an answer," McKenna said. "If he approves it, I imagine he'll want to be present at this meeting."

"Then I hope you have some influence with him, because Monsieur Picard was very specific on one point. He wants to meet with you, and you alone."

"I don't know if that will fly."

"Please try. When might I expect your answer?"

"Can't say for sure, but I'll call you as soon as I can."

"I'll be waiting here until I hear from you."

Bara appeared very unhappy when McKenna explained the meeting and Picard's conditions, but he said nothing. Bara was the boss, but he had bosses, and McKenna knew he would be on the phone with Gene Shields before he vented his position.

Cisco, on the other hand, didn't really believe he had bosses, and he was quick to state his position. "Doesn't this Picard know who I am?" he asked McKenna.

"I'm sure he does, but it's possible that he doesn't know you well enough to trust you," McKenna said.

"Then he's an uninformed idiot, but I'll go along for the ride," Cisco said.

"We'll see about that," Bara said, then left. He was gone for an hour, leaving McKenna to deal with Cisco's ego and injured pride. McKenna appreciated Bara's position, and knew he was calling Gene Shields for instructions. By the time Bara returned, Cisco had managed to give McKenna a pounding headache. Bara did nothing to alleviate it. "Call Ibarretxe back and arrange the meeting for tomorrow afternoon," he said. "Afterward, report directly to Mr. Shields."

"What about me?" Cisco asked.

Bara looked at McKenna. "I'd like him to come with me," McKenna said.

"Then I guess he's going," Bara said, and it appeared he was barely controlling his anger. "Apparently, this meeting has been cleared through the State Department, and for some ridiculous reason they think you're in charge of this investigation."

"I guess someone has to set them straight," McKenna offered.

"Someone should, but I've been told to grin and bear it for now," Bara said. He turned and left the room without another word.

"Did he look like he was grinning to you?" Cisco asked McKenna.

"If that was his grin, I sure don't want to see his mean face."

ELEVEN

The meeting was set for 1 P.M. at Ibarretxe's office in the Spanish Mission to the UN. McKenna and Cisco were ready to leave at 10 A.M., when Bara dropped by with the Italian police file on Bombi, and an additional piece of news. The lab results were in, and their golden retriever wasn't *the* golden retriever.

As usual, Cisco was doing the driving, and McKenna read the Bombi file en route. She had been born in Florence in 1965, the only child of a well-to-do avant garde couple who owned a small hotel and operated a tourist guide service there. Consequently, they encouraged their daughter to learn English, French, and German, and this she did well enough that she was able to work part-time as a tour guide in the family business.

But the family business wasn't for Bombi. As a teenager, she had wanted to be a doctor. She was a good student, so good that she was accepted at the Sorbonne in Paris where she continued her studies, majoring in chemistry, with a minor in Romance languages. There she became romantically involved with Giuseppe Gagliardi, another Italian studying at the Sorbonne. Gagliardi was a student radical, and apparently influenced Bombi with his views. Both were arrested by the Paris police after a demonstration protesting government policies on immigration, a protest that turned into a pitched battle with the police. Bombi suffered a fractured

skull during the melee, and she was also charged with re-
sisting arrest. The government decided to deal harshly with
the arrested protesters. Both Bombi and Gagliardi were sentenced to six months, with Bombi spending the first months
of her sentence in the prison hospital, and both were expelled
from the Sorbonne. As far as the Italian police knew, she
never returned to Florence.

During a broad-daylight assassination of an Italian politician in 1988, Gagliardi was killed during a shoot-out with
the man's bodyguards. The politician, however, was shot by
a woman later identified as Bombi, and she escaped the
scene.

In a 1989 plea-bargain deal, a captured member of the
Red Brigade implicated Bombi in three bombings and another two assassinations, and a warrant was issued for her
arrest. Many other members of the Red Brigade were subsequently arrested and convicted, but not Bombi. An informant within the Red Brigade placed her in Libya in 1991,
and until now, the Italian police had assumed she was still
there.

But she wasn't in Libya long, McKenna reasoned. Bombi
spoke Basque, reportedly one of the most difficult languages
to learn, and the only place it is spoken is in the Basque
Country. He figured that Bombi had been with the ETA for
some time—long enough to learn the language and rise to a
position of authority in the organization.

McKenna took a few moments to study the Italian police's
old WANTED poster. It featured Bombi's French prison photo
taken by the Paris police fifteen years before, and she looked
young, pretty, and innocent. Then he compared the WANTED
poster photo to the photo taken by the ambassador's bodyguard. He noticed that her nose and lips had been altered by
plastic surgery, and her eyes were somehow different, but
the procedures had not detracted from her appearance in any
way.

Young and pretty before, mature and beautiful now. Mc-
Kenna wondered how such a nice package could go so bad.

. . .

Cisco had just passed the New Paltz exit on the Thruway when Bara called at ten-thirty. A major problem had developed. At about 9:45 A.M., an overnight letter package had been delivered through the U.S. mail to Sandra Bullmore's apartment in the Spanish ambassador's building. Sandra was in the living room when Daniela opened the package, and it exploded. Sandra and Daniela were very shaken up, their apartment was a mess, but they weren't injured. It was a dye bomb, similar to the type given by bank tellers to robbers as part of the cash haul during bank robberies.

"Any postmark still readable on the package?" McKenna asked.

"No, the package was wrapped in flash paper. Everything burned when the bomb went off. Your Bomb Squad is on the scene, so I should have more information soon," Bara replied. "In any event, do you know what this means?"

"Sure do. Sandra's identity and address weren't released to the press, so it means we have an important leak someplace. There's a lot that doesn't make sense to me yet, but somebody in the ETA has been reading my reports, either here, in Spain, or in France."

"That's what I figure. I've already started an internal investigation here, but I can't imagine the leak being on our end."

"Me neither," McKenna said. "That means the ETA has an inside look being provided by somebody in either the French police or the Guardia Civil. They've been operating successfully in both Spain and France for over thirty years, and they've developed a good police source in one of those countries."

"But why would they tip their hand to us with this bombing? They just about shouted to us that they've got an informant somewhere," Bara said. "They could've killed both Bullmore and her maid—two witnesses against them in our case—but instead they elected to just piss them off, and maybe scare them."

"And embarrass us along the way," McKenna added. "It's a question we have to answer, but nothing's coming to me now."

"Keep thinking about it," Bara said, and McKenna did, but then Cisco gave him something else to think about. He put the red light on the roof, activated the siren, brought the speedometer up to ninety, and kept it there.

When he wasn't thinking about survival, McKenna concentrated on the other problem. The only conclusion he could draw was that, for some reason they considered important, the ETA wanted to substantially alter the cooperative effort between the French police, the Guardia Civil, and the Joint Terrorism Task Force. He was sure the bomb had done that. Until the source of the leak was discovered, Bara wouldn't be sending any further reports overseas, and McKenna was sure that communication between the French police and the Guardia Civil would also soon cease. It seemed to him that the ETA had gone to a lot of trouble and possibly burned a source to achieve that result.

Cisco dropped McKenna off in front of the Spanish Mission to the UN at twelve fifty-five, just in time for his meeting. The NYPD had beefed up security considerably at the embassy, going from one uniformed cop posted outside to five cops and a sergeant. Once again, McKenna was met in the lobby by one of Ibarretxe's aides, and he was escorted through the busy embassy and the security checkpoints to Ibarretxe's office.

Picard was already there, sitting in an armchair across the desk from Ibarretxe. Although McKenna hadn't seen Picard in over five years, it appeared to him that the man hadn't aged at all. Dressed in a sports coat with an open-necked shirt, Picard looked at ease and confident as he rose to greet McKenna—so confident that it might have been his office, and he added to that effect when he dismissed the aide with a nod.

The aide looked to Ibarretxe for confirmation, and again

received a nod. He then left, closing the door behind him.

"So good to see you again, Detective McKenna, although I wish it could have been under different circumstances," Picard said as he shook McKenna's hand. "You're looking well."

"You, too, Monsieur Picard," McKenna said. "I regret it's been so long since we had a chance to chat."

"We'll more than make up for that today," Picard said, then turned his attention to Ibarretxe. "Mr. Deputy Ambassador, I'd like to speak to Detective McKenna in private."

"Irregular, but I understand," Ibarretxe said. He got up from his desk and headed for the door.

"Mr. Deputy Ambassador! One moment, please," Picard said, stopping Ibarretxe.

"Yes?"

"I assume that you intend to respect my wishes, but sometimes I'm wrong. We will be discussing matters that neither you nor any members of your government will really want to hear."

A look of confusion passed across Ibarretxe's face, and was then replaced by an embarrassed smile as he stood there, saying nothing.

"Before you go, please disable any recording devices that might be operable in this room," Picard said, and Ibarretxe did as he was told. He went to his desk, opened the middle drawer, and pressed a switch.

"Thank you," Picard said, and Ibarretxe left without another word.

There had been a briefcase next to Picard's chair, and he picked it up and placed it on the desk. He then sat in Ibarretxe's chair, and McKenna sat in the chair vacated by Picard. "Let's get down to business," Picard said. "I assume we share the same goals."

"Free the ambassador here, and then get Carmen back," McKenna stated.

Picard revealed his approval with a smile. "To whom will you divulge the details of our meeting?" he asked.

"Only four people, all people I'd trust with my life. My

partner, my wife, the police commissioner, and the man I'm working for now."

"Mr. Bara?"

It surprised McKenna that Picard knew who Bara was, but he tried not to let it show. "No, I wasn't referring to Tommy Bara, but I'm sure he'll be told the details anyway," McKenna said. "I was referring to Gene Shields, the director of the New York office of the FBI."

"As it turns out, Mr. Shields must be included in our undertaking if we're going to succeed. You'll see that telling him involves a necessary risk for me, but it's one I'm prepared to take," Picard said. "How do the others feel about this matter?"

"Angelita feels exactly the way Cisco does—Carmen must be returned, no matter what. As for Commissioner Brunette, he feels that getting Carmen back would be the optimal result—but forget the 'no matter what' part. For him, there must be at least some semblance of legality."

"We should be able to grant him that semblance, eventually."

"But not today?"

"No, not today," Picard said. "Some things have happened in Spain and France that he might consider crimes if they are looked at narrowly. However, as the police commissioner of New York City, these matters shouldn't be his concern."

"Maybe not, but he doesn't condone crimes anywhere."

"An important point, but one we don't have to consider right now," Picard said. "I believe that all links in this case with the French police and the Guardia Civil have been severed, or soon will be?"

He's talking about the bombing, McKenna realized, and that caused a suspicion to pop into his mind. "Correct."

"Tell me about the victims."

"Sandra Bullmore and her maid, Daniela. Good friends. One rich and wacky. The other one not rich, but probably just as wacky."

"Were there any injuries?"

"Minor injuries to the maid, but she's tough and thinks

nothing of it," McKenna said. "There was property damage. Nothing structural, but expensive to repair."

"Just money, and you'll find that money won't be a problem for us," Picard said, brushing aside McKenna's concern. "How are they handling it emotionally?"

"Emotionally? Just fine. Matter of fact, by the time this is over they'll probably think it's the best thing that ever happened to them."

"And it will get better for them. Sandra Bullmore will be compensated for her property losses, and her maid will be as rich as her employer when this is over."

How do I handle this? McKenna wondered. Picard has just admitted in so many words that he's responsible for the bombing. Seems to me that he's risking a lot just to sever our cooperation with the French and Spanish police. There must be more to this, other reasons, and it's time to find out what they are. "Okay, we're not talking to the French and the Spanish, and they're probably not talking to each other," he said. "Why is that so important to you?"

"You're aware that families of ETA fugitives have been kidnapped in the Basque Country?" Picard asked.

"Yes, we are. Are you responsible for them?"

"Yes, and continuing cooperation between the French police and the Guardia Civil would make things inconvenient for me. Besides, since the French police can no longer be of any assistance to us, I've decided that we should do without them."

McKenna guessed Picard's meaning. "The Paris ambassador is no longer in France?" he asked.

"I've learned that he was moved across the Pyrenees Monday night. He's being held somewhere in Spain, and it's my guess that he's now with Carmen."

"How did you learn that?"

"I am a man of some influence on both sides of the Pyrenees, and I have many friends," Picard explained. "People talk to me."

"Do the French or Spanish police know that he's now in Spain?"

"I don't believe so. The people who spoke to me make a living guiding fugitives through the mountains. They would be reluctant to speak to police from anywhere."

"Do you have friends in high places in the Guardia Civil?" McKenna asked.

"A few."

"Is that how you learned Sandra and Daniela's address, and their role as witnesses?"

"People talk to me."

"How about the murders in France and Spain? Are you responsible for them?"

"I had no hand in that."

"Then who? The GAL?"

"Yes, them. They're using this opportunity to run amok and settle old scores, but they've made mistakes that serve our purposes."

"Why?" McKenna asked. "Because public confidence in the Guardia Civil is declining?"

"Vanishing, and I have friends in the press who will keep their mistakes and shortcomings in the public eye. Once you free the ambassador here, putting you in a position of authority in Spain won't be too difficult."

"Why would you want to involve us?" McKenna asked. "Is it that you don't believe the Guardia Civil could find Carmen without our help?"

"They might be able to find out where she's being held, if everything went right for them. However, if the wrong people were in charge of the rescue operation, my fears concern what might happen to her in the process."

"And if she were killed during the operation?"

"The Guardia Civil would have license to wipe out the ETA and everyone who ever supported it. Some in the Guardia Civil might consider that a good thing."

"Do you know who those people are?"

"Most, but not all. Not important. With you in charge, my concerns for her safety are minimized."

"Do you know this Colonel Segovia?"

"Yes. A good man, I believe. He's experiencing some

difficulties now as a result of the GAL murders, but he'll soon be working for you."

"So you consider this a done deal," McKenna observed.

"Once you free the ambassador here, yes, it's a done deal. Might I offer you some help in that regard?"

"Sure."

"Would it help if you knew the names they were using here?" Picard asked.

"I'm sure it would," McKenna said, "but how would you know that?"

"I've talked to the person who made them their new passports and other identity papers. He didn't know they'd be working against my interests when he made them, but he got to me as soon as he found out."

"What are the names?"

Picard opened his briefcase, and took out a large envelope. From that, he took out a smaller envelope and passed it to McKenna. "You're dealing with ten of them. The names they're using here are all in there, along with the passport numbers they used to enter the country," he said.

"Can you tell me about the woman?" McKenna asked, deciding to test the depths of Picard's knowledge.

"Judi Manfreddo?"

"Yes, Bombi."

"She's fairly new to the ETA. Before this operation, I had no knowledge of her existence, but I've been directing a few discreet inquiries since you uncovered her role. There isn't much known about her, but I have managed to find out that for the past two years she's been sharing an apartment off and on in San Sebastian with Raoul Marey."

"Raoul Marey? The guy suspected of running the Carmen operation?"

"Yes, him. I know that he went to Libya for training some years back, and I assume that's where they met."

"Do you know Raoul Marey?"

"I've had dealings with him."

"Are Marey and Bombi lovers?"

"Presumably."

"Did you know she speaks Basque?"

"I've heard she can get by in the language, but I'm sure she's not fluent. It's a very difficult language. On to the next point," Picard said, and he passed McKenna two envelopes. Each had a Basque name written on the outside. The envelope for "Colqui Guarlzadi" was on top. Since Gaurlzadi's wife had been kidnapped Monday night from her home in San Sebastian, McKenna suspected what the envelope contained. He looked to Picard before opening it, and Picard nodded his assent.

McKenna was right. Inside were two Polaroid photos of a woman tied to a chair with tape over her mouth. She appeared to be terrified, but otherwise unhurt.

"Guarlzadi's in prison where?" McKenna asked.

"At the moment, doing life in El Redondo Prison. The Canary Islands."

"At the moment?"

"To make things easier for you, I'm endeavoring to have all the high-ranking ETA prisoners transferred to the same prison."

"How high-ranking is Guarlzadi?"

"The highest ranking ETA prisoner the government has right now, and I'm certain he still has some influence."

"What was he convicted of?"

"Kidnapping and murder."

So Picard's kidnapped a kidnapper's wife, McKenna thought, and presumably he'll want me to deliver a murder threat. No good. "So I show him the pictures, and tell him what?" he asked.

"Just that I have her. He knows me, and knows how I feel about Carmen. Show him the pictures, and just let his imagination wander."

"What will happen if Guarlzadi doesn't help or can't help?"

"Nothing, but he can't be permitted to suspect that."

"Before I'll consent to be part of this, you have to promise me that all the people you've had kidnapped will be released, no matter what."

"Released unharmed, eventually—no matter what happens to Carmen. You have my word on that," Picard said. "Matter of fact, all the people in those photos know they're in no danger, and right now they're all living in some comfort."

"Then why does this woman look so terrified?"

"Because the photos were all taken immediately after they were captured. They didn't know then, but they do now."

The second envelope had the name "Ducho Herriguandi" written on it, and McKenna knew what that envelope contained. Herriguandi's parents had been kidnapped from their farm outside Jaca, so McKenna opened the envelope and saw them. They also were tied to chairs, and they also appeared to be terrified.

"Ducho is also doing time for kidnapping and murder," Picard said. "He might be the second-highest-ranking ETA prisoner the government has."

"What next?" McKenna asked, although he wasn't sure he really wanted to know, since Picard had already made him an accessory to kidnapping if he went through with the plan.

"Mr. Shields, a high-ranking federal official. Are you aware that your National Security Agency has the ability to monitor all trans-Atlantic telephone traffic?"

"I've heard that rumor, but our government denies it. I've also heard that they use computers to monitor the calls for catch words associated with espionage, drug sales, and money-laundering."

"Let's hope the rumor is true, because it stands to reason that the kidnappers here are in touch with whoever's in charge in Spain."

Picard didn't have to say more. If the rumor were true, the NSA's computers would have to be tuned and adjusted to record any trans-Atlantic telephone traffic in the Basque language. "I'm meeting with Mr. Shields right after I leave here."

"Good. Since I won't be seeing you again for a while, let's get on to your logistical support," Picard said, and he passed McKenna another envelope. "Among other things, your pilot's cell phone number is in there. He's at your beck and call twenty-four hours a day, to get you to Spain once I've clarified your role there with the Spanish government."

"My pilot?"

"Your Learjet is at Kennedy Airport right now."

Don't mess with the very, very rich when they have people like Picard looking after their interests was the thought that flashed through McKenna's head as he opened the envelope. He knew he was right when he took out the six certified checks. All were drawn on Carmen's account at the Banco Real de Madrid, and all had been signed by Picard—but McKenna had never seen certified checks that looked anything like the ones he was holding; the payee and the amount were blank. "What am I to do with these?" he asked.

"Use them as you see fit. In the event Colqui and Ducho don't care much for their families, you might have to appeal to their baser instincts. You may write the checks in any currency necessary, and they will be honored at any Banco Real branch by whoever presents them, no questions asked."

"Up to what amount?"

"You have no budget. If you write small, there is room for ten numbers in the amount space."

One penny short of a billion dollars and no cents, McKenna thought, and I've got six checks. Six billion dollars? I'd say that's no budget.

"Naturally, you may cash any of the checks to purchase anything you need along the way," Picard added. "You have total discretionary power, and you're now, in theory, one of the richest men in the world."

"Is there anything else I can promise Colqui and Ducho to get them cooperating?"

"Yes," Picard said. "You may tell them that if the information they provide leads to Carmen's rescue, then their cases will be quietly reviewed."

"And then they'll be released?"

"Possibly, but the review process will take a few months."

"When will I see you again?"

"That depends. If Mr. Shields decides to charge me with some crime in connection with my actions, I'll be here in this building until you get Carmen back. This embassy is technically Spanish soil, so I'll be immune to arrest here."

"And after we get Carmen back?"

"I'll walk out and surrender, but I don't think it will come to that."

Neither do I, McKenna thought. Picard's already proved that he has the support of the Spanish government and our State Department, so why would Gene Shields charge him? And charge him with what? Picard gave me the photos, but he's made no incriminating statements. Under the circumstances, most juries would probably acquit him if he offered any barely plausible story on how he came into possession of the photos. "How will you know whether or not Mr. Shields intends to charge you?"

"I'm hoping you'll give me a call here after your meeting with him and let me know."

"And if I don't call?"

"Then I'll stay here, but that would slow down our efforts to get Carmen back."

"I agree. If Mr. Shields permits it, I'll make the call," McKenna said. "Now, would you mind answering a personal question?"

"That depends. Let's hear it."

"What will be Carmen's attitude when she learns of your actions?"

"She'll be shocked and horrified, and may never speak to me again. I'd be miserable for the rest of my life, but it's the price I'm willing to pay to get her back."

TWELVE

Cisco was a hard man to impress, but McKenna thought he had the ammo to pull it off this time. He gave Cisco the details of the meeting, and then showed him the blank certified checks. He was disappointed at Cisco's blasé attitude about them. "So she's got plenty of gelt, and Picard wants her back real bad" was Cisco's response. "We already knew that."

"Then how's this?" McKenna tried. "Picard's got a private Learjet waiting for us at JFK to take us to Spain."

"Now I'm impressed," Cisco said. "Cisco finally gets to travel in a manner befitting his stature."

McKenna was happy. He next called Bara and gave him the list of names being used by the ETA team.

"It's time to make a move," Bara said. "We've been over every road within fifteen miles of Tannersville twice, at least, so they must have the cars hidden in the woods someplace. This afternoon, I'm gonna have every real estate agent around questioned on these names. Hit them all at the same time, and try to throw the fear of God into them. We'll be taking a chance, but we'll have to keep them from spreading the word around town that we've been talking to them."

"Then suppose we do some work while we're down here? Just in case they didn't rent through a realtor, we'll visit *The New York Times* and get their real estate classified ads from February and March. We'll run down the phone numbers, and see if anybody rented their house upstate to anybody on that list."

"That's a deal. Stay in touch."

Cisco stopped at *The New York Times* building on their way downtown to the meeting with Shields. McKenna went to see John Harney, an old *Daily News* reporter pal who had accepted an editor's position with the *Times*. He was back in the car fifteen minutes later with a stack of classified sections, and he went through them as Cisco drove. He was a third of the way through them and had a list of eighteen "Houses-for-Rent" in the Tannersville area by the time Cisco pulled up in front of the FBI offices on Federal Plaza.

"You coming up?" McKenna asked.

"No. You chat with your pal, and I'll work," Cisco said. "Give me that list, and I'll start calling the owners."

Shields was waiting for McKenna and met him at the door when he was escorted to his office. McKenna knew something was up when he saw the large map of Spain spread on Shields's desk. It took McKenna fifteen minutes to report on his meeting with Picard, and he was interested in how Shields would react to Picard's actions in France and Spain. "Got to admire that tough, cagey old bastard. He really turned the tables on the ETA, giving them a strong dose of their own medicine," Shields said.

It was the exact attitude McKenna had been hoping for from Shields. "You're not planning on giving Picard any problems?" he asked.

"On neither the bombing nor the kidnappings," Shields said. "I couldn't get him indicted on the bombing if I tried, and there's no harm done there anyway. As for the kidnappings in France and Spain, not our jurisdiction, and he's seen to it that we're no longer cooperating with them anyway."

"Do you mind if I give him the call he's expecting?"

"Do it after you leave here, and get him back to his business. I have a feeling you're going to need him if you get to Spain."

"Sounds to me like you're pretty certain we'll be going," McKenna observed. "You know something I don't?"

"I know that the State Department wants you to go, and that they're just awaiting the official invite from the Spanish government."

"Why is the State Department anxious I go?"

"The political situation is deteriorating in Spain, and getting Carmen back will right it and go a long way toward ending the ETA problem. We'll look great in the eyes of the Spanish if you can do that."

"What makes the State Department think I can do it?"

"Me. I told our director that if anyone could do it, it was you. Then he told the secretary of state the same thing."

"So you want to send me, too."

"Yes, but for a different reason. Picard was right, and the rumor is true. The NSA has developed certain information that we can't admit to having. With you there, we can use it without admitting where it came from."

"Who told the NSA where to look and what to do to develop this information?"

"I did," Shields said. "Through the director and the attorney general, of course."

Smart man, and I'm glad he's on our side, McKenna thought. "They've intercepted some trans-Atlantic telephone conversations in Basque?" he asked hopefully.

"Two that are important. One on Wednesday, and one this morning. Cell phones on each end, calls from the U.S. to Spain."

"Locations?"

"The one here is being relayed from a Sprint cell in Tannersville. Subscriber is listed as Antonio Ramirez. He bought the phone in Manhattan on March seventh, and got international service with a three-thousand-dollar deposit. Paid cash."

"Who are they calling?"

"Same number in Spain both times. Eurotel subscriber,

but I'm sure the phone can't be traced to whoever's using it. On Wednesday he was in Pamplona, and this morning he was outside Burgos and traveling south. Whoever he is, it looks like he's got Carmen and the other ambassador with him."

"Can we get Ramirez's cell phone records to find out who else he's been talking to with that phone?" McKenna asked.

"In a pinch we could, but not legally. We couldn't get a court order for them without telling the judge how we know about those calls, and that would never do. National security issue."

McKenna understood, and he knew that he could get the phone records himself in hours from any PI worth his salt—and he knew one PI who was better than any of them. However, it was Shields's show and his decision, McKenna decided, and he would play it his way. "Have you got the transcripts of the calls?" he asked.

"Uh-huh." Shields lifted a corner of the map on his desk and gave McKenna the three sheets of paper that were underneath. All the pages were stamped TOP SECRET in red at the top, and there was an NSA log number and spaces in the box underneath the stamp for signatures. Shields had signed each page.

The Wednesday call to Pamplona at 9:01 A.M. Eastern Standard Time was short, and the transcript took less than a page. They used no names, and the conversation was circumspect, but it was easy for McKenna to infer the meaning. The Basque male in Tannersville asked the Basque male in Spain if there had been any negotiations with the government. He was told there hadn't been, and that the situation in the Basque Country was very unsettled. The one in Spain was awaiting the arrival of the second package, and he feared it would be necessary to activate the contingency plan.

The call at eight fifty-nine that morning to the same Basque male, this time outside Burgos, was longer and the transcript took almost two full pages. The Basque in Tannersville again asked if there had been any negotiations with the government, and he was told that there hadn't been. Then the one outside Burgos said that the second package had arrived, and he then initiated a litany of complaints and concerns. Police activity in the Basque Country had become too intense, and support was low and becoming suspect. Therefore, he had been forced to activate the contingency plan. They had traveled all night with the packages, but there were police checkpoints everywhere, so they had been forced to use back roads. Travel was slow and difficult, and morale was getting low since one package had infected his men. They hadn't said so, but he feared that they wanted to return that package.

Then came two questions from Tannersville that McKenna found alarming. The Basque male said that Bombi wanted to know why he wouldn't consider returning that package to lessen the pressure. "Impossible at the present time" was the reply, along with a terse message for Bombi: she should just do her job, and only worry about things that directly concerned her.

The second question from Bombi did directly concern her, and McKenna as well. She insisted that negotiations were necessary, and she wanted to put additional pressure on the government to talk. She requested permission to open her package, and she would then leave the contents in a place where they would be found.

Bombi was told that her suggestion was being considered, but in any event it couldn't be implemented until they reached their destination. Wait, and she would have her answer in a few days.

McKenna read the transcripts again, and then tried to give them back to Shields. "Not good enough. Strict rules," Shields said. "You've seen them, so you have to sign underneath my name."

"What are the other rules?"

"You can't tell anyone the contents of those transcripts, or that they even exist."

"Then I'll deny it later, but I'm telling Cisco, and I'll tell Ray if he asks about it."

"No need. I'll deny it, too, but I already told Ray," Shields said.

"How about Bara?"

"I'll tell him, too, but let's keep it at that. Five of us who know, and not another soul."

"Fine." McKenna signed each page, and gave the transcripts back to Shields.

"Let's make sure we're both getting the same info from these pages," Shields said. "They talk to each other every couple of days around nine in the morning. That's three P.M. in Spain. They're on what they think is a secure phone link, but they're still being vague."

"All that package nonsense? Easy enough to see through that, as long as you know who they are and what we're dealing with," McKenna said. "So on Wednesday they've got Carmen someplace in Pamplona, and later they're joined by the Paris ambassador and his kidnap team. We're talking about twenty-or-so bad guys, all in one place."

"That's a lot of people to hide in one place," Shields commented.

"Too many, apparently, and they couldn't do it when the pressure was really on. Their support is eroding and they have to be suspicious of everyone. So they're on the road and heading south with Carmen and the ambassador. We don't know how many people they've got making the trip, but it's slow going, and morale is fast becoming a problem because . . ."

"Because Carmen is getting to them."

"Yeah, Carmen, and she has a way about her," McKenna said. "I'm sure that kidnapping her wasn't a universal decision, and I'm just as sure that everyone realizes by now that it might have been a monumental mistake. If they decide not to release her soon, I'm going to work on that morale problem of theirs."

"How?"

"Don't know yet, but getting the crew here will certainly dampen their spirits there."

"You might have less than two days to do that," Shields

noted. "Bombi gets the green light, and that's it for our Spanish ambassador."

"Then we might have to pull out the stops, and maybe stop being so careful."

"Wrong. We have to be more careful than ever," Shields said. "It would greatly complicate matters if any of our people are killed or seriously injured when we find the ambassador and free him. We can kill all the ETA people we have to, but we can't suffer any casualties."

"That's Bara's department. I'm sure his plan will be well-thought-out, but what's your point?"

"Right now, the ETA team here is guilty of murdering two Spanish nationals and kidnapping another, all persons with diplomatic status. We have laws that empower federal authorities to arrest persons killing American diplomats anywhere. That means we can arrest them wherever they're hiding—anyplace in the world—and then we can bring them to the U.S. to stand trial here."

McKenna was beginning to see the point. "Does Spain have such a law?"

"Yes, and the State Department feels that, once we free the ambassador, Spain will seek the right to try our prisoners in Spain. That request would be granted, unless police here were killed or seriously injured taking them."

"I agree. Cops killed or injured here, and we'd try them here," McKenna said. "What would happen to the prisoners after their Spanish trial?"

"They'd be additional political pawns in the peace process. The State Department doesn't think the Spanish government is going to give in to the ETA's demands right now, but there will still be negotiations on the release of the ambassadors and Carmen—and that's a start. Since the ETA's demands aren't terribly unreasonable, it's possible a peace will eventually be negotiated based on them."

"Possible, but only as long as there aren't ten ETA prisoners doing life in American jails?" McKenna ventured.

"That's the feeling. On the other hand, they'd do just five

years in Spain, and come out of jail to a peaceful Basque Country."

So there's a lot more riding on our operation than just freeing the ambassador and arresting the ETA team here, McKenna realized. Eventual peace in the Basque Country if we do it right, or many more years of bloodshed if we don't. How's that for a little more pressure?

McKenna put those thoughts out of his mind, and got back to the events in Spain. "Let's see if we can figure out where they're going," he suggested, and he examined the map. "Looks to me like Burgos is about a hundred miles southwest of Pamplona."

"One hundred thirteen miles, and only a hundred fifty miles from the Portuguese border," Shields said. "Can't see them heading to Portugal, though. Open country, and I'm sure the border is tightly guarded right now."

"Then where do they plan to be in two days? Someplace where they feel they'll be safer than they were in their home base in the Basque Country. South of Burgos, but where?"

"Could be anywhere in Spain, and it's a big country," Shields said. "We haven't been passed the ball yet, so why don't you just concentrate on the task at hand? Get the job done right in Tannersville, and then we'll put our heads together."

THIRTEEN

Cisco was parked across the street from the federal building when McKenna came out, and McKenna could see that he was on his cell phone and writing. He was also smiling, so McKenna knew good things had happened in his absence. Cisco ended the call and started the engine when he saw McKenna coming. "Who were you talking to?" McKenna asked as soon as he got in.

"Mr. Gary McCook, a Nassau County correction officer and our new best friend," Cisco replied.

"Would our new best friend be the owner of the house in Tannersville where our enemies are presently hiding out?"

"On Boy Scout Road in East Jewett, but his house and our enemies are exactly five point two miles from the Tannersville Post Office."

After three days of searching the back roads around Tannersville, McKenna knew where Boy Scout Road was. "We drove Boy Scout Road from one end to the other. Remember?"

"Of course Cisco remembers. Rural road a half mile north of East Jewett. About a mile long, maybe ten houses along the way, ends at the Tri-Mount Boy Scout Camp."

"Does the house have a garage?"

"No, but it's on four acres and there's an old logging road that runs into the woods from the backyard. I bet if you take a little walk down that road, you'll soon stumble across a Lincoln Town Car and a white Ford van."

"Tell me about our wonderful new friend."

"We'll be meeting him in about two and a half hours at our motel. He's driving up now, still Mr. Wonderful to us, but he'll be a little pissed off by the time we meet him."

"Pissed off? Why?"

"Because by then he'll have figured out that he might have to declare an extra four thousand dollars on his taxes this year. Can't fool around once the FBI knows he got the money for renting the house."

"Who gave him the four thousand? Ramirez?"

"Uh-huh. On Friday, March first, McCook placed an ad in the *Times* offering a rental on the house. Ramirez called him the same day. The next day McCook picked him up in front of the apartment building in Queens and drove him up there to look the place over. Ramirez liked the place, and he gave McCook his dream price—four thousand dollars in cash for a two-month rental, plus a two-thousand-dollar security deposit, plus another thousand for use of the phone and cable TV. Then McCook drove him back to Queens."

"They must have talked a lot on the way there and back," McKenna said. "What kind of story did Ramirez give him?"

"A great one, backed up by documentation. Ramirez said he was a dental surgeon just in from Spain, and that he was going into a partnership with another dentist who already has a practice in Queens. Then he showed McCook his Spanish passport and his license to practice dental surgery in Spain."

"What about family?"

"Ramirez said he had a large family coming from Spain, and that's why he needed the house. He called it a cheap place to stay while he got organized here and got his New York State licensing requirements out of the way."

"That's a good story all right," McKenna agreed. "Has McCook been up to check on the place since he rented it?"

"He took a ride up a couple of weeks ago. Visited a pal for a few beers, went to the Tannersville Post Office to get his mail, and stopped by the house to make sure they had enough firewood. Didn't go in, but he said there was a white van in the driveway."

"Did McCook get a phone bill for the place yet?"

"Not yet, but he said it should be in his box at the post office."

"How long has he had the house?"

"Almost twenty years, but says he just uses it for ski season. Rents it out for as much of the rest of the year as he can. Doesn't like paying a real estate commission, so he always places the ads in the *Times* classifieds."

Cisco put the car in drive, and McKenna took out his phone. "Who you calling?" Cisco asked.

"Bara. Got to bring him up to speed."

"You do, but he shouldn't be your first call."

"Who should I be calling first?"

"Our pilot. Tell him to warm up his engines and chill the champagne. We'll be on our way soon."

Cisco made good time getting to the motel, and McKenna told him about the NSA transcripts along the way. He also called both Picard and Bara to give them the news they had been hoping to hear. McCook was coming from farther away, and he wasn't driving at ninety miles an hour, so Cisco and McKenna got to the motel before him.

Bara was waiting for them at the motel, and he had some good news and bad news. There was a fire spotter's tower on the Boy Scout camp, and Bara had posted agents on top with high-power binoculars. It was a quarter mile from the house, but the agents had a good view of it.

The bad news was that they reported that the ETA team had sentries posted in the woods on both sides of the house. The agents had watched a changing of the guard at 3 P.M., and saw that the sentries had rifles and radios.

Bara had called Shields with a request for the FBI SWAT team. He was told they should be at the motel with all their equipment sometime before seven. Bara had also requested arrest warrants for the man known as Antonio Ramirez et al to cover all occupants of the house, a search warrant for the house, and an eavesdropping warrant for McCook's phone. Shields said he would have the U.S. attorney running ragged, but all the warrants would be faxed to Bara's room as soon as possible.

McCook soon arrived at McKenna's room. He was in his fifties, looked like a tough guy, and it was immediately apparent from one look at his face that Cisco had been right. McCook had done plenty of thinking on the drive up, and he had questions and concerns.

Cisco had told McCook only that a wanted federal fugitive had rented his house, so it fell to McKenna to give him the whole story. Ten well-armed international terrorists wanted for two murders and a kidnapping was quite a jump for him, and he didn't take it well. "What's gonna happen to my house?" was his first question.

"Depends," McKenna said. "A decision hasn't been made yet on whether we're going to try to talk them out, or just go in and free the ambassador."

"The 'just go in' option would involve a lot of shooting, wouldn't it?" McCook asked, apparently not liking that idea.

McKenna decided there was no way to sugarcoat it. "Presumably. Stun grenades and gas bombs will probably be used as well."

"So what are we looking at here? Total destruction of my house?"

"I wouldn't go that far. Substantial damage, maybe, but not total destruction."

"Do I have anything to say about this?"

"Not really, but there is a consolation prize. I'm sure the federal government will pay for any damages, and the bad guys are paid up for another month on their rent."

"Plus you've got their security deposit," Cisco added. "If there's breakage—and I'm betting there'll be plenty—just keep their deposit. They won't be in a position to complain."

"Two thousand won't cover the type of damage we're talking about," McCook said, his voice rising. "How long will it take the government to pay for the damages?"

"Can't say, but probably not as long as it would take you to pay them the taxes, interest, and penalties on all that undeclared income you've been making renting that place for years," Cisco said.

McKenna thought it was a low blow, but he had to admit that it did have the desired effect. It took the bluster out of McCook, and he sat on the bed. "It doesn't have to come to that, does it?" he asked meekly.

"If you're gonna make noise, you're gonna be heard," Cisco said. "Sometimes you'll be heard by the people you shouldn't have been shouting at."

McKenna felt sorry for McCook, but then he got an idea that would make McCook happy and help the cause as well. *Unlimited budget to do anything that brings him closer to freeing Carmen,* he remembered, with total discretionary power as well. "What do you think that house is worth right now, with everything in it?" he asked McCook.

"I dunno. Maybe two hundred fifty thousand," McCook replied.

"Minus the land?"

"Maybe one fifty."

"Okay," McKenna said. "I'll guarantee that we'll write you a check for any damages up to that number."

"You've got a deal, but a hundred and fifty thousand is a lot of cash to come up with in a hurry. You're gonna have to tell me how you intend to pull it off."

McKenna did, after swearing McCook to secrecy and showing him one of Carmen's certified checks. The deal was: "Tell anybody about the check before Carmen was freed, and all bets were off."

Good deal, as far as McCook was concerned, and he became a willing participant in a number of ways. He had keys for the house, and he gave them to McKenna. It was a three-story chalet-style ski house, and he drew detailed plans for each floor.

Since more than an occasional car traveling on Boy Scout Road was bound to be noticed, McCook was also helpful in that regard. He knew the area well, and drew a map of the old logging road that ran about one hundred yards behind the house, almost parallel to Boy Scout Road. McCook even offered to guide the SWAT team on foot up the logging road and to the house, but McKenna didn't know if that would fly with Bara.

McCook had made a detour to Tannersville to pick up his phone bill for the house, and he presented it to McKenna. There were two calls made during the March billing period, and both were international calls to country code 34, which McKenna knew to be Spain. However, neither call was to the cell phone being used by the persons holding Carmen and the other ambassador, so McKenna didn't know if he'd be able to make any use of the information.

The disappointment on McKenna's face must have shown as he examined the bill, and McCook was a perceptive guy. "No help?" McCook asked.

"Not much," McKenna replied. "They might be using a cell phone to call other people we're interested in."

"Not from my house, they're not," McCook said. "It's in a bad spot, right between two mountains."

McKenna's heart skipped a beat at that news. "Your cell phone doesn't work from the house?" he asked.

"Usually not, except late at night. And when you can get service, the reception is always horrible."

"Who's your carrier?"

"Sprint right now, but I've tried them all. None of them works worth a damn at that house."

"How far from the house would you have to go to get service with good reception?" McKenna asked.

"Not far. I usually either walk or take a drive to the bottom of the road. Gets you out of the shadow of the mountains, and there's a big meadow on the other side of the county road."

"And you get good reception there?"

"Perfect."

McKenna considered that great news as a plan began forming in his mind. Then came the bad news. McCook had installed two motion-activated spotlights at each corner of the house. Between the sentries and the spotlights, McKenna realized that sneaking up on the house at night was going to be very difficult.

James Rego was the FBI's SWAT team commander. Recently promoted to the job, he had been in the team for years and had distinguished himself during many assaults. Since the black eyes the team had sustained at Waco and Ruby Ridge, he had instituted a tough training regimen. When the team wasn't otherwise engaged, they would plan theoretical assaults and then conduct training exercises at the FBI Academy at Quantico, as well as at military bases all over the country. Consequently, the team was regaining the fine professional reputation it had enjoyed before the two bungled operations.

McKenna found Rego discussing logistics with Bara in Bara's room. He delivered the house keys, the floor plans McCook had drawn, the phone bill for the house, and told them about the logging road and the motion lights.

"Where is McCook?" Bara asked.

"Having dinner with Cisco."

"Could you bring him in here when they get back? We need to talk to him," Bara said. "I'm also gonna get him a room, if there are any left."

"Sure." McKenna considered that a dismissal, so he went back to his room. He hadn't seen any of the SWAT team's vehicles in the parking lot, so he figured that Rego had arrived ahead of his men.

Cisco and McCook returned to McKenna's room at seven-fifteen, and Cisco had been kind enough to bring McKenna a dinner order. As instructed, McKenna brought McCook to Bara's room, and left him with Bara and Rego. Then he returned to his own room and ran his thoughts by Cisco while he ate.

"I agree completely," Cisco said. "For us, this is just a sideshow. We shouldn't take the crew here until we know approximately where that other bunch of dirtbags is holding Carmen."

"So we wait for them to call?"

"We wait, but we have to be in position and ready to jump them if they give Bombi permission to whack the ambassador here."

"That's the big problem," McKenna said. "You know how we'd look if we watched them for two nights, and then they kill the ambassador right under our noses?"

"Like shit. We can't tell anybody about the NSA intercepts, so Shields, Bara, you, and Lord-knows-who-else will have to stand still, close your eyes, and take your lumps from all the second-guessers Congress and the media can muster."

Cisco was right, McKenna knew, and he himself had already reached the same conclusion. Waiting would take a courageous political decision. McKenna knew that Shields certainly wasn't lacking courage. But which was more important to Shields: rescuing the ambassador and looking good, or rescuing Carmen?

The ambassador might still be rescued unharmed if they waited, but maybe not; if Bombi received her permission to kill him, an instant daylight raid fraught with risks would be necessary to free him. The potential for enormous negative political repercussions was there.

Cisco watched McKenna worry, and guessed the reason. "Don't worry," he said. "Shields is your pal, and he's also a good man. He'll make the tough decision, and most of us will get a good night's sleep tonight." Then Cisco got up and went to the door.

"Where are you going?" McKenna asked.

"To bed."

Shields called McKenna at nine-thirty, and caught him still refining his plan. "Already gave this to Bara, but those two calls to Spain from the house are to hostels, one in Sevilla, and the other in Jerez."

"Interesting," McKenna said. "The calls were made before

Carmen was kidnapped, but both those cities are south of Burgos, in almost a straight line if you're heading from there to the Spanish coast. "How did you find out the numbers belong to hostels?"

"Had a Spanish-speaking agent call them. When he found out they were hostels, he got the addresses from the desk clerks."

"Did you give this to the Guardia Civil?"

"No, we haven't given them anything. I will if you want me to, but I haven't yet."

McKenna gave it a minute of thought. Was it possible they were holding Carmen in one of those hostels? If they are, the Guardia Civil would go in and get her, but I wouldn't be there for that, and Picard's fears on the GAL might come true. "No, don't give it to them. I'll work on it when I get there."

"Okay, on to more important matters. I already know your answer, but I want to hear you say it yourself," Shields said. "Do we go in tonight and get them, or do we wait until Sunday morning?"

"I'd say we wait," McKenna said.

"I thought so. And suppose they give her permission to kill the ambassador?"

"Makes no difference, if we can grab whoever has the phone fast enough. Don't forget, they'll be at least a half mile from the house."

"Suppose the phone-bearer gets time to make a call to the house before we grab him?"

"Worst scenario. It'll be a bloodbath, but we have to be ready for that. We go in right away, and we might sustain some casualties along the way."

"And then their war goes on forever, even if you manage to free Carmen later," Shields commented.

"Like I said, worst scenario."

"And if they don't give her permission?"

"Best scenario, but there will still be casualties for the ETA if you like my plan."

"The sentries?" Shields asked.

The question told McKenna that they were thinking alike. "First thing we do is take them out. That'll give us two less terrorists to worry about, and it'll also show them we mean business. Then we give them an ultimatum, and try to talk them out."

"You think they'll be prepared to listen?"

"I hope so. They're not Muslim fanatics, and the ETA has never shown any suicidal tendencies. They'll listen, but I can't absolutely guarantee how they'll react."

"What would you tell them?"

"Free the ambassador, and come out in ten minutes with your hands up. If you do, you'll all be extradited to Spain."

"Good ploy, and probably true if they surrender," Shields said. "That'll give them some hope."

"Especially since they know their pals are still holding two big chips in Spain," McKenna added. "If the ETA succeeds in their negotiations there, they'll all be out of jail in five years."

"What's our hole card?"

"We tell them that if they don't free the ambassador unharmed, we're coming in to get them. Some of them won't survive, and those will be the lucky ones. The rest will be facing the death penalty here at best, or life in solitary in Marion at the worst."

"And we wind up with prisoners for you to grill."

"Like I said, best scenario," McKenna replied.

"I need some time to think this over, and then I'll talk to the director. I'll call you back in an hour or so."

"Suppose the director and you agree with my plan?"

"Then you go talk to Bara and Rego," Shields said. "By that time, I'll have talked to them, and they'll be prepared to listen to whatever you have to say."

FOURTEEN

Saturday was a day of preparation and additional planning. First thing in the morning, Bara sent most of the Joint Terrorism Task Force back to the city for three days off. Many didn't want to leave, but Bara was the boss, and that was that. As long as he had the sixteen-man SWAT team, he felt that his additional manpower would just complicate matters and draw too much attention to the operation. He kept just McKenna, Cisco, and twenty of his own people.

The plan was already set, but Bara and Rego spent the day refining it and preparing for all contingencies. McKenna and Cisco would be doing the negotiating with the ETA the next day, if it came to that. They would also be assigned with four Joint Terrorism Task Force members as the team designated to take whoever made the phone call to Spain with the cell phone. Six of Bara's people would be assigned with state police units to block the roads leading into East Jewett when the action began, and the other ten would maintain the surveillance on the McCook house until then.

The U.S. Attorney in the city had obtained all the warrants Bara had requested, and a wiretap on the McCook phone at the house had been installed from the Verizon office in Saugerties. A relay had been established so that the McCook phone could be monitored from the motel, and Bara had assigned two of his agents to the job.

During a morning of meetings with the state police commander—and he turned out to be a willing participant, as well as a big help—Bara and Rego initiated other moves as part of their plan. Not wanting to repeat one of the major mistakes made by the FBI at the Branch Davidian Compound, they wanted the entire available complements of the East Jewett, Hunter, and Tannersville volunteer fire departments in their fire houses, dressed for action and with their engines warmed up, ready to go at 8:30 A.M. the next day. The East Jewett Fire Department could make it to McCook's house within three minutes.

The state police commander said he would take care of it, and the firemen would all be in place on time.

Medical contingency plans were also made. Bara wanted the volunteer ambulance crews from Tannersville and Hunter waiting behind the East Jewett firehouse with their ambulances and equipment at 8:30 A.M. At that time, he also wanted doctors standing by on alert at Catskill Hospital, thirty miles away. For more serious medical cases, Bara also requested that at that time two state police helicopters be airborne over the Thruway, five minutes' flying time from McCook's house.

Once again, the state police commander said he would see to it, and he assured Bara that it would all be done.

Rego also had some work for the state police commander. Since they would be dealing with a terrorist unit headed by someone nicknamed "Bombi," he requested the presence of the state police's Bomb Squad for 8:30 A.M., in force. He wanted three of their units, including their bomb disposal truck, parked on a side road on the other side of East Jewett. According to the state police commander, the Bomb Squad would be there as requested.

Bara and Rego also had some work for the FBI's communications section. They wanted a direct phone link to Shields, and another one to the National Security Agency's headquarters in Silver Spring, Maryland. Standing by there they wanted a Basque interpreter, ready to relay to them the translation of the ETA team's phone call to Spain as it occurred. They also needed a direct link to the phone in the

McCook house for any negotiations with the ETA that might occur. Since the operation would be run from the fire spotters' tower, they needed all the lines for the direct links installed there. They put their requests through Shields, and he told them it would all happen.

Rego did some minor planning on his own to ensure that his SWAT team would be ready and rested when it came time for them to begin deploying at 2 A.M. the next morning. They had arrived at the motel on Friday night, and Rego had given them the day off with instructions to eat well, have a few drinks if they wanted to, and sleep as much as they could. It seemed to the Joint Terrorism Task Force members that the SWAT team was following Rego's orders, because not much had been seen of them all day.

Meanwhile, McKenna and Cisco were in the fire spotters' tower watching McCook's house, and had been there since before dawn. Just getting to the tower had proved to be a job in itself. The only road leading to the large Boy Scout camp on which the tower was located was the one that ran past McCook's house, and Bara didn't want an increase in vehicular traffic on that road. So an overland route had been established the day before and marked with stakes with iridescent orange ribbons attached. This route began at the county road two hundred yards from the entrance to Boy Scout Road and ran through the woods straight uphill to the tower. McKenna and Cisco had never claimed to be woodsmen, and they had lost their way in the dark a few times during the trip up.

Complicating matters for McKenna and Cisco was the fact that Bara was a perfectionist; he had them dressed in green forest ranger uniforms, complete with Smoky-the-Bear hats, which they thought made them look ridiculous. Bad enough, but Bara had made it even worse than that. The top of the tower was visible from McCook's house, but he knew his men were too far away to be easily seen by the sentries once they were inside. However, he didn't want them to be seen climbing up and down, so McKenna and Cisco would be stuck in the tower until after dark.

Once inside the tower, it wasn't too bad until Cisco insisted they keep their hats on. McKenna complied, only because he got a giggle every time he looked at Cisco. However, the work was easy because they had the tools. They were equipped with high-power binoculars and a Nikon camera with a 1,000 mm telephoto lens. They soon verified that the sentries outside the house were changed every two hours.

At 9:00 A.M. they watched and photographed another changing of the guard, and Duchess came out of the house with one of the reliefs. Like most golden retrievers, she was playful, and loved to fetch. She bounded around the backyard for a few minutes, and then she found a stick and brought it to her master in the woods. He dutifully took it from her and threw it onto the front lawn. She retrieved it, and they repeated the toss-and-fetch process for five minutes. Then he tired of the game, and ignored her.

Duchess wasn't deterred; she simply ran around the house and brought the stick to the sentry in the woods on the other side. He also played with her, but after a few minutes he too got tired of throwing the stick, and he refused to take it from her.

Duchess thought she knew what to do, but she was wrong. She ran around the house again with the stick in her mouth, and brought it to her master. He patted her on the head, but ignored her after that. She looked dejected as she lay down at his feet, but then amused herself by chewing up the stick.

"I think we're looking at the guy who shot Jorge Dominguez and Roberto Hernandez," Cisco said to McKenna, and he had a hard sound in his voice.

"That's what I'm thinking," McKenna replied.

"No matter what happens, let's make sure he doesn't get away."

"He won't."

"Doesn't it bother you that if everything works out according to plan, that scumbag will only do five years in Spain for murdering those two good men?"

"Yeah, it does, but that's the game we're in."

"Cisco knows the game, but he doesn't like the rules."

McKenna knew what Cisco was thinking and how he felt. He also knew that Duchess's master was in a lot of trouble if push came to shove with him and Cisco.

A few minutes passed in silence as Cisco kept his binoculars trained on Duchess's master. McKenna thought it was time to change the subject. "They must have people inside assigned to watch the ambassador all the time. There's ten of them, but between inside and outside, twenty-four hours a day, that's a lot of guard duty."

Cisco lowered his binoculars and looked at McKenna. "So what's your point?"

"No point, really," McKenna said. "All I'm saying is that they must be getting tired and bored."

"Probably right. It's been a trying five days for them since they kidnapped the ambassador," Cisco replied, and then a thought hit him. "I wonder if Bombi ever draws guard duty."

"Probably not. We've had people in this tower since yesterday afternoon, and nobody's seen her yet."

McKenna and Cisco watched another changing of the guard at eleven, and then Bombi showed herself in an unexpected way when she came out the front door just before noon. She was dressed in nylon shorts, a Palermo Marathon T-shirt, jogging sneakers, and a baseball cap. She also had a canvas waist-pack strapped on, and it appeared to be full.

Bombi did five intense minutes of stretching exercises on the front lawn while McKenna, Cisco, and the sentries silently admired her form and figure. Then she checked her watch and took off down the road at a good clip.

The Palermo Marathon T-shirt interested McKenna. He checked his own watch. 12:02. Bara had agents in East Jewett, ready to block the road to the McCook house if the need arose, and McKenna radioed them to let them know that Bombi could be headed their way.

She was. At 12:08 the agents reported to McKenna that

Bombi had just passed them, running strong down the road to Tannersville.

"How far is East Jewett from here?" Cisco asked.

"A mile, I'd say."

"A six-minute mile? Not bad."

"No, it's not, but the first mile is mostly downhill. If she's headed to Tannersville, she has a lot of steep uphills between here and there."

Bara had heard the radio transmissions, and he assigned agents in Team T-2 to watch for Bombi in Tannersville. At 12:34 Team T-2 reported that they had her in sight. At 12:35 Team T-2 was heard from again. Bombi had jogged in place while she checked her watch in front of the Tannersville Post Office in the center of town. Then she had turned and headed back to East Jewett, again running fast.

"What's her speed?" Cisco asked.

"Thirty-three minutes. Five point two miles from here to Tannersville, so she's still doing six-minute miles," McKenna replied. "Not world class, but still impressive."

"What would be your speed for that distance, if you don't mind my asking?"

"Seven-minute miles at best, maybe a little more with the hills."

Cisco liked the answer. "So if you two started off together on that run, she could be finishing lunch in the house by the time you got back."

"Maybe, if she can hold the pace."

"I'll bet you ten dollars she can," Cisco offered.

"No bet, thank you."

Cisco was right, and McKenna had saved himself ten dollars. At 1:04, right after another changing of the guard, Bombi returned. She was drenched in sweat, but she had run up the steep-inclined road so fast that McKenna was absolutely sure she had earned that Palermo Marathon shirt herself.

The sentries had her routine down, and knew she would be returning about then, so all four of them were there to clap when she stopped on the front lawn. She checked her watch again, acknowledged their applause with just a wave, and then walked around the lawn for a few minutes to catch her breath while she did breathing exercises.

"I know how she feels," McKenna said. "That girl must be really beat."

"She doesn't look beat to me," Cisco observed, and once again he was right. While they watched, Bombi did fifty slow push-ups and two hundred quick sit-ups. Then she got up, brushed the grass from her shorts, and went back in the house, apparently none the worse for wear.

"How can a strong, tough girl like her who looks so good be so goddamn bad?" Cisco asked.

McKenna didn't know, so he didn't answer.

By the time McKenna and Cisco left the tower at 7:30 P.M., they had managed to photograph all ten members of the ETA crew. They were relieved by two agents from the Joint Terrorism Task Force, and they had with them a technician from the FBI's communications section to install the phone lines to the top of the tower.

It had been a long day, so McKenna and Cisco were ready for a good dinner and a fair night's sleep. The SWAT team would be up and around at midnight, but McKenna and Cisco's tour of duty the next day didn't begin until 6 A.M.

FIFTEEN

McKenna and Cisco were used to tension and knew how to
correctly cope with it; they were still sleeping fitfully in the
motel when Bara climbed the tower at 2 A.M. Almost a mile
below him, Rego and his SWAT team began the quiet trek
that would eventually put them into position. They were being guided by McCook as he led them up the old logging
road behind his house. Everyone in the group was wearing
night-vision goggles, so the going was rather easy. Fifteen
minutes later, they stopped two hundred yards behind the
house, and McCook left them to return to his car parked at
the side of the county road. His job was done.

From that point on, it was Rego's show, and he spread
his eight-man assault team along the road. All of them were
experienced, well trained, and well-equipped. They wore
heavy protective vests, Kevlar helmets that had radio headsets and mouthpieces mounted in them, and each man had a
gas mask in a pouch on his belt. Their primary weapon was
a Ruger MP-9 submachine gun capable of single shot or full
automatic fire, but they had more firepower than that. Each
team member also had slung over his back an H&K 40 mm
grenade launcher capable of firing either stun grenades or
tear gas grenades.

They were ready, with particular assignments when the
time came to kill and do damage. They had memorized the

house plans to the smallest detail, and each had in his pocket a full-length photo and a head shot of the ambassador. They had studied those two photos until they could distinguish him in an instant from any of the ETA crew, whose photos they also had studied for hours. They lay down and waited for the signal to advance, and they hoped it would be a long wait. According to the plan, it should come some minutes after 9 A.M., but they knew it could come at any time if something went wrong with the sniper teams.

Rego then returned to the rest of his men, the eight who had been waiting for him on the logging road. They were his four sniper teams, with each team consisting of a marksman and his spotter. They, too, were experienced and well-equipped and wore night-vision goggles. They also carried binoculars and sensitive radios with headsets that clearly transmitted the slightest whisper they uttered. The spotters were armed with the same small MP-9 submachine guns that the assault team carried, but their snipers carried M40-A1 scope-mounted USMC sniper rifles with silencers attached, their weapon of choice for this particular mission.

The snipers and their spotters were also dressed for the occasion, wearing camouflage fatigues with so many leaves and branches attached that McCook had thought they looked like walking bushes. They were also smeared with dog repellent and insect repellent. At a signal from Rego, they left the road in a slow crouch and advanced twenty-five yards toward the house. Then the sniper teams got down on the ground, and they began crawling forward.

Since the sentries were stationed in the woods on either side of the house, the sniper teams had to get close enough to get a clear shot through the trees. To minimize the chances of a miss or an obstructed shot, two sniper teams were assigned to each sentry.

After a tough hour of slow crawling, one of the sniper teams reported they had found the Lincoln Town Car and the Ford van parked about a hundred yards from the house on a rutted cut-off leading to the logging road. The vehicles were covered by tarpaulins, with branches and leaves thrown on top for good measure.

As they got closer to the sentries, the going got even slower for the sniper teams. To minimize the noise, they advanced only ten yards between 4 and 5 A.M. Just before dawn, all four teams reported they were in position, fifty yards from their targets, with a clear line of fire.

Rego thought everything was great, but then a problem developed—Duchess knew they were there, and the sniper teams reported they could hear her crying in the house and scratching at the back door. Since they were well past the point of no return, Rego radioed the men in his assault team and told them to get ready to move.

Two minutes later, somebody in the house opened the back door, and Duchess bounded out. She sniffed around the ground in the backyard for a minute, quickly did her business, and then she ran into the woods on the left side of the house and found a stick. She picked it up and ran to the sentry stationed there. He patted her on the head, but ignored her as she wagged her tail and shook her head from side to side.

Duchess soon tired of his treatment. She looked around, and then ran straight to two more potential playmates. The sniper and his spotter were flat on the ground, with good sight picture on the sentry. They were horrified to see Duchess standing over them, wagging her tail with the stick in her mouth. Then she caught a whiff of the dog repellent, and she decided that these smelly guys weren't worth the trouble. Off she went, directly to the other sniper team on that side of the house. No response there, either, and she didn't stay long with those smelly guys.

The sentry was watching Duchess's antics with casual interest, but he didn't see the sniper teams. When Duchess returned to him with the stick, he said something low and soft to her as he patted her again on the head.

Duchess stayed with him another few minutes, but he wasn't playing and he wasn't any fun. Off she went again, this time into the woods behind the house. A minute later she was on the logging road, and she greeted each prone member of the assault team in turn. She received a few kind words, a few pats on the head, and even a hug or two from them as she went down the line, but nobody made a move to take her stick.

Duchess hung around with her new pals for a while, but then the back door opened again and a man stepped into the yard. "Duquesa!" he yelled, and then he whistled. Duchess took off at a hard run, and a minute later the back door closed behind her and her master.

Rego had only one comment on the situation. "I don't care how many of those pricks we have to splatter today, but under no circumstances is that dog to be harmed" sounded over sixteen headsets.

He got no argument, because most of them were thinking the same thing: When this is over, that dog is coming home with me.

At 8:45 A.M. Bara requested by radio another status report from the three teams assigned to capture whoever made the phone call to Spain, and Cisco answered in turn. Nothing had changed, and all were in the same location they had been for Bara's last status report. Team T-8 was parked on the county road a half a mile on the other side of Boy Scout Road from Team T-9, McKenna and Cisco.

Team T-10 was stationed on foot in the woods at the edge of the large, hundred-acre meadow located where Boy Scout Road ended at the county road. They had binoculars, and their job was to track the phone-bearer as he walked along the county road. When the phone call to Spain was completed, Teams T-8 and T-9 would drive in and take him.

The next transmission from Bara came a minute later, and it perplexed them. "Bombi's outta the house, and it looks like she's getting ready to take another run," he transmitted. "She's wearing blue nylon shorts, yellow shirt, baseball hat, and sneakers. She's got some kind of bag strapped around her waist, and she's doing some stretching exercises."

"What the hell?" Cisco said. "Don't tell me she's gonna take a run while her lackey's talking to the boss in Spain. Maybe we've got this wrong."

McKenna gave it a moment of thought before answering. "No, we don't. She's gonna walk the phone-bearer down here. She'll take her run after the call."

"Oh! Now I understand," Cisco said. "First she gets her exercise routine out of the way, and then maybe she gets a chance to whack the ambassador when she gets back. Perfect day for her, very refreshing."

Five minutes later, Bara had another transmission. "There's another one outta the house, and he's got the dog with him. Green shirt pulled out, black pants. Looks like the kind of shirt they were wearing when they took the ambassador."

"And when that one killed the chauffeur and the body-guard," Cisco added to McKenna. "Same guy, same shirt, and probably the same gun tucked into his pants underneath it. Perfect day for us, too."

"They're walking down the road, and the dog's going with them. Team T-Ten, let me know when you see them," Bara transmitted, and then he had another order to give. "Task Force CO to all blocking units. Institute roadblocks."

Bara received four responses. The roadblocks were going up, and the area two miles around Boy Scout Road would be free of the press and the curious.

It was another few minutes before Team T-10 reported again. "Team T-Ten to Task Force CO. We see them now, rounding the curve, still walking down Boy Scout Road. They'll be on the county road in two minutes."

It was just under two minutes. "Team T-Ten to Task Force CO. They made a left on the county road, headed toward East Jewett, but the dog's not going with them. She's sitting at the end of Boy Scout Road."

Another minute. "Team T-Ten to Task Force CO. She just gave him a cell phone from that bag she's wearing on her waist. He's dialing . . . Still dialing . . . He's talking."

Cisco got ready. He took his radio off the dash and stuffed

it in his belt, started up the truck, and removed his pistol from its holster and held it in his left hand.

McKenna also took out his pistol, but he still held his radio in his other hand. As he waited, he felt the adrenaline rush. It seemed to him that the phone call was taking a long time.

"Team T-Ten to Task Force CO. He's done talking. He's giving the phone back to her . . . She's putting it in that pouch on her belt . . . They're talking together . . . She's got her finger in his face . . . Looks like she's yelling at him."

Cisco put the pickup in drive and got on the county road, going slowly toward Boy Scout Road.

"Task Force CO to Teams T-Eight and T-Nine. Take them," Bara transmitted a moment later.

Cisco accelerated, then kept the truck at the thirty-five-mile-per-hour speed limit.

McKenna brought the radio to his mouth. "Team T-Nine to Task Force CO. Did she get permission?"

"Yeah, Brian, she got her permission to whack the ambassador," Bara answered.

They crossed a short bridge, rounded a curve in the road, and saw Bombi and their male target talking together on the road, a quarter mile ahead. It was a straight stretch of road that ran along the large meadow to their left, and a half mile ahead they could also see Team T-8 approaching in their gray four-door Oldsmobile.

So could Bombi. She stopped talking, looked in McKenna and Cisco's direction, and then turned and looked down the road at Team T-8. Casual as can be, she left the man standing there, climbed a short rock wall that paralleled the road, and kept walking into the meadow.

"Savvy bitch," Cisco noted. "Don't worry about her, she's headed toward Team T-Ten. Let's get the guy first."

McKenna didn't know why, but he said, "Your call, but let's not shoot him unless we have to."

Cisco just smiled, and then McKenna knew why he had said it.

The man in the road appeared to be indecisive as he

looked up and down the road. Both units were closing in on him at thirty-five miles per hour when he finally decided to get off the road and follow Bombi.

He had waited too long. He was climbing the wall, but stumbled and fell as the two cars screeched to a halt behind him. McKenna was out of the truck in an instant and saw that Bombi had taken off running without looking back when she heard the scream of their brakes. Cisco remained seated with his gun aimed out the window.

Like McKenna, the passenger half of Team T-8 was also out of his car with his gun raised as the man struggled to get up. As he rose, he was trying to remove the pistol from his belt. The driver of Team T-8 was just getting out when his partner yelled, "Police! Don't Move!"

The man hesitated, and then Cisco added his two cents, yelling in Spanish, "You filthy coward, you don't have the balls! Do it!" And the man did, turning with the gun raised in his hand to meet Cisco's single shot through his heart. He was dead before he hit the ground.

The agents from Team T-8 stood there, astonished, but not McKenna. He had his eyes on Bombi. At the sound of the shot, she reached into her pouch as she ran. She took out the phone, and began dialing on the run.

"McKenna to Bara, she's dialing her phone. Cut the phone service to the house!" McKenna yelled into his radio, forgetting all radio protocol.

Bara's response came a second later. "Bara to McKenna. Done. They've got no phone."

Then McKenna saw the two men from Team T-10 stand up in the woods, and so did Bombi. She made a right and put on the speed as she ran up the meadow with Team T-10 in pursuit on foot. She threw down the phone and once again she was trying to get something out of her pouch. McKenna saw that Team T-10 didn't have a chance of catching her, and her lead was widening.

"Get in!" Cisco yelled.

McKenna hesitated.

"You think you can catch her?"

"Not a chance," McKenna replied, and he got into the truck.

"Do you like this truck?" Cisco asked.

"Not particularly."

"Neither do I. Hold on tight." Cisco engaged the 4-wheel-drive and accelerated down the road. When he was parallel to Bombi, he made a sharp left that McKenna considered suicidal—but only for a moment. He braced himself against the dashboard as they left the road, hit the low stone wall, and somehow made it over. Then Cisco set a course to intercept Bombi before she made it to the woods at the far end of the meadow.

Bombi first heard them, then turned and saw them. She put on a burst of speed that McKenna found amazing, but the pickup was too fast and she must have figured that she wasn't going to make it. She surprised McKenna and Cisco when she stopped and faced them when they were still about a hundred yards away from her.

McKenna hadn't seen her remove the small silver automatic from her pouch, but he saw it then. Bombi was in a police combat crouch, with her pistol in her right hand, and her right arm extended and pointed toward the truck. Her left arm was held tight across her chest, with her left hand in a fist. She fired a shot, and they heard it hit someplace in the grille.

The sound of the shot wasn't loud, so McKenna figured it was a .25-caliber pistol, at most. "Please stop, Cisco," he said, and Cisco did. Both men ducked as low as they could under the dashboard and still see Bombi. They watched as she turned right, still in her police combat crouch. She then fired one shot at her pursuers from Team T-10. They were too far away for her aim to be accurate with the small pistol, but they got her message and dropped to the ground.

Then Bombi was back to McKenna and Cisco, still maintaining her police combat crouch. Her single shot hit the windshield high and broke it, and that got them so low under the dashboard that their noses almost touched.

"You realize, of course, that she's attempting suicide, don't you?" Cisco asked.

The same thought had occurred to McKenna, and he had been trying to put himself in Bombi's head when Cisco asked the question. Bombi wasn't a Basque, and she wasn't even Spanish, he reasoned. She was a dedicated revolutionary wanted in Italy, among other places. Therefore, she knew that if she were captured, she wouldn't be included in any deal Spain eventually made with the ETA. She might do her five years in a Spanish jail, but then she'd be extradited to Italy to do her life sentence there.

Bombi also knows that our presence here means her U.S. venture is doomed. That means her glory days are over, McKenna reasoned further.

Then they heard another shot. It hadn't hit the truck, so he knew Bombi had momentarily returned her attention to Team T-10.

"So what do we do?" Cisco asked.

"She'd be our most important prisoner, so I don't want to kill her," McKenna said.

"A tough, good-looking babe is what she is. For that reason—and only that reason—I don't want to kill her, either."

Another shot went through their windshield, and then another, and then yet another.

"Team T-Ten to McKenna" came over their radios. "She's advancing toward you, but she stopped to reload. Do you want us to take her out?"

"Team T-Ten. How far away from us is she?" McKenna asked.

"Maybe fifty yards. She's done reloading, and coming toward you again. I say again: Do you want us to take her out?"

Three more rounds came through the windshield at two-second intervals.

"Well?" Cisco asked.

"Team T-Ten, are you sure you can hit her?" McKenna transmitted.

Yet another round came through the windshield.

"We've got two Glocks loaded with twenty-eight nine-millimeter parabellum rounds, so we'll get her with at least one of them" was the next transmission from Team T-10. "She's getting real close to you, maybe twenty-five yards, but moving slow. So what do you say? Take her out?"

McKenna looked to Cisco, and he nodded, so McKenna gave the go signal. "Please do."

Instantly, there was a very loud five-second fusillade consisting of, McKenna figured, about twenty rounds.

"Team T-Ten to McKenna. She's down, multiple hits. You can come out now."

McKenna and Cisco raised their heads over the dashboard and saw Bombi lying facedown on the ground, twenty yards in front of the pickup. They could see three bloody hits on the right side of her body—one in her thigh, one in her hip, and one in her side. She wasn't moving, and she didn't appear to be breathing. Team T-10 was up and walking toward them.

McKenna and Cisco were about to get out of the truck when the next series of transmissions stopped them all. "Sniper Team One to Task Force CO" came over the radios in a whisper. "Our target heard the shooting, and he appears jumpy."

"Sniper Team Four to Task Force CO. Same message as regards our target" was the next whispered transmission.

"Task Force CO to Sniper Team One. Do you have your target acquired?"

"Affirmative. We have target acquisition."

"Fire and report."

"Sniper Team One to Task Force CO. Our target is down" was transmitted a second later.

"Task Force CO to Sniper Team Four. Do you have your target acquired?"

"Negative, Task Force CO. We had him a second ago, but we don't have him now."

"Sniper Team Three to Task Force CO. We have target acquisition" was the next whispered transmission.

"Task Force CO to Sniper Team Three. Fire and report."

"Task Force CO, target is down."

Everyone on the air realized that two more lives had just been snuffed out, but that was only the signal for the next part of the plan. "SWAT Commander to Assault Team, deploy to Position One," Rego transmitted. "Sniper Teams, deploy to Position One-A."

"Well, it looks like what started out as a beautiful morning is turning into a rather messy day," Cisco observed. "Wouldn't you say?"

"Yes, I would," McKenna replied.

"Don't worry. There's still six of them left, and we always get a break—eventually. Let's go see what those wise-guy federal brutes did to our favorite murderous beauty, shall we?"

"Let's."

Bombi's face was turned to the side, her eyes were closed, and the small automatic had fallen out of her hand and lay next to her. She had kept her police combat crouch as she had fallen forward, with one arm still across her chest underneath her body. Bombi looked dead, but she wasn't yet. McKenna saw bubbles forming in the blood around the bullet hole in her side; she was lung-shot. He placed his hand on her back and felt a slight, rapid up-and-down movement.

McKenna raised his radio, called Bara, and requested an ambulance in the field opposite the place where Boy Scout Road ended.

"Friend or foe?" Bara asked.

"Foe."

"Task Force CO to McKenna. We're kinda busy right now, but I'll get your ambulance there."

The two Team T-10 agents arrived, and at that moment Bombi opened her eyes. They were unfocused, but her lips moved as a trickle of blood dripped from her mouth.

"Don't try to talk, Bombi," McKenna said softly. "We've got an ambulance on the way."

Bombi either didn't listen or couldn't hear him. Her lips moved again.

McKenna got down on his hands and knees and put his

ear next to her mouth. Bombi told him what was on her mind, and he got up.

"She's not gonna make it," Cisco said, and he was right. She shuddered once, and died quietly.

"What'd she say?" one of the Team T-10 agents asked.

"She said, 'Ba, fongu.' You do the translation," McKenna replied.

"Tough to the end," Cisco observed.

Then Rego transmitted again. All his men were in position, and he was awaiting instructions. Bara told him to stand by.

McKenna bent down and picked up Bombi's pistol. Then he looked at her pouch, and saw there was still something in it. He opened it up, and took out a hand grenade. It was small, green, and standard issue to U.S. troops—an M-29 fragmentation grenade. McKenna knew he was witnessing yet another reason why they called her Bombi, and he again raised his radio. "McKenna to Task Force CO."

"Task Force CO. What now, McKenna?"

"Cancel the ambulance and send the Bomb Squad. We've got a small problem down here."

"I'll do it, but I've got a big problem up here," Bara transmitted back. "I need my negotiators pronto, so get up here now—and bring your pal with you."

"McKenna to Task Force CO. We're on our way."

"Stay with the body, but don't touch it," McKenna said to the Team T-10 agents. He tossed the grenade to Cisco, and it received a casual examination from him before he dropped it into his suit pocket. Then McKenna turned and headed for the pickup, with Cisco following.

"Wait a minute!" one of the agents said. "What's our small problem?"

It was Cisco who answered. "Didn't that combat crouch of hers strike you as strange?"

"Yeah."

"You wanna know why she held that arm across her chest, with her hand in a fist?"

"Tell us."

"It's because she had her other grenade in that fist, with the pin pulled. Still does."

"You're kidding."

"No, I'm not. She was tough to the end, but she also had this little mean streak she kept to the end."

The two agents looked at each other, but said nothing.

"If you don't believe me, turn her over," Cisco added. "Just give us some time to get outta here first."

The Team T-10 agents backed far away from the body.

Cisco turned the pickup around, and they headed back across the meadow, retracing their route in. He stopped before the rock wall. The pickup had knocked off the top layer of rocks at the place where they had broached it, but the wall still looked formidable to McKenna.

"You still don't like this truck, right?" Cisco asked.

"Actually, I was beginning to like it," McKenna replied.

"Too bad." Cisco gunned the engine, and took off. They hit the wall, but this time the truck didn't go over the obstacle—it went through it, and they heard the sound of metal grating against rock. Cisco made the right onto the county road and stopped at the entrance to Boy Scout Road. Duchess was still sitting there.

"You wanna give her a ride?" Cisco asked.

"Sure."

McKenna got out, held the door open, and whistled. Duchess jumped right in. Then he smelled the oil. He bent down, looked under the truck, and saw the oil pouring from the ruptured oil pan. He pushed Duchess over, and got back into the truck. "You better hurry. The oil pan's shot," he advised.

"Think it'll do another mile?" Cisco asked.

"I hope so."

"Me, too, because that's all we need."

The oil pressure warning light came on bright red as Cisco took off up the hill. He stopped in front of the driveway of the McCook place just long enough to see that all Rego's men were deployed in the woods around the house, and they had all manner of weapons pointed at it. As an added touch for the folks inside, Rego had the bodies of the two sentries displayed on the lawn on either side of the house. Each had been killed by one high-velocity shot to the head, a very messy sight.

By then, all the warning lights on the dashboard were glowing, but Cisco ignored them. "Wouldn't want to be in that house right now," he commented, and then took off again up the road. They made it to the Boy Scout camp, but the engine finally seized when they were on the dirt access road leading to the fire spotters' tower. They got out and ran toward the tower. Duchess stayed with them for a while. Then she left the access road and ran into the woods.

"Easy come, easy go," Cisco said, but he was wrong. Duchess caught up to them a few moments later, and she had a stick in her mouth. Cisco surprised McKenna when he stopped, took the stick from her, and threw it down the road. Cisco had a great arm, and he got good yardage.

Duchess took off after the stick, and they continued running toward the tower. By the time they got to the bottom, Duchess was once again with them, the stick in her mouth. "That's my new dog," Cisco announced, but Bara didn't give him time to expand his point. He was leaning over the side, and looking down at them. "Get up here, you two," he shouted down. "And make it fast."

"Cranky, isn't he?" Cisco asked McKenna.

"Stressed, I'd say."

"Then I'm going to raise his medication as soon as we get up there," Cisco said.

McKenna didn't want to hear that, and Cisco didn't give him time to argue. He started climbing up the tower ladder fast, and McKenna followed. Then came a ripping sound that stopped them both. "Don't tell me," Cisco said.

McKenna looked up, and saw the source of Cisco's fears. The seat of Cisco's fitted Barney's suit pants had ripped open to expose his white boxer shorts, decorated with little red hearts. The sight gave McKenna a giggle, and he struggled for a moment to suppress it before he answered. "Somebody has to tell you."

"Damn! This sure is turning into one miserable fuckin' day," Cisco said, and continued climbing.

That simple statement told McKenna just how annoyed Cisco was. As first-grade detectives, they were at the top of their game, and held in godlike awe by most other detectives. Quite naturally, first-graders felt that profanity was only used by lesser beings as they struggled to express themselves.

Got to keep a tight lid on him for the rest of the day, McKenna thought as he followed Cisco up. Cisco stepped onto the tower platform, and McKenna expected to hear a stream of sarcastic invective from him directed toward Bara. That didn't happen, and McKenna saw why as soon as he stepped onto the platform himself. Bara's face was red with rage, and Cisco was leaning against the rail to hide his new source of embarrassment. He gave McKenna a small smile and a nod that said it all, and McKenna got the message: Never poke an angry tiger with a stick when the cage door is open.

The tiger backed up the message with a roar. "You know what we got down there, McKenna?" Bara yelled, but he didn't wait for a reply. "I'll tell you what we've got. A houseful of fuckin' dopes, that's what we've got."

Uh-oh. Bara's annoyance level is certainly higher than Cisco's, McKenna thought. How do I calm him down? "Having problems with the negotiations, Boss?" McKenna tried, as reasonably and as softly as he could.

That didn't work. "Problems? How's this for problems?" Bara yelled. "Only one of those fuckin' dopes speaks any kind of English, and my only hope is that he's the stupidest of the lot. Those idiots don't have the brains to make any kind of decision, even one that would save their lives."

"Their leader is dead, and I guess she made all the decisions for them," McKenna said. "Want me to give it a try?"

"Why do you think I've got you up here?" Bara asked, but he didn't wait for an answer. He led McKenna to his communications center, a table that had been set up on the far wall of the tower. Along with a large radio transmitter, there were four phones on it. One of the phones was labeled

NSA, one was labeled MR. SHIELDS, one was labeled OUTSIDE LINE, and the fourth was labeled HOUSE. The phone service to the house had been restored.

McKenna was familiar with the setup on the house phone. It was the standard device used in most communications in hostage situations. The receiver had a push-to-talk button in the handle, and the phone was attached to a small console. There was a red light blinking on the console, indicating that the line was open, and next to the light was a ring button. When pressed, the phone would ring in the house, even if the line were open.

Bara offered him the house phone receiver, but McKenna had a question first. "Did they threaten to kill the ambassador?"

"No," Bara said, shaking his head. "It's their only card, and the dopes don't know how to play it."

"Good." McKenna took the phone, and pressed the push-to-talk button. "Hello?"

No answer.

"Hello?"

Still no answer, so McKenna pressed the ring button and held it a few seconds.

"Sorry, I'm back," a male voice said in heavily accented English.

"Where were you?" McKenna asked.

"I had to use the bathroom."

"Do you think that was appropriate, under the circumstances?"

"Huh?"

McKenna switched to Spanish and repeated the question.

"Well, I had to go," the man said, following McKenna's switch to Spanish. "I was talking, but nobody was talking to me, so I went."

"What is your name?"

"Elodi."

Elodi? The one Bombi had called *stupid* in the park? McKenna thought. Looks like she was right. "Elodi, this is Detective Brian McKenna of the New York City Police Department. Do you know who I am?"

"Sure I know. We all do."

"I want you to do me and everybody else in there a big favor."

"What favor?"

"Look around, and answer one question for me. Do you see somebody who might be smarter than you?"

"Maybe."

"What's his name?"

"Sanko."

"Thank you. Put Sanko on, please."

"Are you sure? Sanko doesn't speak any English."

Bara also had the scoop on Elodi, McKenna thought. This guy sure is a dope. "So Sanko doesn't speak any English. Too bad," he said. "By the way, what language are we speaking in right now?"

"We're speaking in Spanish."

"And are you having any difficulty understanding me?"

"No, you speak good. Like a teacher."

"And does Sanko speak Spanish?"

"Of course. We all do."

"Then I'm very sure I want to speak to Sanko. Please put him on."

There was a short, heated conversation in Basque in the background before Sanko came on the line. "Hello?"

"Hello, Sanko. This is Detective McKenna."

"I know."

"How are you gentlemen doing in there?"

"How are we doing? What do you think? Did you see what they did to Reynaldo and Huaxa?"

"Are those the two gentlemen lying outside with big holes in their heads?"

"Yes, and they never shot nobody."

"Then that's too bad, but it doesn't have to get worse. Listen to me, and listen well. Your house is surrounded by many very mean, very tough men armed with horrible weapons—and they want to put holes in all of your heads. Do you believe me?"

"Sure I believe you, but you're forgetting one thing."

"What am I forgetting?"

"We have the ambassador. If we die, he dies."

And this is the guy I wanted to talk to? McKenna thought. Maybe a mistake, but let's see. "Then try this one out, Sanko. If the ambassador lives, you live. Does that sound better?"

There was a pause and more conversation in Basque before Sanko answered. "Of course it sounds better, but you won't come in and kill us while we have him."

"Of course we will."

"You will?"

"Sure we will, because you're not allowed to kill the ambassador."

"Why not?"

"Because Bombi told us you're not. She wanted to, but she says that some ETA boss in Spain says she's not allowed to kill him. This boss told her that it's very important that the ambassador is alive and happy, or the Spanish government will break off the negotiations."

"You have Bombi?"

"Yes, but she's hurt."

"What happened to her?"

"She was running away from us, and she slipped and fell down a cliff. Broke her leg bad, and she's being brought to the hospital right now."

"What else did she say about the negotiations?"

"That they're going well, and you know what that means to you."

There was another pause, and another Basque conversation in the background. "I know," Sanko said, "but do you?"

No, you don't, stupid! They've been kept totally in the dark, McKenna thought. I wonder who ties their shoes for them. "Yes, I know what it means to you."

"What?"

"What it means to you is that, after you surrender to us

very soon, we put you all on a plane to Spain—as long as the ambassador is all right."

"When would we be going to Spain?"

"It's too late to go today without reservations, so I'd say tomorrow at the earliest."

"Tomorrow?"

"Or the next day."

"And then what?"

"And then you go to jail in Spain for five years."

"Five years? That's all?"

"If the negotiations are successful, and Bombi seems to think they're going pretty good. As part of the peace agreement, all ETA prisoners who have been in jail for five years are to be freed. All others—and I'm talking about you and your pals—can only be sentenced to five years, maximum."

"I know we wanted that, but you're saying we're going to get it?"

"No, I'm not saying it. It's Bombi and whoever the boss is in Spain who are saying it, and you know what that means to you?"

"No, what?"

"If you harm the ambassador, the deal is off. That means that all ETA prisoners in jail in Spain stay in jail because of you and your pals."

"Wait a minute," Sanko said. "If we kill the ambassador, do we still go to jail in Spain?"

"You're not listening, Sanko. If you kill the ambassador, the men outside kill you. Wait a minute, please." McKenna released the push-to-talk button and turned to Bara. "I'm gonna give them twenty minutes to talk it over and surrender. All right with you?"

"Are they going to come out?" Bara asked.

"It's a done deal."

"Then make it ten minutes."

"Okay, ten minutes," McKenna said, and went back on the line with Sanko. "Sanko, are you there?"

"I'm still here."

"Then listen to me good, because you might not be able

to talk to me later. You have ten minutes to send the ambassador out, and then come out with your hands up. Ten minutes, and that's it."

"Suppose we don't?"

"Then bad things will begin to happen to all of you."

"Very bad?"

"Not too bad at first, but it will get very bad after that. Talk to your friends, and I hope you make the right decision. Good-bye."

"Wait a minute! Where are you going?"

"I have to pee. Good-bye." McKenna ended the call. Since Bara didn't speak Spanish, it took McKenna five minutes to explain the conversation to him.

"So I was right," Bara said. "Real dopes."

"You were right. Their IQs are someplace between a potato and a tomato, but let's hope they're at least smart enough to retain a survival instinct," McKenna said, and then he brought up the subject that had been on his mind all morning. "Did the NSA tell you where in Spain that call got picked up this morning?"

"Near the southern coast, just west of Algeciras, and the ETA boss was moving while they were talking."

"Moving?"

"From one cell to another in Spain, always headed east. NSA estimates they're traveling at about forty miles per hour."

"So they still haven't reached their destination?"

"Not yet. According to the boss in Spain, he's had lots of problems. Says that Carmen is really getting to his people, and he's had some dissension."

"Did he admit it was a mistake to take her?"

"No. The bad news is that he's committed to keeping her, and seeing this thing through."

"How about negotiations with the government?"

"According to him, there still aren't any," and then Bara turned to Cisco and the subject foremost on his mind. "What exactly did you say to that guy before you shot him?"

McKenna knew there was a problem. He hadn't heard

anything over the air about it, so he realized the agents in Team T-8 must have called Bara directly with their concerns.

Cisco realized it as well. "Didn't your crybaby agents tell you?" he asked.

"They have some ideas on what you said, but they don't speak Spanish."

"But I do," McKenna interjected. "He said, 'Drop the gun, and turn around slowly. Don't make us kill you.' "

"That's not exactly what Cisco said," Cisco stated, horrifying McKenna.

"Then what *exactly* did you say?" Bara asked.

"You must understand that Cisco is very polite, and sometimes Brian forgets that. Cisco's *exact* words were, '*Please* drop the gun, and turn around slowly. We don't want to kill you, so *please* don't make us do it.' "

"I see," Bara said, but both McKenna and Cisco knew that Bara was a sharp guy, and that he really did see.

Then Bara checked his watch. "Eight minutes," he said, and then keyed the large radio on his desk. "Task Force CO to SWAT Team commander."

"SWAT Team commander, standing by," Rego transmitted.

"If they're not out in two minutes, go to Phase Two."

"Understood, Task Force CO. Two minutes to Phase Two, and counting. SWAT Team commander to Assault Team, Phase Two on my signal. Acknowledge."

Rego received plenty of acknowledgments.

"What's Phase Two?" Cisco asked.

"Tear gas, and plenty of it," Bara said, and then went to the rail to watch the action at the house.

"Can I try them one more time?" McKenna asked.

"Suit yourself, but they've only got a minute left," Bara said over his shoulder.

McKenna picked up the receiver and pressed the ring button. Sanko came on the line at once. "This is Detective McKenna again. You have less than one minute to send out the ambassador, and come out with your hands up."

"Maybe we will, but we're still talking. We need more time."

"How much more time?"

"Maybe ten minutes. Can we have it?"

"That depends."

"On what?"

"Can you hold your breath for ten minutes?"

"No."

"Then you don't have ten minutes."

"SWAT Team commander to Assault Team. Phase Two, now!" McKenna heard Rego transmit, and his order was instantly followed by the pops of many grenade launchers and the sound of windows breaking.

"What's happening?" Sanko asked, and there was terror in his voice.

"It's only tear gas. It'll hurt your eyes, but it won't kill you. Remember, don't do anything stupid. Come out, now."

"It burns like hell," Sanko yelled. "I don't know about the others, but I'm coming out."

McKenna put down the phone and joined Bara and Cisco at the rail. What he saw satisfied him, in a perverse way. All the SWAT team members were wearing gas masks, and they were grabbing each member of the ETA crew as they ran from the house by the front and rear doors. It was an easy job since all of them ran out of the house with their hands over their eyes, rubbing furiously.

Tear gas was billowing through all the broken windows, and there were many. The smell would hang around for months, so McCook would get his damages.

As McKenna watched, the last two ETA holdouts came out the front door in a state of panic, and they too were quickly subdued by the SWAT team.

"That's six of them," Bara said. "Where's the ambassador?"

"The idiots forgot him inside," Cisco said.

Rego figured as much, and he led two of his men into the house. They emerged two minutes later carrying the ambassador and the chair to which he was tied. He was in the same shape as his former captors, but he was allowed to wipe his eyes and run around the front yard after Rego cut the ropes binding him to the chair.

"Well, it looks like we've got prisoners aplenty," Cisco said. "Think they'll do us any good?"

Those dopes? They're worthless! McKenna almost said, but then he noticed that Bara was looking at him closely. "Stupid as they are, you and me will get something out of them that will help us."

SIXTEEN

Huaxa, one of the sentries the snipers had killed, was the man who had adopted the name Antonio Ramirez, and Mc-Kenna considered that bad luck. Since Ramirez had served as the ETA team's advance man, McKenna had him pegged as Bombi's second-in-command, and someone she might have confided in.

The tear gas was still lingering inside, so McKenna and Cisco wore gas masks while they participated in the search of the house. Nothing McKenna considered useful was found, but there were many items of interest. The ETA crew had been heavily armed, and casualties could have easily been incurred in taking the house. Found inside were nine AK-47s, three rocket-propelled grenade launchers, and plenty of ammo and grenades for each. Also found were three .38 S&W revolvers and the Remington scope-mounted rifle that had been used when the ambassador was kidnapped. In the room McKenna assumed was Bombi's, he found another six M-29 hand grenades.

As it turned out, Bara's decision to use scrambled radios had been a good one. On the dining room table was a police scanner, and it was still on when the search team entered the house.

The ETA team had stockpiled enough food to last them a month, and apparently had been prepared to sit out the crisis in some comfort while negotiations with the Spanish government proceeded.

After the search of the house was completed, the prisoners were brought to the state police substation in Tannersville, and McKenna was anxious to question them. Because of Bombi, that questioning had to wait a few hours. An investigator from the state police's Bomb Squad had suited up in his full blast-protection gear, and he had inserted his hand under Bombi's body to verify that she did have a primed grenade in her hand with the pin pulled.

Since he was wearing bulky blast-protection gloves, the Bomb Squad investigator didn't have the manual dexterity to reinsert a pin in the grenade. Bombi would have to be rolled over, and it was decided that would have to wait until rigor mortis set in. When that happened, in theory at least, Bombi's dead, stiff fingers wouldn't release the grenade when she was rolled over.

It was one o'clock before Bombi was stiff enough for them to proceed, and it was a perfect photo opportunity for the news crews. Reporters from all the New York City newspapers were there by then, along with news crews from CNN and all the New York City TV stations. They set up on the county road, two hundred yards from Bombi's body, with telephoto lenses attached to their cameras.

The Bomb Squad had attached hundred-foot-long ropes to her outstretched right arm and her right leg. McKenna watched through binoculars as two Bomb Squad investigators pulled on the ropes and rolled Bombi's stiff body over.

McKenna was braced for the explosion, but it never came. He could see that Bombi was still holding the grenade, and her grip hadn't loosened. It took only another minute for a Bomb Squad investigator to insert a pin in the grenade, and then pry it from her fingers.

McKenna wanted to be present at the search of Bombi's body, so he and Cisco walked over to join the Bomb Squad investigators standing over her. McKenna thought Bombi was a sad sight—stiff, with her eyes open and glazed over. Gravity had been at work while she had been lying facedown on the ground, and the blood inside her body had flowed to the lowest points so that her face was purple. Blood had congealed at her mouth, and the flies had found her and were buzzing around her open wounds.

As McKenna looked down at her, it was hard for him to imagine that she had been so alive and beautiful just four hours before.

Ibarretxe brought Señora Clavero to Tannersville for a joyous reunion with her husband. The ambassador was interviewed many times by the press, and he was patient with them and always effusive in his praise for the Joint Terrorism Task Force. He said he had been well-treated during his captivity, and he had been allowed to read and watch TV whenever he wanted.

After his press interviews, the ambassador had a long chat with McKenna over coffee. He identified Bombi as the leader of the ETA crew, and he thought that Antonio Ramirez was her second-in-command because—even though he sometimes assigned himself to sentry duty—it was Ramirez who made the guard assignments.

The ambassador's account of his kidnapping verified most of the assumptions McKenna had made. Just blocks away from his building, he had been transferred to the white Ford van and driven upstate. He had been blindfolded at the time, but he knew they had stopped for a while in a rest area on the Thruway because one of his captors had left the van and returned with food for the rest of them.

The ambassador didn't know who had picked up Bombi in the park, but she was in the Lincoln Town Car that he figured must have been behind them for most of the trip to Tannersville.

The ambassador was able to identify the three men who had been the main players in the kidnapping since he had spent a few minutes in his Mercedes with them immediately after. Two of them were still alive and among the prisoners, and he identified Sanko as the man with the rifle. As for the man who had been waiting around the corner on East 80th Street, the ambassador identified a man the others called *Julio*.

To McKenna's relief, Cisco had been right about the man he had shot. The forged passports had been found in the house, and McKenna showed the ambassador the passport photo of the dead man. The ambassador verified that he was Duchess's master—the man who had killed Roberto Hernandez, shot Jorge Dominguez three times in the back, and driven the Mercedes in the escape after the kidnapping.

The ambassador described his captivity as uneventful. He had spent many evenings playing chess with Bombi, and he said he usually lost to her. She was always pleasant with him, but he also said that she was arrogant and bossy with the other members of the ETA crew. He felt that she held them in contempt.

The ambassador also had something else to report that made McKenna doubt the prisoners had much useful information to give. Although he been kidnapped, he hadn't been robbed, and he had $230 in his wallet when he was taken. He frequently joined in his captors' card games, and he had $2,210 in his pocket when he was released. "They're all losers," he told McKenna, "and none of them are very bright."

"Did they ever win?" McKenna asked.

"I won every time I sat down with them."

"Do you consider yourself a good card player?"

"Mediocre. My wife beats me most of the time, and Señor Ibarretxe beats me all the time."

"If you had to pick out the brightest among them, who would it be?"

"Without a doubt, Sanko."

"Why?"

"Because after the first game, he never played cards with me again."

Before the prisoners were interrogated, Sandra, Daniela, and José Gomez were also brought to Tannersville to verify the ambassador's identification of the players during the kidnapping. Señora Clavero and Gomez were also shown the passport photo of the man Cisco had shot. Both identified him as the man who had shot Roberto Hernandez and Jorge Dominguez.

Next came a series of lineups, and McKenna was delighted that the ambassador's identification of the other two players was also verified by the other witnesses. Señora Clavero couldn't identify the man in the park with the rifle, but Gomez, Sandra, and Daniela could. In three separate lineups, they all picked out Sanko.

Señora Clavero was more helpful when it came to identifying the man who had held her on the sidewalk, the same man who had hit Gomez on the head with his gun. She picked out the man her husband had identified as Miguel, and so did José Gomez.

Next came the press interviews, and Bara figured he would handle that task in front of the Tannersville police station, with McKenna, Cisco, and the SWAT team in the background. He made a brief statement for the press as the TV cameras rolled, and was then prepared to field questions. The problem was that the reporters had none for him; it was to McKenna they addressed their questions. McKenna answered most of them, but issued the standard "That matter is still under investigation" for the few questions he felt would shed any light on events occurring in Spain.

Bara tried smiling through McKenna's question-and-answer session, but McKenna felt it was a poor attempt.

McKenna thought that he would take the lead in interrogating the prisoners, but Cisco wasn't so sure, and thought that Bara planned to have his agents conduct the questionings. "He thinks we have to be put in our place," Cisco said with conviction. "The problem is, he can't bring himself to admit that our places are always first place and second place."

Cisco had McKenna worried, but their fears were resolved after they watched Bara take another phone call from Shields. It was a one-way conversation, and Bara's part consisted mostly of "Yes, sir."

McKenna and Cisco were momentarily mystified as they watched Bara painfully replace his grimace with a smile after he hung up. Then he called them over.

"You know, I'm pretty happy with you two," he said.

"No, I didn't know that," Cisco said. "When did you get so happy?"

"Just now."

"Why?"

"Because Mr. Shields just told me I'm happy, and said I should show it," Bara admitted. "Said I appeared too grumpy on TV, and also said it's a bad look for me."

"Did he say anything else?" McKenna asked.

"As a matter of fact, he did. Despite whatever the press thinks, he said that he knows that I'm in charge of this investigation—and so does the director and the attorney general. They think I should be commended, and Mr. Shields agrees."

"Congratulations," McKenna said, and Cisco was quick to follow suit.

"There's more," Bara said, "and I take it the new official attitude will ultimately be affecting your travel plans in a way you'll like."

"We're being sent to Spain?" Cisco asked.

"Not yet—but soon, I'm sure."

"So what's next?" Cisco asked.

"Interrogating the prisoners. Mr. Shields wants a report as soon as you're done with them."

"Will we be able to offer them anything to talk?" McKenna asked.

"A trip to Spain. The Spanish ambassador in Washington has informally advised the attorney general that his government will seek to have them extradited to Spain to stand trial there, but here's a proviso nobody's ever heard before: You, Detective McKenna, are to have the final say on who stays and who goes."

"Stay here and face life, or go to Spain to probably do five years?" McKenna said. "That's a big bargaining chip."

"Then go play it."

SEVENTEEN

McKenna and Cisco wanted to wrap up the Tannersville episode, get what they could from the prisoners, and move on to the mission they considered more important. However, the legal amenities had to be observed; the prisoners were entitled to legal representation before being questioned—if they asked for a lawyer after being advised of their rights. Both knew that the presence of even the greenest lawyer would throw their investigation into "park" for weeks because that lawyer would automatically advise his or her clients not to talk. It was part of the lawyers' creed: No questioning of clients until the evidence was examined at length, the case was dissected in a search for the most minute of flaws, and the possibility of a deal with the prosecutor was explored.

So lawyers would be avoided until the stage was set, McKenna and Cisco decided. The work had been done right, their case against the prisoners was almost airtight, and the Spanish government had given them a strong trump card. It was just a matter of showing the prisoners exactly where their best interests lay, and then convincing them that the presence of a lawyer at an inappropriate time would cause them nothing but more misery.

Cisco was ready to do his part. He had anticipated that the efforts in Tannersville would be successful, and he had planned ahead. He had brought with him what he called a "motivational video," a twenty-minute presentation prepared

by the Bureau of Prisons featuring the maximum-security
facility at Marion, Illinois. The surviving members of the
ETA crew were in for a show, and Cisco was prepared to
make it interesting and personal for them.

The prisoners were brought handcuffed into the substation's briefing room, and McKenna addressed them briefly
in Spanish. He told them that it was possible that some of
them would soon be going to Spain, just as he had promised
during the negotiations, but there was something they had to
do before that could happen. He then turned the floor over
to Cisco.

The prisoners were shown the video while Cisco interpreted the narration into Spanish for them. Then he ex-
pounded on the points he had found interesting. He talked
about the sterile six-by-nine cells where prisoners spent
twenty-three hours a day without seeing another human being, he lamented the fact that only three hours of closely
supervised visitation was permitted per month, and he explained that entertainment for the prisoners consisted of one
book a week. At Marion, they had no rec room, no weight
room, no counseling, and no rehabilitative therapy. Prisoners
were sent there to do their time, and almost nothing else.

Then Cisco connected the dots for them. As members of
a foreign terrorist organization that had committed capital
crimes in the United States, thereby arousing public ire and
alarm, Marion was where they would be going if they didn't
cooperate. But for how long would they be going? Cisco
asked no one in particular, and then he gave his considered
opinion. Since they had been heavily armed while holding a
hostage after committing two murders in a cause that held
little or no interest for Americans, they would probably
spend the rest of their lives there.

Since he had the prisoners' total interest at that point,
Cisco decided to give them his informed assessment of the
political climate in Spain. He pointed out that support for the
ETA, even in the Basque Country, had virtually vanished
since Carmen's kidnapping. He went on to say that, since
the ETA's ability to influence public opinion in a positive

way was close to nonexistent, they had been working and taking unacceptable risks for a basically defunct organization. Furthermore, they could expect little or no sympathy in Spain when they were sentenced to life without parole in Marion.

Cisco had shown them the stick. Then McKenna again took the floor, and he produced the carrot. He stated his opinion that the Spanish government would eventually negotiate in good faith with the ETA on the issue of prisoners and sentences. He made no attempt to back this opinion up with facts, but he added that he thought the ETA demand of a maximum five years in prison for offenses committed by its people would eventually be the basis of an agreement to end the violence once and for all.

After having sat through Cisco's gloomy projections on their fate, the prisoners' moods lifted visibly as McKenna told them what they wanted to hear. Then McKenna made himself the most important man in their lives when he told them the Spanish government would soon request their extradition, but he had been given the absolute power to decide who would stay and who would go. He explained the dilemma that power had placed him in: The FBI had to justify the enormous manpower commitment and expense generated in locating and freeing the ambassador, so at least two prisoners would have to stand trial in the United States in order to satisfy the American public.

So how would he decide which of them was to spend life in Marion, especially since he didn't care if they all did? McKenna told them he had talked it over with Cisco, and they had decided that the only fair way was to have a contest. The smartest prisoners go to Spain, and the dopiest stay.

All of the prisoners appeared intensely interested, so McKenna went on to explain that the objective of the contest would be to determine which four prisoners possessed the best information on the kidnapping of Carmen and the Spanish ambassador to France, and that was it. He told them that freeing Carmen was his only real concern, and added that he cared nothing about other crimes and political events in

Spain. Therefore, he promised that the specific source of the information would never be revealed, nor would he provide to the Guardia Civil any information learned in Tannersville that would assist in the prosecution of other members of the ETA.

McKenna next explained how the contest would work. Each prisoner would be brought to an interrogation room by him and Cisco, and he would be read his Miranda warnings. If the prisoner decided that he wanted a lawyer present before answering any questions, fine, but he would be disqualified and the contest was over for him. Then the three of them would talk for an hour about soccer, or politics, or anything else the prisoner had on his mind before the next contestant was selected.

There were other contest rules, of course, but they were simple. McKenna explained that there would be no points awarded for bravado, and lying on even the most minor of points would result in disqualification.

The contestants were then separated and fed dinners brought in from a Tannersville restaurant, while Cisco and McKenna went out to eat and refine their strategy. They decided that going from the dumbest to the smartest would be the order of contestants, and they relied on the ambassador's opinion as to what the lineup would be.

Since the English-language skills of the four prisoners questioned so far were poor, the interrogations were conducted in Spanish. After four hours of questioning, McKenna and Cisco knew quite a bit about the ETA and the kidnappings because of a lucky twist for them. It seemed that the ETA had shrunk into something of a family affair with a vested interest, and all of those questioned had close relatives held in prison and other relatives in the Spain and France kidnapping teams. Three of the four prisoners questioned had been active in the ETA for under a year, and all had wanted to end their involvement after almost any kind of deal had been worked out with the Spanish government on the ETA prisoners it held.

All details of the New York kidnapping had been cleared up, and what had at first appeared to be an operation by ruthless and dedicated terrorists had not been that at all. They had been well-led by Bombi, and the operation had been well-planned by her, but most of her crew was poorly trained and lacking in motivation. Bombi and the discipline she had imposed on them had been the critical factors in the successful kidnapping.

What McKenna and Cisco had found interesting was that the little training the prisoners had, they had received in Morocco. In January, they had traveled in pairs from the Basque Country to the city of Algeciras in southern Spain. From there, they had taken a ferry across the Strait of Gibraltar to Ceuta, a city that was part of Spain, but actually located on the Moroccan coast in North Africa. They had been met by an ETA agent at the ferry terminal on the Ceuta side, and transported to a safe house to spend the night.

Since the main mission of the Spanish border patrol in Ceuta is to keep Moroccans out, not keep Spaniards in, they had entered Morocco the next day with no difficulty and were transported to a small ETA training camp in the Atlas Mountains. The camp was disguised as a hunting lodge and was the Berber version of a dude ranch for wealthy Spaniards and Moroccans. Most of the time it served that purpose, but not during those three weeks in January. During that time, the only guests were the thirty ETA fighters who were to take part in the kidnappings.

All of the prisoners questioned so far had described the first week of their stay in Morocco as a pleasant experience. Sanko and his brother Txero were in charge of the regimen. The group spent each morning in weapons training, and all claimed that they had gained some proficiency in the use of the AK-47 and the RPG-7 during that time. Afternoons were reserved for language lessons in English and French, and nights were spent in political discussions with friends and relatives.

Everything had changed dramatically during the second week with the arrival of Bombi and two men known to the prisoners only as Comandante Segundo and Comrade Tercero. However, the prisoners were shown Spanish police photos of Raoul Marey—the man who had led the team that had kidnapped Carmen—and all had identified him as Comandante Segundo. The prisoners were also able to identify Comandante Tercero from the photos; he was Ignacio Uranga, another ETA fugitive.

The ETA fighters had been gathered and told they had been selected for three important missions that would end the struggle and bring peace to the Spanish Basque Country. They had been given no details on these missions, were told they would all be heroes—but first they would have to prove themselves capable and worthy. The picnic was over.

At the end of the training session, the fighters had all been photographed for their passport photos, and they had received some background on the new identities they would be assigned. They had then been transported back to Ceuta on a Spanish tour bus, and on to Algeciras after another night in the Ceuta safe house. They had been left to their own devices to get back home for a week of rest in the Basque Country, and told they would be contacted with further instructions on the missions they were to undertake.

For all the prisoners interviewed, those further instructions had come on March 13, and they were terse. Be at the Iberia ticket counter at the airport in Madrid the next morning at seven, packed for a two-week trip. All had complied, and Bombi had met them there and distributed tickets for New York and passports in their new identities. The ten of them had seats scattered around the 9 A.M. flight to New York, and they had arrived there and passed through Customs and Immigration without incident. Bombi had a van waiting outside, and the driver took them to the house in Tannersville.

What followed were the weekly trips to New York to establish the ambassador's Sunday routine, nightly political indoctrination and training sessions conducted by Bombi, listening to hours of taped English lessons, and not much else.

The men were virtual prisoners in the house, and none of them had been to town.

McKenna and Cisco had no clear indication on where the ETA teams in Spain were headed with Carmen and the other ambassador, but they had to consider Morocco. The ETA had been approaching Algeciras at the time of the last phone call, the coastal city with ferry service to Ceuta on the North African coast. They could be in Morocco already with Carmen and the ambassador, McKenna and Cisco had been forced to concede, and that prospect depressed them.

As for the phone calls made to the hotels in Jerez and Sevilla, all of the prisoners interviewed so far said Bombi was the only one who had used the phone.

At 10:30 P.M. McKenna and Cisco brought Miguel into the interrogation room. He was the next-to-last contestant, and all were still in the game. Miguel had a few more problems than the previously interviewed prisoners. The lifts Walsh had obtained from Señora Clavero's belt buckle matched his left index and ring finger, so, aside from the eyewitness identifications, there was irrefutable physical evidence placing him as a participant in the kidnapping of the ambassador and the murders of his chauffeur and bodyguard. McKenna and Cisco expected to do well with him.

Miguel smiled as he took his seat, and he placed his hands on the table in front of him. He appeared to be in a cooperative mood, and McKenna began the interrogation in Spanish. His first question was, "Do you speak English?"

"Not great, but okay," Miguel replied in English.

Fine, McKenna thought, and he explained to Miguel in English the overwhelming evidence against him. Miguel understood, and McKenna quickly found there was no reason to threaten him. As far as he could tell, Miguel answered all questions honestly in heavily accented English, and it took just half an hour to verify the information received from the other prisoners.

So now what? McKenna wondered. No help so far, so what's the question I should be asking? "How long have you been with the ETA?" he tried.

"Almost five years active," Miguel replied, and he seemed proud of it.

"Do you have any relatives in the other kidnap teams?"

"A brother."

"Do you know if he's in the team that kidnapped Carmen, or the one that kidnapped the Paris ambassador?"

"I can't say for sure, but I think he should be with the one that took Carmen."

"What makes you think that?"

"Because we're from Jaca."

"Why is it that you speak English better than most of the other prisoners?" McKenna asked.

"Because I studied English in high school, and my brother works for a travel agency. We've been to London three times."

"Does your brother speak English?"

"Yes, and much better than me. He went to college in Madrid, and he took more English courses there."

Then why wasn't he assigned to the New York mission? McKenna wondered. He decided it was a question worth pursuing. "Of all the people who were with you in Morocco, how many of them spoke better English than you?"

Miguel thought for a moment before answering. "Counting my brother, maybe five."

"But none of them were assigned to the New York mission?"

"Huaxa was."

"Huaxa? You mean the man who came here as Antonio Ramirez and set everything up?"

"Yes, him."

"Tell me about Huaxa. How long had he been in the ETA?"

"A long time, I think. Longer than me, and he knew Comandante Segundo. I think they were friends."

"Did he ever tell you that Comandante Segundo's real name is Raoul Marey?"

"No. Huaxa didn't talk a lot, and he thought he was a boss."

"Doesn't it seem strange to you that four of the people who speak good English weren't sent to New York?"

"It seemed strange to all of us," Miguel said. "Stupid, even."

McKenna pondered the ETA personnel decision, and then a thought hit him. "Have you ever been to Gibraltar?" he asked.

"Twice."

"And your brother?"

"Many times. He liked to go there to practice his English."

McKenna glanced at Cisco, and saw that he was smiling widely. They were on the same track. "You have any more questions for him?" McKenna asked.

"Why ask any more questions when we've already got all the answers we need?" Cisco replied.

"Do I get to go back to Spain?" Miguel asked.

"Yeah, it looks like you're going back," McKenna said.

Cisco escorted Miguel back to the cells, leaving McKenna to examine their conclusion. The more he thought about it, the more sense it made to him. British territory and British sovereignty over the Rock had always been a serious source of contention between Great Britain and Spain. Gibraltar had been British since 1704, but Spain still laid claim to it.

Cisco returned, ready for discussion. "Are we agreed that they're probably headed to Gibraltar?" he asked.

"I think that's it," McKenna said. "That's why they kept most of the English speakers for the mission they considered the most important."

"Have you ever visited the place?"

"Once, about ten years ago."

"And?"

"Loved it. England on the Mediterranean. Clean and prosperous, great views—and English is the language."

"And the people? What are they?"

"Brits, Scots, and many people of Spanish ancestry. However, nobody there considers themselves Spanish. British subjects and proud of it."

"Do you know how that happened?" Cisco asked.

McKenna was a history buff, and since he liked the place, the history of Gibraltar had always intrigued him. "Britain took it from Spain by force in 1704, and it was legalized in 1713 by a treaty with Spain. It's been one of their major naval bases since, but the Spanish government has been claiming it since the Napoleonic Wars ended. They claim that treaty was made under duress."

"Do they do anything about their claim?"

"They did, and it was quite an inconvenience for the people of Gibraltar. Cut off the water and closed the border for twelve years, beginning in the seventies. Made the people there very anti-Spanish, and I imagine they still are."

"All of them?"

"Just about. At Spain's insistence, there was a plebiscite maybe ten years ago to see what the people of Gibraltar wanted. Stay British, or return the city to Spain. More than ninety-nine percent voted to remain British."

"Is it difficult to cross the border now?"

"Piece of cake when I was there, but it's a very busy crossing. Lots of tourists, and lots of truck traffic."

"Is it easy to get to Morocco from there?"

"Very easy. There's a ferry that goes to Morocco, but the city also has a big pleasure-boat marina. It's only fourteen miles to North Africa."

"Where in Morocco does this ferry go?"

"Tangiers."

"Does the Guardia Civil have any influence in Tangiers?"

"It's a Moroccan city, so I don't imagine so."

"Then I'd say that taking the ferry is what they're planning," Cisco said.

"So would I. I don't imagine they'd generate much notice when they got off in Tangiers, and they'd have nothing else to worry about."

"Then they can't be permitted to get on that ferry. How are the police in Gibraltar?"

"They seemed competent to me, but there's not much for them to do. Pretty much a low-crime city."

"Any military presence there?"

"There's the Royal Gibraltar Guard consisting of the local folks, maybe four hundred of them. There are also a couple of companies of Royal Marines stationed there, but I think they're just there for show."

"How far is it from Algeciras to Gibraltar?" Cisco asked.

"Close. Maybe half an hour by car."

"Meaning that they probably already have Carmen and the ambassador there."

"Good chance."

Like Miguel, Sanko too had been placed by eyewitnesses at the scene of the ambassador's kidnapping, and there was also physical evidence verifying that he had been the man in the park with the rifle—the man who had murdered the ambassador's bodyguard. The lift obtained by Walsh from the hundred-peseta coin matched Sanko's left thumb, and he had a pack of Gauloises in his pocket when he was captured. Once again, when the evidence had been explained to Sanko by McKenna, further threats weren't necessary. Sanko was prepared to cooperate fully, and he did. The interrogation yielded some new information, but not much. McKenna was able to verify Miguel's assertion that most of the ETA's English speakers weren't sent to New York. Another bit of information was that Sanko's brother, Txero, was in one of the other kidnap teams, and he also spoke English.

After the interrogations were complete, McKenna gave the new theory on Carmen's location to Bara, and Bara gave it to Shields. The British government would be made aware of the possibility that twenty heavily armed terrorists with two prominent hostages might clandestinely enter Gibraltar—if they weren't already there. Presumably, the border-crossing procedure between Spain and Gibraltar would be tightened, and boats crossing the strait to North Africa would be searched.

In the meantime, McKenna and Cisco would be accompanying their prisoners back to Spain.

EIGHTEEN

It had taken four days of diplomatic and procedural wrangling before the deal was officially sanctioned by both the Spanish and the United States governments. While McKenna would have no official status in Spain, it was understood that the people in charge there would be prepared to listen to whatever he had to say.

The prisoners were shackled and in leg irons, so guarding them was no problem, and Cisco encouraged congenial political debate during the seven-hour flight. Despite the ETA's platform that the fighting would continue until there was a free and independent Basque homeland, McKenna's prisoners believed that the government-held prisoners were the only real issue that interested the Spanish Basques, and for most of them that level of interest was not high.

As the plane descended for landing, the only passengers awake were McKenna and Cisco. The prisoners awoke as the wheels touched down, and five minutes later the pilot stopped next to eight green-and-white Guardia Civil vans and a Guardia Civil helicopter parked alongside the ramp truck next to the runway.

McKenna took in the scene through the cockpit window while Cisco watched the prisoners, and he saw that the unloading was a high-security affair. The prisoners were to be transported to a prison near Madrid for processing, and the cops were taking no chances; all of them were out of their vehicles, all were wearing heavy flak jackets and Kevlar helmets, and six carried machine pistols.

The ramp truck backed up to the plane's front door. As soon as a flight attendant opened it, a team of eight cops headed by a sergeant boarded the plane. Two of the cops carried shackles and leg irons, but McKenna told the sergeant the Guardia Civil's restraints weren't necessary; they could keep the NYPD shackles, and he gave the sergeant the keys. After paperwork had been exchanged and signed for, the prisoners were taken off the plane and loaded into the vans without incident. The vans took off, and McKenna had expected the Guardia Civil helicopter to fly over the convoy as an aerial escort, but it remained on the ground.

"What's next?" Cisco asked.

McKenna had expected to be met by a high-ranking Guardia Civil officer with instructions or suggestions, but that hadn't happened. "I don't know," he admitted. "Let's see if the pilot knows anything."

The pilot did. He had been contacted by radio by the Guardia Civil pilot, and they were to board the helicopter.

"Says who?" Cisco asked.

"A Colonel Segovia."

"To go where?"

The pilot just shrugged, and that wasn't good enough for McKenna. "Could you get Picard on the phone?" he asked the pilot.

"Sure, but you can do it yourself," the pilot replied. He took a cell phone from his pocket and gave it to McKenna. "That's yours, now. Monsieur Picard is number one on speed dial. I'm told you can get him anytime, twenty-four hours a day."

McKenna took the phone, pressed number one, and held it. After two rings, Picard came on the line. "Detective McKenna?"

"Yeah, it's me. We're in Madrid, and a little confused."

"I understand, and it's good to hear from you," Picard said. "How was your flight?"

"Just marvelous, but let's get to my confusion. There's a Guardia Civil helicopter parked outside, and we have instructions from Colonel Segovia to board it."

"And you should. Colonel Segovia is waiting for you in San Sebastian."

"Are Colqui Guarlzadi and Ducho Herriguandi now in the prison there?"

"Yes. It turns out that most of the government's ETA prisoners will also be there by tomorrow."

"Have there been negotiations?"

"No. It's been decided by the government that there will be no formal negotiations while they're holding Carmen and the ambassador. In tomorrow's papers the prisoner transfers will be characterized as a unilateral good-will move on the part of the government in an attempt to improve relations with its Basque citizens."

"Sounds like it'll fly, but it also sounds like a major concession to me," McKenna said. "Moving the prisoners to the Basque Country is one of the ETA's demands."

"If so, there have been concessions made by both sides. As I said, there have been no formal negotiations, but Colonel Segovia has had a meeting with Guarlzadi."

"Segovia went to the Canary Islands to meet Guarlzadi?"

"Yes, he's been very busy. At some point in their meeting, Guarlzadi guaranteed that none of the ETA prisoners will make any attempt to escape for the next two years if they were transferred to the Basque Country."

"And I take it Guarlzadi's guarantee can be believed."

"I know him, and I believe it. He's a dangerous, uncompromising man who expects his orders to be obeyed."

"So Segovia's taken on the role of the government's unofficial negotiator?"

"Not at all. Segovia's mission is to purge the Guardia Civil of GAL members. He met with Guarlzadi at Guarlzadi's request, and this agreement was a side product of that meeting."

"Why did Guarlzadi want to meet with Segovia?"

"Because he believes the GAL has his wife."

"So what could he tell Segovia that would help him in his fight against the GAL?"

"I really don't know," Picard said.

"Segovia didn't tell you?"

"No."

"Did you ask him?"

"Yes."

The answer surprised McKenna, but then caused him to smile. The man who seemed to know everything happening in Spanish government circles apparently didn't have Segovia in his pocket.

Then Picard reinforced McKenna's impression. "I must ask you to say nothing that would enlighten Colonel Segovia on the matter of those kidnappings until Carmen is freed."

"Because Segovia would arrest you if he knew you were behind them?"

"Presumably. He's not a flexible man," Picard said, but he didn't sound too concerned. "My arrest might hinder our search for Carmen, so it must not happen until after she's freed. Can I trust you on this?"

"I'm here as planned, so you can count on me to keep playing along—but I'm not the one you should be worried about. What if Guarlzadi or Herriguandi squawk after I show them the photos?"

"They won't. I trust you'll convey the impression that bad things will happen to their families if I'm arrested as the result of any ridiculous complaints they might make."

"And after Carmen is freed, and you've released your hostages? Why wouldn't either Guarlzadi, Herriguandi, or your former hostages finger you then?"

"Nothing to stop them then, so in that case I might be charged," Picard said, still sounding unconcerned.

"But not convicted?" McKenna guessed.

"Probably not. After all, I am El Protector, and I am operating in Carmen's best interests—no matter how illegal my acts. I believe a jury anywhere in Spain would forgive and acquit."

McKenna examined Picard's reasoning, looking for flaws.

He didn't find any. "Okay, you have it all figured out," he said.

"There is one more bit of unpleasantness. You must keep in mind that the Guardia Civil is a very old, tight-knit military organization that's in some turmoil right now, so I've insisted on some precautions. On that helicopter are two of my men, Claude DuPont and Ernesto Usandizaga. Both are very competent, and you can trust them implicitly. As a bonus for you, one of them had some experience with bombs."

"An ordnance expert?"

"Of a sort."

McKenna was getting a queasy feeling in his stomach. "What's their role to be, exactly?"

"They'll do anything you tell them to do, but basically their mission is to keep you healthy."

"We have bodyguards?" McKenna asked.

"Just a precaution. As I've told you, freeing Carmen might not be considered an optimum result by some members of the Guardia Civil. On the other hand, you being eliminated by the ETA before that happens wouldn't be considered such a bad thing by those same people."

They had been over some of this before, and McKenna understood. If Carmen died before he could free her, or during a rescue attempt, then the Guardia Civil—including the GAL—would have a tacit free hand to settle old scores. Picard, however, had added a new twist. If the ETA managed to eliminate him and Cisco before they could free Carmen, McKenna realized that the Guardia Civil might get the same free hand. "It's not just the ETA we have to worry about, is it?" he asked.

"Unfortunately, no. Right now, Segovia has the GAL's back to the wall. If you're killed, and it appears the ETA did it, it would take a lot of pressure off the GAL."

"Did Segovia go along with this bodyguard idea of yours?"

"No, he didn't. I believe he considers their presence a personal affront. However, the interior minister does agree with me, so you have them."

What the hell have we gotten ourselves into? McKenna asked himself. Now we have to worry about getting ourselves killed by both the ETA and the cops in the GAL. "Where are you now?"

"Near Gibraltar. I'm in La Línea."

"Doing what?"

"Just looking at the Rock. You may consider me a sentimental old man, but somehow it makes me feel better knowing I'm close to Carmen. Good-bye, Detective McKenna, and good luck."

It took McKenna a few minutes to relay the conversation to Cisco, and Cisco took the news without appearing the least bit concerned. "So everybody wants to blow us up, huh? Let's go see what these bodyguards of ours look like" was his only comment. They retrieved their luggage from the rear of the plane. As soon as they descended the ramp with their bags, two large, tough-looking men in suits left the helicopter and walked rapidly toward them. McKenna could see that both wore large pistols under their jackets. He thought the younger bruiser was about thirty-five, but he could only place an approximate age on the older. Maybe late fifties, early sixties, he decided.

Cisco had also noted the large pistols. "Looks like our bodyguards are armed for bear," he observed.

"Good afternoon, señores. I am Ernesto Usandizaga," announced the younger of the two in Spanish when they reached McKenna and Cisco. "May we help you with your bags?"

"No, thank you. We can manage," McKenna replied, also in Spanish. "Usandizaga? Is that a Basque name?"

"Yes, sir. I am Basque."

"And you are?" McKenna asked, addressing the older man.

"Claude DuPont, at your service."

What McKenna hadn't expected was the accent. DuPont had answered in English-accented Spanish, not the expected French accent. "British?" McKenna asked.

DuPont reacted as if he had been slapped. "Certainly not,"

he replied indignantly, then added, "I am a citizen of France."

Definitely Irish, and probably Northern Irish, McKenna decided as a suspicion formed in his mind about DuPont's affiliations. "And you would be our ordnance expert?" he asked.

"I've had some experience with bombs," DuPont answered nonchalantly.

Making them or disarming them? was the question that popped into McKenna's mind, but he kept it to himself.

McKenna and Cisco were seated across from DuPont and Ernesto in the six-passenger helicopter. DuPont seemed uncommunicative, and he stared out the window as the helicopter flew north. Ernesto, on the other hand, stared at McKenna and Cisco with undisguised friendly interest.

McKenna decided some conversation was in order. "How do you like this job?" he asked Ernesto.

"I am blessed to be in the service of La Tesora," Ernesto answered reverently, and McKenna noticed Ernesto bowed his head when he mentioned Carmen. Uh-oh. Totally devoted fanatic, McKenna thought, and he decided he wanted to learn more about Ernesto. "What is it you do for her, exactly?" he asked.

"Whatever Monsieur Picard wishes."

"Whatever?"

"Of course. He is El Protector, and he enjoys La Tesora's confidence."

"And what were Monsieur's instructions regarding me?"

"You are to be safeguarded at all costs."

"How about me?" Cisco asked. "What were Picard's instructions on my safety?"

Ernesto appeared embarrassed at the question, and he lowered his eyes when he answered. "You weren't mentioned."

McKenna feared whatever response was forming in Cisco's mind, so he thought it time to change the subject. "How did you get this job?" he asked Ernesto.

"By God's grace, my father was in the service of La Tesora's father," Ernesto replied proudly.

"Do you have a son?"

"No, but God has blessed me with a wonderful daughter. My Graciela has won a place in Doña Carmen's blessed heart."

DuPont then indicated that he had had enough of the conversation. Without looking away from the window, he uttered a sharp command in Basque. Ernesto smiled apologetically at McKenna and then turned his attention to his window.

So DuPont's managed to learn Basque, McKenna thought. "I'm impressed, Monsieur DuPont," he said in English. "I've heard that Basque is one of the world's most difficult languages to learn."

For a few moments, McKenna thought DuPont wasn't going to answer. Then he faced McKenna. "Maybe it is, but I've lived for years in the Basque Country on both sides of the border, and I'm not an idiot," he finally said in a deep brogue, and without a hint of a smile.

Definitely Northern Irish, McKenna thought. "Are you as devoted to Carmen as Ernesto is?"

"Good woman, and she certainly treats me well enough, but I work for Monsieur Picard."

"And do you do whatever he says?"

"Best man I know, and I've been to hell and back with him," DuPont replied evenly, and left it at that.

Not much of a conversationalist, McKenna thought. "I bet you'd have quite a story to tell, if you ever felt like reminiscing."

"If I ever did, it wouldn't be to a couple of cops. I'll keep you safe and sound, and I'll do whatever you think needs doing, but let's keep this relationship all business." That was all DuPont had to say, and he returned his attention to the sights outside the window.

But, as McKenna expected, Cisco had something to say. "Don't go wasting any more polite conversation on Mr. Personality, Brian," he advised in a stage whisper. "He's just another wiseass felon with a history who's managed to find a nice place to hide."

McKenna braced himself, ready for the confrontation sure to follow DuPont's response, but it never came. DuPont ignored Cisco, and continued looking out his window.

To McKenna, that suddenly seemed the thing to do. Below them, the semi-arid landscape around Madrid gave way to large farms, and then to the lush green foothills of the Pyrenees. San Sebastian came into view a half hour later, and McKenna admired it from ten thousand feet. He and Angelita had visited the city twice on vacation, and they both thought it one of the most underrated destinations in Europe. The Spanish government had never promoted tourism in the Basque Country, but that was bound to change once the conflict ended. It was a beautiful old city, situated around a horseshoe-shaped harbor near the French border at the spot where the snow-capped Pyrenees splashed into the Atlantic. There was a mountain fronting the sea at each end of the harbor, the air was crisp and clean, the weather was usually balmy, the beaches were pristine and only blocks from the city center, and the views from virtually any corner in town were splendid.

"We'll be landing at the old bullring outside town. I have a car there to bring you to your hotel, and it will remain at our disposal. You'll also have a police escort," DuPont announced out of the blue.

"Which hotel?" McKenna asked.

"The Plaza Amara, about a kilometer from city centre. Big, new, very nice. I've seen to your rooms."

"When will we be meeting with Colonel Segovia?"

"At his convenience—but soon, I imagine. He's also staying at the Plaza Amara."

"Do you know Colonel Segovia?"

"Met him a few times, but he didn't have much to say to me."

"What do you think of him?"

The question caught DuPont by surprise. "My personal opinion? Why are you asking?"

"Because I've already formed an opinion on you, and I'll have to trust him at some point. It could help me to know what a guy like you thinks of a guy like him."

DuPont considered McKenna's request for a moment, and then he smiled for the first time. "I'll make you a deal. If you don't tell me your opinion on me, I'll give you my opinion on him."

"Deal."

"Segovia's smart enough, very efficient, but something of a trite bastard. All business, zero personality."

"You think I'll like him?"

"To your credit, no, I don't think you will," DuPont said, and then he offered McKenna his hand. "I know I can be a little hotheaded sometimes, but I'm sorry we got off on the wrong foot."

"Maybe my fault," McKenna said, taking DuPont's hand. "I understand now that a man in your position doesn't appreciate any cop with questions about his past."

McKenna thought that it would have been nice if DuPont offered to make amends with Cisco, but that didn't happen, and McKenna understood. Most people who knew Cisco— even those who grudgingly respected him—didn't really like him, and that had never seemed to bother Cisco in the slightest.

As they descended, McKenna was surprised to see that the uniformed cops waiting for them in the bullring below were from the San Sebastian police, not the Guardia Civil. McKenna asked DuPont for an explanation.

"Can't be helped," DuPont said. "As part of the autonomy arrangement, most of the Guardia Civil was withdrawn from the Basque Country. Left behind some cops to handle the border crossings and patrol the highways, but that's about it."

"What do you think of the San Sebastian police?"

"Nice guys, and most of them are trustworthy enough

since the ETA murdered a few cops they considered problems."

"Most of them?"

"It's widely suspected that the ETA still has sympathizers in the police here, and maybe a few hard-core agents as well. Might account for the police's lackluster performance in tracking down the ETA. Most of their raids come up with nothing."

"The ETA's being tipped off?"

"Either that, or these cops are totally incompetent."

"Did the ETA consider that San Sebastian sergeant they killed the night before they kidnapped Carmen to be something of a problem?"

"I'm told they did. He was on the anti-terrorist squad, and they thought him a little too competent and hard-charging for their tastes."

The helicopter landed next to the row of San Sebastian police cars, and McKenna saw that there was a shiny black Audi sedan in the middle of the row. DuPont offered to carry McKenna's luggage off the helicopter, but McKenna declined the offer. Nobody offered to carry Cisco's luggage.

The lieutenant in charge of the security detail met them at the helicopter door, and DuPont knew him. The two men exchanged a few pleasantries in Basque, and then DuPont introduced him to McKenna. The lieutenant embarrassed McKenna when he came to attention and saluted. "I am Lieutenant Santiago of the San Sebastian Police Department, and I am instructed to inform you that you have the full resources of our department at your disposal," he said in Spanish, holding the salute.

McKenna self-consciously dropped his bags, returned the salute, and then offered his hand. Santiago shook it, and added, "You also have my personal best wishes and prayers for the success of your mission. The murdering bastards had no business taking La Tesora, and I hope you make them pay."

"Thank you, Lieutenant. I'll do my best."

McKenna picked up his bags, and then Santiago turned

his attention to Cisco. "And señor, you are . . . ?"

"Detective First Grade Cisco Sanchez, NYPD, World's Best Detective. I'm here to make sure Detective McKenna makes no mistakes during his investigation."

Santiago looked confused by Cisco's response, and he looked to McKenna.

"That's who he is, that's what he is, and that's what he does," McKenna said.

"I see, and forgive me for not knowing of you," Santiago said to Cisco, coming to attention and saluting once again. "Welcome to San Sebastian."

Cisco dropped his bags and sharply returned the salute. "Think nothing of it, Lieutenant," he said. "I'm a modest man, and I try to keep a low profile."

They also shook hands, and then Santiago led the group to the Audi sedan. DuPont had the keys. He popped the trunk, and Cisco and McKenna loaded their luggage in. Santiago then detailed one of his men as their driver, but DuPont waved him off and climbed behind the wheel. Ernesto got in next to him, and Cisco and McKenna took the backseats. The motorcade left the bullring and headed toward town with two San Sebastian police cars in front of the Audi, and two following.

"Is this type of security really necessary here?" McKenna asked DuPont.

"I think so. You're dealing with two groups with long memories who don't have much respect for life," DuPont replied. "You've killed three Basques in New York, locked up another six, and disrupted a major ETA operation. You have to be careful around here with your history."

"Is this a Guardia Civil car?"

"No, it's the mayor's. I suggested to him this morning that you should be riding around in style, and he was happy to offer it. Good publicity for him with the good people living here. I checked out the car with a fine-tooth comb, and it's been under guard since then."

"Under guard by who?"

"Parked in the middle of the bullring, being guarded by the local cops."

"Is that good enough?"

"In this case, it is. I've got people here keeping an eye on them."

DuPont didn't have to say more for McKenna. Car bombs were one of the ETA's preferred terror tools, and DuPont considered elements of the San Sebastian police to be suspect.

There were no traffic lights en route to the hotel, and they were there in under five minutes. The Plaza Amara Hotel was the tallest building in San Sebastian, it occupied the entire block, and it was located between a large plaza that featured a fountain in its center and the river that ran through the center of town. The entrance was on the river side, and the motorcade pulled up in front. Ernesto stayed with the car. McKenna and Cisco left their luggage in the trunk and followed DuPont and Santiago inside. Four cops formed the escort, making McKenna feel like a visiting head of state. DuPont had already rented the rooms, so they all took the elevator right up.

For reasons of security, DuPont had rented the entire tenth floor, and he had the hotel management rig the elevator so that a key was needed before the elevator would stop on "10." He gave McKenna and Cisco elevator keys and showed them to their rooms, 1002 and 1004. Each was a nice suite, with a sitting room, two double beds, and two bathrooms. DuPont then dismissed Santiago and his men. Before he left, Santiago offered to station cops on the floor, but DuPont insisted that wouldn't be necessary. All he wanted was two cops parked outside, and another two to guard the Audi in the hotel garage. Santiago assured him it would be done, and then McKenna had a question for him. "Lieutenant, do you have any influence with the authorities running Martutene?"

"The prison? Yes, I have influence with them. What do you need?"

"I'd like to visit it tomorrow morning sometime around ten o'clock. Could you arrange that?"

"As I told you, Detective McKenna, I am totally at your disposal, and will arrange anything you wish."

After the bellboys had delivered the luggage to McKenna's and Cisco's rooms, there was a knock at the door. DuPont opened it and admitted two more large, tough-looking men. McKenna could see that they also had large pistols under their jackets. DuPont introduced them to McKenna and Cisco as René and Rodrigo, and explained that they were part of the security team. They would maintain a watch on the tenth floor, and were staying in Room 1010 at the end of the hall. René and Rodrigo left immediately after the introductions.

"I hope that's everything," McKenna said to DuPont.

"Just about," DuPont replied.

"You know, I haven't been here in years, and I'd really like to go to the old part of town for dinner," McKenna said just for fun, knowing what DuPont's reaction would be.

DuPont, however, didn't get excited. "I think it's a bad idea, under the circumstances, but you're in charge," he said. "I have enough people here to handle it, but it will take me about half an hour to set up the logistics."

"Forget it. You're right, bad idea," McKenna said. "We'll order up from room service."

Then Cisco piped in. "Bad idea for you, maybe, but I'm going out. Looks like an interesting town to me, and I'm going to see it."

If Cisco expected a reaction from DuPont, he didn't get it. "Do whatever you like" was his answer.

NINETEEN

McKenna was jet-lagged, and he was taking an after-dinner nap when he was awakened by a knock on his door. He answered it, and found a short, stocky, balding man in his fifties outside. The visitor was wearing a suit and a scowl.

"Colonel Segovia?" McKenna asked.

"*Sí*. Pleased to meet you, Detective McKenna," Segovia said in Spanish. "Let's get down to business."

Segovia entered without a smile or a nod, and McKenna followed him into the sitting room. Segovia took a seat in the armchair. McKenna sat on the sofa and looked to him, waiting for him to take the lead.

Segovia did, immediately and directly. "What is your proposed course of action?" he asked, staring directly into McKenna's eyes.

Be careful with this guy, McKenna told himself. "First of all, Martutene Prison. Tomorrow morning I'm going to meet some high-ranking ETA prisoners your government's holding there."

"Including Colqui Guarlzadi and Ducho Herriguandi, I presume?"

"Yes," McKenna replied, fearing that he knew Segovia's next question.

His fears were well-founded. "What do you know about the kidnappings of their families?"

"What makes you think I know anything about those kid-nappings?"

"Just answer the question, please."

McKenna didn't answer, he just returned Segovia's stare.

"I see," Segovia said after a long, uncomfortable silence. "By your refusal to answer, I'll presume that Monsieur Picard is behind those kidnappings."

Again, McKenna didn't answer, but that didn't seem to bother Segovia. "One cop asking another about some high-profile, very troublesome kidnappings, and no answer? Rather strange, wouldn't you say?" Segovia asked, but for the first time a hint of a smile formed at his lips.

Dangerous man, but is he friend or foe? McKenna wondered. "I agree. Under most circumstances, I'd say that's strange, but we find ourselves in a peculiar situation."

"Yes, we are. I also see that we're going to immediately discard the pretense that I have some kind of authority over you."

"Just while we're on this subject. Once we get off it, I'm prepared to do whatever you suggest."

"Suggest?"

"Meaning I'll hop to whatever suggestions you whisper or shout that will bring us closer to getting Carmen back, and I'll try to make you and your Guardia Civil look good while I'm at it."

Then Segovia actually did smile, but it was a sardonic grin that appeared natural on him. "It's such a shame that you realize you're operating here in a position of some strength," he said, shaking his head.

"So why don't we set that up on the table and take a good look at it?"

"Go ahead."

"I have the total confidence of my government, I'm here at the invitation of your government, and your Guardia Civil—for whatever reasons—is in something of a mess right now. We have to get Carmen back safe and sound, and that's my only mission here. If and when we do, I trust you'll be able to square things away here after I'm gone."

Segovia looked neither surprised nor disappointed at Mc-
Kenna's assessment of his position. "And the ETA? What's
your position on prosecuting those involved in her kidnapping?" he asked, the smile still on his face.

"Personally, I'm not interested. Your problem. Naturally,
however, I will do whatever my government instructs once
we get her back."

"And how about Monsieur Picard and his involvement?"

"What about it?"

"You have knowledge of crimes he's committed in Spain,
knowledge that could put your government in an awkward
position if it ever came to light," Segovia said.

"If that could be proved," McKenna countered.

"If I work at it long and hard enough, I'll be able to prove
it. You intend to present Guarlzadi and Herriguandi with certain propositions, and they'll talk to me sooner or later if
things go wrong."

"What do you mean, if things go wrong?"

"What I mean is if Carmen de la Cruz is injured or killed
during your rescue attempt—if we get to that."

McKenna knew what Segovia was getting at, but he
wanted to hear him say it. "The ETA has already said that
they wouldn't harm her under any circumstances. Do you
believe that?"

"I'm inclined to believe it."

"So if she is injured or killed, it would have to be as a
result of a bungled rescue attempt on our part," McKenna
stated.

"Many things could go wrong, of course, but I'll be
frank," Segovia said, and the smile left his face. "I can't
vouch for the good intentions of everyone in the Guardia
Civil. Her death could serve many purposes."

It hurt him to say that, McKenna thought, but at least our
cards are on the table. "Your job is to prevent that."

"We can work together," Segovia said. "What do you
need from me?"

"Answers."

"More than you've given me?"

"Yes," McKenna said, ignoring the sarcasm. "What do you intend to do about Monsieur Picard when this is over?"

"If this works out favorably, and his hostages are released unharmed . . ."

"They will be, no matter how it works out. Unharmed, and probably very happy."

"He intends to pay them for their inconvenience?"

"I imagine so. You'll have a kidnapping with no complainant."

"Just as well," Segovia said, surprising McKenna.

"Just as well? Do you like Picard?" he asked.

"Like him?" Segovia asked, then took a moment to think. "No, I don't like anyone who operates outside the law. However, he has been good for Spain, and I probably couldn't find a jury to convict him anyway."

"Then let's get to more important points," McKenna suggested. "What about Carmen?"

"Nothing concrete, but I'm afraid the GAL thinks it would be a good thing if she died—as long as her death could be blamed on the ETA."

"And me? Did my name ever come up as a possible target?"

"Nothing definite, but this information is a week old. We've learned that, should you ever make it to Spain, it would also be a good idea if you were killed."

"As long as the ETA gets the blame."

"Yes."

Something's not adding up here, McKenna thought, but he kept it to himself. He thanked Segovia for his time and promised to report back to him after his jailhouse interviews with Guarlzadi and Herriguandi.

TWENTY

Ernesto was uncomfortable and dirty, but he didn't mind. From his vantage point under the van in the Plaza Amara's garage, he could see the tires of the mayor's Audi as well as the front tires of the San Sebastian police car. The two uniformed cops assigned to guard the Audi were parked in exactly the right place, as far as Ernesto was concerned. It was the spot he would have chosen if he had their assignment—parked at the side of the entrance ramp leading into the hotel's section of the garage. The cops could see the Audi, they could see the door leading to the hotel's elevator at the far end of the garage, about ten meters from the Audi, and they had the vehicular entrance into the garage covered. They could see everything, if they were looking.

Ernesto had taken a peek at the cops a half hour earlier, and saw that the one in the passenger's seat was sleeping while the other was reading a paperback book with the interior lights on. Their windows were all closed, and the engine was running. Not too dedicated, and not too alert, Ernesto had decided hours before. On DuPont's orders, he had slipped into the garage at 4:30 P.M., right after DuPont had checked McKenna and that arrogant Detective Sanchez character into their rooms. The cops guarding the car on the previous tour of duty had been no more alert than the pair guarding it now, so getting into his present position had been easy for Ernesto. He had taken the hotel elevator down to the garage level, got down on his hands and knees, and opened the garage door a crack. He had then slipped through and crawled along the garage wall to the van. One of those cops had been reading a newspaper while the other was eating, and neither of them had seen him enter the garage.

The only thing close to excitement he had experienced during his long, lonely surveillance was when Detective Sanchez entered the garage from the hotel at 6:15 P.M. He checked the doors on the Audi, then asked the cops for the location of a good restaurant in the old part of town. There were many, and it was a long conversation. Then Cisco had astonished him when he walked around that section of the garage, peering into every car. Ernesto could only see his feet, and he held his breath when Cisco reached the car parked next to the van he was hiding under. Cisco had stood there for what seemed like a long time to Ernesto, and then he had almost stopped Ernesto's heart when he bent down and looked under the cars. He saw Ernesto at once, winked at him, then stood up and walked back to the hotel door without saying another word to the cops.

At midnight there had been a change of shift, and the present team of cops had replaced the first two. This team had never left their car.

At 3:30 A.M. Ernesto heard the sound of a car's engine as the vehicle entered the garage at street level, two floors above. The car descended on the ramp, and Ernesto saw its tires when it stopped in front of the police car. The driver kept the engine running, and Ernesto saw a pair of shapely legs when she got out of the car and walked back to the police car. She had a Madrid accent, and Ernesto kept his eyes glued on the door leading to the hotel elevators as she questioned the cops about the room rates and location of another hotel in town, the María Christina.

Ernesto imagined that the woman must be very pretty, because both cops engaged her in animated conversation about the merits of the María Christina Hotel. He also knew that she had a map in her hands, because she asked the cops to point out a few of the tourist locations on it. Both cops got out of their car, and she positioned herself so that their backs were to the door leading to the elevators while they gave her directions and pointed out locations on her map.

Then Ernesto saw the door leading to the elevators open, just a crack, and two pair of feet slip into the garage. He pushed himself from under the van and hid behind it along the garage wall. He peeked around the corner of the van and saw the two men. One was crouched behind a parked car, with a large pistol pointed at the cops' backs at the other end of the garage. The second man was crawling along the wall on the other side of the garage. He also had a pistol in his hand, but in addition he carried a rectangular metal box. He reached the Audi and crawled under it and out of Ernesto's view. Seconds later he emerged without the metal box. Then he crawled back along the wall to his companion, and they left the garage the same way they had entered less than a minute earlier.

Ernesto pulled out his cell phone and dialed while he watched the woman talking to the cops. She was in on it, he knew, because she had been able to see the men while she talked to the cops.

DuPont was two flights up, in the closed bar adjacent to the hotel lobby and the elevators. He answered at once.

"Two men, dark pants, dark shirts, thirties, armed with pistols," Ernesto whispered. "They just attached a bomb under the Audi."

"I see them," DuPont replied. "They just got out of the elevator. They're leaving the hotel. Anything else?"

"There's a woman, a redhead. She's part of the team. Distracted the cops while they placed the bomb."

"Can you slip out and get up here?"

Ernesto continued watching the woman talk to the cops. She certainly was good-looking enough, he decided, but a little too skinny for his tastes. "Not while she's here," he replied. "She would see me."

"Then wait until she leaves, and call me back then. I'll attend to her."

"And the other two?"

"Don't worry about them. Gonzalo and Lavin are follow-ing your bombers. See you soon."

McKenna was awakened at 5:10 A.M. by the sound of many sirens. The sirens stopped, but he could tell they were close to the hotel. He looked out his window and saw three San Sebastian police cars and an ambulance parked a block away, in front of a closed bar. There was a body on the sidewalk near the front of the bar, a man dressed in dark pants and a dark sports shirt, surrounded by cops and the ambulance crew. A small pool of blood was on the sidewalk, next to the man's chest. Even from that distance, McKenna could see that he was dead, and the ambulance crew was making no attempts to alleviate that hopeless condition. While one of the cops bent over and searched the body, a sergeant pounded on the door of the bar with his flashlight.

As it turned out, the bar wasn't closed after all. The door was opened by a young woman dressed in a very short mini-skirt, high stiletto heels, and a blouse that left nothing to the imagination. Behind the door, McKenna could see that the club was very dimly lit. Prostitute, after-hours club, he thought as he watched the sergeant greet the woman and enter. She closed the door behind him.

McKenna took a few minutes to get dressed. When he looked out the window again, he saw Segovia arrive at the scene, walking from the direction of the hotel accompanied by a uniformed San Sebastian cop. A blanket had been placed over the body. The sergeant was outside again. He saluted Segovia and had a short conversation with him. Then Segovia bent down and pulled back the blanket to reveal the face of the dead man. He stared at it for a moment, replaced the blanket, and resumed his conversation with the sergeant.

McKenna went to his door and opened it. A tall, slender man in his sixties and wearing a suit was standing in the hallway facing his door. McKenna could see that he carried a large-caliber pistol in a holster on his belt under his jacket.

McKenna entered the hall, closing the door behind him. "Good evening," he said to his guard.

"Good evening, señor. May I inquire as to where you're going?" the guard replied in Spanish.

French accent? McKenna wondered. "There's a commotion on the street, about a block away, and Colonel Segovia's there."

"And you intend to join him?"

"Yes."

"Monsieur DuPont advises against that. Your presence might complicate matters. It would be better if you discussed the matter with Colonel Segovia in the morning, after he has more information available to him."

"Could you guess what that information might be?"

"Just a guess, but I think he might find out by then that the unidentified body on the sidewalk is a member of his Guardia Civil."

"Could you venture another guess as to what that officer was doing before he was killed?" McKenna asked.

"There shouldn't be any Guardia Civil cops in the Basque Country, so I'd guess that he was up to no good. Besides, it's my understanding that he was in a bar with an unsavory reputation, a place that is frequented late at night by ETA types looking for some illicit fun while they discuss their business."

"Really? But you still think the dead man was a Guardia Civil cop?"

"Yes."

"I see. I think I'd like to get Monsieur DuPont's opinion on that."

"And he'll probably give it to you, in the morning."

"I don't want to wait until then. Where is he right now?"

"I'm sorry, señor. He is unavailable at the moment."

"Then I guess I'll just have to wait," McKenna said in French. "Excuse me, monsieur, what is your name?"

"I am called Josèphe Lavin," he replied in smooth French.

Cisco stepped into the hallway. "What's up?" Lavin left McKenna and walked down the hall.

"Murder, a block away," McKenna said, then related what he had seen and what he had learned from Lavin.

"This Monsieur Lavin seems remarkably well-informed," Cisco said, then told McKenna about Ernesto hiding in the garage.

If Cisco was right, McKenna realized that he had been wrong in his assessment on Segovia's impact on the GAL. Far from being on the run and in disarray, the organization had been able to mount an assassination attempt on short notice. "I'd love to hear what DuPont has to say about this."

"Would you really?"

"Of course. Wouldn't you?" McKenna asked.

"I'm thinking that the less we know about whatever these guys are doing for us, the better. We don't know who all the bad guys are yet, but we know they're the good guys, as far as we're concerned. Unless DuPont's dying to blab, I'd suggest we keep our questions to ourselves."

Cisco might be right, McKenna thought. DuPont must be in touch with Picard, and that cagey old bastard's orchestrated everything pretty effectively so far. Mainly illegally, but still effectively, so why should we be asking questions on the circumstances surrounding the murder of a cop—questions that will have answers that are sure to be embarrassing for us to know about? "Okay, we don't want to know," McKenna said, and then he filled Cisco in on his meeting with Segovia.

"Segovia's doing pretty good, but we could be doing better" was Cisco's assessment on the meeting.

"We?"

"As usual, Brian, you're not thinking evil enough, and this time you have to. Your mission is to free Carmen, and their mission is to kill you before you do. If I'm right about what happened here, they've already tried once, and they're dedicated. They'll try again. Therefore, Cisco's mission has changed somewhat."

"Carmen's no longer your mission?"

"A mission, but no longer the main mission. Cisco will be frank with his friend. Those knuckleheads have apparently been fooled by Cisco's modesty. They don't realize that he is the real brains in our team, so they are trying to kill you instead of him. Unfortunately, when they place a bomb in your car to kill you, and Cisco is also riding in that car, then they have inadvertently tried to kill Cisco. That makes him angry."

And he really is angry, McKenna knew. He had long ago realized that whenever Cisco was angry or felt insulted—or sometimes just for fun—he talked about himself in the third person. Then he was absolutely at his most annoying, but McKenna had also learned that Cisco should be taken very seriously during those irritating times. "The point, please, Cisco? Your new main mission?"

"While you go about finding and freeing Carmen, Cisco will get the GAL before they get us."

Never could do anything to change Cisco's mind once he's decided on a course of action, McKenna thought, so there's really only one thing I can say to shut him down and keep my life bearable. "Okay."

TWENTY-ONE

McKenna had plenty of questions that he hoped Guarlzadi and Herriguandi would be answering, and he wanted to be prepared when they did. He packed the Guardia Civil's bulky files on Raoul Marey and the other top ETA leaders into a large briefcase, along with the photos and checks he had received from Picard.

At ten o'clock, McKenna and Cisco were escorted from their rooms and to the lobby by two of DuPont's men whom they hadn't seen before. Outside, the Audi was parked in front of the hotel, in the middle of a line of four San Sebastian police cars. Their escort to Martutene Prison consisted of Lieutenant Santiago and seven of his cops. All were out of their cars and appeared alert when McKenna, Cisco, and their two bodyguards emerged from the hotel. Ernesto was standing near the lead car, talking to Santiago. DuPont was behind the wheel of the Audi, and he got out as Ernesto left Santiago and walked to the Audi.

"Nice day," Cisco observed, and McKenna had to agree. It was in the seventies, there wasn't a cloud in the sky, and a gentle breeze carried the scent of the ocean. The weather, however, wasn't on McKenna's mind as he looked around for Segovia. He wasn't there.

Ernesto opened the rear door for them, and McKenna noticed that he hadn't gotten much sleep, if any. Ernesto appeared alert enough, but his eyes were red and there were bags under them.

So Ernesto had a part in the activities last night, McKenna thought, and then he looked to DuPont. DuPont was wearing sunglasses, and McKenna suspected he was in the same shape as Ernesto.

McKenna wasn't looking forward to another tight ride in the back of the Audi, and he decided to make this trip as comfortable as possible. "Could you pop the trunk, and we'll put this in?" he asked Ernesto, holding up his briefcase.

The simple request apparently caused Ernesto some consternation, and he looked to DuPont with his mouth open.

"It's a short ride," DuPont said to McKenna, softly and in French. "Would you mind riding with your briefcase on your lap?"

Ernesto's reaction and the strange request puzzled McKenna, but only for a second. "What is it we have in the trunk that we don't want these cops to see?" he asked, also in French.

"Another passenger. Sorry, but we had no place else to put him, and I thought it might be fun."

"Alive?"

"In some discomfort, I'm sure, and probably terrified and thinking furiously, but yes, very much alive."

"Guardia Civil?"

"Yes."

"And what's he thinking?"

"That this car is going to be blown up before we get to Martutene, or on the way back."

"But it's not?"

"No."

Well, it looks like we're gonna hear the story we didn't want to know about, McKenna thought as he looked around. Santiago and the other cops were staring at them, and waiting.

McKenna got in the backseat and placed his briefcase on his lap. As DuPont and Ernesto got into the front seat, McKenna noticed that Cisco was trying to conceal a smile, and failing in the attempt. Damn! Let's get this over with, Mc-Kenna thought. "Cisco, you are the greatest. With just a few facts available to you, your assessment of this situation was brilliant."

Cisco treated McKenna to his most regal smile. "Very perceptive, Brian. Most Exalted Detective First Grade Cisco Sanchez thanks his loyal acolyte for the compliment, and promises to teach him even more as we go along."

"You're being insufferable, Cisco."

"Am I? Sorry. Cisco will try to be more gracious."

The motorcade took off in line, and it didn't appear that DuPont was inclined to talk as he concentrated on driving. As DuPont had pointed out, it was a short trip, and McKenna figured he could wait for the details. That wasn't good enough for Cisco. "Let's have it, DuPont," he said. "Short and sweet, if you don't mind."

"What's important is that the GAL had us all scheduled to die today, and now that's not going to happen," DuPont replied evenly as he kept his eyes on the police car ahead. "Are you sure you want to know more?"

"Yeah, now I'm sure."

"Detective McKenna?" DuPont asked.

"Tell us," McKenna said.

"All right. As your friend probably told you, last night we were watching the cops who were watching this car. At three-thirty they were distracted by a woman who drove in and swamped them with tourist-type questions. She was good-looking and dressed very expensively, so they were happy to answer all her questions while two armed men snuck into the garage from the hotel entrance and attached a bomb to our undercarriage, on top of the muffler. Six pounds of Goma Two, the ETA's favorite explosive, packed tight in a metal magnetic case, rigged to be remotely detonated by radio signal."

"Where's that bomb now?" McKenna asked.

DuPont said something to Ernesto in Basque. Ernesto reached under his seat, removed the metal box, and passed it back to McKenna.

"It's nothing sophisticated, but it would've blown us all to kingdom come," DuPont said. "I've removed the blasting cap, so it's quite safe right now."

"The dead guy was one of the people in the garage?"

"Yeah, the guy in the trunk is the other. After they planted it, they took the elevator up to the lobby, left the hotel, and walked to the bar. It's a Basque place, and its name roughly translates to The Night Owl. Fairly legitimate place during normal business hours, but after hours it's a cathouse frequented by a few of the local toughs. ETA sympathizers and wanna-bes, mostly, and occasionally a few legitimate terrorists as well."

"Seems to me you know the place well," Cisco said.

"Used to visit on business from time to time, but I haven't been there in years."

"Did you visit it last night, after the police left?"

"No reason to. Monsieur Picard knows the owner well, and she would never cross him. I knew that we'd find out about everything that happened in there."

"And did you?" Cisco asked.

"Yes. I met her at her house at seven this morning, after Segovia released her."

"What did she tell him?"

"Nothing of any consequence."

"And what did she tell you?"

"The two guys came in, and she knows one of them. Iker Eizmendi, a Basque guy who's rumored to be a hired killer who used to be with the ETA."

"Is he the dead one?" McKenna asked.

"Yeah, but I thought he was Guardia Civil until I talked to the owner this morning."

"Why? He could have just as easily been ETA."

"Because this is the guy in the trunk." DuPont reached into his coat pocket, removed a shield case, and passed it back to McKenna.

McKenna opened it. Inside were the shield and photo ID card of Sargento Javier Ruíz of the Guardia Civil. He was thirty-nine years old and had been a member of the Guardia

Civil since 1988. There was also a platinum Visa card in the case in the name of Luís Perez. "What's the story on the card?"

"Luís Perez is one of the aliases of Manel Bengoechea, an ETA fugitive. I'd say the GAL caught up with him in the past couple of days. Killed him, disposed of the body, and now they're using his alias and his car for their dirty business."

"The car the woman used is also registered to Luís Perez?"

"Yes."

McKenna passed the shield case and the Visa card to Cisco. "Okay, get back to the bar. What happened next?"

"Eizmendi orders a couple of drinks for himself and the sergeant, and then he chitchats with the bartender in Basque for a while. About an hour later, their female accomplice comes in and joins them."

"Do you know where she had been in the meantime?"

"In the sergeant's hotel room, eight-sixteen."

"He charged it on the Visa card?"

"Uh-huh."

"How did you know what room she was in? Did you follow her from the garage to the eighth floor?"

"Didn't have to. Yesterday morning I introduced myself to the hotel's security chief and explained to him who I represent. The Plaza Amara is fairly new, with state-of-the-art security. You can't see them, but there are video cameras covering all the elevators and hallways. After she parked her car in the garage, she took the elevator up. I was in the security chief's office by then, watching her progress on the monitors. She got off at eight, went straight to the room, and used the keycard to get in."

"Was the security chief with you while this was going on?"

"No, off duty, but he had given me a key to his office. Nice man, very sensible."

"What was she doing in that room for the hour before she went down to meet her pals in the bar?"

"Changing clothes, for one. She was dressed classy when she distracted the cops, but that would be way out of character for her in The Night Owl. She had to change into the type of clothes they're accustomed to seeing her wear there, something cheap and slutty."

"She's a hooker?"

"She's worked for the owner off and on for two years, prefers to turn her tricks with the local toughs. According to the owner, she's become quite a favorite of theirs."

"Including the ETA people?"

"A few, which leads me to believe that hooker business is just a tough cover job for her, but one she does well. What we have here, I think, is a very unusual lady."

"What we have here? Do you have her, too?"

"Tied up and under guard in her room."

"Is she Guardia Civil?"

"She won't talk, and she had no official ID on her, but I'd say that's likely."

"Why's that?"

"Because of the other thing she was doing in that room during that hour. She made a two-minute phone call after she was up there for twenty minutes. Unlisted number, but I found out it belongs to Mendosa Viajes. Big travel agency in Madrid, but according to Monsieur Picard, it functions primarily as a GAL money laundering operation."

"By any chance, were you able to listen in on her call?"

"Unfortunately, no. By the time I figured out the security chief's phone console, she was off the phone. However, I did try the number this morning."

"And?"

"All I got was a noise that sounded like a fax tone."

McKenna's heart skipped a beat. "A fax tone is what you get when you dial up a computer. Does she have a fax in that room?"

"No."

"Now, please tell me she has a laptop computer in that room, and that you have it."

"Okay. She has a computer up there, and we have it."

"Really?"

"Don't know much about computers, but I do know that it's an IBM ThinkPad."

Just then, the lead car turned into a side street, and the rest of the motorcade followed. McKenna wanted to hear the rest of DuPont's account, but he could see the prison at the end of the block and knew he didn't have much time. "Quickly please. How did Sergeant Ruíz wind up in the trunk?"

"It's not a long and complicated story, but I don't think we have time," DuPont said.

DuPont was right, McKenna quickly saw. The motorcade had stopped in front of the prison's front gate, and the cops were instantly out of their cars. Santiago took a quick look around, and he then focused on the Audi as he stood by his car, waiting.

"Honest answer on Iker Eizmendi's death, and I need it right now," McKenna said to DuPont. "Was that murder, or self-defense?"

"Self-defense. When we tried to take him and the sergeant, Eizmendi was a little too quick for his own good. He broke away and got his gun out, and I knew he would use it. He had to go."

"Did the police recover his gun?"

"I presume so. We were in something of a hurry, and we just left him there when we took Ruíz. The gun was next to him on the sidewalk."

"Can these circumstances be reported to the police?"

"Eizmendi was the type of guy who won't be missed much, but Monsieur Picard says no, not right now."

McKenna saw that Santiago had left his car and was walking toward them with a puzzled look on his face. "Who killed Eizmendi?"

"I did," DuPont said.

So here I am, a cop with direct knowledge of one killing and two kidnappings, McKenna thought. Worse, both of the people being held by DuPont are agents of the Spanish government, and one of them—a sergeant, no less—is in the trunk right behind me. We're surrounded by cops, I'm an official guest in this country, I'm supposed to be acting in an official capacity, and here comes a lieutenant from the local police. So what do I do? Tell Santiago and stay straight with the police, or follow Picard's advice and, consequently, put myself and Cisco in some heavy-duty official jeopardy?

Santiago had reached the Audi, and he stood waiting at McKenna's door. McKenna decided he needed more information before making a decision. "What were Monsieur Picard's instructions regarding telling me all this?" he asked DuPont.

"To tell you only if you insisted on knowing, and then to do whatever you say."

"Suppose I bring you to Colonel Segovia and ask you to repeat everything you just told us."

"No problem. I've been in some pretty tough jails in my time, and the thought of going to one of the comfy prisons in vogue nowadays doesn't scare me much at my age."

"You don't trust Colonel Segovia to believe you and then straighten out this mess in a manner that will keep you out of jail."

"Trust Segovia?" DuPont responded, smiling. "I don't have many rules in life, but here's a big one I live by: Never trust anyone who doesn't trust Monsieur Picard."

McKenna looked to Cisco for his reaction, and got one. "We know Picard, we like Picard, and we both think he's a sharp guy. So far, he hasn't given us a reason not to trust him or his judgment," Cisco said, then nodded toward Santiago. "These clowns we don't know at all, but you should take into account that a bomb was attached to our car while two of them were guarding it."

That pretty much sums it up, McKenna thought, feeling better that Cisco agreed with the decision he was inclined to make himself. Then Cisco decided to lower McKenna's confidence in their decision. "While you're in there, see if you can reserve a couple of their better cells for us, just in case."

"You're not coming in?"

"It's Carmen stuff you'll be doing in there. Your mission,

remember? Mine is the GAL, and it looks like I've been activated."

"So what will you be doing?"

"Me and my new pal Monsieur DuPont will continue this little chat, and then I'll be about my business."

Santiago knocked lightly on the window, but McKenna ignored him. "Wouldn't you rather wait for me?" he asked Cisco.

"Bad idea. Everyone's watching you like a hawk here, and you can't make a move. Nobody, however, seems to be paying quite that much attention to me. I'm going to be up to some things that need doing, things you might not agree with and shouldn't know about."

"Maybe not agree with, okay. That's never stopped you before," McKenna said, not liking the direction Cisco was taking. "But not know about? Why?"

"Deniability, partner. No reason for both of us to go down if things go wrong. If they do, Segovia will have a few embarrassing questions for you, and you won't have the answers."

"He won't believe that."

"He will after you pass that lie detector test you'll agree to take for him."

"And how about you?"

"Don't worry about me. If things go bad, I'll be gone."

"Gone? Gone where?"

"Someplace nice, I'm sure," Cisco said, then nodded toward DuPont and Ernesto. "These guys seem to be pretty well connected, and money won't be one of my problems. Give me one of those checks, please."

"Picard's checks?"

"Matter of fact, give me two."

"How much will they be for?"

"Does it make a difference? However much they're for, I'm sure Carmen will be happy to cover them after you do your job."

He's right, McKenna was forced to admit. And Picard did

give me total discretion and authority in spending Carmen's money, didn't he?

Santiago rapped on the window again, a little more force-fully this time. McKenna held up his hand, indicating that he would be another minute. Santiago nodded, and stepped back to wait.

McKenna opened his briefcase. He removed the envelope containing the checks, and took a last look at the top two signed and certified, but unaddressed checks that were each good for a large fortune. He passed them to Cisco, closed his briefcase, and opened the door.

"Thanks, partner, and good luck," Cisco said, and then he lightly punched McKenna's arm. "See ya."

When? McKenna wondered, but he didn't want to look at Cisco to ask the question. He got out of the car and was immediately joined by Santiago. "Sorry for the delay," Mc-Kenna said.

"No problem, and no rush. We are totally at your disposal," Santiago said pleasantly.

McKenna took a moment to take in the prison. Martutene appeared to be a modernized medieval fortress, but small for a prison by American standards. The thick yellow walls were thirty feet high, and there were glassed-in guard towers on top, spaced every fifty yards. Only every other tower was manned. There were two guards in each of the manned tow-ers he could see, both with large automatic weapons slung across their chests. One guard faced the inside of the prison while the other watched the exterior, and there were many gunports cut into the glass to give the guards free fields of fire in all directions.

The prison had a front courtyard enclosed by a fence with ten-foot-high bars. There was a guard shack at the wide courtyard entrance, and the lone guard there had his attention focused on Santiago. Inside the courtyard, a large prison van was backed up to the main entrance in the walls. The driver and another guard were standing at the open rear doors of the van.

Along the far side of the courtyard fence, a line of hundreds of people stretched the full length of the fence, with more arriving in twos and threes and taking their places at the end of the line. Most were women, and many had children with them. Families of the newly arrived ETA prisoners who had been transferred from the distant prisons all over Spain, McKenna figured, here to visit the husbands, sons, and fathers they hadn't been able to see in some time.

As McKenna watched, the steel prison doors slid open, and a line of ten handcuffed and shackled prisoners emerged and were loaded into the van under the supervision of two guards. Then another prison van pulled into the yard. That van was loaded with ten more handcuffed and shackled prisoners, and then both vans took off with the prisoners and two guards in each. The rest of the escorting guards reentered the prison, and the steel doors slid shut behind them.

They're transferring ordinary prisoners to make room for the many new ETA arrivals, McKenna reasoned. From what he could see, he thought the security at the prison might be adequate under ordinary circumstances, and that a breakout would be difficult. He thought, however, that a determined, well-armed ETA assault from the outside to free their comrades within would have a good chance of success, as long as they had enough explosives to breach the walls and were prepared to sustain many casualties in the process.

When McKenna had seen enough, he took out his pistol and handed it to Santiago, who accepted it without question and put it in his belt. The two men then walked toward the prison. McKenna had thought they would have to check in with the guard manning the shack at the entrance to the exterior courtyard, but Santiago didn't slow down and simply shouted something in Basque to the man as they passed. The guard saluted, but didn't reply, and the steel prison doors were opened.

Inside was a passageway leading to a large reception area. At its entrance was another guard manning a walk-through metal detector. Santiago walked around the machine, and McKenna followed him, but the guard sprinted in front of them, blocking their path. "I'm sorry, Lieutenant, but I need some ID from this man," he said. "Then he'll have to pass through the metal detector, and his briefcase must be searched."

McKenna certainly didn't want the guard to see the checks and the photos of Picard's hostages that he had in his briefcase, but Santiago barked at the guard for a full ten seconds and demanded his name, which was Guiterrez.

Guiterrez appeared cowed as he backed off a step, but Santiago wasn't done with him. "Go get the warden, and bring him here at once," he ordered.

"Please, sir, he's on an inspection tour, and I can't leave my post."

"Why not?"

"Because I have to prevent unauthorized persons from entering, and I have to inspect any packages coming in."

"Nobody at all is coming in while I'm here. Go."

"And I have to prevent unauthorized persons from leaving," Guiterrez added.

"Haven't you heard that Colqui has guaranteed that there will be no escape attempts for two years?"

"Yes, sir."

"I'll admit that Colqui is a misguided, murdering fanatic, but even an idiot like you should believe him when he guarantees something."

"Yes, sir. I do."

"So you really don't have much of a job, and this post isn't necessary at all," Santiago shouted impatiently. "What are you still doing here? Go get the warden this instant."

"But we still have some ordinary, decent criminals here," Guiterrez protested. "They might try to escape."

"Not while I'm here. Go."

"Yes, sir," Guiterrez said, and headed toward the reception area.

"Wait!" McKenna shouted, and Guiterrez stopped. "If you don't mind, I'll go with him, and get a tour of the prison while I'm at it," he said to Santiago.

"Whatever you wish, of course," Santiago said.

"Follow me, please, señor," Guiterrez said to McKenna,

and walked through the reception area to a door leading to the prison interior.

McKenna followed, and quickly caught up with Guiterrez. "Sorry about that scene back there," he said.

"Think nothing of it," Guiterrez replied, shrugging off the incident. "Lieutenant Santiago is a good man, and I've heard that he's usually very nice to everyone, but I've also heard that he's been out of his mind since they took La Tesora. He's devoted to her."

"He knows her?"

"And she knows him, too. He's instrumental in Vascos Contra la Violencia, and he's the founder of the police chapter."

That explains a lot about Santiago, McKenna thought, but not everything. "It seems to me that, for a lieutenant, he wields an extraordinary amount of power," he observed.

"Of course he does. He's the cardinal's nephew, so people pay attention when he talks."

That gave McKenna something to think about as Guiterrez led him through the two visiting rooms. The rooms were separated by a corridor, and in each was a table with seats for three prisoners and three visitors. Running along the center of the table was a three-foot-high Plexiglas barrier to separate the inmates from their visitors, and although each room was monitored by a video camera, McKenna didn't consider the security provisions to be adequate for dealing with high-risk prisoners.

At the end of the short corridor was a steel door with a video camera mounted over it. There was a bell next to it, but the door swung open before Guiterrez could ring it, leading McKenna to believe that the guards were on their toes. As soon as they passed through the door, rows of cells were visible on the left of the long corridor, and McKenna's nostrils were assailed by the odor common to prison-cell areas everywhere. In this case, however, the odor was stronger than he had ever experienced before. Martutene Prison smelled like the inside of a giant rancid sneaker, but it took McKenna a moment to notice there was something missing;

noise was a constant irritant in any prison he had ever visited, but instead of the shouting, complaining, arguing, and loud bantering, only the faint murmur of subdued conversation emanated from the direction of Martutene's cell area.

Guiterrez led McKenna to another steel door on the right of the corridor, and this one also swung open as they approached. It led to a stairway, and they climbed two flights to the top. It was a floor of more corridors staffed by many armed guards, and as McKenna toured it, his opinion of Martutene's security procedures climbed slightly. The cells below them had barred ceilings, and the corridors were situated above the passageways that separated the rows of cells. There were windows spaced every fifteen feet that provided a complete view of the crowded cells.

McKenna stopped to take a look. There were two beds per cell, but each cell held six prisoners, who appeared to accept their condition. Some sat on the beds, conversing or playing cards with their cellmates, a few were reading, but most stood idly at the bars. None looked up at the guards' corridor above them.

McKenna tapped the window. "One way glass?"

"Yes. We can see everything they're doing, but they can't see us," Guiterrez replied. "They never know when we're watching them."

"How about at night?"

"It's always daytime in here. Lights are always on."

"Any problems so far?"

"None. Every time we get a batch of new arrivals, Colqui talks to them. Tells them to be good, and be patient. They all listen."

"What are the guys at the bars waiting for? Visiting hours?"

"Yes, but visiting minutes would be a more correct description. So many visitors all at once, and we're not yet equipped to handle it. We can only allow ten-minute visits for now."

"When will that be corrected?"

"Maybe another week, if we can all continue working this

overtime. The warden is building another temporary visitors' area in one of the cell blocks, but it takes manpower to watch them during the visits."

"And the overcrowding?"

"The same, another week. This prison is designed to hold nine hundred forty-five inmates, and we now have twelve hundred."

"Can you show me Colqui and Ducho?" McKenna asked.

"It will be a bit of a walk. They're being kept in one of the empty cell blocks on the other side of the prison."

"In the same cell?"

"That's what they wanted, and the warden agreed. He believes that as long as they're kept happy, we'll all have fewer problems here. Seems to be working."

The trip through three cell blocks took ten minutes, and McKenna received word from one of the guards manning a checkpoint that the warden had been informed he was in the prison and wanted to know where McKenna would like to meet him. McKenna decided that the corridor overlooking Colqui and Ducho's cell would be fine. They arrived there before the warden, giving McKenna time to inspect his adversaries.

From their Guardia Civil files, McKenna knew every small fact about the two men, and he had expected they would be tough, hardened fanatics. The men sitting on the beds in the cell below, however, didn't appear to fit his preconceptions. Both men were intently reading—Colqui a newspaper, and Ducho a news magazine—and they were apparently oblivious to each other. Newspapers and many books were neatly stacked in a corner of the small cell, and they had made it home. Each had a footlocker at the end of the bed, and framed photos covered the lids. On a small writing desk was a TV tuned to a news station, but both men ignored it.

McKenna knew that Colqui was fifty-nine, but his years in prison had not been kind to him. He was pale, painfully thin, balding, and he appeared to be in his late sixties. Ducho, on the other hand, was ten years younger than Colqui, but looked to be half his age. He was also pale, but he had a full head of black hair and was slightly overweight. He had a kind face, and he wore thick glasses that made him appear studious and intelligent.

Then Ducho looked up from his magazine and his gaze focused on the window above. McKenna knew Ducho couldn't see him through the one-way glass, but he got the impression Ducho was staring directly at him. A moment later, Colqui placed his newspaper next to him on the bed and also looked up at the window.

"They don't know we're here, do they?" McKenna asked Guiterrez.

"I don't think so, but you never can tell with Ducho," Guiterrez replied. "Some people say he has ESP, and always knows what everybody around him is thinking."

Since I have to question this guy and find out what he's thinking, that's not great news, McKenna thought. It might take quite an act to convince him that Picard will harm his parents if he doesn't cooperate with me.

McKenna's ruminations were cut short by the sound of hurried footsteps on the stairs. A short, stout, casually dressed man in his late thirties rounded the corner and continued walking quickly toward McKenna and Guiterrez. "It's the warden," Guiterrez whispered. "Señor Asturez."

"Detective McKenna, so sorry to keep you waiting. I had just gotten back to my office when I heard you were here," Asturez said as he approached.

McKenna thought Asturez appeared too young and too nervous to hold such a position of authority, and he decided to try to put him at ease. "My fault, señor. Of course your office would be the proper place to meet," he said as he extended his hand.

Asturez appeared relieved as he reached McKenna and shook his hand. "I've been instructed to cooperate fully with your wishes, and will be happy to do so," he said. "I could have saved myself some time if I would have just waited for you here. I was talking with Colqui and Ducho when I was informed of your arrival."

"Really? Did they know I was here?"

"I can't say for sure. The guard whispered the message to me, but they might have heard him."

So maybe Ducho's ESP isn't so uncanny after all, McKenna mused, feeling better. He heard I was here, and suspected I might be watching him. "How have you been getting along with them?" he asked.

"Very well, considering the circumstances. They've been somewhat reserved, but pleasant enough. I give them a lot of credit."

"Why?"

"Can you imagine the stress they must be under since the GAL kidnapped their families? It must be difficult for them to keep functioning the way they are."

"That just means they can take misery as well as dish it out," McKenna commented. "Is it all right with you if I use your office to interview them?"

"Of course. Would you like to see them both at once?"

"No. One at a time. Colqui first."

Asturez turned to Guiterrez. "See to it, please."

TWENTY-TWO

Asturez's office was large enough for McKenna's purposes, but spartan and unimpressive. The furniture was polished and serviceable, but old, and the linoleum floor was badly in need of replacement. Attesting to the fact that Asturez had been busy recently were the stacks of inmate personnel files and signed prisoner transfer orders on his desk.

While waiting for Colqui's arrival, McKenna made small talk with Asturez, which consisted mostly of listening to his complaints. Although it was only April, the arrival of the ETA prisoners had already adversely affected many lines in his annual budget: His yearly overtime allotment was almost expended, the construction of the additional visiting area was exhausting his miscellaneous-expense line, and the overcrowding meant that the funds allotted him for prisoners' meals would run out in September.

McKenna listened sympathetically until Asturez's phone rang. It was Guiterrez reporting that Colqui wanted to know if McKenna would also be interviewing Ducho.

"Tell him yes," McKenna told Asturez, and he waited while the answer was relayed to Colqui.

It was another minute before Asturez reported a problem that required an immediate decision. "Colqui says that you may interview them both, but only at the same time."

McKenna understood the reasons behind Colqui's demand. Over the years, both he and Ducho had been interrogated many times by the best the Guardia Civil had, and neither had ever given up any information. They were also well-informed, and figured that McKenna was there to offer some kind of deal.

McKenna recognized that he had a reputation as an able interrogator, but to get any information from these two acting as a team would be a real test, one he would have to take. Asturez was looking at him, waiting for a reply. "Tell him it's a good idea," McKenna said, sounding as confident as he could. "It'll save some time."

Asturez relayed the message, and then McKenna brought up an unpleasant point. He didn't like throwing the warden out of his own office, but it had to be done. "I don't mean to offend you, but when they get here it's necessary that I talk to them alone."

"I'm not offended in the slightest. I understand," Asturez replied at once.

"And I'd like to have their handcuffs removed."

"Handcuffs? They won't be wearing any."

"They won't?" McKenna said, surprised.

"Not necessary. Since Colqui has guaranteed that there will be no escape attempts, he and I have reached an accommodation to avoid problems and make life easier for all of us. He basically has the run of the prison—under guard, of course—and then we talk over points that trouble him and his men."

Sounds to me like the foxes are running the henhouse, McKenna thought. "Suppose you were a little less compliant, and suppose he wasn't so reasonable and understanding? Considering his no-escape-attempts pledge, what problems could he cause you?"

"Massive, and not just for me. He could put out word through one of the visitors, and we'd have demonstrations outside daily. It would be just a matter of time before some violent incident occurred, and that wouldn't help our national situation at all."

"Really? I thought the ETA's support was declining to the point were it's almost negligible."

"Declining, but far from negligible. About fifteen percent of the Basques are hard-core nationalists, meaning that if they weren't ETA supporters, they were at least ETA sympathizers. True, support and sympathy for the ETA and its methods has declined since they kidnapped La Tesora, but that hasn't affected the nationalism issue. That same fifteen percent still wants an independent Basque homeland, and many of them would still support the ETA, no matter what they do."

If Asturez is right with his numbers, then he might be right in his approach to Colqui and Ducho, McKenna thought. We're in the Basque Country, and maybe the ETA could still get a wild crowd outside. Since tensions are easing now, who needs that?

McKenna was ready by the time Guiterrez appeared with Colqui and Ducho. He was seated behind Asturez's desk with Picard's envelopes in front of him, had two chairs set up facing him, and his script was prepared. Neither man was handcuffed, and they nodded to the warden as he left with Guiterrez, closing the door behind them.

McKenna thought both Colqui and Ducho looked too confident for his taste, and he hoped to change that. "You know who I am?" he asked.

"Yes, we know," Ducho said.

"Good. Please be seated. I have an important issue I'd like to discuss with you."

"Important to who?" Colqui asked.

"Among others, me, you, and your families."

Colqui and Ducho exchanged a glance, but McKenna could detect no reaction. Then they nodded to each other, took the seats in front of the desk, and looked at him without a hint of interest or passion.

"I believe you know Monsieur Picard?" McKenna said.

"Not well, but we know him," Colqui said.

"Know him well enough to realize how much he values Carmen de la Cruz?"

"Everyone knows of his devotion to her," Colqui said.

"I'd say it's more than a devotion. I'd call it a crazed obsession with her happiness and welfare."

If they got the point, they weren't showing it. Colqui and Ducho still appeared disinterested as they returned McKenna's gaze. "You realize that Monsieur Picard is a man of many resources?"

"We know his history."

"Would you characterize him as a vengeful man without scruples, a man who can be counted on to make good on any threats he may make?"

"He can be counted on to do whatever he says he'll do, but I wouldn't say he's particularly unscrupulous or vengeful," Ducho replied, then reflected on the question for another moment.

"Wrong. I thought I knew him too, but he's changed since your ETA took his treasure, and that's not good for your wife," McKenna said, nodding to Colqui. "Not good for your parents, either," he continued, turning his attention to Ducho for a moment.

The dispassionate facade fell from both Colqui's and Ducho's faces, but only for a moment before it returned.

Finally got their interest, McKenna thought. "We want Carmen back," he said. "Monsieur Picard believes you know something about her kidnapping, maybe enough to help us."

"We've been in prison for years. What could we possibly know about the current operations of our comrades?" Colqui asked.

It seemed to McKenna that the question was asked tongue-in-cheek. "I've seen the way you run the prison here, so I'm inclined to agree with Picard. I think there's not much that goes on in the ETA that you don't approve, or at least know about. If we're going to talk, let's be forthright with each other," he said.

"What makes you think we'll have anything to talk about?" Colqui asked.

"This," McKenna replied. He took the photos of Picard's kidnapping victims from the envelope and, clasping them tightly by the top edges, held them up for Colqui and Ducho to see. This time the facade was completely abandoned as they both leaned across the desk to study the predicament in which Picard had placed their loved ones. As he judged the changes occurring on their faces, McKenna thought he knew the emotions flashing through their minds: first concern, then rage, and finally, he hoped, an objective assessment of the situation. After half a minute, it seemed to McKenna that Colqui had reached the last stage, but not Ducho. "Picard will pay for this," he whispered through clenched teeth.

"Maybe eventually, but he doesn't care," McKenna said. "Stop your threatening, and start thinking."

Ducho looked at Colqui, and received a disapproving smile from him. It took another thirty seconds, but Ducho followed McKenna's advice. He stared at Picard's photo of his parents, apparently lost in thought.

"Do you mind if we hold these photos for a moment?" Colqui asked. McKenna hesitated until Colqui added, "I promise we'll give them back."

McKenna passed them the photos, and focused on Colqui's reaction as he stared at the picture of his wife. Colqui was outwardly calm, but McKenna could almost feel him thinking. Then Colqui gave McKenna back the photo, and Ducho followed suit. McKenna took a lighter from his pocket, touched the flame to the photos, and dropped them on the linoleum floor. The three watched without a word as the evidence quickly burned to ashes.

It was Colqui who broke the silence. "An observation, if you don't mind. You are a police officer sworn to uphold the law. Yet here you are, apparently advancing the interests of a man who has made himself a criminal."

"I don't condone Picard's acts, but I'm a cop in the United States—not here," McKenna retorted. "His crimes were committed in Spain, and the Spanish government hasn't requested my help in solving them."

"So they've only officially requested your help in finding Carmen de la Cruz?" Colqui asked.

"That's it, and I didn't find anything in the request that

specifically asked for my help in arresting her kidnappers."

"If that's true, it's probably just an administrative oversight," Ducho observed, watching McKenna closely.

"One that might suit me just fine," McKenna said, returning Ducho's stare. "I'm not interested in your dirty little war here, and I won't take sides unless you force me to. Carmen is a friend of mine, and I feel I owe her for killing her husband. All I want is to have her back."

"State it in plain words, please," Ducho insisted. "Are you interested in arresting those who took her?"

"No, but I'll help the Guardia Civil arrest anyone I think can help lead me to her."

"How does that position reflect on your status here?" Ducho asked.

"My status here is quasi-official, I guess, but just between us, my involvement is strictly personal."

Colqui looked at Ducho, and Ducho nodded. "Okay, we believe you," Colqui said. "What is it you propose?"

"Tell me where Carmen's being kept, and your families will be released unharmed and compensated for their inconvenience."

"Compensated by who?" Colqui asked.

"By me, through Monsieur Picard. He's given me access to Carmen's money."

"How much access?"

"Suggest a number."

"He's taken three hostages, so I'd say three million U.S. dollars would be a fair amount."

"And Monsieur Picard's involvement?"

"Forgotten."

"Three million? Fine," McKenna said, feeling he was getting a bargain. He had already decided that, if he had to, he would negotiate to get Picard off the hook. Colqui had cut to the chase, making further bargaining in that department unnecessary. He took two of Picard's checks from the envelope and held them up for Ducho and Colqui to see. "Certified checks that will be honored by whoever presents them at any Banco Real branch worldwide, no questions asked," he explained, then focused on Ducho. "Do you mind if I put your parents' two million on one check?"

Ducho kept his eyes on the check for another moment, and then turned to Colqui. Both of them had a look on their faces that McKenna hadn't seen before. They're confused, he thought, and that could mean something bad. "You don't know where she's being held, do you?" he asked.

"No. We were aware of the general plan, but not the specifics," Colqui admitted, then asked, "How many of those checks do you have?"

"Three, but that no longer concerns you," McKenna said as he stuffed the checks back in the envelope. "If you can't or won't help me find Carmen, we really don't have much to talk about."

"We'll see. What were your instructions from Picard?" Colqui asked.

How much should I tell these two? McKenna asked himself. Since I suggested we be forthright with each other, I should follow my own advice. "Get Carmen back, no matter what it costs. If I do, and information you give me helped me get her, your cases will be reviewed. It might take a few months, but you'll be out."

"Suppose we all put our heads together and come up with something that helps you find her," Colqui said. "Are you willing to follow Picard's instructions and offer more?"

"Getting a little greedy, aren't we? You want more than a million dollars for each of his hostages?"

"Much more. We want enough to end the struggle."

"Under no circumstances would I give you enough to win your war. Carmen would hate me for life if I did that."

"I didn't say win the war, I said end the struggle."

"Explain, please."

"Except for a few details, the struggle is already basically over. The moderate Basque nationalist parties won the last election in the Basque Country with fifty-two percent of the vote—and that doesn't count the fifteen percent that voted for the Euskal Herritarrok party.

"Your political arm?" McKenna asked. "From everything

I've heard and read, support for the ETA has declined dramatically since you took Carmen. Big mistake, and you'll never achieve power."

"Was it a mistake? We'll admit that we didn't agree with the plan when it was first presented to us, but now we think we were wrong. If Carmen hadn't been kidnapped, would you be sitting here with us now, ready to negotiate with all that cash at your disposal?"

"No."

"And would the case for Basque independence be catching world attention?"

"No."

"And would myself and all our comrades have been transferred to this prison in the Basque Country?"

"Probably not," McKenna conceded. "But support for the ETA has still gone down."

"True, and it may be worth the price. The ETA is only the disagreeable means to an end, and that end is Basque independence. Whether myself and people like me achieve power when that happens isn't important. What is important is that, with world attention finally focused on us, Spain can't hold on to the Basque Country forever against the will of the majority of the people who live there."

"Suppose that does happen. What becomes of you and all your pals in jail?"

"Those are the details you and we will work out now. With a majority of the Spanish Basques now favoring independence, we realize that we're a big stumbling block preventing meaningful talks between Madrid and the Basque government."

"I'm not in a position to negotiate for the Spanish government," McKenna noted.

"Sure you are. Right now, many in Spain are calling for negotiations, including some elements in the Spanish press. Sounds good, but the politicians in Madrid believe in self-preservation, and they aren't stupid. They know that if they negotiate away the Basque Country in the heat of the moment, their political fortunes will suffer in the long run."

"So where do I come in?"

"If you free Carmen, you'll be a national hero—but still a foreigner. The press will hang on your every word, and you could be the one to say that Basque independence doesn't sound like such a bad idea. The Madrid politicians couldn't get away with that, but you could—and the Spanish people might be inclined to listen."

"I would never do that without the approval of our State Department."

Colqui indicated with a sardonic smile that he was unimpressed with McKenna's refusal. "Better yet, maybe Carmen would say something positive, if you talked to her," he suggested.

"Maybe," McKenna replied, hoping he didn't sound too noncommittal. "Let's get back to Carmen."

"Let's, because she's the key to peace."

"And you and your people are the stumbling blocks," McKenna countered. "As I understand it, even if there is independence, the Basque people aren't crazy about you walking around free. Most of them see you as a bunch of crazy kidnappers, murderers, and thugs. Nobody wants revolutionaries around once the revolution is over."

"That's where Carmen comes in, with your help. If she agrees that what we're proposing regarding prison sentences is fair . . ."

"Are you talking about the five years max?"

"Yes, meaning that many of us who have been in prison for years will be freed, but Carmen can see to it that we're not a problem for the Basque people to worry about, and we'll even suggest something additional that will make the Spanish government feel more comfortable about releasing us."

"What's that?"

"Two years of closely supervised probation after release, with a promise of no political activity during that time."

"Is that just *you* you're talking about, or everyone who's released?"

"All our people."

"Closely supervised by who?"

"The Guardia Civil, if the government likes."

"But the Guardia Civil's presence in the Basque Country is negligible," McKenna countered. "You're not proposing bringing them back, are you?"

"Of course not."

"Then how would it work?"

"The Canary Islands, the place where myself and many of my comrades have already spent years in prison. We'll agree to go back there to do our time, and remain there for our two years' probation."

"Are you agreeing just for yourselves, or for everyone in the ETA?"

"Everyone, including those the Spanish government classifies as fugitives. As long as the government agrees that they'll be tried in the Basque Country, they'll turn themselves in to the police in the Basque Country."

"And then you think they'll be acquitted by the Basque courts?"

"Not necessarily. The Basque government will be eager to show the world that justice prevails in the Basque Country. Since most of our people have committed at least some of the crimes charged, they'll be found guilty, and then sentenced to do their five years in the Canary Islands."

"You seem to have this pretty well thought out, but getting your prisoners transferred to the Basque Country to be close to their families was one of the main points you were fighting for," McKenna said. "I don't see how you can get your people to agree to it."

"They'll agree, if you agree to spend Carmen's money— and lots of it."

"How?"

Colqui nodded to Ducho for the explanation.

"Redondo Prison is horrible and must be renovated so that those of us who still have time to serve can do it under humane conditions, but the climate is perfect," Ducho said. "Our families will also have to be moved there, so housing, schools, and jobs must be provided."

"What are we talking about?" McKenna asked. "Four hundred families?"

"More or less," Ducho said, shrugging off the number. "A drop in the bucket for Carmen. The initial expense might seem high, but Picard has always found a way to make money for her. He'll establish some industry or another there, and our families and those on probation will work for him for a fair wage."

"And those who won't?"

"Will be disciplined."

"By who?"

"Not your concern, so don't spend too much time worrying about it. We Basques have always had a reputation as an industrious people, and we're quick learners," Ducho said proudly. "That's why the Basque Country is the most prosperous region in Spain."

This all sounds too good and too simple, McKenna thought. All these terrorists are going to turn themselves into hardworking, law-abiding citizens of the Basque Country. What's the catch? he wondered, but only for a minute. "So what's your plan after you get off probation, if Madrid grants the Spanish Basque Country independence? Turn your attention to terrorizing the French Basque Country?"

It was Colqui who answered. "Some will be inclined to work toward joining the two Basque regions."

"More bombings, kidnappings, and murders?"

"Maybe, but we would advise against that, and discourage it if we could."

"You would? Why?"

"Because we recognize that, for the moment, most French Basques are content to remain French. We believe that, in time, that attitude is bound to change once the Spanish Basques have their own homeland."

"What do you envision would be responsible for that change?"

"Peace, prosperity, and national pride. Madrid now takes much more in taxes from the Basque Country than it returns in services. Once we're in charge of our own destiny, the

Basque Country will become even more prosperous. The French Basques will see the wisdom in joining us."

So it's peace through Carmen's money that they're proposing. But is it a dream or a possibility? McKenna wondered. However, if it is a possibility, I have to admit that she'd love it. Back to basics. "All very nice ideas," he said, "but nothing's on the table unless you can help me get Carmen back."

"If we can help, will you discuss our proposal with Monsieur Picard?"

"That's a deal. What do you know?"

"First tell us what you know," Ducho insisted. "What did you learn from our people you took in New York?"

"They're a pretty dumb and uninformed group, but we were able to piece together at least a little of Marey's contingency plan."

"*Contingency* plan?"

"We think he planned to stash her and the ambassador somewhere in the Basque Country, but it's become too hot for them there. Support is drying up, and he's got trouble in his ranks, so he's taking them south under heavy guard. Last definite fix we had on him was Algeciras, but that was days ago. We figure he was headed to Gibraltar."

Colqui's face remained impassive at the mention of Gibraltar, but McKenna saw something pass over Ducho's. Then Ducho nodded, almost imperceptibly. Surprise, or recognition of a fact? he wondered.

"And after Gibraltar?" Ducho asked.

"I think they were planning to take her on the ferry to Tangiers, but the British prevented that. If they have a new plan, I think it's to lay low for a while, then a short nighttime voyage to one of your training camps in Morocco."

Ducho nodded again, and this time it was a distinct nod of agreement. "I assume you have Gibraltar buttoned up tight by now?" he asked.

"The British do. All approaches and exits—land, air, and sea. Trouble is, we think Marey and his crew already have them there. Slipped in somehow before the noose tightened."

"I see," Ducho said, and then he turned to Colqui. The two men exchanged a look that McKenna couldn't fathom, and then they remained silent for a few minutes, obviously thinking.

Colqui finally broke the silence. "We think we can help, but Ducho and I need a few minutes alone to discuss this."

"Take your time," McKenna said, and got up. McKenna found Asturez and Guiterrez waiting down the hall from the office. McKenna took a moment to tell Asturez that Colqui and Ducho would be alone in the office for a few minutes, but Asturez saw no reason to send Guiterrez in to watch them. McKenna then excused himself and walked to the other end of the hall to call Picard.

Somebody else answered the phone. "Detective McKenna for Monsieur Picard, please" was all McKenna said, and Picard came on line seconds later. "Are you still at Martutene?" he asked.

So DuPont's keeping him informed, McKenna thought. "Yes, I am, but I shouldn't be here too much longer."

"How are you doing?"

"Colqui and Ducho have agreed to help."

"And have they?"

"Not yet, but I think they'll tell me everything they know. Their personal price is release of the people you're holding, and three million for the inconvenience you've caused them."

"Fair enough. Matter of fact, a bargain."

"I also got you thrown into the bargain. I haven't nailed it down tight yet, but I think their families aren't going to remember being kidnapped. Just a big mistake, really."

"Not important. You can tell them that if you believe they're sincere with whatever information they give you, their people will be released within the hour. Am I going to pay the families, or are you going to use the checks?"

"I think it better if I pay Colqui and Ducho myself."

"Whatever you think best," Picard said. "You said three million was their *personal* price. What's the rest?"

"Very expensive, I imagine," McKenna said, and then he explained Ducho and Colqui's proposal.

"Plausible idea, and La Tesora would love it" was Picard's reaction. "As for renovating Redondo Prison, she can visit it once she's free. If she would make a few comments on the conditions there, I believe renovation work would be planned the next day."

"So if it turns out their information is good, I can tell them it's going to happen?"

"You can do better than that. If you believe they've told you everything they know, you can tell them that by four this afternoon a corporation will have been formed in the Canary Islands with five hundred million in its escrow account at the Banco Real branch there. How does the Canary Islands Personnel Redevelopment Corporation sound?"

"Fine, I guess."

"And it's not such a bad idea they have, speaking strictly business. I've been looking at the Canary Islands for some time, and I always considered it undeveloped as a tourist location. If things work out, we can market it as the new Australia. Another nice place made possible and more pleasant by importing convicts."

"It's up to you how you do it," McKenna said.

"Good. You can also tell them they'll be on the corporate board, and that I'll be sending the necessary documents to them for their review and signature. Anything else?"

"Just one more item. It's possible I've spent even more of Carmen's money."

"The checks to your partner?"

DuPont's keeping him very well informed, McKenna noted. "Yes, two of them, with no limit."

"As I've already told you, you have total discretion and authority with those checks. Besides, I hear he's a sensible fellow. A little tough to get along with, but totally dedicated to you and to getting La Tesora released. Good luck, and please keep me up-to-date," Picard said, then hung up.

Cisco totally dedicated to *me?* Never considered that angle, McKenna admitted to himself. Maybe Picard knows something I don't—or maybe he's just smarter than me.

Colqui then poked his head out of Asturez's office and

beckoned to McKenna. "You come up with anything that will help?" McKenna asked him on his way in.

"We think so," Colqui replied.

McKenna took his seat behind the warden's desk. Colqui and Ducho occupied the same chairs as before. As McKenna looked at them, their faces told him they did have something. "Well?"

"We have both been to Gibraltar before," Ducho said. "We find it to be a convenient, safe place for us when we're operating in the south of Spain and things get hot."

"The British aren't too accommodating to people like yourselves, are they?"

"They've rarely been aware of our presence there. All that's necessary are good documents and a car with Gibraltar plates, and we have access to both. Then the border crossing is perfunctory."

"Never a problem fooling the British?"

"They consider us to be purely a Spanish problem. Considering the relations between Spain and England when it comes to Gibraltar, it's not a problem they're overly concerned with."

"How about the Guardia Civil at the border?"

"Sometimes a disguise is necessary for some of us to get by them. Then it's just a matter of timing," Ducho explained. "Since many Gibraltarians find it much cheaper to live in La Línea, the border crossing is very busy during rush hour."

"I see, but I don't think Raoul Marey and his heavily armed crew slipped two hostages in that easily."

"Nor do I. Too many people to transport in our car right now," Ducho agreed. "However, we also have access to a large truck and driver. This driver enters and leaves Gibraltar routinely once a week. Been doing it for years, and he's well-known to both the British and Spanish border guards. Friendly type, very funny, and he usually passes without question—and always without inspection."

"Is he Basque?"

"No, Irish."

"IRA?"

"When they were active, we always got along very well with them, and shared the same ideology. Different enemy, but a similar situation. Besides, many of us believe that their Saint Patrick was really a Basque missionary."

"What type of deal did you have with them?"

"Loose, a matter of mutual convenience. Exchange of intelligence, discussions on tactics and new products becoming available on the arms market. Occasionally we helped each other out with weapons procurement, and they've used our training camps in Morocco from time to time."

A few Guardia Civil files in McKenna's briefcase contained speculative reports on those aspects of the ETA's cooperation with the IRA before the Northern Ireland peace process took root, and it made him feel confident to hear those suspicions confirmed from Ducho's own lips. These two can be trusted, he decided. "How about safe houses?" he asked.

"We used to provide them with sanctuary when things got too hot for some of them in England and Ireland."

"Sanctuary in Gibraltar?"

"Years ago, but no longer."

"Why not?"

"In '88, British Intelligence found out some IRA people were there as guests of ours. Also knew their schedule, and the SAS set up an ambush. Massacred all five IRA people at a gas station in Gibraltar, and that set off quite an international stir."

"I remember. Well-run operation, but it was criticized as mass murder in some quarters," McKenna said. "Who provided British Intelligence with the information? One of your people, or one of the IRA's?"

"We looked very deeply into the matter, and we're fairly certain it wasn't one of our people."

"Back to your truck driver. What's his name, and what's his cover?"

"Goes by the name of Liam Kilkenny, and for years he's worked for a British dairy company. Seems that the people living in Gibraltar don't like or trust the Spanish dairy products, so he makes a weekly run back and forth from England. Brings in a load of milk, cream, cheeses, and other British specialty products."

"Refrigerated truck?"

"Yes, but it's bearable inside if you're dressed right. Keeps it at about five degrees centigrade."

McKenna did the math. Forty degrees Fahrenheit. Could be made comfortable enough inside, behind the milk and cheeses. "Does he leave Gibraltar empty?"

"No. The Costa Brava northeast of Gibraltar is a big destination for the British. Lots of tourists, and many British retirees live there. After he leaves Gibraltar, he delivers to a number of hotels and supermarkets that cater to the British market."

"What's the name of Kilkenny's dairy company, where does he live, and where does he stay when he's in Gibraltar?"

"Don't know, offhand, but we could find out. Do you want us to make some inquiries?"

Do I? McKenna asked himself, and quickly decided it was too risky. Word could get back to Marey that there were inquiries on Kilkenny, and that would be bad. "Don't bother. I have a friend in British Intelligence, and I'll have him look into it. What else do you have for me?"

Colqui answered, but with a question. "Do you know about Bombi's parents?"

"Something about them. Run a small hotel in Florence. Avant-garde thinkers, possibly politically sympathetic to radical causes, but otherwise legitimate."

"Maybe legitimate once, but no longer," Colqui said. "Old-time Communist ideologues, and in Bombi's case the apple didn't fall far from the tree."

"So how does that help me?"

"Communists, maybe, but they have a pure capitalist streak when it comes to their own finances. They cater to the British and American tourist trade in Florence, and they've been so successful that they decided to expand. They travel quite a bit, and they've bought interests in a number of hostels catering to English speakers. Since Bombi joined us, these hostels have been offered to us for our use in emergencies."

"Do they have hostels in Jerez and Sevilla?"

Both Colqui and Ducho looked surprised at the question. "Yes, as part owners," Colqui said. "How did you know?"

"Because Bombi made calls to those hostels from the house your people rented in New York. We couldn't figure it out, and assumed she had been talking to ETA people in Spain. Now I know we were wrong."

"I understand that our people have used those places a few times, but not recently. So she was . . ."

"Talking to her parents," McKenna said. "I assume they also have interests in a hotel in Gibraltar?"

"A nice one, we believe. However, to our knowledge, our people have never used it."

"But you know the name of this hotel?"

"Unfortunately, no. We haven't had news on operational matters in years, and we never ask for specific details on any proposed plan."

"So what is your role while you're in prison?"

"Approve or disapprove general plans and concepts, enforce discipline in prison, and provide guidance on political matters," Colqui explained. "Should we try to find out the name of the Gibraltar hotel?"

"No, I'll find out on my own. Do you have anything else for me?"

"No," Colqui replied, and turned to Ducho.

"Nothing else I can think of," Ducho said. "Have we given you enough to satisfy our end of our bargain?"

"Yes, you have." McKenna removed two of Picard's checks from the envelope. He made one out for one million, and gave it to Colqui. He wrote the other for two million, and gave it to Ducho. "You can give them to whoever you like and fill in the bearer names when you do," he said as they briefly examined their fortunes. Both looked content, but they weren't done with McKenna. "And the Canary Islands?"

"Approved," McKenna said, and then told them about the

Personnel Redevelopment Corporation, their roles on the corporate board, and the money soon to be deposited in the
corporation's escrow account in the Canary Islands.

"How about renovating Redondo Prison?" Ducho asked.

"According to Picard, Carmen will see to that once we
get her back," McKenna said, then stood up. "I think that
concludes our business."

Colqui and Ducho remained sitting. "Almost, but there is
something else you should know," Ducho said.

McKenna sat down again. "What's that?"

"Raoul Marey. We're committed to the struggle, but he's
a complete fanatic. Won't rest until the French and Basque
countries are united in one independent homeland. Dangerous man, and he'll be especially dangerous for you."

"Bombi?"

"Yes. According to our information, he was hopelessly in
love with her. He's a vengeful, eye-for-an-eye type, and you
were responsible for her death."

"Thanks. I'll keep that in mind," McKenna said, and got
up again.

So did Colqui and Ducho, but Colqui had one more item
to discuss. "Please keep something in mind for us," he said.
"We believe you when you promised you would cause the
least damage possible to our people when you try to get
Carmen back, but it's not necessary to us that Marey emerge
in one piece."

Some revolutionary intrigue going on here? McKenna
wondered. "Why's that?"

"Peace will come, and he'll always be an irritant when
that happens," Colqui advised. "Maybe even an impedi-
ment."

"I'll do whatever necessary to get Carmen back, but I'm
not going to take Marey out for you."

"Unless it's necessary?"

"Exactly."

"We know him, and you don't," Ducho said. "It will be
necessary, so keep yourself ready for that. We have a lot
riding on you."

"I appreciate your concern."

. . .

Santiago was waiting for McKenna in the reception area. Once outside, they walked through the courtyard together, and McKenna noted the Audi was no longer parked outside the prison. He had expected that, but had to ask. "What happened to my car?"

"I'm told that Picard's men and your partner left soon after we went in," Santiago replied.

"Without a word of explanation to anyone?"

"None. I guess you'll be returning to the hotel with us."

So Cisco's off on his mission with Picard's men, McKenna thought. But doing what?

By the time they reached Santiago's car, McKenna realized that Cisco had been right. Whatever it was that Cisco was doing, McKenna didn't want to know.

TWENTY-THREE

After McKenna had entered Martutene with Santiago, Cisco sat in the Audi for the few minutes it took DuPont and Ernesto to relate how Sargento Ruíz had wound up in their trunk, and why he was still there.

It had been a simple matter of logistics. None of Picard's men were from San Sebastian, and they didn't have a car available to them when Ruíz and Iker Eizmendi were followed to The Night Owl bar after they had placed the bomb under the Audi. When the bombers were joined there by their female accomplice, DuPont phoned Picard for instructions. "Take them, find out who sent them, and keep the police out of it," DuPont was told.

Taking the woman wouldn't be much of a problem, DuPont had figured. He knew she would be returning to the hotel sooner or later, and she could be dealt with by the two men DuPont had stationed on the eighth floor, waiting for her. Taking the men, however, required a car.

Ernesto had sneaked out of the garage by then, and DuPont sent him back for the Audi with instructions to tell the cops guarding it that he was taking it out to gas it up. That worked, and Ernesto rejoined DuPont with the car moments later. DuPont had another two men on the scene—Lavin and Gonzalo—and they all waited around the corner from the bar.

The street was deserted, and DuPont didn't anticipate any

problems. They watched the woman leave, and DuPont received word minutes later that his men in the hotel had met her when she got off the elevator on the eighth floor, and they had her tied up in her room, the one rented by Sergeant Ruíz.

Taking the sergeant had not been so easy. When Ruíz and Eizmendi finally left the bar, DuPont approached them from the left, Lavin and Gonzalo from the right. Ruíz and Eizmendi must have suspected they were in danger because they froze for a moment, uncertain what to do next. When Ernesto turned the corner in the Audi, Eizmendi and Ruíz went for their guns. Eizmendi was quicker, and he paid for his speed. He had just managed to clear his pistol from his holster when DuPont shot him.

At that point, Ruíz knew just what to do. He raised his arms and surrendered. DuPont quickly disarmed him, and huddled him into the Audi without further incident. DuPont then sent Lavin and Gonzalo back to the hotel, and had Ernesto drive him and Ruíz to the outskirts of town. En route, Ruíz was questioned by DuPont, but the sergeant refused to talk.

DuPont needed more time with Ruíz, but knew he didn't have any. Ernesto had to return the car to the garage before the San Sebastian cops assigned to guard it became alarmed, and DuPont had no secure place at that moment to stash Ruíz until he could be questioned further. The trunk of the mayor's Audi was the only place available, so DuPont had Ernesto drive to a twenty-four-hour convenience store and buy two rolls of tape and some clothesline. Ruíz was quickly tied, gagged, taped, and placed in the trunk, and that was where he remained.

"Did you threaten him when you questioned him?" Cisco asked DuPont.

"No, I didn't think that was necessary. Remember, he had just seen me kill his partner."

"Tough nut?"

"Dedicated, I'd say, and not a coward. I don't think he's afraid to die for his cause."

"Would you be able to crack him if you had more time?"

"Time enough to apply some pain?"

"That's not going to be our way of doing things," Cisco insisted.

"Good," DuPont said, nodding his assent. "Never was my way."

"Did you promise him anything?"

"No. I'll leave that to you."

"Does he know that you found the bomb?"

"We didn't tell him anything," DuPont replied.

"So he doesn't know you have the girl?"

"No."

"She had the transmitter to detonate the bomb?"

"Yes. We found it in her room."

"So Ruíz might think this car is still set to blow?"

"I don't know what he's thinking right now, but that's a possibility."

"Since you've given him some time to think and contemplate his existence, let's test his dedication."

"Now?" DuPont asked.

"Yeah, now. On the way here I noticed a nice stretch of woods along the highway. Let's talk to him there."

DuPont started the engine, put the car in gear, and waved to Santiago's men as he cruised out of the prison courtyard. They looked perplexed, but a few of them waved back, and none made a move to stop the Audi.

Cisco spent a few seconds looking around and congratulating himself before he got out of the car. It was a nice spot he had chosen for the business at hand. DuPont had pulled the Audi far enough into the trees to hide it from cars traveling the highway behind them, and the few houses visible in front of them on the other side of a small river were at least a quarter mile away.

Cisco asked for the bomb, and Ernesto gave it to him. When he and DuPont got out of the car and walked back to the trunk, Ernesto slid behind the wheel in case a quick exit became necessary. Cisco placed the bomb on the ground under the back bumper, and then nodded to DuPont. DuPont opened the trunk and pulled back a blanket to reveal Ruíz.

Although Cisco admired the way DuPont had Ruíz secured and helpless, he found himself a little surprised at the tinge of sympathy he felt for the man who had tried to kill him and his partner. Ruíz was lying on his side with his arms tied behind his back and his legs tied together with clothesline. A taut length of rope stretched between his wrists and his ankles kept him in the fetal position, and tape covered his mouth and all the knots. He appeared to be terrified as he looked up at Cisco, squinting.

"You look like you might have something to say," Cisco observed. "Do you?"

Ruíz nodded as much as he was able, so Cisco reached down and pulled the tape off his mouth. "Where are we?" Ruíz asked at once.

Cisco detected a Madrid accent. "On the highway between Martutene and San Sebastian," he replied.

"And where are we going?"

"Back to the Plaza Amara. Sorry, but you'll be spending some more time in the trunk until we can figure out what to do with you."

Ruíz opened his mouth to speak, then stopped himself.

"What is it you want to tell us?" Cisco asked.

Ruíz remained silent as he stared up at Cisco, so Cisco reached up, grabbed the trunk lid, and slammed it.

Ruíz's response was immediate. "Wait! Don't go!" he screamed from inside the trunk.

Cisco waited a moment before opening the trunk again. "Why not?" he asked. "We're pretty busy, you know, and we don't have a lot of time to spend on you."

"Because this car is going to be blown up as soon as you get close to the hotel," Ruíz replied. "There's a bomb attached underneath."

"Really? How would you know that?"

"Because I put it there," Ruíz admitted.

"How is it set to detonate?"

"Remote control. Radio signal."

"Since it wouldn't be you who's setting it off, you must have an accomplice. Who is it?"

Once again, Ruíz remained silent.

"Okay, we'll talk about that later," Cisco said. "Do you know who I am?"

"You're a New York cop. McKenna's partner."

"And what was the purpose of the bomb? To kill me?"

"No, McKenna."

"Why?"

"I don't know. I just do what I'm told."

"And who in the GAL tells you what to do?"

Again silence.

"Is it the girl in your room on the eighth floor in the hotel?" Cisco asked.

Ruíz appeared surprised for a moment to hear that question, then dismayed. "You have her?" he asked.

"Yes."

"Is she hurt?" Ruíz asked, and there was concern in his voice.

"She's just fine. Maybe a little uncomfortable, but not as uncomfortable as you are," Cisco said. "How would you like to get out of there?"

"Very much."

"Fine, but first a question. Would you agree that confession is good for the soul?"

Ruíz managed as much of a shrug as he could, under the circumstances. "Sometimes."

"Okay, sometimes. But once you start confessing, *sometimes* doesn't it make things better to keep at it?"

"That would depend on how much trouble the sinner is in, wouldn't it?"

"And on his chances for forgiveness. Let me show you something," Cisco said, then reached under the bumper, picked up the bomb, and held it up for Ruíz to see.

Ruíz appeared surprised for a moment, and then he recovered and put a blank look on his face. "Okay, you got me started confessing. Let's see where we go from here."

"Let's," Cisco said, then nodded to DuPont. DuPont took a folding knife from his pocket, opened it, and began cutting through the ropes and tape holding Ruíz. It took some time, but Ruíz ignored DuPont and kept his eyes on Cisco.

When DuPont was finished, he stepped back, and Ruíz slowly climbed out of the trunk. However, when he tried to stand, his legs buckled, but Cisco caught him before he hit the ground. "My legs fell asleep," Ruíz said.

"Understandable," Cisco replied, still holding Ruíz. "Let's walk it out."

Cisco took one arm, DuPont the other, and they walked Ruíz around the car until he could stand on his own. Then they sat him on the ground with his back propped against a tree. "Why don't you rub your legs to get the circulation going again?" Cisco said.

Ruíz didn't reply, but he did begin rubbing his legs.

"Mind if I give you my position on this mess you find yourself in?" Cisco asked.

"You're in charge," Ruíz replied noncommittally as he continued rubbing his legs.

"Yes, I am, and try to keep that in mind. First of all, I don't care a bit about your dirty little war here. Don't care who wins and who loses. Far as I'm concerned, you're just a cop who went bad, but I do need to know what makes people like you tick."

"You wouldn't understand. It's all about patriotism and honor."

"Patriotism, honor, and revenge?" Cisco suggested.

"Maybe for some."

"But not you?"

Ruíz stopped rubbing his legs and thought a moment before answering. "Maybe me, too," he admitted.

"Now let's get to you and your problems," Cisco said. "If I was acting in a police capacity here, I'd have you and your female accomplice real good. There were supposed to be four of us in the car, so that's four counts of attempted murder with your bomb for starters."

"For starters?"

"There's also the murder of Manel Bengoechea, once his body turns up."

"If he's dead, I had nothing to do with it," Ruíz protested.

"Maybe, but you'd have a hard time convincing a judge of that. You're GAL, he's ETA, and you used the credit card and the car he had in his Luís Perez alias when you set up this bombing."

"I didn't have anything to do with killing him, if he is dead," Ruíz repeated.

"Not too important, considering. Just one less major crime, but your life could still be ruined. Disgraced and in jail, with a good job gone. Do you have a family?"

"Divorced, two kids."

"Then you should start thinking about those kids, because it doesn't have to be that bad for you. Might even be good, in the long run."

"I don't understand. Are you telling me that you won't report all this to Colonel Segovia?" Ruíz asked, eyeing Cisco suspiciously.

"That all depends on you. You tell me everything you know about the GAL, and all is forgotten—as long as I believe you're telling the truth, and as long as your female pal takes the same deal."

"You haven't talked to Esmeralda yet?"

"She's next, but listen closely because this is very important to you. If she doesn't talk, I'm not mad at you, but I'm going to use whatever you tell me to put her deeper in the box."

"That means I'd be arrested," Ruíz said.

"Probably, but you'll be able to get a good deal with the prosecutor when you testify against her."

"But I'd still go to jail, and have no job and no life when I get out."

"No job, true, but you'd still have a life," Cisco countered, "because if it comes to that, I'll give you two hundred fifty thousand dollars American. That's a quarter million, a nice start."

"You can do that?"

"Sure," Cisco said. He took one of Picard's checks from his pocket and showed it to Ruíz. "This check could have your name on it," he added.

That got Ruíz thinking, and Cisco left him alone. When Ruíz finally reached his decision, it was one that surprised Cisco. "No deal. I'd never testify against Esmeralda."

"You care for her that much?"

"She's a great woman."

"Love her?"

"Don't get to spend much time with her, but yes, I think I love her."

"Does she love you?"

"Maybe she could, if she gave herself a chance. Her whole life has been committed to the cause."

"Another patriot?"

"No, she's Basque. Esmeralda Loyola. Famous Basque name, and with her, revenge is definitely the motive. She hates the ETA and everyone in it."

"Why?"

"Because her mother was killed before her eyes in '88, when they blew up the Guardia Civil station in Pamplona. They were just walking by, shopping. Wrong place at the wrong time."

"Was Esmeralda hurt?"

"Some scars, but nothing you would see unless you were looking for them. She was next to her mother, and her mother's body took most of the blast. Shielded Esmeralda."

"How old was she then?"

"Fourteen."

"Pretty drastic," Cisco commented. "Maybe even drastic enough to make her into a prostitute for the GAL to get information on the ETA. What is she, a Guardia Civil or an informer?"

"Guardia Civil, of course. Only twenty-eight years old, but already a sergeant. If this didn't happen, she'd be a lieutenant before long," Ruíz replied proudly.

"Not bad, but all of that will be gone unless both you and her come clean with me."

"You want me to tell you about her, too?" Ruiz asked.

"That's right."

"Can I talk to her before I decide?"

"Not the way it's going to work. Don't want you two getting a story together so you can feed me a pack of lies."

"Then how is it going to work?"

"First you tell me all you know, here and now. Then I go back to the hotel and give her the same deal."

"Will I be going with you to the hotel?"

"If you want, but you're free to go after I'm done with you here. You have two minutes to decide. It's talk to me, or have Colonel Segovia talking to you."

It took Ruíz less than a minute. "What do you want to know?"

"What do you do in the Guardia Civil?"

"Bomb Squad, attached to the Madrid barracks."

"Figures. How long you been with the GAL?"

"Two years."

"Why did you join?"

"Always been sympathetic to them, but nobody ever approached me on membership. Then three years ago a judge was ambushed by the ETA outside Madrid. My cousin was one of his bodyguards, and he was killed in the ambush. We were very close, grew up in the same neighborhood, and we joined the Guardia Civil together."

"Then what happened?"

"Then I was approached by Esmeralda. I joined, and was assigned her team. Ours had four people, counting Esmeralda. She's the team leader."

"Who are the other two?"

"Both Guardia Civil. One from the Valencia barracks, and one from mine."

"What are their names?"

"I won't tell you that," Ruíz said.

"Then forget that question. Are they here in San Sebastian?"

"No. They're regular highway cops, and they couldn't get off from work. Most of the Guardia Civil is on forced overtime manning roadblocks and checkpoints since they kid-napped La Tesora."

"Is that where Eizmendi fits in?"

"Eizmendi?"

"Iker Eizmendi. The thug my pal here killed when they took you last night."

"Sorry, didn't know his name. When the other two couldn't make it, Esmeralda had to hire him."

"Do you know if she ever used him before?"

"She didn't say, and I didn't ask. Esmeralda's very close-mouthed when it comes to GAL business."

"What else have you been doing for the GAL since you joined?"

"Not much, until La Tesora was kidnapped. Meetings, training sessions, political discussions. Met about once a month."

"And after they took Carmen?"

"One other mission, a failure. There's an ETA safe house on the other side of the border, in the mountains near Foix. We staked it out for three days, but nobody showed."

"And suppose somebody would have shown?"

"If they were on the ETA fugitive list, kill them."

"Was everybody in your team on that mission?"

"No. Just me, Esmeralda, and the guy from my barracks."

"Do you know anybody else in the GAL?"

"Not a soul. Who's in and who's not is a very big secret."

"How often is Esmeralda up here?"

"Varies a bit, but it's usually two months here and a month in Madrid."

"Was it Esmeralda who gave you the assignment for this mission?"

"Yes. Called me at work yesterday afternoon. Managed to get today off before I left, then met her at a rest area outside Pamplona."

"Was she driving Bengoechea's car?"

"Yes. To answer your next question: I don't know where she got it from, and I didn't ask."

"Was Eizmendi with her?"

"No. We picked him up at The Night Owl after we registered at the Plaza Amara."

"How about the bomb? Did you bring that with you?"

"No. I put it together just in case we needed it for our last mission, but Esmeralda kept it when we didn't get a chance to use it."

"Do you know how Esmeralda gets your assignments?"

"No."

"Now tell me why she was slated to be a very young lieutenant in the Guardia Civil."

"It's because she's smart, hardworking, and more dedicated than you could possibly imagine."

"Dedicated to what? The Guardia Civil or the GAL?"

"Dedicated to doing whatever she can to get the ETA. To get information, she risks her life doing things no other woman you know could or would do."

"Undercover assignment?"

"Yeah, a dangerous, sleazy undercover job that's ruined her reputation with the good people in the Basque Country. They think she's an ETA sympathizer, and she's made herself into a rented girlfriend for many of those murderous scum. She's in big demand with them, and Lord knows what she does for them to get them talking."

Cisco could see that it bothered Ruíz to talk about Esmeralda's assignment, but he needed to know more. "What kind of information does she get?"

"More than you'd expect, not that it does the Guardia Civil much good. Who's around the Basque Country and who's not, who got promoted in the ETA, and sometimes she gets whoever she's with bragging about what crimes he's done for their cause."

"Why doesn't her information do the Guardia Civil much good?"

"Because, no matter how good her information, we can't officially act on it."

"Because the ETA might suspect where it came from, and Esmeralda is too valuable a resource to risk blowing her cover?" Cisco guessed.

"That's one reason we can't officially make much use on the information she gets. Another is that we're not allowed much of a presence in the Basque Country anymore, and we learned long ago not to trust the local cops with any kind of operation."

"You keep saying 'officially.' I take it that means the GAL makes pretty good unofficial use of the information she gets?"

"Lately we have. When she goes frolicking with one of her pals, he frequently brings her to one of their safe houses to have his fun with her. She knows the locations of most of the ETA safe houses in the Basque Country."

Cisco couldn't think of another question for Ruíz, except for the obvious one. "You hungry?"

"Starving. Haven't eaten a thing since yesterday afternoon."

"If you're coming with me back to the hotel, I'll call room service now and have two sandwiches waiting for us."

"With a few beers to wash them down?"

"Good idea."

TWENTY-FOUR

DuPont left them as soon as they got to the hotel. After lunch, Cisco left Ruíz in his room with Ernesto, took the elevator down to the eighth floor, and knocked on the door of room 816. Lavin answered it, and he looked as tired as the rest of DuPont's crew. "Been expecting you for a while," Lavin said.

"DuPont told you I was coming?"

"Yes. Filled me in, and told me you were in charge."

"What's her state of mind?"

"Sleeping now, but mean and defiant. This one's a tiger," Lavin said, then led Cisco inside.

Esmeralda was sleeping, slumped in a stuffed chair with her wrists tied to the chair's arms and tape across her mouth. Cisco took a moment to take her in. She was still dressed as a floozy, but a good-looking one. Her black skirt was short and tight, her red blouse low-cut and skimpy enough to reveal her stomach. She had kicked off her high pumps, and they were lying on the floor in front of her. Black fishnet stockings completed the clothing part of her disguise, and her choice of jewelry put the finishing touches on it. Around her neck was a gold chain with some pendant that disappeared into her cleavage, her ears were pierced with more earrings than Cisco could count, she wore rings on most of her fingers, and her nails were long and painted in many iridescent colors, none of which Cisco could name if he had to.

Bad look for such a pretty woman, Cisco decided, and then he studied her face. He thought her red hair was too bright, and she wore too much makeup for his taste, but he also noticed that she hadn't been easily taken by DuPont's men. Her makeup was smeared in spots on her face, there was swelling under her left eye, and she had a bruise on the right side of her neck.

Cisco ripped the tape from her mouth, and she opened her eyes. For a few seconds she appeared groggy and confused, and she strained at the ropes on her wrists as she looked around the room. Then she focused on Cisco, totally alert. "So you got me. What's the plan?" she asked.

Her voice surprised Cisco. It was soft, sweet, and cultured. "Do you know who I am?" he asked.

"McKenna's partner. Detective Sanchez of the New York City Police Department. Do you know who I am?"

"Yes, and you're quite a piece of work. Esmeralda Loyola. Guardia Civil sergeant with a difficult undercover role, and also the leader of your GAL team."

Surprise passed across Esmeralda's face, but only for a moment. "So we have a traitor somewhere. Who gave us up on this operation?"

"Nobody gave up your operation, you were just dealing with some sharp people," Cisco said, and nodded to Lavin. "Monsieur Picard's people."

"You're being guarded by El Protector's people?" she asked, and there was some emotion in her voice that Cisco couldn't precisely define.

"Yes. And now, as it turns out, so are you," he replied.

"Do you have my team, too?"

"We have Ruíz, and the devil has Eizmendi."

"He's dead?"

"Yes. He made a bad move, and he had to go."

Esmeralda shrugged, unconcerned. "No great loss. He was a common thug, and not very bright. Now tell me, if you would, how do you know so much about me?"

"Ruíz told me."

"Ruíz talked? That surprises me," she said, although she didn't look surprised. "How did you do it, threats or money?"

"There were some threats, and there could be some money involved, but that wasn't it. He talked for two reasons. One was that his life was over if he didn't, and the other is that he loves you. I made him see that the only way to save you was to come clean, and he did."

"He loves me? He told you that?"

"Yes, and I believe him."

"You shouldn't. I'm soiled goods, not his type at all. He might be a traitor, but he's also a very moral man."

"A moral man ready to commit murder?"

"You wouldn't understand. As far as he's concerned, he's a soldier fighting a just war."

"Like you?"

"No, nothing like me. I can no longer think of myself as a moral person, and I'm fighting this war in my own way and for my own reasons."

"I know. He told me about your mother."

"Then I guess he told you just about everything he knows. So tell me, how does him spilling his guts save me?"

"You recognize that your life as you know it would be finished if I turned you over to Colonel Segovia?"

"Of course, not that it matters much to me. But since you haven't done that yet, you probably won't."

"Why not?"

"Spain is still a country of laws, and holding a female prisoner tied up and helpless for many hours in a hotel room before arrest processing and official interrogation isn't the national custom."

"So what do you think my options are?"

"Threaten me to get me talking, but that won't work. Offer a deal, but that won't work, either," she said, sounding confident. "In the end, you might have to kill me to cover up your own role in this."

She's smarter than Ruíz, Cisco realized. Smarter and tougher, so he decided to put all his cards on the table. "Kill you? Don't worry about that. Murder isn't one of my options."

"Why? Too sanctimonious to get your hands dirty?" she asked, looking amused.

"Because I'm not like your GAL brand of police. I'm a cop, and in my mind that means I'm with the good guys. To be the good guys, you have to act like you're the good guys."

"So where does that leave us?"

"I could just let you go. If I did, you wouldn't be in a position to complain to anyone."

"Nice option, one I hadn't considered."

"I think it's the one I'll take, but my conscience won't permit me to leave you free in Spain, murdering and bombing after I leave here."

"So what's your brilliant new plan?" she asked, appearing unconcerned.

"We have your bomb, we have your detonator, we have Sergeant Ruíz, and we have a credible witness to your attempt to blow myself and my partner to smithereens. So there will be letters to the press and Colonel Segovia after I leave, letters accompanied by sworn statements and all the evidence we have."

"So I'll be a fugitive?"

"Still free to carry out your vendetta, but not as free as you were before."

"What about your Sergeant Ruíz?" she asked. "Wouldn't this plan of yours put him in official jeopardy?"

"I know you don't believe me, but he's still *your* Sergeant Ruíz," Cisco said. "He only talked to save you because he foolishly thought you'd see the hopelessness of your situation and come to your senses."

"Why he's a traitor doesn't concern me," Esmeralda countered, and she didn't look concerned. "He made a deal with you, but you'd still give him up just to make my life miserable?"

"To slow you down, yes, I would. He didn't think it would come to that, but if it does, he'll be well paid for the few years he might have to spend in jail."

"Paid by who?"

"By me. My partner and I have an unlimited budget."

"To do what?"

"His part is easy. He has to free Carmen de la Cruz, and he can spend as much as he thinks necessary to do it. My end, as usual, is the hard part. First of all, I have to stop your GAL from killing us and blaming it on the ETA before he finds Carmen. Then, once he does find her, I have to stop the GAL from killing her during the rescue."

For the first time Cisco got a noticeable reaction from Esmeralda, and it delighted him. "Wait a minute!" she said, sitting upright in her chair. "You can't really think we would try to kill La Tesora."

"Of course I do, and somehow you'd find a way to blame that one on the ETA, too."

"Kill La Tesora? Why?" Esmeralda asked, disbelieving.

"Do you really want to discuss this?"

"Yes. I'd be interested in hearing what brings you to that ridiculous conclusion."

"Then let's discuss it in some comfort." Cisco began working on the knot holding Esmeralda's left wrist to the chair, but his efforts were unnecessary. Lavin produced a knife, and Cisco stood back as Lavin quickly sliced through both lengths of rope holding her wrists to the chair. Then Lavin looked at Cisco, and Cisco indicated with a nod toward the door that he should leave them. Lavin was gone at once, leaving the room without a word.

"Back to business?" said Cisco.

"So we're going to try to kill La Tesora?" she asked. "Tell me why we'd want to do something like that, and how we'd pull it off."

"It seems the prospect really disturbs you," Cisco observed.

"It does. She's a good woman, and there's nothing I don't like about her."

"A good woman? I've heard her described by some as a living saint."

"Maybe she is."

"Are you a religious person?"

"I'll admit that I'm not a very good person, but I am a church-going girl."

Cisco knew he had hit a note, and he focused on the chain around Esmeralda's neck. "Is that a medal you're wearing?"

"A crucifix," she replied, and pulled up on the chain to reveal a small gold crucifix. "It's my mother's. She was wearing it when she was killed, and it's been around my neck since the day of her funeral. Helps keep me focused."

"Focused on what? Revenge and murder?"

Esmeralda just glared at him without answering, so Cisco decided to change the subject. "While you're thinking, think about why you were ordered to kill my partner," he said.

"That's an easy one. To discredit the ETA, of course."

"How about this? Maybe whoever's running the ETA thinks we might foil the plan, and they decided to get rid of us before we do."

"I think you give yourself too much credit," she said. "What are you offering?"

"In exchange for everything you know about the GAL?"

"Yes."

"What do you want?"

"Out. It's known by now by my superiors that we botched this operation, and I didn't report in."

"You reported in after you placed the bomb, didn't you?" Cisco asked.

"Yes, but I was also supposed to report in after I set it off. Eizmendi's dead, so my superiors must suspect that Ruíz and myself have been either killed or captured. If we resurface, we'll be viewed as a definite liability, people who talked their way to freedom. We have to get out of the country."

"Money and a new identity until it's safe to come back?"

"A new identity that will last forever. It will never be safe for me to come back to Spain."

"Then I'll see to it that you get a complete new identity you'll like. You'll just disappear. As for the money, I'm offering the same I offered Ruíz. Will two hundred fifty thousand dollars American do it for you?"

"It would, but how can a cop guarantee these things?"

"Monsieur Picard has people who can do anything."

"And the money? Does that come from him?"

Cisco took out the checks, showed her one, and explained their power. Then he began. "How do you usually get your GAL assignments?"

"Most of my operations are self-initiated, so I usually don't get assignments," she replied. "I e-mail my superior for approval beforehand, and then I e-mail him a report with the results when it's over."

"Are these messages encrypted?"

"Yes. I was given a computer when I first joined, and showed how to use the e-mail function and the encryption program."

Cisco then asked the big question. "Who is your superior in the GAL?"

"You're probably not going to believe me, but right now I don't really know."

"Then how did you get in?"

"As soon as I finished my training after joining the Guardia Civil, I was invited in by a lieutenant. He became my team leader in the GAL."

"Where's this lieutenant now?"

"In jail."

"And he never talked?"

"Nobody ever talks," Esmeralda stated, and then she smiled after reflecting a moment on her own situation. "Until now, I guess," she added, "but I'm sure the others were never offered anything like the deal you're giving us."

"So how did your new superior contact you? By e-mail?"

"Yes, and that's the only way we've ever communicated. The only thing I can tell you about him is his e-mail name. Patria and Valor."

It was not the answer Cisco expected, and it prompted another question. "Do you know any other GAL team leaders?"

"Two, and yes, they also report to Patria and Valor by e-mail, and they receive their assignments from him. They don't know who he is either."

"Conclusion?"

"There's only one big boss in the GAL, and we all report to him," Esmeralda said.

"When did you get your assignment to kill McKenna?"

"Yesterday morning."

"What did the e-mail message say?"

"To kill him, preferably with a bomb, and make it look like the ETA did it. Also that he was staying in this hotel, and would be using a black Audi which would be in the garage, under police guard."

"Anything about Martutene?"

"No. Is that where you went today?"

"Yes. Where did you think we were going?"

"No idea, but the message said that McKenna would be going somewhere this morning in the Audi, and that he would be coming back sometime today."

"It seems that Patria and Valor had quite a bit of information for you. Also seems that you formed a good plan and put it together pretty quickly—a plan that would have worked if it weren't for Monsieur Picard's men."

"Is that a compliment?"

"I admire courage, brains, and initiative, especially in a beautiful woman," Cisco said, smiling. "You would have been the one to detonate the bomb to kill us?"

"From the corner outside, as soon as the Audi came into sight on the return trip from the prison."

"And Bengoechea's car? Parked close to where the blast would go off?"

"Yes. It's in a lot near the corner."

"With things in it that would connect Bengoechea to the blast?"

"Same type of detonator, and a kilo of Goma Two plastic explosive with the same chemical signature."

"Show me your computer, please."

Esmeralda got up, took her computer from her suitcase,

placed it on the desk, and powered it up. A password was required, and she entered hers, REVENGE. The in-box of her e-mail program contained in plain text the latest Patria and Valor assignment she had described. "And all the other messages you've received from him?" Cisco asked.

"Deleted, and so are my reports to him."

"Show me how your encryption program works."

Esmeralda did, and Cisco found that it was a simple program to operate. When he was sure he understood it completely, he had just one more matter to discuss with Esmeralda. "Who killed Manel Bengoechea?"

"Why would you need to know that?" Esmeralda asked.

"Because I'd just like to know how much trouble I'll be in if word gets out that I let you go."

Esmeralda took a moment before answering. "Fair enough. You'll be in lots of trouble."

"You killed him?"

"I needed his car and his credit cards to connect him to the bombing. Met him yesterday afternoon, gave him some fun in one of their safe houses, and then he feel asleep," she explained, then smiled. "That's when I slit his throat."

"And the body?"

"It'll never be found. He's just another ETA fugitive who totally disappeared."

The matter-of-fact way she explained the murder bothered Cisco, but a deal was a deal. Then came the matter of payment, and he took out one of Picard's checks. "Mind if I put it all on one check?" he asked. "You and Ruíz can square accounts after you cash it."

"Why one check?" Esmeralda asked. "You have two, don't you?"

"Yeah, but I might need the other one for myself."

Esmeralda understood, but she had another concern. "If we're going to have new identities, what names are you going to use for us? We don't want to have any trouble cashing it."

"Makes no difference. If these checks are as good as Monsieur Picard says they are, I can make it out to Mickey Mouse and Minnie Mouse."

Ruíz and Ernesto were playing cards when Cisco entered his room. "How did you do with her?" Ruíz asked.

"Fine, but we'll talk about that later. Go wait in the bathroom until I'm ready for you."

Ruíz didn't look happy, but he did as he was told, closing the door behind him.

"I have a few requests I'd like you to relay to Monsieur DuPont," Cisco said to Ernesto.

"Anything you need, señor."

"Good, because I need a man who's very good with computer hardware here this afternoon, and it would help if he's also a great hacker."

"I'm sure Monsieur DuPont will have the best such man in Spain here for you," Ernesto replied. "Anything else?"

"Yes, and it might be a problem. I also need a master keycard for this hotel, the kind the maids use."

"I'm sure you'll get it."

TWENTY-FIVE

McKenna got to know Lieutenant Santiago a little better on the trip back from Martutene, and found him to be a candid, opinionated character. He admitted to being a Basque nationalist who, for many years, had been tolerant in his attitude toward the ETA. Before becoming involved in the peace movement, he had viewed them as a necessary evil, and he attributed the Basque Country's autonomy largely to their efforts. Carmen's kidnapping, however, had outraged him. According to him, the ETA had divorced itself from the heart and soul of the Basque people, and therefore it had to go, by whatever means necessary.

McKenna was dropped off in front of the hotel, and since none of DuPont's men were there, Santiago insisted on escorting him inside. McKenna stopped at the desk for messages, and received one he hadn't expected. The wife of Spain's ambassador to France, Señora Anita Navarra, was waiting for him in the piano bar.

McKenna excused himself from Santiago and headed for the bar. Since it was lunchtime, the place was crowded, but Señora Navarra spotted him as soon as he entered. She stood and waved from her table along the far wall. She had a clear drink in front of her, but it was untouched.

McKenna had seen her pictures in the Spanish and French press after her husband was kidnapped, but as he approached her table he decided that the photos hadn't done her justice.

They had been taken immediately after the kidnapping while she was still in shock, and they made her appear much older than the woman in front of him. He knew her husband was fifty-eight, but Señora Navarra didn't appear to be much over forty.

"Thank you for seeing me, Detective McKenna," she said as she offered her hand. "I can only imagine how busy you must be."

McKenna reached across the table to shake her hand. "The pleasure is mine, señora, and I can only imagine how worried you must be," he said.

"I'm very worried. That's why I came as soon as I found out you were here. Do you have a few minutes for me?" she asked, indicating the chair facing her.

"Of course. You have as much of my time as you want." As soon as they sat down, a waiter approached, but McKenna waved him off. He thought he knew what was on Señora Navarra's mind, but he waited for her to put it into words.

She did at once, and he was right. "What worries me most about this whole affair is that nobody seems to care much about what happens to my husband," she said. "He's hardly been mentioned in the press this week. Everything is Carmen, Carmen, Carmen, and it's gotten so that I can barely stand to see her name in print."

"I've noticed the same thing, and I understand how you feel."

"I hope you do, because I'm also worried about the way you regard his kidnapping. The ETA has promised not to harm Carmen, but they've said nothing about what they will do to my husband if their demands aren't met."

She's right, McKenna thought, and she should be concerned. The ETA was set to execute the ambassador in New York just to make a point, meaning that her husband might still be in grave danger. So what do I tell her? McKenna wondered as she watched him. As much of the truth as I can, he decided. "I promise you that getting your husband back safe and sound will be one of my highest priorities."

"But not your *highest* priority?"

"No. I'm primarily here to get Carmen back."

"I guess I should thank you for being so candid," Señora Navarra said, and McKenna's heart went out to her as he watched the tears form in her eyes. "So where does that leave my husband?"

"If things work out the way I think they will, in pretty good shape."

"Can you tell me why you believe that?"

"You certainly deserve to know, but I'm in a delicate position. Before I can tell you anything, I need a promise from you that you won't ever reveal any of what I tell you to anyone without my permission."

"Does this *delicate position* of yours mean that you find yourself working against the interests of Spain?"

"No."

"Then you have my promise, and you can believe it. I am the wife of a high-ranking diplomat who has always trusted me and confided in me on matters big and small. I have never violated his confidence, and I would never violate yours."

McKenna decided to trust her. "For reasons I won't go into, I have been less than forthright with your government regarding the progress being made on this case. I know that your husband is being held with Carmen, and I believe that they're being held in Gibraltar."

Señora Navarra's face lit up at the news. "Gibraltar? That's a small city," she said. "It shouldn't be too hard to find them there."

"I'm hoping it won't be."

"Do you have the cooperation of the British authorities?"

"Yes, and when I leave you I'm going to get even more cooperation from them. It's possible that I'll soon know exactly where in Gibraltar they're being held."

"And then?"

"I'll cross that bridge when I come to it. If conditions are right, we'll take them by surprise. If not, I guess we'll negotiate, but we'll be in a stronger position than we are right now."

"Taking them by surprise still entails quite a bit of risk for my husband, doesn't it?"

"And so does negotiating. I'm going to be frank with you, but you probably already know what I'm about to tell you. Your husband is not their most valuable negotiating chip, and they might consider him expendable."

"You mean that you think they'd kill him to make a point?"

"If we had them cornered, yes, they might. They were about to kill your ambassador to the UN right before we rescued him."

"I see," Señora Navarra said, and a blank look came over her face. "So you really have no good news for me, do you?"

"No, just that the end is in sight."

"Will you be in charge of the rescue effort?"

"No. I expect I'll have something to say, but the operation will probably be run by the British police."

"Will the Guardia Civil be involved?"

"On Gibraltar? I don't imagine so."

"Thank God for that, at least."

The statement from a woman McKenna believed to be a Spanish patriot surprised him. "Why's that?"

"Why?" she said, and mulled the question over for a moment. "I'll tell you, but first I need the same promise from you that you got from me. You can't repeat what I tell you to anyone."

"You can have my promise, if you'll accept one exception. I'd feel obliged to tell my partner. He's completely trustworthy, and would never violate a confidence."

"Then I'll trust you on him, so here it is," Señora Navarra said. "If the Guardia Civil had been doing its job correctly, I think that none of these kidnappings would have happened. Somebody there dropped the ball, by either accident or design."

"Are you telling me that the Guardia Civil should have known about the ETA's plans in advance?"

"I'm saying more than that. I'm saying that maybe they

did know about the plans, and then they did nothing to prevent them."

It was an incredible statement that rocked McKenna's mind and got him thinking furiously. "How could they possibly have known?" he asked, then answered his own question. "They have an informer high up in the ETA."

"Yes, I think so—and so does my husband."

"What brought you both to that conclusion?"

"Two years ago my husband helped negotiate the cooperation agreement between the Guardia Civil and the French police. To help convince the French that a real problem existed, he was given access to many Guardia Civil reports which contained information on ETA and Iparretarrak safe houses in France, as well as the names of the terrorists hiding out there. Once the agreement went into effect, they were all arrested, and most were extradited to Spain. For the next year, the Guardia Civil forwarded even more information to the French on Iparretarrak- and ETA-planned operations in France and along the border, and even more arrests followed."

"And this information was so detailed that your husband and you concluded that it could only have come from an informer?" McKenna asked.

"If you saw the reports, you'd have to draw the same conclusion."

"That the Guardia Civil has somebody high up in the ETA on their payroll?"

"Yes."

"Couldn't a lot of it have come from prisoners they turned?"

"Some of it, I guess, but not a lot. The information was always very current. It seemed the Guardia Civil knew everything the ETA was up to in France, and my husband was kidnapped in France."

She's a smart woman, McKenna thought, and she has a good point. Is it possible that the Guardia Civil—or at least someone in the Guardia Civil—knew about the ETA's kidnapping plans in advance, and then allowed them to proceed?

If so, why? Maybe to cause this national backlash against the ETA was one reason that immediately came to mind, a backlash that even extends into the Basque Country. "I need some time to think about this, señora," he said. "Where are you going to be?"

"Wherever you want me."

"Could you check into this hotel?"

"I already have. Room six-ten."

McKenna wanted to talk over with Cisco the suspicions that were forming in his mind, but there were other pressing matters at hand. After ordering lunch from room service, he called Scotland Yard and asked for Inspector Sidney Rollins. He was informed that Rollins wasn't in at the moment, but he was expected back soon. McKenna left his number and an urgent request that Rollins call him as soon as he got in.

Rollins was essential to the plan forming in McKenna's mind. Although Rollins was technically with the police, McKenna had worked with him on a previous case, and consequently he knew better. Rollins was actually with British Intelligence, and was one of their leading experts on the IRA.

McKenna was hungry, but when lunch arrived he hardly tasted his food as he ate and mulled over the information he had received from Señora Navarra. If she was right, there had to be somebody in the GAL who had withheld information that would have prevented her husband's kidnapping. If so, McKenna was sure that person was a fanatic, a totally reprehensible character who would do anything to realize the GAL's goals—and he was succeeding. Support for the ETA was at an all-time low, but the price was high. Among the five people killed when the ETA took the ambassador in Paris was his bodyguard, a sergeant in the Guardia Civil, and the GAL had allowed him to be sacrificed in order to achieve their political goal.

The phone rang. "Good to hear from you, old boy, and I'm delighted you called," Rollins said.

On a personal level, Rollins wasn't exactly McKenna's

cup of tea, and he couldn't imagine what it would take to actually *delight* the always composed and condescending Englishman, so he had to ask. "Delighted? Really?"

"Yes, really."

"Why's that?"

"I've been following your endeavors in New York with some interest, and now it seems that you've managed to involve me in your caper. So just when I was meaning to call you, I find that you've called me first."

"You're already involved?" McKenna asked.

"It would appear so. My superiors in Whitehall were in a bit of a panic over this Gibraltar business and the implications it could pose regarding our relations with Spain, and it just got worse for them. I've just returned from a meeting where I was told that a Spanish cardinal has requested a meeting for tomorrow with the Archbishop of Canterbury. Rather unusual, wouldn't you say?"

A Roman Catholic cardinal requesting a meeting with the head of that heretic Church of England? Very unusual, McKenna decided, and he saw Picard's hand in it. "Did the archbishop agree to the meeting?" he asked.

"Tomorrow, at noon in Canterbury."

"Were you assigned to find out what the subject of that meeting would be?"

"In so many words. A connection to Gibraltar is feared, and they know I'm friendly with you. Do you have any idea what might be on that cardinal's mind?"

"No, but maybe I can find out—if you'll agree to help me out with a few things I need. Do you know who Henri Picard is?"

"Monsieur Picard? Of course I do. What about him?"

"I know he'd have access to any Spanish cardinal he'd like to talk to, so he might be behind this meeting."

"Now that is interesting. Would you talk to him for me?"

"Yes, but I don't know how much he'll tell me."

"Just the effort is worth anything I can do for you," Rollins said. "What do you need from me?"

"Do you know of a man named Liam Kilkenny?"

"Liam Kilkenny? Former IRA, did six years in Long Kesh for gun-running back in the eighties, but he hasn't popped up on our screens since then. What about him?"

"He drives a dairy truck from England about once a week. Brings British cheese, cream, and milk to Gibraltar and a few other places in Spain where your folks have settled down. On the return trip he sometimes brings back guns from the ETA, and probably does a few other favors for them."

"Like what?"

"Uses his truck to smuggle ETA fugitives into Gibraltar when Spain gets too hot for them."

"I've heard of this type of cooperation before," Rollins said. "You believe that he's the one who brought Carmen and the ambassador into Gibraltar for them?"

"Along with maybe twenty ETA soldiers. If Gibraltar is where they are, it's probable that he's the one who brought them in. It would be nice to know exactly where he dropped them all off."

"Any idea where he is now, or the name of the company he's working for?"

"That's what I need you for."

"Shouldn't be too hard for me to find out. I'll have our people in Gibraltar question the people running the super-markets until they find someone who knows him. Once I have the name of his company, I'll pay them a visit. Then, if he's in the U.K. at the time, I'll have him for you. If not, I'll have him held at the border in Gibraltar the next time he shows up. Good enough?"

"Yes, but there's more. Sometime during the past couple of years, Bombi Manfreddo's parents have gotten into the act. Bought shares in three hostels or hotels that the ETA has been using as hideouts. Two of them are in Spain, but one of them is in—"

"Don't tell me. Gibraltar."

"*Yes*, Gibraltar. I need to know the name of that hotel."

"And you shall. Don't they own a hotel in Florence?"

"Still do, as far as I know."

"Has the Guardia Civil been looking into their places in Spain?"

"No. I haven't told them about those places."

"Why not?" Rollins asked.

"Because there's something rotten going on here, and I'm going to keep the Guardia Civil in the dark until I find out who's responsible."

"You have any idea yet who that might be?"

"An idea, yes, but it's nothing I can prove."

"Too bad. Please get back to me right after you talk to Picard."

After hanging up, McKenna spent a few minutes trying to think of a plan for handling Picard. He couldn't come up with one, and realized that the straightforward truth was the only way to go.

Picard answered the phone himself this time, and he congratulated McKenna for managing to remain alive.

"I have you and your men to thank for that," McKenna replied.

"I'm not so sure," Picard countered. "I've heard that your partner had the insight to visit the garage last night. He expected to find one of my men there, and I suspect he only left when he found he was right."

"Yeah, Cisco's good. The problem is that over the next few years I'm probably going to hear about that garage visit so many times that I might wish we had been blown up," McKenna predicted, and then got to the business at hand. "I need to know why your cardinal is visiting the Archbishop of Canterbury."

McKenna was gratified that, for once, he had Picard at a loss for words—but not for long. "Your source of information, please?" Picard asked curtly.

"A pal of mine in British Intelligence. You have Whitehall quite upset with that stunt, and he's been assigned to find out what's up."

"Because he's a pal of yours?"

"I'm sure that has something to do with it. He's also, incidentally, the person who is going to help me find out exactly where in Gibraltar they might be holding Carmen."

"That would make him a very valuable pal indeed. I take it you made progress with Colqui and Ducho?"

"It's going to cost you, but yes, I made progress."

"Tell me about it, please."

"You first, monsieur. The cardinal."

"I have no problem with the British government, but I'm a little disappointed at the lack of progress on their part in Gibraltar. It's a small city, Carmen is there, and they haven't made sufficient efforts to find her."

"I believe they're doing all they can."

"I disagree. They could do more, but they haven't."

"Like what? A house-to-house search, maybe?"

"Exactly what I had in mind."

"Never. Britain is a democracy, and the people of Gibraltar are British citizens. The police in Gibraltar could never do anything like that, even if we had strong proof that Carmen was being held there."

"They can't, but I can—and I will because I've decided you need a little more help. That is what our cardinal is going to advise the archbishop, purely as a courtesy. Hopefully, next Sunday, he and his people will explain from the pulpit that our intentions are peaceful, we will pay for any damages, and we will leave immediately after we have Carmen back."

"*We?* Who's *we?*"

"Myself, and probably more than a million Spaniards and Basques. Next Sunday it will be announced at every mass in Spain and the Basque country that Carmen is being held in Gibraltar. Also announced at that time will be a peaceful demonstration on Monday in La Línea to protest her captivity. I imagine that demonstration will be extremely well-attended."

"Sunday? That's the day after tomorrow," McKenna exclaimed, horrified. "And what happens then? You march on Gibraltar?"

"In essence, yes. I think it would be a nice touch if all our people—including women and children—are carrying candles and singing hymns for the benefit of the world press.

Properly organized, we have our house-to-house search from one end of Gibraltar to the other. We'll find Carmen, and bring her back with us."

"If she's there," McKenna said.

"I have faith in you, and I've analyzed your conclusions. She's there."

"And what about the people of Gibraltar? How do you think they'll react to this search of their homes?"

"With understanding. Most of them are of Spanish descent, and overwhelmingly Catholic. Once they understand that the sovereignty of Gibraltar isn't being seriously threatened by us, they'll just stand by and watch."

"And the Spanish government will permit this?" McKenna asked, already knowing the answer.

"Permit it? They'll love it!" Picard replied. "The government's official position is that Gibraltar is part of Spain, and this is just a case of Spaniards freely visiting a city in their own country. Of course, the government will station extra Guardia Civil at the border to placate the British, but they will also expect that those cops will be peacefully swept aside."

Good God! Rollins is just gonna love this, McKenna thought. Can it be prevented? "I don't like it, and I need more time. Give me a chance to get Carmen back without an international incident," he said.

"You have two days."

"Yes, but I've only been here two days."

"All right. You have three days. The demonstration will be on Tuesday."

"One last question," McKenna said, taking a chance with the confidence of Señora Navarra. "Have you ever heard about a possible Guardia Civil informer high up in the ETA?"

"No, I haven't. Why not just ask Colonel Segovia?"

"I could, but I'd rather not."

There was a long silence before Picard replied. "Are you losing confidence in him?"

"That might be an understatement."

"I'm surprised to hear that, but I'll trust your judgment once again."

TWENTY-SIX

McKenna had a raging headache by the time he got off the phone with Rollins, but he was sure his headache was nothing compared to the one he had given Rollins. Next was a call to Segovia's room. McKenna didn't really want to talk to him, but knew a courtesy call was in order. Fortunately, Segovia wasn't in, so McKenna left a brief message saying that he had been successful at the prison, and that he would be in his room if Segovia wanted to talk to him.

Since McKenna didn't want to talk to Cisco until Cisco wanted to talk to him, for the first time in a long time he found himself with nothing to do. Under the circumstances, a nap seemed in order.

A knock at the door at six o'clock awakened him, and he let Cisco in. "How'd you make out at the prison?" Cisco asked.

"Got what we came for, and a little more. Also had an interesting conversation with Señora Navarra that leads me to believe we might have a real problem here."

"Colonel Segovia?"

"Yeah? How'd you know?" McKenna asked, surprised.

"Because I have a few facts you don't yet, and I agree with you. Having the head of the GAL as our supposed boss here could present us with a real problem."

"You realize, of course, how ridiculous this sounds. The

respected Guardia Civil colonel who's in charge of smashing
the GAL is actually in charge of the GAL?"

"Perfect position for him, if you think about it," Cisco
countered. "Places him above suspicion, and all the intelligence information he needs to run successful GAL operations is made available to him. Along the way, he gets to
know who all the squealers are in the Guardia Civil, and he
always knows who's hot and who's not in the GAL. Then,
if too much suspicion falls on one of his people, he bags
him, makes sure he talks just enough, and enhances his own
position and prestige in the process."

"It would take a certain kind of man to pull that off,"
McKenna said.

"Yeah. A real devious scumbag, so let's keep that in mind
as we deal with him. What put you on to him?"

"A few things got me started thinking. First of all, DuPont
doesn't trust him, and he seems a good judge of character to
me. Then there's the fact that the GAL put their bomb plot
against us in motion so very fast. They had to have some
inside information to know about the Audi and where we
were staying, and Segovia had it."

"So did the San Sebastian cops," Cisco countered.

"True, but they don't strike me as a particularly cunning
bunch. Then there's the fact that our colonel didn't make the
trip with us to Martutene this morning."

"Big point, and now he must be going out of his mind.
He doesn't know that Eizmendi was on the hit team, but he
must know who he is, so that call to view his body last night
must have got him thinking. Then add in that we're still here,
and the last report he got was that the bomb was in place.
Since he sent them an e-mail two hours ago that hasn't been
answered yet . . ."

"He did?" McKenna asked.

"Sure did," Cisco replied, "so he must figure they're dead
or captured—and he's probably hoping dead and not talking.
So what does that leave us with?"

"If he's the one, a very nervous, confused, and probably
desperate colonel," McKenna surmised. "He had me fooled

last night, had me thinking he had laid it all on the line for me. The great, sanctimonious champion struggling against that evil GAL. What he was really thinking was that he could tell me whatever he wanted to set me at ease because we'd both be dead today."

"Have you heard from him today?" Cisco asked.

"No. Called him when I got back from Martutene, but he wasn't in. Left a message, but he hasn't returned my call."

"Not surprising, considering the stress we have him under," Cisco said. "He doesn't know how much we know, doesn't know if we suspect him, and he's in no hurry to find out."

"Do you know where he is?"

"He's been in and out a few times today, but right now he's in his room putting down a bottle of Scotch."

"How would you know all that?" McKenna asked, but too fast, he thought, because the answer came to him immediately. "The hotel's chief of security?"

"Wonderful man, and a very compliant fellow. Mention Picard's name, and he just about snaps to attention. Does whatever our Monsieur DuPont wants, and asks no questions. Segovia's in room four-oh-nine, so we fast-forwarded through the tapes of the fourth floor's security camera. He was in and out a couple of times before we were on to him, but at three twenty-eight he left carrying—"

"A computer case," McKenna guessed.

"A briefcase, actually, but there was a computer in it."

"How do you know that? Did you follow him?"

"No, too risky. I thought he'd be too nervous and too wary by now. Besides, I figured I knew where he was going, and I was right. There's only one Internet café in town, and I had one of DuPont's men there to watch him enter, and then leave after he sent his e-mail to Esmeralda."

"Esmeralda?" McKenna asked.

"The babe DuPont's people captured. She showed me how to run her encryption program, so we read his message. He marked it urgent, wanted a status report."

"You didn't send him a reply, did you?" McKenna asked.

"Thought flashed through my mind, something to really shake him up, but I held back. He went back to the Internet café at five-forty to check and see if he got a reply from her. Since he didn't, he bought a bottle of Scotch on his way back to the hotel, and I imagine he's working on it now."

"Tell me about this Esmeralda," McKenna said. "Did you turn her completely?"

"Both her and the sergeant. Got them eating out of my hand. Unfortunately, it's caviar they're eating, but it's worth it for us."

"How much?"

"Two fifty apiece, plus freedom, plus new identities from Picard's pals."

"Interesting story they had to tell?"

"Quite. Ruíz is madly in love with Esmeralda, a woman who slits throats without a second thought."

"Throats?"

"At least one. Manel Bengoechea, and I doubt his was the first throat she slit for the GAL. Dangerous woman."

"Didn't you ask her if she did any other murders?"

"No. Since I was letting her go anyway, why bother clouding your conscience with more details you wouldn't want to know?"

He's right, McKenna thought. We paid a murderer for information we needed, and then set her free. Tough move, one we'd have a hard time justifying in most circles.

There was a knock at the door. McKenna answered it, and tried to look happy to see Segovia. "Come in, Colonel, please," he said.

If Segovia had been drinking, it wasn't evident to McKenna. He didn't smell alcohol on him, and Segovia was composed and seemed as steady on his feet as ever. He did look tired, but as usual he was all business. He gave Cisco a curt nod, and then addressed McKenna. "Sorry I didn't get back to you sooner," he said, "but I've been busy all day. Had a murder right down the block last night. Local tough with some ETA connections was shot dead, and the police here managed to involve me in it."

"Anything to do with our investigation?" McKenna asked.

"Not as far as I can tell," Segovia said, then changed the subject. "I take it things went very well for us at Martutene today."

"Better than expected. How did you know?"

"Because Guarlzadi's wife and Herriguandi's parents checked into a very nice hotel in Biarritz about two hours ago, looking remarkably healthy and happy. Seems they had been in the mountains—hiking, of all things—and they had just heard this ridiculous story that they had been kidnapped. They asked the desk clerk to call the French police to straighten it out, and a couple of detectives arrived to interview them. They didn't have much to say, even when pressed, but one thing they did say was that they expected to remain on holiday in France for another week. The detectives noted before leaving, however, that their clothes and luggage looked new—and expensive."

"Will you be going there to talk to them?"

"That's the other thing they had to say, specifically told the detectives that they didn't want to speak to me under any circumstances."

"That's to be expected," Cisco said. "If you're doing your job right, you can't expect to be popular."

Segovia didn't bother to answer, or even look at Cisco. He kept his attention focused on McKenna. "Care to tell me what deal you made with Guarlzadi and Herriguandi to get Picard to release their families in such style?"

"I won't go into specifics, but I now have a pretty good idea where Carmen and your ambassador are being held."

"Are you going to tell me that, at least?"

"Gibraltar."

"Gibraltar?" Segovia said, apparently surprised. "How sure are you of that?"

"Better than fifty percent."

"Gibraltar," Segovia repeated, and then remained silent and focused on the floor while he thought. "Makes sense, if they managed to make it there," he said after a minute. "Lots of traffic in and out, it's out of my reach, and the British make a point of never showing too much interest in our affairs."

"I'm sure the ETA took all that into consideration before they headed there."

"And I assume you know that the ETA has good connections in Morocco, just a short boat trip away?"

"I've spoken to a friend of mine, a big shot with Scotland Yard. The British now have the harbor and the straits under close watch."

"Are you going to Gibraltar?"

"Sometime tomorrow morning."

"So I guess that leaves me out of it."

"Not necessarily," McKenna said. "You know the ETA better than anyone I have available to me, and I wouldn't mind having you along."

"I don't know," Segovia said, shaking his head. "The British won't like it."

"They'll see things my way, and I'll make sure you're treated well."

"I'll have to clear it with the minister of the interior first."

"Then do that. Is ten o'clock good for you?"

"Fine. I can't land a Guardia Civil helicopter there, but I can bring you to La Línea and arrange transportation from there. Would that be all right with you?"

"Perfect, and thank you."

Segovia then turned and left without another word.

"Are you sure you want to keep that treacherous, double-dealing bastard involved in this?" Cisco asked.

"Remember what the Godfather said?"

"I know. Keep your friends close, but your enemies closer. Might be good thinking, but I'll tell you one thing: We're not flying anywhere in that helicopter of his unless he's sitting between us."

"So what's next?"

"His computer is the key," said Cisco. "Resurrect his e-mail to his GAL people, and we've got him. Find out everything they've all been up to, and maybe even who they all are."

"Suppose he's deleted all his messages?"

"He's a careful guy, so he probably has. A problem, but one that can be overcome with the right equipment and the right people. DuPont is supplying me with a guy he touts as the best computer nerd in either Spain or France. Simon LeBarre, a discreet man willing to take risks for money."

"So, in addition to letting murderers go, now we're going to do a burglary?" McKenna asked.

"We're strangers in a strange land. You see another way to put Segovia in check?"

McKenna didn't. "When will Simon get here?"

"Eight o'clock, but I've spoken with him over the phone. According to him, nothing can be completely deleted from a hard drive. There's always a shadow of text left that can be partially reconstructed."

"So we're gonna steal Segovia's computer?"

"Just his hard drive, but he'll never know. Simon is going to copy his hard drive onto another one he's bringing. Then we take Segovia's, and leave the duplicate installed in his computer."

"Won't that take a long time?"

"Half hour, tops."

"You've got a keycard for Segovia's room?"

Cisco took a hotel keycard from his pocket and showed it to McKenna. "A master key. DuPont got it from our security chief."

"And a plan to get Segovia out of his room?"

"A pretty good one, I think. Let me show you." Cisco took McKenna to the window and pointed to the parking lot on the corner. "See that brown BMW parked on the end?"

"Uh-huh."

"It's Manel Bengoechea's car, and the trunk is loaded with goodies. Explosives, blasting caps, and a detonator. Sometime tonight, at our convenience, the San Sebastian police are going to receive a call about it. It's open, so they can pop the trunk from inside and find the stuff. I'm sure they'll call Segovia to show him, and in his state of mind, he'll want to see it."

"Very impressive, Cisco. Good plan."

"Glad you like it."

"Don't you want to hear what I've been up to?"

"Only if you've made progress, and then only if it's interesting."

How do I put up with this guy? McKenna wondered for the umpteenth time. "I have made progress on my end, and I humbly think it will interest you."

"I'll be the judge of that. Let's hear it."

Simon had arrived on time. He looked intelligent, but possessed no personality or social graces whatsoever. Cisco left him stashed in his room, where he was amusing himself reading a technical computer manual as quickly as a teenager could read a comic book.

At ten-thirty, Cisco had Ernesto anonymously phone the San Sebastian police and report that he had seen an unknown suspicious man constructing what appeared to be a small bomb at the trunk of Bengoechea's BMW.

As McKenna and Cisco watched the lot from McKenna's window, they learned that the police in San Sebastian took their bomb threats very seriously. They arrived in force, blocked traffic, and cordoned off the block. When a sergeant popped the trunk and saw the Goma Two plastic explosive and bomb components inside, they went even further and quickly evacuated the building behind the parking lot. For a few minutes, McKenna and Cisco were afraid they were even going to evacuate the hotel, but the cops contented themselves with clearing the ground floor while they awaited the arrival of their Bomb Squad.

They didn't have long to wait. The Bomb Squad arrived minutes later, and quickly determined there was no risk of detonation. That was when Segovia appeared on the scene, escorted from the hotel by a uniformed cop. And that was when Cisco left to bring Simon to Segovia's room.

McKenna kept watch on the lot below, ready to call Segovia's room and alert Cisco if the colonel returned to the hotel, but that didn't happen. When detectives arrived and Segovia went into conference with them in one of their cars, McKenna knew it had been discovered that the car belonged to Bengoechea.

McKenna's phone rang twenty minutes later. "Mission complete," Cisco said. "I'll be up in five minutes."

And he was, six minutes later, carrying a computer. "How'd we do?" McKenna asked.

"Had some password difficulty getting Segovia's computer activated, but our man is good. IBM has a few secret password bypass codes installed in their computers for people who forget their passwords, and he knew them."

"Were you able to access his e-mail program?"

"Not yet. Another password. Simon says he'll be able to bypass it, but he couldn't tell me how long it would take him."

"How about the accounting program?"

"It's there, complete with another password. He'll get around that one, too."

TWENTY-SEVEN

McKenna was awakened twice by phone calls during the night, but he didn't mind at all. Every time he hung up the phone, he felt he was closer to freeing Carmen and bringing his case to a successful resolution.

First to call was Rollins, at 3 A.M. As Rollins had predicted, getting the information McKenna wanted on Kilkenny hadn't been at all difficult, but it had been difficult for all the people interviewed by him and the Gibraltar police since they had to be visited at home in the dead of night.

It turned out that Kilkenny was well-known to the supermarket managers in Gibraltar, and according to the police there, he was also well-known to many of the bartenders and barmaids in town. He worked for Edgecombe Dairies in Surrey, and Rollins had visited the home of the company's manager. Kilkenny had worked for the company for six years, and the manager described him as a good, reliable employee who enjoyed himself thoroughly whenever he wasn't driving. On Thursday Kilkenny had left England on his regular route through the British retirement communities in France, Spain, and Portugal. Since the manager knew Kilkenny liked to spend Saturday night and most of Sunday in English-speaking Gibraltar, he figured Kilkenny would be arriving there sometime during the next afternoon, Saturday.

Rollins had then asked the manager the most important question of the interview: Did he have the details on Kilkenny's last run through Europe? The manager did, and it just about verified McKenna's theory that Kilkenny had transported Carmen and the ETA into Gibraltar. Due to the traffic delays encountered at the many checkpoints established by the Guardia Civil, Kilkenny had arrived in Gibraltar one day late the week before, on Sunday at 8:15 A.M. instead of Saturday afternoon. Therefore, taking the time difference into account, Kilkenny had been in or near Algeciras when Bombi had made that phone call to the ETA traveling team right before she had been killed, and Algeciras was the city the ETA team had been passing through at the time.

That piece of information had been enough to convince Rollins's superiors that he should go to Gibraltar to take charge of the investigation there. Rollins himself would be at the border, waiting for Kilkenny to arrive.

As for locating the hotel in Gibraltar in which Bombi's parents had bought an interest, Rollins had been less successful with that assignment. Since McKenna thought it possible that Carmen and the ambassador were being held there, Rollins had thought it too risky to send the Gibraltar police to the many hotels in town to interview the managers and determine ownership. Complicating matters was the fact that Gibraltar was an offshore tax haven, so banking and real estate transactions there were not transparent and easily inspected unless the proper paperwork was meticulously in order.

Rollins assured McKenna that he would drag a local magistrate into court as soon as he arrived in town, and he would soon have the proper court orders. Then, all that remained for him to complete his assignment was to get civil servants and banking officials into their offices on a Saturday to do the research and provide the information mandated by the court order. He promised that by sometime the next day the paper chase would be complete, and he would know which hotel it was.

Rollins had one additional good piece of news for McKenna. He had booked him and Cisco into the five-star Rock Hotel, the city's best.

Then McKenna gave Rollins what he thought would be a piece of bad news. Without going into specifics, he asked permission to bring Segovia along, and was surprised when Rollins said it was a good idea. Irregular, he added, but Segovia knew the ETA better than anyone in Gibraltar, and it wouldn't hurt the political situation to have a high Spanish police official involved.

The second call was from Cisco at 6:05 A.M., two hours before McKenna's wake-up call. "Simon cracked one password, and resurrected the deleted messages from the hard drive. Took him all night, and he couldn't get it totally word for word, but we were right," Cisco announced.

"Segovia's the head of the GAL?" McKenna asked.

"And has been for three years. The GAL never really stopped functioning, but there wasn't much traffic until this month. Then they broke out and got bad."

"Any indication on the number of people he has?"

"Looks like he's been communicating with six hit teams, counting Esmeralda's."

So the GAL is a small organization, McKenna thought, and the way Segovia has it set up, everything goes through him. The teams don't know each other, so when we chop the head off, the GAL stops functioning. "How about the accounting program?"

"Simon hasn't cracked that password yet, but he says he will," Cisco said. "He has to get some sleep first. I'll stay here with him, so it looks like you'll be going to Gibraltar without me."

"When will you be coming?"

"As soon as we have enough to put Segovia in the box, and keep him there."

When the porter arrived with his trolley for McKenna's luggage, DuPont and Ernesto were with him. "Gibraltar won't present the same security problems for you as we had here, so it will be just me going with you today," DuPont said.

Figuring that the GAL couldn't operate quite so easily

there, McKenna agreed. However, he wanted more information from DuPont. "Will your people be getting a couple of days off?" he asked.

"Yes, and they need it."

McKenna thought so, too. Most of DuPont's people had been working for two days straight, but he had another question. "And then they'll be with Monsieur Picard in La Línea?"

"Yes," DuPont replied, then helped the porter load the suitcases on the trolley.

Although DuPont obviously wasn't inclined to say more, Picard's reasoning made sense to McKenna. He would want his most trusted people with him to help keep his planned march on Gibraltar properly organized, and he would want them well rested.

When they got to the lobby, Segovia was there with Santiago, and McKenna noted that Segovia traveled light; at his feet were just one suitcase and his briefcase. "Where's your partner?" Segovia asked McKenna.

Let's give him something to think about, McKenna thought. "He had a few things to do. He'll be joining us later in Gibraltar," McKenna replied, and left it at that.

If that information worried Segovia, he didn't show it. He just shrugged his shoulders, picked up his luggage, and headed for the police cars waiting outside.

The trip to the bullring and the waiting Guardia Civil helicopter was again by motorcade. McKenna rode in the Audi with DuPont and Ernesto, and Segovia rode with Santiago. Ernesto remained with the Audi when McKenna, DuPont, and Segovia boarded the helicopter. Once they were seated, Segovia took a stack of reports from his briefcase, and McKenna got a glimpse of the laptop computer inside. Then, without a word to McKenna or DuPont, Segovia began going through his reports.

McKenna thought Segovia's conduct rude and antisocial, but it was fine with him since he hadn't been looking forward to making small talk with Segovia during the flight.

· · ·

The helicopter was cruising at eight thousand feet when the
pilot called McKenna to tell him Gibraltar was in sight. Mc-
Kenna went forward and stood between the pilot and copilot,
marveling at the spectacular view in front of them. Gibraltar
was perched at the end of a peninsula jutting from Spain,
and to the ancients it marked the end of the known world,
that place where their well-traveled Mediterranean Sea ended
and the unexplored, perilous Atlantic Ocean began. It was a
clear, cloudless day, and visible beyond Gibraltar and across
the strait was the mountainous coast of Africa and Mons
Abila, the Moroccan mountain which, together with Gibraltar, formed the Pillars of Hercules.

As the helicopter approached, McKenna could better distinguish the geographic features created by man. West of
Gibraltar and across its famous harbor was the larger Spanish
city of Algeciras, and north of the Rock was La Línea de la
Concepción. From the air, the three cities appeared to form
one large, busy metropolitan area. The harbor was crowded
with ships, and there was a steady flow of vehicular traffic
along the Spanish coastal highways leading in and out of the
cities.

When the helicopter was over La Línea, McKenna asked
the pilot to hover for a minute, and he complied while Mc-
Kenna studied the features of the famous Rock. The city of
Gibraltar was located mainly on the western edge of the
mountain, the Atlantic side, and it stretched from the harbor
halfway up the mountain's steep slopes. At the base of the
eastern side of the rock were the city's beaches. They faced
the Mediterranean, and there should have been plenty of people swimming and taking in the sun on this very nice day,
but McKenna saw no sign of people there. To prevent an
ETA escape by sea from the beaches, the British had obviously closed them.

At the tip of Gibraltar, facing Africa, were the naval base
and the old military fortifications England had used to control

access to the Mediterranean through countless wars during the past three hundred years.

McKenna could see that the city had grown larger since last he was there, grown in the only way it could. Landfills had been used to expand the city's pleasure boat marinas and the industrial area at the edge of the harbor, and new, sun-drenched warehouses and luxury apartment buildings there indicated to McKenna that Gibraltar was a prosperous place.

Then McKenna noticed an RAF transport plane landing at the airport, the most curious landfill project in a city where space was at a premium. It was constructed a hundred yards from the border crossing, and the only access road into the city crossed the middle of the runways, meaning that all traffic into and out of Gibraltar had to be halted every time a plane took off or landed.

As the transport taxied toward the terminal, McKenna was curious as to who the passengers were. He suspected they were troops flown in to reinforce the city's garrison in response to Picard's plan, but he decided it wouldn't be polite to keep the helicopter hovering long enough to find out. He thanked the pilot, and told him he had seen enough.

Segovia had one of the Guardia Civil's vans transport them to the frontier from the La Línea barracks, and they found Rollins waiting for them there. Rollins, as always, was meticulously dressed in a blue pinstripe suit. He was in his fifties, tall, thin, balding, and he had an aristocratic air about him. He appeared surprised when he saw DuPont, and DuPont appeared just as surprised to see Rollins, but they greeted each other politely. Then Rollins managed to surprise McKenna when he greeted Segovia in schoolboy Spanish, and added how pleased he was to have such a high Guardia Civil official as a guest in Gibraltar.

Segovia managed a perfunctory reply, but McKenna could see that his attention was focused on the unusual scene on the British side of the border. To annoy the British, from time to time the Guardia Civil slowed traffic to a crawl at

the border by thoroughly inspecting the documents and vehicles of all persons leaving Gibraltar, but this time it was
the British who were annoying the tourists and the citizens
of Gibraltar. Usually there were only four constables stationed on the British side, and their regular function was
simply to wave cars through to the Spanish border station.
Not today. Traffic was backed up to the airport because there
were eight constables checking the documents and searching
the vehicles of all persons leaving Gibraltar, and they were
backed up by two squads of Royal Marines deployed in full
combat gear. Also visible were another two squads of troops
deployed around the airline terminal down the road.

When Segovia had seen enough, he turned and walked
back to the Spanish border station. "How long has this been
going on?" McKenna heard him ask one of the Guardia Civil
cops stationed there.

"Six days, sir."

Since McKenna had led Segovia to believe that it was
only the night before that he had formed his suspicions that
Gibraltar was where Carmen and the ambassador were being
held, he expected some explosive comment from Segovia
when he returned, but he was pleasantly disappointed.
"When this is all over, we really should talk" was all he said
to McKenna, and his tone was cordial.

"When this is over, Colonel, I assure you we will," Mc-
Kenna replied, just as cordially.

Rollins had a police van manned by a constable waiting
to drive them to the hotel, and they all climbed in after load-
ing in the luggage. Rollins was sitting next to the constable,
and McKenna was anxious to learn whether he had made
any progress. "How are you making out with our truck
driver?" he asked as soon as the van took off.

"Fine," Rollins said without turning around, and then he
took on the role of tour guide, pointing out the sights as they
crossed the runway and proceeded through town along the
narrow, winding streets.

Rollins's short response puzzled McKenna until he gave
the matter some thought. At first he figured Rollins didn't

know whether or not Segovia spoke English, and Rollins didn't want to give a Guardia Civil colonel a progress report on a British investigation. Then McKenna came up with another explanation that, knowing Rollins and DuPont, made more sense to him. It seemed Rollins and DuPont had somehow recognized each other. Therefore, since Kilkenny was IRA and Rollins worked for British Intelligence, DuPont must have some IRA connection. Rollins didn't want to discuss one IRA man in front of another.

The Rock Hotel was perched in the middle of its own park halfway up the mountain, next to the city's casino, and its balconies provided a better view of the city and the harbor than any building in town. After checking in, McKenna unpacked, and then stood on his balcony while waiting for Rollins to call. There was a lot to see that interested him. First there was the courtyard of the Kings Barracks near the end of the peninsula; two companies of Royal Marines were formed up there with their sea bags at their feet, and McKenna guessed they had just arrived on the RAF transport plane. Then there was the naval activity in the harbor and offshore; a destroyer slowly cruised in the strait, and McKenna could make out two large patrol boats in the strait as well as three police launches in the harbor. He could also clearly see the city's two marinas and the commercial docks, and there were many police and military vehicles parked along the water's edge. It was evident to McKenna that the British were totally on board, and there was no way the ETA was leaving town with Carmen and the ambassador by land, air, or sea.

McKenna was making his second cup of coffee when he answered a knock at the door. "Do you know who it is you've brought with you?" was the first thing Rollins said once he was in.

McKenna was ready for the question. "Yeah, a capable guy who saved my life, and who, incidentally, was probably with the IRA sometime before I was born. He's now the trusted right-hand of the most respected man in Spain. He's not a problem for you."

McKenna had caught Rollins by surprise, and for once the upper-crust, unflappable IRA expert was at a loss for words. "Forget I asked," he said when he found his tongue.

"I can't forget until you tell me he's in the clear with you," McKenna said.

"It hurts me, but he's in the clear. What hurts even more is that I can never mention this to anyone."

"Was he that bad a guy?" McKenna had to ask.

"Let's just say that pinching a man everyone thought has been dead for twenty years would make me a legend," Rollins replied, shaking his head and appearing forlorn. "His work was classic, and we still can't figure out the technical aspects of some of his bombs or how he placed them where he did."

"How did you recognize him?"

"Easy for me. I carried his picture in my hat for ten years when I first started out in this business."

"So you recognized him, but it seemed to me he also recognized you," McKenna noted.

"Just means he's a careful man who keeps track of his enemies. My picture has appeared in the press many times, and it's on the jacket of the book I wrote on the IRA," Rollins said, managing to sound modest.

McKenna was anxious to get a progress report from Rollins, but thought that first the Segovia issue should be addressed. "Okay, so DuPont's a sharp guy who's not a problem for you. But the other guy I brought with me is a problem, maybe for both of us."

"Colonel Segovia? Seems an odd sort, but I'm prepared to treat him quite well. I'm sure he'll leave with a better impression of us."

"I want him to leave with a terrible impression of us," McKenna countered. "Segovia is the head of the GAL."

McKenna had expected a reaction from Rollins, but Rollins was back in character. "Head of the GAL? Quite peculiar" was all he said.

"You're not surprised?"

"Not really. The politics of Spain has always been mired in intrigue prompted by misguided patriotism. The Spanish thrive on it," Rollins observed, and then he waited for McKenna to explain the reasons behind his accusation.

McKenna did, and then Rollins had some comments he expected. "So you expect to have him wrapped up tight, but I'm not sure you'll be able to proceed against him. The evidence you're accumulating against him comes as a result of illegal acts on your part—a burglary and the theft of his property, to be precise—and I'm not sure such evidence would be admissible in Spain. I know it couldn't be presented in your country."

"It couldn't if I were acting as a cop in an official capacity, but my status in Spain is murky," McKenna countered.

"You're splitting hairs. In any event, you and your partner could be subject to charges there. It probably wouldn't happen, I realize, but your professional reputation would certainly be damaged."

"I'm more worried about staying alive and getting Carmen back in one piece than I am about my reputation. That's why I have him here with me now."

"To keep an eye on him?"

"No, so you can keep an eye on him."

"You want me to have him followed?"

"Whenever he has his briefcase with him. He keeps his computer in it. When he starts e-mailing his people, I'll know I've got another problem coming," McKenna said. "Do you know the chief of security in this hotel?"

"Yes. Retired assistant superintendent, Scotland Yard, doing quite well for himself here."

"Good, because I also need a wire on Segovia's phone."

"This security chief is not what you would call a risk-taker. We'd need a court order for that."

"Then I guess we'll have to get one."

"You realize, of course, that you would have to tacitly admit your misdeeds in front of a magistrate in order to explain your underlying basis for the wiretap order, don't you?"

"I'll do that if I have to, but aren't there some provisions in your National Emergencies Act that would allow me to avoid that?"

"If such an emergency were declared, yes, there are."

"Then you better look around. You have troops running around in battle gear, some interesting naval maneuvers offshore, imminent threat of invasion, and twenty desperate and heavily armed terrorists holed up someplace in your town. Wouldn't you call that an emergency?"

"They're at the Canon Hotel."

"Forget that, for now. Do we have an emergency here, or don't we?"

"I would say we do, but it's not my call. That would be up to the governor-general."

"Do you know him as well?"

"Slightly. Met with him when I arrived this morning, and once before that years ago."

"Then I think you should talk to him seriously, and maybe even become buddies, because if Carmen is killed here, either by accident or design, this nice little town you have here is going to be the number-one priority on your big neighbor's hit list."

It didn't take Rollins long to digest McKenna's assessment. "I understand. I'll talk to him."

"If we're going to do this by the book, we might as well get everything we can. You should also tell the governor-general that we need a wire on every phone line in every Internet café in town."

"Quite a tall order, but suppose he goes for it. If Segovia does send an e-mail, the message will be encrypted, and not much use to you."

"Wrong, if you have a computer expert available here. Do you?"

"I imagine so. Gibraltar is a major banking center, and banks use computers. What's your plan?"

"I have Esmeralda's computer with me, and it's loaded with the same encryption program Segovia's using."

"Ah, I see. If the right person is on the wiretap with her

computer, he should be able to read Segovia's message."

"That's what I'm hoping. Then I won't have to wonder what Segovia's up to, I'll know, and we'll be ready for him."

"Then let's save some time. I'll take that computer with me."

"Fine." McKenna took Esmeralda's computer from his luggage, turned it on, and explained the password procedure to Rollins. Then he got to the more important matters on his mind. "You've made progress?"

"First of all, we did very well at the border this morning," Rollins said. "Got Kilkenny coming in at eight, and the Manfreddos trying to leave an hour ago."

"Have any of them talked?"

"Not yet, and I really don't have anything to charge them with at the moment. Everything bad we know about them comes from the unsworn statements of two terrorists doing life in a Spanish prison, and a prosecutor would never draw up a complaint on that basis alone. Kilkenny's truck was clean, and the Manfreddos are saying they're just foreign citizens conducting business in Gibraltar. They're acting quite outraged, and their outrage would be understandable to an uninformed observer."

"Understandable? Why's that?"

"They were driving back to Florence to bury their daughter. Her body has been released by your medical examiner, and it's arriving there the day after tomorrow."

That could be some *quite* understandable outrage to the uninformed observer, McKenna realized. Their daughter was killed by the police, and now the police are preventing them from burying her. "How long can you hold them for without charging them with something?"

"In Kilkenny's case, for a while. The Manfreddos, a matter of hours. They've already retained a barrister, and he's about to petition for their release."

"Have you explained to them that you can't really hold them now, but that once this is over, you'll have plenty on them? After we hit the hotel and take prisoners, one of those ETA characters is going to talk and implicate them. When he does, they'll do substantial time for aiding and abetting terrorists."

"I left them with that thought."

"And did you offer them anything?"

"The usual. Reduced charges, special consideration when their cases come up for sentencing."

"Not good enough. We need everything they know right now, so I think you should offer them a free pass."

"A what?" Rollins asked.

"A free pass. Tell us everything they know, and all is forgiven."

"They wouldn't be charged with anything?"

"Not even if they pissed on the queen's statue."

"That would be quite a deal for them, considering that we don't need much from them anyway."

"Because we already know the Canon Hotel is where they're staying?"

"Precisely, and I didn't need them to find that out. It took some tedious plodding, but your information was enough to confirm that's where they are."

"Is it confirmed?"

"Not visually, but in my mind it is. Right after I learned it was the Canon Hotel that the Manfreddos owned, I called there to make reservations for two rooms for a week, beginning tonight. It's the off-season, and most of the hotels here have under fifty percent occupancy now—but the desk clerk at the Canon told me they were booked full through the week, and they weren't accepting reservations."

"What steps have you taken so far?"

"Preliminary ones. The hotel is difficult for us, located in the center of the old part of town. The local police are quietly setting up observation points in buildings around the hotel, I have a company of Royal Marines on standby in case the ETA tries to leave, and I have a squadron of SAS en route from the U.K."

"Good preliminary steps, but do you have a plan for freeing Carmen and arresting the terrorists?"

"Not yet. That's one of the things we have to talk about,

and whatever we come up with will be subject to review by the governor-general."

"In any event, there's the strong possibility that the hotel will be assaulted."

"Yes."

"And it will be a messy affair?"

"Yes. If it comes to an assault, there will be casualties. Most of them theirs, hopefully, but it will be messy."

"Then we do need Kilkenny and the Manfreddos. We need from them names, numbers, weapons, and dispositions. Who are the terrorists, how many are there, how are they armed, where are they in the hotel, and most important, where are Carmen and the ambassador being kept? Whatever the price, we need that information to properly plan an assault."

"All right, Kilkenny and the Manfreddos get their free pass if they talk," Rollins said, and McKenna could see it hurt him to say it. "That also will have to be cleared by the governor-general."

"Well, you were going to see him anyway, weren't you?"

"Yes, right now. What are your plans for the rest of the day, if you don't mind my asking?"

"I haven't been here in years, so I'm going to take a stroll around town. Might pass by the Canon Hotel while I'm at it."

"Do you have a cell phone?"

"Yes," McKenna replied. He gave him the number, and got Rollins's cell phone number in return. Rollins went to the door, opened it, and then turned to face McKenna. "Is he going with you for your jaunt around town?" he asked, nodding toward the hall.

"Who?" McKenna asked, and then it came to him. "Is DuPont out there?"

"Sitting on a chair at the end of the hall."

"Then I guess he'll be going with me."

"Is he armed?"

"Yes."

"Then please don't let him shoot anybody while he's here. I'd look quite the fool if he did."

Wouldn't that be something? From legend to fool, just because he followed my advice, McKenna couldn't help thinking. "But you'd still be a regular guy in my book."

"And what would that get me?"

"I'll be your best friend, and I'll call for you every day."

"Pardon?"

Competent, stand-up guy, but absolutely no sense of humor, McKenna decided.

McKenna had changed from his suit to a casual sports shirt and cotton slacks, and he was about to leave when Cisco called from the Plaza Amara. "It took Simon longer than he thought it would, but we're into Segovia's accounting program," Cisco announced. "We have him nailed down tight."

"The transactions aren't in code?" McKenna asked.

"Nope, it comes down to a simple checkbook. Dollar account, the universal currency. Wrote six huge checks to someone over the past year, comes to a total of four hundred twenty-five thousand dollars."

"Segovia has that kind of money?" McKenna asked.

"Had, Brian, had. Bank of Andorra account. Started with over nine hundred thousand dollars when he took it over in '99, but because of one very expensive person on his payroll and a few other incidentals, he's now down to fifty-two thousand and change."

"Would this expensive person be an informant?"

"One possibility. Another is that it's somebody in the Guardia Civil who somehow got on to Segovia, and is now blackmailing him."

"I don't know. Segovia seems too sharp a guy to let himself fall into that type of situation."

"You're forgetting one of the rules, Brian: No matter how sharp you are, there's always somebody sharper—except in my case, of course."

"Of course. The details on the checks, please?"

"Whoever he is, and whatever he's doing, this guy impresses me with the very regal name he's chosen for himself. Six checks to Augustus Sanchez—Sanchez the Lesser, I call him—for a total of four hundred twenty-five thousand. Segovia began writing him checks two years ago, but the big one was dated April first of this year—one hundred thousand even."

"Two weeks before Carmen was kidnapped. That's something to think about," McKenna noted.

"We'll think about it together."

"When are you getting here?"

"As soon as you attend to an issue that requires your attention. Lavin has arranged Carmen's helicopter for me, but my pilot tells me that he can't land in Gibraltar unless you get special permission for him."

"He can't? Why not?"

"It's that old Spanish–Brit thing over Gibraltar. Planes taking off from there can't land anywhere in Spain, and so the Brits formed their own rule: Spanish-registered planes can't land in Gibraltar."

"I'll take care of it," McKenna said. "When can I expect you?"

"Around midnight."

"Don't get too used to this lifestyle, Cisco. Remember, after this is over, we go back to being ordinary detectives again, doing ordinary things."

"True, but in an extraordinary way, as is our custom."

TWENTY-EIGHT

Gibraltar had grown at the edges, McKenna noted as he and DuPont walked around, but the old part of town was still the same—very quaint, very British, and very clean. Although the major British department stores were represented at corner locations, most of the streets were narrow, winding pedestrian malls lined on both sides with restaurants, pubs, and boutiques. Signs in shop windows proclaimed Gibraltar's tax-free status, and it seemed to McKenna that the local residents had taken advantage of the lower prices; most were well dressed, and browsing through the shops seemed to be a local pastime.

Bits of conversations McKenna overheard caused him to smile. It seemed to him that the Gibraltarians had leisurely merged two languages into one, going from British-accented English to Spanish, and then back to English, all in the same sentence. He heard many other languages as well, and most of the tourists were also well-dressed and middle class, with one exception. Gibraltar had become a Mecca for Britain's young punk-rock class, and he saw bizarre getups and hairdos that would have stood out anyplace else except in the U.K. But even those folks were well behaved, and they received barely a glance from the other people browsing the shops.

They did, however, receive frequent notice from DuPont, and he had a comment every time they passed a group. "Ah!

Here's another batch of citizens from the imperial British Empire" was one of his favorites, closely followed by, "Here's some more superior Brit culture for you."

Then, quite by accident, McKenna noticed they were passing the Canon Hotel. It was a small hotel set in the middle of the block, with shops on both sides and across the narrow street. All of the buildings were four stories tall, and McKenna glanced up at the apartment windows above the shops as they continued down the street toward the harbor. He didn't see any sign of the police observation posts in those apartments, and was glad for that.

As they crossed the next street, McKenna noticed two young men talking on the corner, and their attention was focused on two attractive teenage girls across the street who were licking ice cream cones while they window-shopped.

Something about one of the young men caught McKenna's eye. He had a knack for spotting concealed weapons that, in his younger days, had led to record numbers of arrests for illegal possession of a firearm. His gun-collar record had not been seriously threatened by any cop in the NYPD since then, despite some impressive efforts. His knack had become legend in the NYPD, although some unsuccessful contenders for the record title had since dismissed it as magic that couldn't be duplicated. Far from New York, McKenna found that knack was serving him again; both of the young men wore pullover three-button short-sleeve sports shirts, and neither man had his shirt tucked into his pants. With just that brief glance, two factors made McKenna sure that one of them had a pistol tucked into the front of his pants, covered by his shirt. What first caught his attention was the alignment of the young man's clothes; his fly should have been aligned with the three buttons on his shirt, but it wasn't because the weight of the hidden pistol tucked into the left side of his pants had pulled his fly to the left. Years of experience had taught McKenna to look next for the corresponding bulge under the man's shirt, and it was there—barely discernible, but still there. "ETA lookouts," McKenna said to DuPont as they continued down the street. "Two of them."

"I was thinking that maybe they were, but they're not much to worry about, are they?" DuPont replied casually.

"Why's that?"

"Well, here you are, that famous detective whose face is plastered all over the newspapers and the telly, the one who swore to everybody who'd listen that he was gonna get them, and you walk right past them in broad daylight without getting as much as a raised eyebrow."

"Maybe we were just lucky those girls were there to distract them," McKenna offered.

"Maybe they're just incompetent," DuPont countered.

"That still makes us lucky, doesn't it?"

"Still a maybe. If there's two on that end of the block, there has to be two we missed on the other side of the hotel."

"I didn't notice them," McKenna admitted, "but it figures they're there."

"Then let's hope they didn't notice you."

McKenna and DuPont continued walking toward the harbor, and two blocks later they found themselves at a small plaza, where they could see the police station on the other side. There was a small fountain in the middle of the plaza, along with two old cannons and two statues of military men long dead.

McKenna noticed that DuPont's eyes were misty. He tried to ignore it, but DuPont knew he had seen the tears. "There, I've gone and done it," DuPont said as he wiped his eyes with his sleeve. "Now you're probably asking yourself, What kind of tough guy is this I'm stuck with?"

"I'll admit I'm surprised, but I wasn't asking myself any such thing," McKenna said. "What is it? Carmen?"

"Yeah, Carmen, and I'm more surprised than you. That nonsense hit me when I realized we were just within a hundred feet of her."

"You don't strike me as a religious person."

"By God, I'm not. Can't afford to be, because if there's a hell, I know that's where I'm headed."

"Then for you, it's just Carmen the person?"

"That it is. She's just so, so . . ."

"Good?"

"She is that, for sure, but I was gonna say nice. Nice to everyone, no matter who—including old, hard sorts like myself who don't deserve much kindness. It's been a long two weeks for her—and for us, as well."

"So it's just that you miss her?"

"Yes, it is that, and I'll trust you to never mention this display of mine to another living soul."

"You have my promise. You hungry?"

"Famished."

"I'll meet you in that pub over there," McKenna said, indicating The Captains Table, a small place they had just passed. "What do you feel like having?"

"Am I gonna be taking another stroll past the hotel?"

"I *would* like to know for sure if there's another two lookouts on the other side, and if our passing generated any panic in them."

"Then I'll be back in ten minutes. Order me whatever you're having, but make sure I get a pint of Guinness with mine."

"Before you go, I have one request from Inspector Rollins. He asks that you don't shoot anyone while you're in town."

DuPont broke into a smile and shook his head. "Ah, that Rollins is a cagey bastard. Recognized me, did he?"

"Right away, but you have nothing to worry about from him. For some reason, he holds you in high regard."

"Then, if my name ever comes up again while you're talking to him, you might tell him the feeling is mutual. He's a smart one, and he's tough, but I've heard from some old mates of mine that he's a fair man."

DuPont left, and McKenna took a window seat in the pub. The waitress came over with the menu, but he had already decided on the special advertised on a sign over the bar; he asked for two orders of fish and chips, with the Guinness for DuPont and a Coke for himself. When she left, he turned his attention to the police station, and quickly found it was a good time to be there. It was four o'clock, changing of the tour, and a line of constables emerged from the front door with military precision.

McKenna looked around the plaza to see if anyone else was especially interested. Two more young men lounging behind the fountain in the center of the plaza were totally focused on the police station. They were too far away for McKenna to make any judgment on whether they were armed or not, but he noted that one of them had a fanny-pack strapped around his waist that was large enough to conceal a pistol.

Five minutes later, the ETA had their own change of tour. The young men behind the fountain were joined by another two, and the four of them stood talking while keeping an eye on the police station.

It was then that DuPont returned to the scene. He entered the pub, but stood in the doorway looking out, and McKenna noticed that he also was focused on the four men. Then he came over to McKenna's table and sat down. "You see we got another four outside?"

"I see them. First two being relieved by the second two."

"You have it right. Four lookouts at the hotel, and I watched their changing of the guard. They breathe, walk, and talk, but they're unconscious. Never noticed me noticing them."

"You have to admit it's good planning, though," McKenna said. "Station lookouts on both sides of the hotel, and another two at the police station to report on any signs of unusual police activity."

"Good planning, lousy execution. Did you order?"

"Fish and chips, and your Guinness."

"Excellent choice. Good Brit food and good Brit drink in a good Brit place."

"Guinness is British?"

"Old Brit family pretending they're Irish, and fooling most of the folks while they're at it. Good beer, though."

McKenna was aware that the IRA had once kidnapped the heir to the brewery fortune, but he didn't want to discuss politics with DuPont—or whoever he really was. "You gonna follow those two back to the hotel?" McKenna asked, nodding toward the fountain.

"Not all the way back. Just far enough to make sure that's where they're going."

"Okay, but be careful."

"Careful? From what I've seen of this crew, I could follow them in a bleeding ambulance with the lights and sirens on, and they'd never know I was there."

"You have to forgive them," McKenna said. "They're all new to this business."

"How new?"

"For most of them, this is their first job."

"Any training?"

"Three weeks."

"Not enough for this group. If you have to hit that hotel, they should be a pushover," DuPont predicted.

"Pushovers ready to kill, if ordered," McKenna countered.

"That's no feat. Killing's easy, and it doesn't take much in the way of brains."

Their food arrived, and conversation was put on hold for a few minutes—but McKenna did want to talk to DuPont. Since seeing the lookouts, McKenna had already formed the basis of a plan, and he decided DuPont was just the man to offer a critical analysis. "Would you like to hear how I'd hit that hotel, if I were in charge of the operation?" he asked.

"Wouldn't mind at all. Wouldn't mind knowing if you're the smart guy everyone seems to think you are," DuPont replied. "The lookouts go first?"

"Uh-huh, and it might involve a lot of killing. Catch them at their changing of the guard. That would take twelve of them out right away."

"Leaving what inside the hotel to deal with? Eight?"

"More or less."

"That's the way I'd do it," DuPont said. "And since they're pulling a lot of guard duty, some of those eight would probably be sleeping when you hit the hotel."

"Probably."

"Any ideas on exactly how you'd hit the hotel?"

"Not yet. Need more information on how they're deployed inside."

"Are you gonna get that information?"

"Hopefully."

"And does Rollins have the SAS coming in?"

"Yes."

"Then here's my piece of advice to you: Leave that part of the planning to their commander. They're damned bloody efficient when it comes to this type of thing."

McKenna decided at that moment that he would follow DuPont's advice. When it came to urban assaults, the SAS had a proven track record and plenty of experience gained in Northern Ireland. However, one thing disturbed him; he had promised Colqui and Ducho that he would attempt to free Carmen with minimum casualties to the ETA, and he had just proposed killing twelve of them right at the start of the operation. DuPont liked the plan, but McKenna hoped somebody would come up with something better.

Then two things happened in quick succession. The relieved ETA team headed back toward the hotel, so DuPont left his meal to follow them. Next, McKenna's phone rang, and he answered it. "We now officially have our state of emergency, so you have all your wiretaps approved," Rollins said. "They're being installed now."

"How about my computer person?"

"You have that too, and from a surprising source. There's a man on the SAS team who is trained for just that type of thing. Real expert. He explained to me how it's done, but I didn't understand much of it. It has to do with servers and other Internet components, but what it comes to is that we'll have Segovia under control."

"Excellent. Is your whole SAS team in?"

"In town, and ready to go. Their commander is anxious to get a planning session scheduled."

"We need more information before we do that."

"And we should have it. The governor-general has also authorized your free pass for Kilkenny and the Manfreddos, and I'm about to talk to them. Would you like to be here for that?"

"Where's *here?*"

"I'm at the police station. John Mackintosh Square."

Directly across from where I'm sitting, and I didn't see him go in, McKenna thought. "Did you go in by the back door?" he asked.

"Had to. The ETA has lookouts stationed on the square. Damned inconvenient, had to tell our constables to pay no mind to the two terrorists watching them come in and out."

So the local police observers hidden around the hotel are on their toes, and they've been doing a good job, McKenna thought. They saw the lookouts leave the hotel, and followed them to the square. They're so good, in fact, that we never saw *them.* "So I guess you also know about the lookouts the ETA has posted around the hotel?"

"And the one they have on the hotel's roof as well. Also know that you and DuPont are sitting in The Captains Table. They tell me that the fish and chips are excellent there, if you haven't ordered yet."

"Then you can tell your people they're right. We have ordered, and the fish and chips *are* excellent," McKenna was happy to say, but then a disturbing thought hit him. "When you brought Kilkenny and the Manfreddos in, was it by the back door?"

"Fortunately, yes. The cells are in the back, and that's where all prisoners are brought in."

"So we got a lucky break," McKenna said. "The ETA still doesn't know we have them."

"Yes, we were lucky. Would you like to be here when I talk to Kilkenny and the Manfreddos?"

"No, you're on your own with that one. My presence would just complicate matters with the Manfreddos. I'll leave it to you to get everything they know, and then we'll schedule our planning meeting."

"Would nine o'clock at the hotel be all right?"

"Love your confidence. Nine will be fine."

"Good, and since the governor-general might be in attendance, we should make it a civilized affair," Rollins said. "The hotel has an excellent conference room, and I'll arrange that we'll be able to order dinner from there. The Rock Hotel's restaurant is really top shelf."

"I like your way of conducting meetings, and I'd like to have Segovia there as well."

"Dangerous game you're playing, but it's your call."

McKenna was glad he had already cleared the Segovia invitation with Rollins, because he and DuPont ran into Segovia an hour later. He was in the center of town, getting out of one of the tour operator's vans with a map under his arm when McKenna spotted him. What he didn't spot with a casual look around was the Gibraltar police surveillance team assigned to follow Segovia, but he assumed they were there.

As McKenna had come to expect, not the slightest bit of surprise registered on Segovia's face when he saw them. "How did you like the tour, Colonel?" he asked.

"Very informative. Have you ever taken it?"

"Years ago, but I have some time to kill. I think I'll do it again," McKenna said, and turned to DuPont.

"Fine by me," DuPont said. "I've never been here before, and it's never too late for an education."

"Are you free at nine?" McKenna asked Segovia.

"Yes. What do you have in mind?"

"A planning session."

"Attended by whom?"

"You, Inspector Rollins, the commander of the SAS unit, myself, and possibly the governor-general."

"SAS?"

"Special Air Service. British commando unit. Rescuing hostages is one of their specialties, but they've never dealt with the ETA before. I'm sure your input would be appreciated."

"And I'd be happy to give it. I take it that you believe you know where Carmen is being held?"

"In a hotel just blocks from here."

"Then I'll be there. Where is this meeting planned?"

"The Rock Hotel's conference room, and Inspector Rollins has it planned as a dinner session."

"Ah, the British," Segovia said, shaking his head. "Not black tie, I hope?"

Is that possible? McKenna wondered. If the governor-general is going to be there, that just might be what Rollins had in mind. "If it is, we can both hate Rollins."

Segovia had been right, McKenna and DuPont agreed. The tour certainly had been informative, and their guide had been excellent. The tour of the city had been a history lesson, with a geology and zoology lesson thrown in when they toured the Rock itself. The baboons who inhabited the upper reaches of the Rock—except for man, the last of Europe's great apes—were friendly, and the tour guide knew them all by name. One of them had even ridden in the van with them as they drove from the Sergeant-Major's Cave to St. Michael's Cave.

It was during the cave tours that McKenna decided the adage "As steady as the Rock of Gibraltar" might be overstating the steadfastness of the mountain. Gibraltar was composed largely of limestone, and it was riddled with caves, both man-made and natural. The British had dug many caves into the mountain during the past three hundred years, and these had served them primarily as platforms for artillery emplacements and ammunition storage warehouses. The tunnel network connecting the guns was extensive—but nothing compared to the natural caves. St. Michael's Cave was the largest of these, with sections so wide and high that they had been used as churches in the early Christian era. The cave was also deep, so deep that the Romans had considered it bottomless. The Arabs who had conquered Gibraltar in 711 had another theory about the cave; according to their legends, the cave continued under the Strait of Gibraltar all the way to Morocco.

There were other tunnels running through the base of the mountain, part of a British engineering marvel. These had been constructed in 1980, when Spain had cut off Gibraltar's water supply. British engineers had constructed a reservoir on the Mediterranean side of the mountain, with water tunnels leading through the mountain to the city on the other side.

The result was that, according to the tour guide, the Rock of Gibraltar was really just a hollow shell, and McKenna was inclined to agree.

TWENTY-NINE

After the tour, McKenna and DuPont returned to the hotel. McKenna showered and changed into his best suit, but he still had two hours before the meeting. He decided to spend the time getting to know his enemies better. Since Raoul Marey was Comandante Segundo, and Ignacio Uranga was Comandante Tercero—the leaders of the ETA teams holding Carmen and the ambassador—he took their Guardia Civil files from his briefcase and began studying them.

First was Raoul Marey's, and McKenna spent some time staring at Raoul's photo, trying to get a feel for the man. It was a French prison photo taken in 1988, and it showed him standing as he glared back at the camera. If McKenna had to categorize in one word the expression on Marey's face, he would opt for *determined*. It was the face of a tough guy, McKenna decided, with a body to match. He was wiry, and there wasn't any flab visible on his five-foot-ten frame.

Then it was on to Ignacio Uranga's file, and McKenna was reminded that Uranga had led an interesting but violent life. He had spent thirteen of his forty-two years in Spanish and French prisons, and was currently wanted by the French as a result of his escapade a few years before. Uranga had been in a car with two other men crossing the border from France into Spain at Hendaye when the documents of one of Uranga's companions were found suspect by the gendarmes. The men were ordered out of the car, and at that point Uranga bolted, pulling a pistol from under his shirt as he ran across the border into Spain. Both the Guardia Civil and the gendarmes opened fire, and it was returned by Uranga. In the exchange, a gendarme, a Spanish cop, and Uranga were all hit. Uranga managed to make it to a car waiting on the Spanish side and he escaped, but the Spanish cop subsequently died.

There were tales of bombings, kidnappings, and murders as McKenna read through Uranga's file, and then McKenna came across an item that stopped his heart for a moment. It was on the page that listed Uranga's known aliases, and number four on the list of seven names was *Augustus Sanchez.*

What did I do? Uranga is on Segovia's payroll—his inside man on the ETA's kidnapping team—and I just told Segovia that we know where they're holding Carmen and the ambassador, McKenna thought as he struggled to bring his panic under control. What did I tell him, exactly? A hotel a few blocks from where I met him?

Then McKenna reached some conclusions that made things seem not quite so bad. First of all, he hadn't told Segovia which hotel, but that didn't matter much. The well-known Guardia Civil colonel couldn't just walk into the Canon and ask for Comandante Tercero without setting the world ablaze, and he couldn't call the hotel for the same reason. The ETA knew they were very hot in Gibraltar, and any call to the desk at the Canon would be regarded at this point with great suspicion. So Segovia knew, but he couldn't get word to Uranga, unless . . .

The panic was back as he dialed Rollins's cell phone, and it increased as the phone continued to ring. Then Rollins finally answered.

"Where's Segovia now?" McKenna asked.

"Really, old boy. I'm in the middle of interviewing Mrs. Manfreddo, but I keep getting interrupted by phone calls," Rollins replied in his most condescending tone. "Is this an emergency?"

"Yes, goddamn it. Where is he?"

"Give me a moment to excuse myself here," Rollins said

to McKenna. "So sorry for the interruption, Mrs. Manfreddo. I'll be back in a minute or two," McKenna next heard through the phone, followed by the sound of a door opening and closing. "Last report I received was thirty-five minutes ago. He was leaving the Rock Hotel."

"With his briefcase?"

"Yes," Rollins said, and McKenna's panic increased. "Where is he now?"

"I'll have to check with the surveillance team, and get back to you."

"Then I hope it's not too late. Tell them that, no matter what, he should not be permitted to send any e-mails."

"Why not?" Rollins asked calmly. "He'd just be sending the message to us."

"He would? You mean, that e-mail wouldn't go through to the person he thinks it will?" McKenna asked, and he felt his heart slowing down.

"No. The way the SAS has the wiretaps set up, as I understand it, is that any message he sends will be deflected to a server in the Barclays Bank here. From there, it goes to Esmeralda's computer for deciphering."

"Thank God! Please find out what he's doing, and then get right back to me."

"So he should be permitted to send any e-mail messages he likes?" Rollins said, and McKenna detected a patronizing tone in his voice.

"Yes, Sidney, of course. You've arranged things masterfully, and I can see now that my fears were ill-founded."

"Thank you. You'll be hearing from me shortly, and I would be interested in hearing what prompted those fears."

"Just a mistake on my part," McKenna admitted. "An oversight, really."

"An oversight, is it? And no harm done?"

"No, no harm done."

"Splendid. Then it's nothing that need be mentioned again," Rollins said. "By the way, aren't you interested in hearing how I'm doing with Kilkenny and the Manfreddos?"

"Of course. How are you doing with them?"

"Very well. They responded nicely to our free pass offer, and—"

"Sorry, Sidney. I can hear this later," McKenna said, trying to sound as apologetic as he could. "Colonel Segovia first."

"As you wish," Rollins said, and ended the call.

Hurt his feelings, I know, after he's been just so splendid. I'll soothe him good later, McKenna thought, then sat down to ponder the Segovia–Uranga relationship. Within minutes, he had a theory on how it had begun; Uranga might have escaped from the border after being shot, but McKenna was willing to bet he didn't get far.

Uranga probably made it to a safe house, McKenna thought, but he wasn't safe there. Hendaye is right next to San Sebastian, and thanks to Esmeralda, Segovia knew where all the ETA safe houses in the area were. So Uranga's wounded and vulnerable, and then he's captured by Segovia's people. That's when Uranga turned, and began receiving checks from the GAL account. That last hundred-thousand-dollar check was a big payment for something, and I think I know what. It's likely that Segovia knew about all three kidnappings in advance, and he let them proceed anyway.

McKenna examined his theory from every angle and finally concluded he was right. Then he stood by the phone, waiting for it to ring, with one thought to comfort him: Sanchez the Greater had also previously read Uranga's file, and he hadn't made the connection between Uranga and his Augustus Sanchez alias, either.

McKenna was so lost in thought that when the phone finally did ring, it startled him. "He went to the only Internet café in town, the King's Internet Emporium," Rollins said. "Looks like he's on his way back to the hotel now."

"The message, please," McKenna said.

"It's addressed to BraveInside at Eurotel dot com, and it's quite curious: 'I have the rest of your money, but they know where you are. Kill her, and get out.' I would say Segovia has someone in the hotel," Rollins said.

"He does. Ignacio Uranga, Comandante Tercero."

"The leader of their Paris team?"

"Yes."

"And you had figured this out?"

"Yes. Should have figured it out earlier, but it only came to me right before I called you."

"That's the oversight you mentioned?"

"Yes, and I've learned to live with it," McKenna said, then moved on. "More important for us right now is that we have enough legally obtained evidence to arrest Segovia."

"Arrest a Guardia Civil colonel in Gibraltar?" Rollins said, shocked at the idea. "Are you mad? Even if I were to go along with it, I'd be overruled by Whitehall—and severely criticized as well."

"Even though we can prove he's the head of the GAL?"

"As bad as he is, and as good as our case might be, there's national sensibilities to be considered. The Spanish are very sensitive when it comes to us being in Gibraltar, and the arrest here of any Guardia Civil colonel by British authorities would be considered a slap in the face."

"I see. So they wouldn't want you cleaning house for them under any circumstances?"

"Absolutely not, and they also wouldn't be pleased to accept any incriminating information from us. National pride, and all that."

"But it could come from me?"

"Yes, but not while you're here. At the moment, you're one of their national darlings, and you should have been even more endearing to them after we rescued Carmen."

There was something in Rollins's voice, and quite a bit in his statement, that concerned McKenna. "You sound like that rescue might be in doubt," he observed.

"If it happens, it won't be immediate. Carmen, Marey, and an ETA soldier named Txero left the hotel early this morning with a couple of knapsacks, and they hadn't returned by the time the Manfreddos left. We know they're still in the city, so we'll get them eventually, but it appears it won't be the same Carmen we'll be returning to the Spanish."

"They've hurt her?"

"Not physically, but they've certainly changed her. Remember when the SLA kidnapped Patty Hearst in California years ago?"

McKenna shuddered, precisely because he *did* remember everything about the case of the pretty young heiress kidnapped by a crazy group of revolutionaries. Patty had been so physically and emotionally abused that she had been eventually brainwashed into joining her captors, and she later served time for helping them do a bank robbery. "Are you saying that Carmen has joined them?" he asked.

"That's the impression the Manfreddos have, and even Kilkenny is inclined to believe it. It seems to them that she comes and goes as she likes."

"She leaves the hotel?"

"She's been to mass every morning since they arrived in town. Goes by herself, and Marey only sends one of his men to follow her—usually that Txero character. When they got back this morning, Txero told Mrs. Manfreddo that Carmen had passed two of our cops on her way to church, and she made no effort to contact them. Didn't even slow down."

"And your cops didn't recognize her?"

"From what I hear, no one would recognize her, maybe not even you. She's gone punk on us, and bizarrely so."

"Punk? Do you mean punk rock?"

"Exactly what I mean. Purple-and-black hair cut short, tattoos, pierced eyebrows and nose, more earrings than Mrs. Manfreddo could count, and as many rings on her fingers as well. Fingernails and toenails painted all sorts of crazy colors, and her clothes are just as bizarre. Black pedal-pusher slacks, multi-colored blouses she wears with no bra, and those high-platformed open-toed heels."

"Did the Manfreddos and Kilkenny know who she is?"

"Kilkenny's a little sharper than the Manfreddos. He picked them all up at the Manfreddos' hotel in Jerez, and he admits not recognizing her at first. It was only when he stopped in the woods for supper and saw how most of them treated her that he realized she was Carmen."

"How do they treat her?"

"With total reverence and respect, the same way she treats them. According to Kilkenny, most of the ETA guys were tripping all over each other to make sure she was warm enough after she came out of the lorry, comfortable enough when they sat in the woods, and very anxious that the food they were cooking were things she liked."

"And her reaction to all of this?"

"Thanked them all by name at every turn, but here's the kicker. A few of them asked her to lead them in a prayer before the meal, and she suggested that it should be Marey, their real leader, who should lead them. Then she said she would be happy to join in and pray for all of them, and added that she would pray especially for their safe return to their families. That caused quite a stir, and quite a bit of dissension in the ranks."

"Don't tell me Marey refused to lead them in prayer," McKenna said. "They're terrorists, and some of them are murderers, but most Basques are devout Catholics, and the ETA has always professed an allegiance to the Church."

"That's just what Marey did, at first. Refused, and then Carmen told him she wasn't really hungry. Turns out that thirteen of his men weren't really hungry, either, and they also refused to eat. That's when Marey came to his senses, said a short prayer, and suddenly Carmen and everyone else were starved. Ate good, and then Carmen prayed silently on her knees for hours. Must have put Marey into shock when that same thirteen got down on their knees next to her, but he had learned something. Didn't say another word, even when the ambassador knelt down and joined in. He just waited until she was done praying. Then they all got up and climbed back into the lorry."

Marey had complained to Bombi that Carmen was infecting his men. I guess this is what he meant, McKenna thought. "So when was it the Manfreddos found out they had Carmen for a guest?"

"Tuesday, they said, two days after they all arrived."

"Did Marey tell them?"

"No, he didn't tell them anything. Very circumspect fellow, and very morose. According to them, he hasn't been the same since their daughter was killed, and has said barely a word to them. He's hurting, and spends most of his time by himself. Goes out by himself every morning, and everybody was pretty glad to see him go."

"Had the Manfreddos met him before?"

"Twice before, at their hostel in Jerez, just before and just after their training trip to Morocco. Bombi brought him to meet the family, and the Manfreddos could see they loved each other."

McKenna wanted to get off the Raoul–Bombi subject, and stay off it. "So how *did* the Manfreddos know it was Carmen they had in their hotel?"

"Pretty much the same way Kilkenny found out. They noticed the way everybody treated her, and the way she treated them. Then there were the prayer sessions in her room. Very well attended, until Marey discouraged them. By then the Manfreddos knew."

"How'd he discourage the prayer sessions?"

"Txero did that for him. Personable guy, this Txero, but tough enough, and he's a respected character with the rest of them. He seems to be the one Marey trusts the most, and Txero is apparently not taken with Carmen at all. Every time any of them goes anywhere near her, Txero bores them with some revolutionary rhetoric until they give up and leave."

"Where's the ambassador through all this?"

"Tied up and under guard in his room."

Rollins had given McKenna a lot to think about. "Can you come up to my room before the meeting?" he asked Rollins.

"To tell you the truth, I'm going to be quite busy. Why don't you come to my room when you're ready? Room six-twelve."

"Sure, but busy doing what?"

"Changing, of course. The governor-general will be at the

meeting, and one should be properly dressed for such an occasion."

"Don't tell me it's black tie, because I don't have a tux with me," McKenna said.

"Nor do I, so it's nothing you have to worry about."

"Then what will you be changing into?"

"My dress uniform. It might surprise you to learn that I'm a lieutenant colonel in the Welsh Guards. Honorary position, of course, but with it goes a dress code and certain responsibilities for an occasion such as this."

McKenna didn't want to hear more. "Fine, Lieutenant Colonel Rollins. Your room. See you later," he said, then hung up.

Who to call next? The Segovia matter still had to be addressed, and Rollins's fears on Carmen's behavior had to be explained. McKenna had some ideas on both issues, but at that point he wanted sound advice from someone he trusted. In this case he thought that list should be limited to Shields, Brunette, Angelita, and, though he hated to admit it, Cisco.

Cisco knew Carmen and all the dirty laundry involved in the case, but he was in Carmen's helicopter someplace over Spain at the moment, so he was out. Angelita also knew Carmen, but McKenna knew she would simply dismiss all the complications that could arise from the crimes he and Cisco had committed. In her mind, Carmen had to be rescued, no matter what it took—so Angelita was out. Then there was Shields, an old friend and the man he was technically working for on this case. Not the best choice, McKenna decided; Shields didn't know Carmen personally, and McKenna wouldn't feel comfortable telling him about everything he and Cisco had done in Spain.

So that left Brunette, McKenna's closest friend through thick and thin for over twenty years. True, Brunette also didn't know Carmen personally, but McKenna considered him the best judge of human character he had ever met. And as for the dirty laundry, McKenna was confident Brunette would see it the same way he did—serious violations of law in a foreign land, but under the circumstances, things that certainly had to be done.

McKenna called Brunette's office, and the police commissioner was in. "Haven't heard from you in a while, buddy," Brunette said. "Thought I'd have to be content to follow your progress in the press, but there's not much there, either."

"We've been busy, and we're making progress, but we've had to do some things you won't like."

"Lots of things go on that I don't like, but I've been around long enough to realize that some of them are necessary. What'd you do?"

"A burglary, freeing a murderer, and then helping her to escape."

"Are you gonna ask me to do a cover-up?"

"No. If it comes up, don't deny it, because Cisco and I will admit to it."

"And then?"

"Maybe we'll take a few slaps in the New York press."

"But not a bashing?"

"No, because it happened in Spain, and the Spanish won't be pissed at all. Besides, what we did could go a long way toward ending the war here."

"Then it's a case of no harm, no foul. Tell me about it."

McKenna did, from beginning to end, and then he waited for Brunette's comments. When they came, they were direct and to the point, starting with Esmeralda. "You *had* to let her go to get what she knows, and that's a shame. She's made for TV, and she has a long story to tell. Matter of fact, get her trial on Court TV, and you could knock *Law and Order*, *The Sopranos*, and all the soaps right off the air."

"And the end result of that trial, if it were held in the U.S.?"

"Depends where in the U.S. Acquitted in New York, sentenced to death in Texas. Big question is, What would she have gotten in Spain?"

"Participated in many murders, but I'd say just five years—if she got any time at all."

"Then it's not a big concern. On to the burglary. Had to be done under the emergency circumstances and in the hostile, uncertain environment you were operating in. Couldn't condone it here, but it happened there, and the Spanish won't mind much—as long as you get Carmen back, safe and sane, and then put Segovia down."

"Carmen first. What do you think of Rollins's theory?" McKenna asked.

"That she's gone over to the enemy? Forget what it looks like, I don't buy it. That lady has been through a lot in her life, but she's always come out as Carmen in the end. She knows who she is, she doesn't condone violence in any form, and she's not gonna change—no matter what they put her through."

"I agree, which leads us to the *why* questions. Why does she have the run of the hotel, basically unguarded? And why didn't she alert those cops she passed on the street yesterday?"

"Yeah, why? All she had to do was identify herself to them, and this thing would be eighty percent over," Brunette said. "You know her, and I don't, so give me your thoughts."

"All right. We already know about the promise she made to them when they took her: Don't shoot that cop, and she would cooperate in every way and never testify against them. Then add in the ambassador, and what do you think Marey told her?"

" 'You've got the run of the place, but if you try to escape, he dies.' We're on the same page," Brunette said. "On to Segovia?"

"Please," McKenna said.

"You've got him good, but the Brits want nothing to do with it. You're technically working for Shields now, so according to procedure, you should have him go through the State Department to turn over your evidence to the Spanish authorities. But you don't want to do that?"

"No. He'd have too many questions on how I got this evidence, questions I'd rather avoid if I could."

"It seems you've worked up quite a relationship with Ibarretxe. Do you trust him?"

"Yes."

"Then go through him to get Segovia. He's a diplomat, which means he has to be discreet and results-oriented."

It was just the solution McKenna had in mind, but he wanted to hear Brunette say it. "You'll help me smooth things with Shields when this is over?"

"Gene's a pal, remember? While him and his FBI are basking in the glory over your success, I'll whisper in his ear that there are some things he doesn't want to know about in this affair."

"And that will work?"

"He's no dope. When it comes from me, he just won't want to know," Brunette said, dismissing the issue. "When will I be reading about you again?"

"If I were you, I'd get tomorrow's papers bright and early."

THIRTY

It was tough, but McKenna managed to keep a straight face when Rollins opened the door. Rollins's dress Welsh Guards uniform consisted of sharply creased black trousers with a red stripe running down the side, a bright red short waistcoat with epaulets and many, many brass buttons, and a pillbox-type brimless hat with chin strap. Completing the picture were the rows of medals on his left breast, and, of course, the swagger stick tucked under his arm.

"Well, how do I look?" Rollins asked as he adjusted his hat to a cocky angle.

"Like you're ready to run up Bunker Hill."

"Is that good or bad?"

"Bad if you're in the front, good if you're in the back," McKenna replied.

"We won that battle, didn't we?"

"Technically. Do you always pack that uniform and bring it with you, wherever you go?"

"Only when I'm traveling to civilized locales. Been to America many times, for instance, and never saw the need to bring it with me."

"I see," McKenna said, and he decided to let Rollins have the last word on that subject. "I thought you'd like to know that you no longer have to worry about the Colonel Segovia issue."

"Say no more, because I wasn't worried. As I explained

to you, he isn't an issue with us," Rollins stated, and then had another thought on the matter. "Will he still be attending the meeting?"

"Yes."

"Rather tacky, wouldn't you say?"

"Yes, but I'd like him to feel comfortable and very much at ease."

"Of course. He's a guest, and simple courtesy demands that. If you can, though, try to position him so that he doesn't appear in too many of the photos."

"There'll be a photographer?"

"Please realize that this meeting is an important event, and it must be properly recorded."

"Okay, so the photographer's a *must*. Do you still have access to the Manfreddos?"

"Yes. Under the agreement I've worked out with them, they're being held under guard and incommunicado in this hotel until we do something about their hotel."

"They told you that Marey left every morning?"

"Yes."

"For how long?"

"Hours."

"What was his condition when he returned?"

"His condition?"

"Was he dirty, were his clothes disheveled, did he look beat? Another question would be, 'Did he carry a knapsack with him?' "

"Sorry. I never thought to ask."

"Then please do."

"Now?"

"Yes, now."

Rollins thought over McKenna's request for a moment, and then understanding dawned on him. "I see where you're headed. Interesting questions, and very careless of me not to have asked them," he said as he picked up the phone.

A minute later, Rollins had his answers. "You're right," he said to McKenna as he hung up the phone. "He returned to the hotel beat and soiled every day, with his knapsack. Marey has Carmen someplace in the caves."

"That's what I think."

"But to what purpose?"

"To keep him and her safe and hidden until his boat can pick them up off the beach."

"The beach is closed," Rollins countered. "Access totally blocked."

"Are the beaches patrolled?"

"No. Why patrol them if nobody can get to them?"

"Marey can. He's figured out a way."

"What way?" Rollins asked, but before McKenna could answer, Rollins had another question that went a long way toward answering the first. "Do the caves connect to the old reservoir tunnels?"

"I'm betting they do. Those caves are all interconnected, and what is the reservoir right next to?"

"The beaches, of course."

The governor-general, Sir David Rand, was also in a dress uniform which McKenna found almost as ridiculous as Rollins's. Rand held a colonel's position in Her Majesty's Second Highland Regiment, so his uniform included a green kilt, a bright red waistcoat with an impressive array of medals on the left breast, and a green plaid sash. The SAS commander, Major Reginald Bower; the chief of the Royal Gibraltar Police, Commissioner William Martin; and the commander of the Royal Marines detachment, Major Horace Greer, were also in dress uniforms that included bright red coats, swords, and plenty of medals. Six waiters wearing tuxedos with red bow ties and red cummerbunds stood at attention along the wall at various points around the large conference room, which contributed toward making McKenna feel as if he were a lowly extra on a set of *The Charge of the Light Brigade*.

During the course of the introductions, McKenna noticed that Rollins was referred to by everyone as *Sir* Sidney, which prompted McKenna to ask him when he had been knighted.

"Actually, I have you to thank for that, in part," Rollins replied. "Our last case together received some favorable notice, and a month later I was Sir Sidney."

Segovia was the last to arrive. He was wearing a simple brown suit, and for the first time McKenna felt a kinship with him. McKenna introduced him to Rand and Martin, and learned that the governor-general and the police chief spoke perfect Spanish. They told Segovia how simply delighted they were to be graced with his presence in Gibraltar, and for once Segovia appeared to be pleased and flattered. Then he ruined it when he told them he would be just as gracious as they were if *they* were visiting *him* in Gibraltar, which is the way, in his opinion, the political situation should be.

Segovia's undiplomatic comment on who should control Gibraltar was overlooked by Rand and Martin, and Segovia managed to restrain his patriotism when McKenna introduced him to Major Bower and Major Greer. Their comments to Segovia were polite, but reserved.

Then it was on to dinner, which infuriated McKenna when so many pressing matters were yet to be discussed. As McKenna was finishing his salad, however, he did receive a piece of news that caused him to smile. There was a nominal admission charge to enter St. Michael's Cave, and during his tour of the cave McKenna had noticed a counter on the turnstile at the entrance to the cave, and another counter on the turnstile at the exit. At his suggestion, Rollins had sent a constable to locate the cave's admission clerk. That constable had done his job, and came into the conference room to report to Rollins. Three more people had entered the cave that day than had left it, so McKenna knew he was right in his theory. Those three people were Marey, Txero, and Carmen, and they were still in the cave complex.

It was after they had all ordered their main courses that Rand finally got down to business. He asked the waiters to leave the room, and then nodded to Major Bower. The SAS commander stood up, straightened out his uniform, and cast an impassive glance around the room.

McKenna thought Bower to be an impressive figure, and obviously a weightlifter since he had the V-shaped physique usually seen only on specimens at the beach, in the gym, and hanging out in front of gay bookstores. Except for McKenna, the rest of the room remained in silence as Bower explained his plan for assaulting the hotel and freeing the ambassador. McKenna translated in a whisper for Segovia as Bower spoke.

Bower first outlined the situation at the Canon Hotel. Since pedestrian traffic on the streets died down considerably at night, the ETA had a different nighttime lookout procedure. The two lookouts constantly stationed at each end of the hotel's block would be noticed at night, so since eight o'clock they had been stationed on the roofs of the buildings at the corners. It was an easy location for them to access since every building on the block had four stories. To arrive at their posts, they simply walked across the roofs from the Canon Hotel's roof.

As for the lookouts at the police station, their routine also changed at night. Instead of remaining stationary in the square fronting the station house, they walked around the area, frequently strolling past the police station. These lookouts had a radio, and it appeared that they reported in hourly.

Bower had the plans of the Canon Hotel and all the information the Manfreddos had supplied to Rollins, so he hadn't been operating blind as he explained his plan. The interior of the Canon was laid out like a Disney World hotel. The sunlit lobby rose to a large circular skylight built into the roof, and the rooms were reached by means of a balcony that formed a circle on each floor. The front desk was in the middle of the lobby, positioned so that the desk clerk could see the door of each of the hotel's twenty rooms, and there were two guards always stationed there, one of whom played the role of desk clerk, and the other the part of bellboy. There were two AK-47s loaded and ready for immediate use behind the front desk. There was also a radio behind the desk, and it was to the guard stationed there that the lookouts at the police station reported.

The elevator and the stairway to the balconies were behind the desk. The hotel's small restaurant, bar, and lounge were all on the ground floor. The front door was kept locked, and a large NO VACANCY sign posted on it discouraged visits by tourists looking for lodging.

According to the Manfreddos, the ambassador was being kept in Room 20 on the top floor, a room that faced the street. The ambassador was handcuffed with the cuffs in front, and he was always guarded by one armed ETA soldier stationed in his room. The meals for both the ambassador and the guard were brought to them from the hotel's restaurant.

Counting Marey, there were originally nineteen ETA soldiers, but his departure with Txero left seventeen for the SAS to deal with. According to the Manfreddos, Comandante Tercero was in charge of assigning all the guard details, and his men were bored and at the point of exhaustion since each of them was assigned twelve hours of guard duty a day with no days off. The Manfreddos had indicated that morale was low among the ETA troops. The troops were not armed as they walked around the hotel and during meals taken in the restaurant, but each had a loaded AK-47 in his room. The Manfreddos had not seen any other weapons.

Then Bower outlined his plan to free the ambassador, and McKenna thought it was relatively simple—and very bloody. One thing that annoyed him was that the major used the euphemism *neutralize* for kill, and there would be much neutralizing going on before the ambassador was freed.

First to be neutralized would be the lookouts, and to inflict the maximum number of casualties, that would happen at the changing of the guard. Eight SAS snipers had already used backyard back doors to sneak into the police's observation points in the apartments opposite the hotel, and Bower proposed using them to neutralize the lookouts on the roofs opposite. To distract the lookouts while his snipers were sneaking into their rooftop positions, there would be a bright and noisy fireworks display in the harbor that would last a few minutes. The lookouts near the police station would be the responsibility of the Gibraltar police.

Bower had his assault team in position in the building next to the hotel, and they also had gained access by using the building's backyard door. Once the lookouts were neutralized, a two-man SAS team would go to the hotel's roof, rappel down to the top-floor room where the ambassador was being held, fire a stun grenade through the window, and neutralize the guard.

The remaining SAS troops would blow the hotel's front door, fire a rocket into the hotel desk, and neutralize any remaining ETA soldiers who tried to leave their rooms.

Bower estimated the assault should take under a minute, and his plan was met with murmurs of assent. McKenna, however, had participated in three such assaults during his police career, and he wasn't happy with the plan. The major then opened the floor for discussion and comment.

McKenna stood, and was acknowledged. "This plan will work, Major, but I think the number of casualties will be excessive."

"I disagree, Detective McKenna," Bower countered. "We have already evacuated most of the residents of the block through the back doors, so there shouldn't be any civilian casualties. And as it so happens, we have trained for this exact scenario, and we've practiced the assault I've just outlined in excess of one hundred times. The highest number of simulated casualties we've sustained in our training exercises was three."

"I'm not talking about your casualties, Major, I'm talking about the ETA's casualties. At the end of this assault, there probably won't be many of them left alive."

"Is that a problem?"

"For me, it is. I've already dealt with these guys in New York, and I wouldn't characterize many of them as experienced and committed terrorists. Matter of fact, for the most part, they were untrained bumblers, and we know this group is from the same lot. They're tired, their morale is low, and Carmen has affected them. If the facts were correctly presented to them, I think they'd free the ambassador and surrender."

It was apparent to McKenna that Bower didn't like his suggestion. The police chief had been translating for Segovia as McKenna spoke, and it was also apparent that Segovia didn't like it, either. "So you propose giving them notice, and then talking them out?" Bower asked.

"Yes."

"What do you estimate your chances of success would be if we went with your plan?"

"Possibly seventy-five percent."

"And the chances for success with my plan?"

"That you'll kill most of the ETA soldiers, that's almost one hundred percent certain. However, that the ambassador will survive the assault is nowhere near certain."

"Why should you care how many of those terrorists are killed?" Segovia asked.

McKenna waited until the chief had translated the question into English before he answered. "Because killing always produces hate and more killing is one consideration. Another is that, in exchange for the information that brings us to this point, I promised Colqui Guarlzadi and Ducho Herriguandi that I would try to keep ETA casualties to a minimum when we finally located the kidnappers."

"As it turns out, that was a promise you weren't authorized to make," Rand noted, and his comment was followed by approving nods from everybody except Rollins.

"I would also like to add that giving the ETA notice loses the element of surprise for us, and that would entail the risk of higher casualties on our part," Bower added, and his appraisal was followed by a chorus of more approving nods.

"You're in the business of taking risks, aren't you?" McKenna asked.

"Yes, *necessary* risks. Your plan burdens us with, in my opinion, unnecessary risks."

"On the contrary. If my plan succeeds, there will be no casualties on either side."

"The final decision will remain mine, but I suggest we put it to a vote," the governor-general said. "All in favor of Detective McKenna's plan, please raise your hand."

Only Rollins raised his hand, slowly, and then only after he had looked around the room.

"Major Bower, when would you be ready to proceed?" the governor-general asked.

"Right after dinner."

"So the decision is made?" McKenna asked.

"No, I'd like to give the matter some more thought," the governor-general replied. "I'll have a decision for you after dinner."

"Sir David, might I add that in my dealings with Detective McKenna, I've always found *him* to be a very persuasive negotiator," Rollins said. "I think he'll be able to talk them out, without casualties."

"Thank you, Sir Sidney," Rand replied. "I'll certainly take your opinion into consideration before I make my decision."

"Then let me give you some more to consider while you're eating," McKenna said. "Whenever I make a promise to anyone, I do everything in my power to keep it. Therefore, if you go with the major's efficient-but-bloodthirsty plan, you'll be reading about my opposition to it in all the American and Spanish newspapers once it's over—and I won't hold back at all. Unnecessary, premeditated, British imperialistic mass murder, I'll call it, and I think it's likely Carmen will say the same once she's freed. I'm sure you all remember the fuss the press raised after the SAS took out that IRA team here in the eighties, and that'll be nothing compared to this."

Everyone, including Rollins, greeted McKenna's threat with a look of horror, and he easily read the thought on each face: Not exactly cricket, Old Boy.

Most of the lights were out in the Canon Hotel rooms facing the police's observation point across the street. It was a nice apartment, McKenna thought. Three bedrooms, and the windows from one of the bedrooms and the living room faced the hotel. With him were Rollins, the governor-general, and their radio operator, an SAS sergeant in black battle gear.

Rollins and Rand had changed clothes, and appeared to be normal people.

Bower was with his heavily armed, black-clad team in the building next to the hotel. If reinforcements proved necessary, Major Greer had a company of Royal Marines loaded into trucks at their barracks, just minutes away. Commissioner Martin was with a police team that had under surveillance the ETA lookouts wandering around the police station. Those lookouts would be the last order of business.

From the bedroom window, McKenna couldn't see the ETA lookouts on the roofs across the street, but he knew they were there. At five minutes before midnight, he saw two young men leave the hotel and begin their walk to the police station to relieve their comrades there. The radio operator reported their departure to Bower, and the operation was put into motion.

At a signal from McKenna, Rand called the harbor master. A minute later, the sky was lit up by the fireworks and rockets set off from a ship in the harbor, and the sounds of the explosions awakened most of the ETA soldiers in the hotel. Many more lights came on in the rooms facing McKenna.

A report came over the radio that the lookouts on the roofs were watching the fireworks display. During the course of the next two minutes, the snipers reported one by one that they were in position, and had their targets acquired.

When the fireworks display ceased, McKenna picked up the apartment's phone and called the Canon Hotel's front desk. It rang for a minute, but wasn't answered. McKenna hung up, waited for another minute, and then called again. This time it was answered on the first ring. "Canon Hotel. How may I help you?" an ETA soldier said in Spanish-accented English.

"This is Detective McKenna of the New York City Police Department. Do you know who I am?" McKenna asked in Spanish.

There were a few seconds of silence before the ETA soldier answered. "Yes."

"Then listen very carefully, because all your lives depend

on it. Your hotel is surrounded by a couple of hundred heavily armed, bloodthirsty Royal Marines. If you radio your lookouts on the roof, they will be killed instantly, and thirty seconds later the rest of you will be dead. Do you understand?"

"Yes, sir."

"And you won't murder your comrades on the roof by radioing them, will you?"

"No, sir, I won't."

"Good. Now go get Comandante Tercero for me."

"Yes, sir."

More lights went on in the hotel while McKenna waited for Uranga. When he finally came on the line, he sounded businesslike and unconcerned. "You've reached Comandante Tercero, Detective McKenna. I was expecting you would call, but I didn't think it would be so soon."

Uranga's statement surprised McKenna. He resolved that he wouldn't be on the defensive for long, but his curiosity was piqued. "You'll have to explain that to me, Ignacio."

"Certainly. The recent spate of military and police activity at the border and at the harbor indicated that the British suspected we were someplace in Gibraltar. When I read that you had arrived in Spain after foiling our plans in New York, I suspected that you were behind the activity here. You see the type of personnel I'm forced to work with here."

"Your lookouts?"

"Yes. Common sense, experience, and our training manual dictate that they be assigned those duties. I also knew that if you were any good, it wouldn't take you long to spot this bunch and find out we were here."

McKenna didn't feel it necessary to explain he had a lot of help from the Manfreddos in that department. "Did Marey agree with your assessment?"

"Yes. As a matter of fact, he came up with it."

"Is that why he left with Txero and Carmen for the caves this morning?"

McKenna knew he was back on the offensive when it took a few moments for Uranga to answer. "Very good, Detective

McKenna. I can see that your reputation is well-deserved, because you've just managed to astound me—and that's a very hard thing to do."

"Then I have some even more astounding things to tell you, but that can wait until later."

"If I'm alive to speak to you later," Uranga said.

"I already know that you're a very sensible man, so I'm sure we'll have that chat."

"We'll see. Situation and terms, please."

"Your men on the roof are covered by eight very efficient SAS snipers, and they'll be the first to go. Then the SAS will be coming in from all angles with guns blazing and grenades popping. They've trained extensively for just the scenario you find yourself in, so I imagine that most of you will be dead shortly after they arrive."

"As well as many of them," Uranga countered.

"Some, maybe, but not many. The weapons they're going to use on you are quite overpowering, and they're facing only your inexperienced, unmotivated bumblers who are armed with only pistols and AK-47s."

"But the ambassador will certainly not survive this attack, so what's the point of making it?"

"You know how the British are. Anything for a good military show, and to tell you the truth, most of the troops you'll be facing are hoping that I can't talk you into surrendering."

"Then please do try and talk me into it," Uranga said.

"All right. First the terms. If you free the ambassador unharmed and surrender, tomorrow you will all be extradited to Spain. Through me, Monsieur Picard has made a deal with Colqui and Ducho, and he's agreed to get behind your suggestion that prison terms for convicted ETA members be limited to five years. He's a man of considerable influence, so I expect his backing will produce results—especially if he has Carmen at his side."

"I agree, but where does that leave us? Half of us are now wanted in France, so we'll be extradited there to do life after we do our five years in Spanish prisons."

"That issue hasn't been addressed yet," McKenna admitted, "but I promise it will be. I think that ETA prisoners in French jails is counterproductive to the peace process, so I will do everything in my power to ensure that the French are brought on board. They would also like to see an end to this war of yours, you know."

"And would it be you alone trying to make this happen?"

"No, it won't be just me. I think Carmen, Monsieur Picard, and many members of the press will be with me in those efforts. I also promise to publicly state my position at every opportunity, and I'll be getting a lot of press both here and in America once this is over."

"I see," Uranga said, and then he chuckled. "So it's possible that our three kidnappings might actually produce the results we intended?"

"Highly possible, and I have even more good news for you when we have a chance to chat under better circumstances."

"If we have that chat. We still have the ambassador, you realize, which gives us a certain bargaining power."

"What you have is a small bargaining point that many are inclined to disregard. I'd like to see the ambassador come out of this in one piece, but he's not the main reason I'm here," McKenna said, trying to sound as noncommittal and unconcerned as he could. Then he checked his watch. "It's now ten minutes after midnight. If you agree to my terms, at twelve-nineteen you will radio your lookouts to throw their guns and radios off the roof. At twelve-twenty, you will send the ambassador out, unharmed, and the rest of you will follow, unarmed and with your hands in the air."

"And if that doesn't happen?"

"Then at twelve-nineteen your lookouts will be the first to die. Most of you inside will be dead shortly thereafter, and the survivors will be spending the rest of their lives in cold and drafty British prisons, far from home and family."

"That's a very concise assessment, Detective McKenna. Maybe we *will* be talking later."

"I hope so," McKenna said, then hung up.

At McKenna's direction, the radio operator gave Major

Bower and the snipers the new timetable for death and destruction. Then McKenna sat down to wait, and he tried to appear confident and unconcerned as Rollins and Rand watched him from the window.

"What do you think your chances for success are now?" Rand asked at twelve-eighteen.

"Excellent, almost one hundred percent," McKenna said. "They'll go for it."

"I hope so, for all our sakes," Rand said. "If not, it will be a bloodbath, and Sir Sidney and myself will be severely criticized for allowing you to proceed in this fashion."

"Goes with the territory. Heavy's the head that wears the crown, Governor" was McKenna's reply, and Rand didn't appear to take it well. The radio transmission seconds later from one of the snipers, however, put a broad smile on his face. "The lookouts are getting a radio message, and they look confused" was the sniper's first report. Quickly following was the second report: "They're throwing guns and radios off the roof," which was followed by "They're standing there with their hands in the air."

McKenna stood up and joined Rand and Rollins at the window. He arrived in time to see the front door of the hotel open and the ambassador emerge, quickly followed by Uranga and his men with their hands in the air.

"Good show, Detective McKenna" was Rand's new assessment of the situation as the SAS team flooded the street to cover the ETA men.

"Really top-drawer," Rollins added. "In fact, splendid."

These guys could really bore me to death, McKenna thought, but that wasn't his reply. "Thank you, Sir David, and so nice of you to say so, Sir Sidney."

The ETA lookouts circling the police station had been jumped and easily taken by the Gibraltar police, and they were placed in the cells in time to greet their comrades when they too arrived at the police station in irons.

Then Cisco arrived at the police station. The taking of the

ETA prisoners was being reported on the local news stations, so had he learned about it from his taxi driver on the ride from the airport. However, Carmen had not been rescued, and he didn't appear satisfied. "Tell me about the mundane tasks you've managed to accomplish in my absence," he insisted.

McKenna told the story, but he didn't expect Cisco to be impressed with his achievements.

Naturally, Cisco wasn't. "Still no Carmen, but I see that all the training I've given you over the years is beginning to pay off" was his take on the matter.

"Very big of you, Cisco. You're my hero."

"As well I should be, my loyal vassal. If you manage to keep up the above-average police work, Cisco will reward you by teaching you even more."

"Please shut up now, Cisco. You're giving me one of those tough Cisco-headaches."

"Then Cisco will." And he did.

McKenna figured that the Gibraltar police station might have been built when the United States was still the Thirteen Colonies, but the interior had been renovated and was thoroughly modern.

Modern, but not civilized, McKenna thought. It annoyed him that there was no coffee available in the station house, just tea, and there wasn't a decent cup of coffee to be had anywhere in town at that hour. However, he decided to bear the inconvenience with a smile.

Rollins had obtained the Canon Hotel's phone records, and there were two calls to Torremolinos, Spain, that intrigued him and McKenna after Segovia ascertained for them that the calls were to a boat dealer there. Segovia then had cops from the Guardia Civil's Torremolinos barracks locate the dealer, wake him up at home, and interview him. It turned out that he had sold a used fifteen-meter boat to an Augustus Sanchez under curious circumstances. The entire transaction had been completed over the phone, and this Augustus Sanchez had purchased the boat, sight unseen. He had wired 6,240,000 pesetas into the dealer's account—roughly $40,000—and the special modifications ordered by Sanchez had been completed that day; the boat had been painted black, extra fuel tanks had been added to give it a range of 250 kilometers at top speed, 90 kilometers per hour, and the radar had been upgraded to provide a range of twelve nautical miles.

The dealer had also sold Sanchez a trailer for the boat, and according to the arrangement he had made with Sanchez, the boat and trailer would be picked up by Sanchez's representative in the morning.

Segovia wanted to have whoever picked up the boat arrested at the dealership, but after some effort McKenna and Rollins persuaded him to abandon that idea and return to the Rock Hotel.

Rollins and McKenna were in an interview room, waiting for Uranga to be brought in, when McKenna's cell phone rang. "Hello, Monsieur Picard," McKenna said. "Yes, we've made considerable progress. We have Señor Navarra back unharmed, and seventeen ETA prisoners."

"Casualties?"

"None."

"Very good, Detective McKenna. And Carmen?"

"Not yet. Marey and another ETA soldier have her in the caves under the mountain."

"Any indication on how she's holding up?"

"Very well. I believe that her influence on her captors was largely responsible for the fact that we were able to take them without a fight."

"I'm not surprised. She's a quiet person, but she has a powerful personality. Affects everyone she meets, and they always leave as a better person than they were before they met her," Picard said. "When will you be getting her back?"

"That depends on Marey, but I would think sometime within the next day or two. The ETA has just bought a fast boat in Torremolinos. I think Marey's still planning on a voyage to Morocco, but I don't have his timetable."

"So you don't know whether or not you'll have her back by Tuesday?"

"Hope so, but can't say for sure. But in any case, it won't be long, and the British have been totally cooperative, so can you call off your invasion?"

"I'll modify my plans. In just a few hours, the public will be informed in every church in Spain about the demonstration in La Línea on Tuesday, and it's too late to change that. However, I will guarantee that it will remain just that—a peaceful demonstration, not an invasion."

"Thank you. I'm sure that news will be well received here," McKenna said.

"You are welcome. I hope you don't think this question presumptuous of me, but why don't you just go into the caves and get her?"

"Too dangerous. First of all, those caves run for miles, and it would take a major military operation just to find three people in them. Then there's the potential for confrontation and gunfire in a confined area, and I don't want Carmen getting hit by any ricochets. And lastly, those caves run downward at a steep angle in places, and Marey would hear us coming. I don't want them running in a panic, because there's always the danger they could fall down one of the precipices. Besides, I'll have the Royal Navy at my disposal, so I'd rather just wait Marey out and catch them in the open."

"I see now that my question was presumptuous, Detective McKenna. As always, I will rely on your judgment."

Uranga was brought in, smiling confidently as the constable uncuffed him, but McKenna knew that smile wouldn't last. He waited until the constable left and Uranga was comfortably seated across from them, and then McKenna turned to Rollins. "I'm going to talk to him first about that matter that doesn't interest you or your government, and you might not want to be here for this."

"You're right," Rollins said, and he stood up. "I'll be outside. You'll call me when you get to matters that do interest me?"

"You'll be back in a few minutes."

Uranga showed some interest as he watched Rollins leave, but the confident smile remained fixed on his face.

"Are you prepared to tell us everything you know?" McKenna asked.

"I don't know if I am. Are we in negotiations?" was Uranga's smiling reply.

"A type of negotiations, I guess, but this will be very different from your deal with Colonel Segovia. You won't be paid for this information, and you'll be allowed to live if you don't care to talk."

McKenna was gratified to see the smile completely vanish from Uranga's face, and it was instantly replaced by a look of abject fear. He waited until Uranga composed himself enough to hang on his every word before he continued. "However, if you don't care to talk to me, then it will be me doing the talking—and I'll be doing quite a bit of it. I'll start by telling all your pals in the cells about how their leader betrayed them for money and to save his own skin. After that, I'll be talking to the press at length, saying some very bad things about you. By the time I stop talking, I think life will have become very interesting for you. Very dangerous, too, I imagine."

"Stop!" Uranga shouted. "Can you prove any of this?"

"To exactly which point are you referring?"

"Can you prove I've been working for the Guardia Civil?"

"Worse than that, for you. I can prove that you've been working for the GAL, and that certainly isn't going to endear you to your comrades."

"For the GAL?"

McKenna was surprised to see that Uranga looked totally confused. "You know, for a guy who's supposed to be pretty smart, you're pretty stupid," he said. "Haven't you figured out yet that Segovia is the head of the GAL?"

That revelation appeared to stun Uranga, and McKenna

let him lose himself in thought for a few minutes. "If you're right, then I guess I should have figured it out for myself when we got this far," he finally admitted.

"I am right, but you're still wrong. You should have figured it out when Segovia let your kidnappings proceed after you gave him advance notice on them."

"Maybe I should have, but I figured he didn't get the plans. I left them in a drop he arranged outside Foix, a drop we had never used before. I didn't hear from him again, and after the kidnappings were successful, I figured I had left the plans in the wrong place."

"Still wrong. He got them, and he's been using you and all your men as pawns in his sick game."

"If you say so. What are you going to do to him?"

"I'm going to nail his murderous, treacherous ass to a prison wall."

"When?"

"Not tonight, but soon."

"That's good, because he's truly an evil man. He excels at torture, and I think he really enjoys it."

Now here's a prime case of the pot calling the kettle black, McKenna thought, and then Uranga had another question. "Are you going to need me to testify against him?"

"Probably. Your answer, please."

Uranga gave the matter only a few seconds of thought before making his decision. "What do you want to know?"

"Let's stick to Segovia for a few more minutes, and then we'll get to Carmen. Did you leave all the details on all three kidnappings at that drop?"

"Total details on my Paris job, but I didn't have all the details on the New York and the Carmen jobs. Marey and Bombi were very secretive, and they knew I was totally against taking Carmen."

"What exactly did you leave him on those two jobs?"

"Just what I knew: that Carmen and the UN ambassador were to be kidnapped on Palm Sunday, the same day me and my team were going to take the Paris ambassador."

"And what did you expect Segovia would do in your case?"

"He knew where my men were staying outside Paris, so I expected they would all be arrested before the job."

"But he didn't know where *you* were staying?"

"No. I might be stupid, but not that stupid."

"We'll agree on that," McKenna said. Then he got up, went to the door, and called Rollins back into the room. As he took his seat, Rollins expressed no curiosity on how successful McKenna had been with Uranga. "Where do we go from here?" was all he said.

"For starters, Ignacio is going to tell us about his new boat, the one Marey is planning to use to take Txero and Carmen to Morocco with him," McKenna said.

A surprised look crossed Uranga's face.

"Who's picking it up at the marina tomorrow, and when and where is he picking up Marey and his passengers?"

"A Moroccan weapons dealer who we've used in the past to transport weapons here for us. He's a man who will do anything for money, and he knows the Gibraltar waters."

"What is this Moroccan's name?"

"To tell you the truth, I don't know his real name. He has so many, so we always call him Sheik. He seems to like that."

"Doesn't Sheik have his own boat?"

"Yes, but it's too big, and not fast enough. My new boat should be faster than the British patrol boats. Not much faster, but still fast enough to outrun them if we had to."

"So you were also going?"

"Sure. My money, my boat, and I had to get away from those morons I had working for me before you got us all."

"How were you going to get to the beaches? Did Marey draw you a map to get you through the caves to the reservoir tunnels?"

"No. He's found a way, and that's how he's getting there, but not me. Those caves scare me. Too dark, too damp, too deep."

"So how?"

"I'm afraid of caves, but I'm not afraid of heights. Do you know the Sergeant-Major's Cave?"

"Was just there. Not a cave really. Man-made tunnel dug by the British for artillery positions to discourage Napoleon from attacking them by land from Spain. Cuts through the rock from the Atlantic side to the Mediterranean side, about halfway up."

"Have you been to that little wooden observation platform on the Mediterranean side of the tunnel?"

"Yes. Great views," McKenna said, and then got Uranga's point. "If you look straight down, there's the reservoir."

"And if you look under the old artillery platform closest to that end of the tunnel, you'll find the two hundred meters of rope I hid there."

"So you were going to rappel down to meet Marey and your boat?"

"That was my plan."

"When were you and he planning to leave?"

"Tomorrow night, when there's no moon."

"To exactly where on the Spanish coast is your greedy Moroccan friend going to trailer the boat before he launches it?"

"That's up to him, but I'm sure it will be only a few kilometers from here. We were supposed to call him from the beach when we were ready to be picked up, and then he would come in to get us."

"Will Marey still be able to call him?"

"He should be able to. He has a cell phone, and he also has Sheik's cell phone number."

"Would he leave without you?"

"Of course he would. We're comrades, not friends."

"You don't like him?"

"He's a very hard guy to get along with. If you get to meet him, you won't like him much either."

"Why not?"

"Because he hates you, and he'll kill you if he can—even if he has to die in the process. Like I said, not a friendly man, but tough enough and brave enough."

"How do you think he's treating Carmen?"

"Not badly, but with indifference. It's very hard to be mean to Carmen, even for Marey. But you should keep this in mind: He's totally committed to the cause, and he's not afraid to die. He might kill her if he's cornered. Might kill her anyway, just to spite you."

Now there's something to worry about, McKenna thought.

THIRTY-ONE

After two days of wandering the caves, Carmen was tired, scared, and she knew that they were still lost, but she was coping reasonably well with Marey through their ordeal. The loneliness and almost total lack of conversation bothered her—Marey wouldn't talk to her, and Txero didn't have much to say—but she found enough solace in her prayers to keep her going. When she talked to God and asked for guidance, she believed it was never a one-way conversation.

She also believed that God had very recently blessed her with more physical strength and stamina than she could ever possibly possess on her own, and she was grateful to Him for those gifts. She didn't say it, but she knew the maps Marey made had been rendered useless after he had guided them through a wrong turn sometime on Saturday afternoon, even though he insisted to Txero for hours afterward that he had been right. Carmen didn't have a watch, but she knew they had climbed down for a long time before Marey finally admitted his mistake. By then, it was too late, and Marey hadn't said another word since. He just led, and they followed, sometimes for hours without stopping. There had been many dead ends, and other obstacles that had first appeared to be dead ends, but Marey kept silently pushing on. They had dug and squeezed through holes in the cave walls she would have thought a rat couldn't have passed through, and they had climbed down—and sometimes up—the many steep precipices they had encountered along the way. The going was always difficult, and frequently dangerous.

Carmen still had no idea about the purpose of the journey, but she knew it had to end soon if they were to survive. Marey had only packed enough food and water for a one-day trip, but Carmen felt some consolation in even that potential disaster. Enjoying their meager rations meant there was less to be carried in their backpacks, and each meal stop made the going easier. Also making their load lighter were the batteries, another disaster in the making. They had started out with many in their backpacks—more than enough to power their flashlights for a one-day journey through the caves—but they had been expending batteries at an alarming rate through their two-day trek. As a result, they were down to three batteries each, and Carmen's backpack was almost empty. She had asked Marey if she could put the batteries in her pocket and discard the backpack, but he, as usual, had ignored her.

Carmen didn't mind. She recognized that Marey was a suffering, misguided soul who was still hopelessly in love with his dead girlfriend, and she felt sorry for him—so sorry that she even prayed for him, asking God to help him get through his suffering and find inner peace.

Txero was also suffering, she knew, suffering because he was worried about his brother Sanko, and his plight concerned her even more than Marey's. Txero loved his younger brother dearly, and he blamed himself for enlisting Sanko in the ETA. After Sanko had been captured in New York by Brian and Cisco, she had tried to comfort Txero by telling him that her friends Brian and Cisco were good, moral men, and she was sure that Sanko would receive fair treatment at their hands. She also had told him that Sanko would be in her prayers, but Txero had remained aloof and apparently disbelieving. His conduct had been noticed by Marey, and it was Txero he assigned to pierce her ears, eyebrows, and nose for all those horrible rings Marey had insisted she wear as part of the disguise he had inflicted on her.

Carmen's flashlight had failed, and she was out of batteries. So were Txero and Marey, but their flashlights still worked; Txero's cast a strong beam, but Marey's was weak. Consequently, he had turned his off and permitted Txero to take the lead. Their rations had run out, so they were thirsty and hungry, and they had only slept hours since entering the caves—and they were still hopelessly lost. Even Marey could no longer deny that fact, because they had just come across the backpacks they had discarded hours before.

Txero then decided they had descended way too deep into the cave, and they were climbing up. Carmen was last in line, so she was following almost blindly, and then she slipped and fell. It had happened many times before, and the fall didn't surprise her, or even cause her to cry out. It was those ridiculous, high-platformed shoes Marey had forced her to wear that had made her so clumsy, she knew, but she didn't blame him. He was a smart man, and he was doing what he had to do in order to lead and survive.

Neither Txero nor Marey had heard her fall, and they hadn't stopped. Carmen could barely make out the reflection of the beam Txero's flashlight produced on the cave walls far in front of her, and she knew she had to hurry to catch up. She put her hands on the cave floor to push herself up, and she felt the moisture. She disregarded it, at first. They had been reduced to licking moisture from the limestone cave walls, but it always tasted bitter. She licked her fingers anyway, and found that this water was different. It tasted sweet, so she got down on her hands and knees and found a rivulet of water running down the cave floor. She wet her hand again and tasted it. Sweet and delicious, but not enough to quench her thirst.

She could no longer see even the reflection cast by Txero's flashlight, so the darkness was total—but she didn't care. Crawling down the cave floor, she traced the tiny stream of moisture to the wall, and suddenly her hand was in a pool that covered her wrist. "Water! Sweet water!" she screamed. "God has given us water."

Txero and Marey heard her, and it was then they realized Carmen was no longer with them. They ran back in the direction of her voice. They quickly found her, and she was waiting for them with water cupped in her hands. "God has given us water," she repeated. "Taste it."

Marey was first, and he drank all the water from Carmen's hands. "Don't worry, there's plenty more," she said, and again dipped her hands in the small pool.

Txero gave the flashlight to Marey, and he drank the water Carmen offered. "Best water I've ever tasted, Carmen. I don't know why, but God has been good to us."

"Don't thank God, you idiot," Marey growled. "If you have to thank anyone, thank Carmen. She's the one who found it."

Carmen was about to protest, but then the strong beam cast by Txero's flashlight suddenly went out in Marey's hands, casting them all into total darkness. He turned it off and on again, and then shook it, all to no avail. They remained in darkness, so Marey returned the useless flashlight to Txero, took his own from his pocket, and turned it on. The beam was weak and flickering.

"Now what do we do?" Marey asked no one in particular, but it was Carmen who answered. "We're in God's hands now."

"God's hands, is it?" Marey screamed. "God's hands? So what do we do about that?"

"I know what to do," Txero said softly.

"What? What is it we should do now, because I'm ready to listen to anything," Marey said, and he was still shouting.

"Don't you see it, because I can," Txero replied. "We should ask Carmen to pray for us."

Carmen was embarrassed by the request, but she still looked to Marey. She could barely make him out by the fading beam from his flashlight, and then he turned it off. She and Txero waited in the darkness for his decision. "All right, Carmen," Marey said softly. "If you would, please pray for us."

She would, and she did, silently praying for so long that Marey asked Txero if she had fallen asleep on her knees. She hadn't, and as she got up she again lost her footing on the slippery cave floor. She reached out in the darkness, and grabbed Txero's belt, but he wasn't ready. As he struggled to maintain his balance and keep Carmen from falling, first his pistol and then his flashlight fell from his belt to the cave floor. The pistol landed in Carmen's pool of water, but the flashlight bounced off the back of her head, and then continued bouncing far down the cave floor. When it finally hit the wall and stopped, it went on and stayed on, and the beam it produced seemed stronger and brighter to Marey and Txero than it had ever been.

"I have another suggestion," Txero whispered to Marey, awestruck.

"What?"

"I think we should let Carmen lead us out of here."

"Good thinking."

It had also been a long two days for McKenna and Cisco since the success at the Canon Hotel, and those two days had been separated by an even longer, very frustrating night. Very few things had gone right for them, and the thing that mattered most to them had gone very wrong; they had nothing to show after a night spent dug in on the beach with the SAS, ready and waiting for Marey's attempt to escape with Carmen and Txero.

That hadn't happened, and events made McKenna realize that time wasn't on his side. After the wasted night spent on the beach, Bower wanted to take his men into the caves to get Marey and Txero, and rescue Carmen. McKenna thought that proposal too risky because, if they even managed to get close to Marey, Txero, and Carmen in the labyrinth, Marey would certainly hear them coming well in advance. Desperate men do desperate things, and Marey was certainly desperate. He would have time to plan his moves as the SAS troops approached, and McKenna felt Carmen's survival would be in doubt if it came to an armed confrontation between Bower and Marey in the caves.

McKenna was very worried about Carmen, and he feared that she, Marey, and Txero were lost in the caves. If they didn't emerge in another day, starvation and dehydration became factors that would have to be taken into account. Permitting Marey and Txero to die of starvation in the caves was an acceptable consequence for the British, but one that certainly didn't apply in Carmen's case—and that meant going back to square one. The governor-general had decided that if Marey, Txero, and Carmen didn't emerge from the caves tonight, then Bower and his SAS squadron would be going in to get them.

McKenna suspected Rand's decision was prompted more by concerns for his own political future than his concerns for Carmen's safety. As expected, the cardinal's call for demonstrations in La Línea tomorrow had been announced at every mass in every Catholic church in Spain on Sunday, but the response from the Spanish and Basque peoples was even stronger than expected. The Spanish press was reporting that every hotel room within one hundred kilometers of La Línea was booked, the highways leading into the city were already backed up with traffic for thirty kilometers, and so the current press estimate was that two million Spanish and Basque men, women, and children would be demonstrating at the Gibraltar border by tomorrow afternoon. The numbers were staggering, the political situation volatile, and the governor-general was not ready to rely on Picard's private assurance to McKenna that Gibraltar would not be overrun.

Whitehall had also voiced concern over the situation to the governor-general, and he had assured the prime minister that Carmen would be rescued by noon tomorrow, no matter what.

THIRTY-TWO

It had rained heavily during their second night on the beach, so McKenna, Cisco, and Rollins were miserable in the camouflaged trapdoor foxhole the SAS had dug for them near the water's edge, fifty feet from the old reservoir's pump house. Despite the foxhole's wooden cover with the sand and the plastic bush attached to the top, the rain had flooded in and they were standing in water past their ankles.

Besides being uncomfortable, they were also worried and discouraged. They had all the logistical support they needed for success if Marey, Txero, and Carmen emerged from either of the three abandoned tunnels behind their foxhole, but it looked to be another wasted, unsuccessful night, despite the support.

In the Mediterranean twenty miles offshore was the HMS *Exeter*, a British guided-missile destroyer. The captain was steaming a circular course that kept his ship out of range of Sheik's radar, but the *Exeter*'s radar was much more sophisticated than that. According to the captain, his radar could pinpoint a beach ball floating on the surface twenty miles from his ship, so he would certainly know the moment Sheik launched Uranga's boat from the Spanish shore.

And the *Exeter* wasn't the only assistance being provided by the Royal Navy. Two fast and armed Island Class Patrol

Vessels, the HMS *Jersey* and the HMS *Guernsey*, were at
their docks in the British naval base on the Atlantic side of
Gibraltar, with their engines idling and their crews on board
and ready. The massive obstruction provided by the Rock of
Gibraltar would also prevent Sheik's radar from picking out
those vessels until they rounded the point of Gibraltar at full
throttle, and by then it would be too late for him.

There was also sufficient support at ground level, and it
was well hidden. Gibraltar's beaches ran for two miles along
the Mediterranean side of the rock, and most of that area was
covered by three companies of entrenched Royal Marines.
The critical stretch, Old Reservoir Beach, was covered by
Bower and his heavily armed forty-man SAS squadron. Two
ten-man squads covered the old tunnel entrances, and two
covered the beach. All the SAS men were equipped with
night-vision goggles.

Since the British had built three desalinization plants on
Gibraltar to provide for the city's water needs, they had allowed the reservoir to dry up. Bower and his radio operator
were in the middle of the reservoir, centrally located between
his four squads. Like McKenna, Cisco, and Rollins, all the
SAS men were also in trapdoor foxholes so skillfully dug
and camouflaged that McKenna could not see even a sign of
the troops once they had silently deployed just after dusk at
the beginning of the evening.

Lighting had also been provided by the British. The Rock
of Gibraltar was a spectacular sight and a source of pride to
the British, so they intended that passing ships of all nations
could always properly see it, day or night. Twelve powerful
searchlights at the base normally illuminated the Mediterranean face of the Rock, but this night only six were used. The
other six were off, but they were manned by Royal Marines,
and their beams had been readjusted to light up Old Reservoir Beach on Bower's command.

Communications were also Bower's province. Each of his
troops had radios mounted in their helmets, and the Royal
Navy vessels involved were tuned to his frequency. Rollins
also had a radio-equipped helmet, and he had been gracious

enough to have Bower provide Cisco and McKenna with the same. There weren't enough night-vision goggles to go around, so Rollins, McKenna, and Cisco had to do without.

Rollins had also been gracious enough to politely reiterate to McKenna and Cisco that their role was confined to being interested observers. McKenna didn't mention it, but under the protocol mandated by the governor-general, Rollins himself wasn't much more than an interested observer. It was to be a military operation, with Bower in charge. Only when Marey, Txero, and Sheik were disarmed would it become a police operation, and only then would command pass to Rollins.

At four-thirty Bower was convinced the night would end without success. He radioed his squad commanders and ordered them to have every other man redeploy to the St. Michael's Cave entrance and relax there.

McKenna knew what that order meant. The SAS was going into the cave at dawn, and Bower wanted at least half his men to be rested, however slightly, when they entered. The cave entrance was on the other side of the Rock and halfway up it, so Bower's men had a distance to go. McKenna lifted the cover of his trapdoor to watch them leave, but it was so dark, and they were so skillful and so stealthy that he wasn't sure if he had seen any of them leave their foxholes. Ten minutes later the squad commanders reported to Bower that his orders had been carried out, and it was only then that McKenna realized he had missed the show.

At four fifty-five there was a hint of sunlight on the horizon over the Mediterranean when a message from the captain of the HMS *Exeter* came over the radio, a message that snapped McKenna out of the depression that had been slowly engulfing him for hours. A small boat had put out from the Spanish shore three miles from Gibraltar, and it was headed for the Rock, hugging the beach.

"Speed?" Bower radioed the captain.

"Fifty-one knots," the captain radioed back.

"Can you estimate the length?"

"I don't have to estimate, Major," the captain said. "The

boat approaching your position is forty-six feet long."

Definitely Sheik, McKenna thought, which means Marey just called him—which also means that Marey and Carmen are very close to us right now.

Cisco also realized it. He lifted the trapdoor a few inches and peered toward the tunnel entrances.

"Can you hear the boat yet?" McKenna asked him.

"No. I hear wind, but in this foxhole with this helmet on, I won't hear it until it's almost on top of us."

Next came a transmission from Bower to his men that chilled McKenna. "Target boat will be arriving in less than three minutes. Lock and load, but fire only on my command."

Bower next ordered the skippers of the *Jersey* and the *Guernsey* to set out. They replied that they already had, and would be rounding the point and coming into view in five minutes.

McKenna took off his helmet and lifted the beach side of the trapdoor a few inches, straining his eyes as he searched the Mediterranean. There was some sunlight on the horizon, and he estimated dawn would come within minutes, but he still couldn't see the boat he knew was there. Then he heard the sound of an engine offshore, but seconds later it stopped. He put his helmet on in time to hear Bower's next transmission: "SAS Commander to *Exeter*. Where is that bloody boat?"

"Just offshore, about one hundred yards in front of you," the captain replied. "The tide's coming in, so he cut his engines. He's going to float in."

"Ah! Quite right, I see it now," Bower radioed back seconds later, and McKenna knew Bower was using his night-vision goggles. He also thought Bower's next transmission to be very wise. The top speed of the *Jersey* and the *Guernsey* was fifty knots, so Sheik could outrun them if his radar picked them up rounding the point. Bower had also figured that out, and he ordered the skippers to slow down. They weren't to round the point until ordered to do so by him.

It was getting a little lighter, and McKenna could finally

make out the boat. It was low and dark, maybe fifty yards offshore, and floating in. With the trapdoor raised slightly on both sides, Cisco and Rollins watched the tunnels while Mc-Kenna watched the boat drift in. The trapdoor was heavy, and McKenna's arms were beginning to hurt when the sound of three quick, muffled shots somewhere close behind him startled him. He dropped his end of the trapdoor.

"What the hell?" Rollins whispered, but by then McKenna had figured it out. There had to be pipes leading from the pump house to the tunnels, and Marey was taking no chances. He, Txero, and Carmen had crawled through the pipes, but had found the pump house locked. No problem. Marey waited until Sheik phoned him to say he was in position, and then he just shot off the lock.

"Don't see them yet, but they'll be passing right by us very soon," Cisco whispered.

Cisco was right, but Bower saw them first from his position with his night-vision goggles. "ETA targets in sight, but hold your fire. Repeat, hold your fire," he transmitted to his men. "Targets have hostage in compromising position" came next from Bower, and then Cisco dropped his end of the trapdoor. "Here they come, and Marey has Carmen around the neck with a gun to her head," he whispered to McKenna and Rollins.

"How does she look?" McKenna whispered back.

"Can't tell, but certainly different."

Then they heard footsteps above them as Marey, Txero, and Carmen passed close to their foxhole on their way to the boat.

McKenna waited a minute before lifting his end of the trapdoor, and he was quickly assisted by Rollins and Cisco. Dawn was breaking as they peered through the opening to see Marey, Txero, and Carmen enter the water. Sheikh had the boat anchored thirty yards offshore, as close as he could get without beaching it. He was standing behind the wheel, waving them on.

Marey was still taking no chances. As he slogged through

the surf with Carmen, he had her around the waist with the pistol still to her head.

Bower then radioed the patrol boat captains and ordered them into their blocking positions. They replied they would be in position in two minutes.

Then Bower radioed the order that McKenna knew would bring the affair to its climax. "Illuminate the beach," he transmitted, and the six powerful searchlights at the Rock's base came on and swung to focus on the boat and the people in the surf. Marey, Carmen, and Txero were ten feet from the boat, and Marey reacted instantly. He switched his grip on Carmen from her waist to her neck, and swung her in front of him so that she was between him and the beach. Shielded behind Carmen with his gun to her head, he waited. Txero and Sheik assessed the changed situation immediately after Marey did, and they were quick to react. Txero crouched in the water behind Marey with his pistol out, and Sheik dropped to the deck of his boat.

As the *Jersey* and the *Guernsey* rounded the point in tandem a mile away, it was ultimatum time, and Bower had a loudspeaker to deliver it from his foxhole. "Marey! You are surrounded by British forces and the Royal Navy," he announced over his loudspeaker in English. "You have no hope of escape. Release the lady, drop your weapons, and surrender."

Does Marey speak English? Possibly a poor choice of language to threaten him, McKenna thought as he watched Carmen. She was filthy, and he had to admit she looked bizarre with her short purple-and-black hair, but she appeared calm. Then McKenna saw her lips move, and he knew she was translating Bower's speech for Marey.

Marey glanced at the approaching patrol boats, now half a mile away, but he still didn't react, so Bower repeated his ultimatum, again in English.

Marey waited patiently for Bower to finish, and then he had an ultimatum of his own. "I don't care who you are or what you want," he shouted in Spanish. "If I see one single person, or if those boats reach me, I blow her brains out."

Then another wise transmission came from Bower, this time to the patrol vessels. He ordered them to cut speed to five knots, and they acknowledged. McKenna focused on the patrol boats, and saw them slow dramatically.

That wasn't good enough for Marey, and he upped the ante. "I'm counting to thirty," he shouted in Spanish. "If those boats haven't turned around by then, it's over for me—but, God help me, it's also over for this good woman, because I swear I'll kill her." Then he began counting in Spanish, slowly and loudly.

Everyone waited for the expected simple command from Bower to the patrol vessels, but Bower had something else on his mind. "Does anyone have a clear sight picture on either of the terrorists?" he transmitted.

McKenna looked to Marey, about seventy-five yards from him. He could see only inches of the man, and even less of Txero, and McKenna knew that he was closer to Marey and Txero than any of Bower's men.

"If anyone tells Bower he has a clear sight picture, he's a goddamn liar," Cisco said, and McKenna agreed.

It took another five seconds of radio silence for them to learn there were no liars among the SAS troops, and Marey had reached eleven in his slow count by then.

"He's going to do it," Cisco said. "That murdering bastard is going to kill our Carmen right before our eyes."

"I know," McKenna replied, and then turned to Rollins. "Do something, for God's sake."

"Sorry, nothing I can do, Brian," Rollins said. "I'm not in command yet."

Marey had reached sixteen, and McKenna knew he didn't have time to argue. Instead, he keyed his radio. "SAS Commander to the patrol vessels. Turn around now."

"Sorry, who's speaking?" was the reply that came seconds later, but by then Marey had reached twenty.

"Detective McKenna, New York City Police Department. Turn around now," McKenna shouted into his headset.

"Unauthorized transmission. Kindly stay off the air" was the reply. The patrol vessels continued their slow approach.

Marey had reached twenty-three. McKenna briefly considered showing himself, and offering himself to Marey in exchange for Carmen, but then he remembered Uranga's opinion: If Marey knew he was there, he would kill Carmen for spite. McKenna could think of nothing else to do, and thought it was too late for Carmen, but then Bower finally transmitted. "SAS Commander to the Patrol Vessels. Turn around now, and do it fast."

The patrol vessels responded instantly. Their skippers gunned the engines, but to turn around they had to go forward a bit.

Marey heard the engines roar, glanced in the direction of the patrol boats for a second, and kept counting. He was at twenty-seven, and McKenna decided he didn't want to see Carmen die. She appeared calm, with her eyes closed, so he also closed his eyes.

As it turned out, somebody did have a good sight picture on Marey, an infinitely better sight picture than the SAS troops could possibly have. When Marey reached twenty-nine, Txero brought his pistol up, placed the barrel at Marey's right temple, and fired.

McKenna winced at the sound of the shot, then opened his eyes in time to see Marey slide into the water with his arm still locked in a death grip around Carmen's neck. He pulled her down and under with him, but Txero was there. He threw his pistol over his shoulder, raised his hands high in the air for a second, and then reached down and disentangled Carmen from Marey. She splashed and struggled to her feet in the waist-high water, and then she embraced Txero. He wrapped his arms around her and was smiling broadly as he held her, apparently the happiest man in the world.

But not for long. McKenna, Cisco, and Rollins took off their helmets and were out of the foxhole in seconds, running for the boat. McKenna was faster, so when he reached the waterline he stopped, turned around, and waited for Cisco and Rollins. He could see SAS troops emerging from their foxholes, and they were cautiously approaching the waterline with their weapons trained on the boat. When Cisco and Rollins reached him, Rollins decided to stay on the beach and take charge. As McKenna and Cisco ran into the water, in the distance they could see that the patrol vessels had followed Bower's orders and were still headed back for the point at full throttle.

Marey's body had floated to the surface, and the tide was bringing it toward the beach. McKenna disregarded it and pushed on, but not Cisco. He stopped to give the body a shove toward shore, accompanied by an assortment of curses in the worst Spanish McKenna had ever heard.

McKenna reached Carmen first, and he stopped short. She had her back to him and was holding on to Txero and sobbing softly into his shoulder. Then Txero released her, but she still held on to him.

"I'm here, Carmen," McKenna said softly. "It's Brian, and I'm here."

For a second, McKenna thought she hadn't heard him. She let go of Txero, softly patted his arms twice, and turned to McKenna. There were tears in her eyes, but she still had a smile for him. "I knew you'd be here, Brian," she said. "I knew you'd find me." She held her arms out, and McKenna held her and rocked her like a baby. She was sobbing again, softly, and McKenna felt his own eyes misting.

By then, Cisco had arrived. "Hiya, sweetie. Good to see ya" was his greeting to Carmen, and then he grabbed Txero by the arm and pulled him through the water to the boat. Still holding on to Txero, he pulled out his gun and knocked on the side of the boat. "Get up, Sheik, and your hands better be in the air," he shouted. "Time to go to jail."

Carmen remained with her face pressed into McKenna's shoulder, but she had something to say. "Please let them go, Brian," he thought he heard her say.

"What?"

Then Carmen pulled her face from his shoulder, and looked into his eyes. "Please let them go, Brian," she repeated softly. "Txero saved my life, and he's a changed man. He shouldn't go to jail, and I promise he won't be a problem for anybody ever again."

Let them go? Can I do that? McKenna wondered as he stared down into Carmen's eyes. Then he said the only thing he could think to say to her. "Okay."

McKenna took another quick look around to take stock of the situation. Sheik was standing in the boat with his hands in the air. Cisco was still standing at the side of the boat, and still holding Txero as he covered Sheik with his pistol. Then Cisco turned to McKenna with a quizzical expression on his face. "What's going on?"

"We're letting them go," McKenna replied, still holding on to Carmen.

"We are?"

"Yes."

Cisco smiled, shook his head, and then turned to Txero. "You heard the man," he said. "Looks like you're going to Morocco after all. Get in the boat." Next he turned his attention to Sheik. "What are you doing just standing there like a dope?" he asked. "Pull up your anchor, and get out of here."

Both Txero and Sheik responded at once to Cisco's orders. The Sheik ran to the front of his boat, and Txero jumped up from the water and shimmied onto the railing. Cisco picked up his legs and pushed him over the side and onto the deck as Sheik began pulling up the anchor.

McKenna noticed that someone had finally given the patrol vessels the word. They had turned around and were heading back at full throttle. Then he heard from Rollins, by loudspeaker. "McKenna, what's going on out there?"

McKenna let go of Carmen and turned to the beach. There were twenty very competent SAS troops there, lined up in battle formation with their weapons trained on the boat. There were also Bower and Rollins, but Rollins had taken Bower's loudspeaker, so McKenna knew Rollins had also assumed command. "They're leaving," McKenna shouted, cupping his hands around his mouth.

"They're *what?*"

"Carmen thinks we should let them go, and now so do I. We don't need any more ETA prisoners."

McKenna watched Rollins think that one over, but knew what his decision would be. Under the circumstances, the British government wouldn't want to displease Carmen in any way, and they hadn't wanted any ETA prisoners in the first place. Then Rollins said something to Bower, and Bower complied with his order. "Stand down," he shouted to his troops, and they lowered their weapons.

THIRTY-THREE

McKenna and Cisco had made plans for Segovia, and they had expected him to check out the next day, but he didn't. Instead, he had remained in his room all day for the third day in a row, and McKenna had learned from the hotel's security chief that it had been a day like the others. Segovia ordered all his meals from room service, and a bottle of Scotch daily.

According to Cisco, Segovia was still in town because, after Esmeralda failed to report in, he suspected the fate in store for him. He knew he would be arrested, and he had decided to enjoy a few days in this mink-lined prison before heading to that harsher environment Spain had planned for him. McKenna agreed that Segovia suspected his game was up because he had abandoned his cautious Internet café strategy to receive his messages. Instead, he plugged his computer into the telephone jack in his room and checked for messages five or six times a day. Since the wiretap on his room was still in effect, they knew Segovia had neither received nor transmitted any e-mail messages, and that's where McKenna disagreed with Cisco.

Despite the daily Scotch orders, McKenna felt Segovia wasn't enjoying his last free days at all. He thought Segovia feared prison and exposure so much that he was worrying himself out of his mind, and he wondered if Segovia might even be contemplating suicide.

If that were the case, Cisco didn't think it was such a bad idea. It was his opinion that Segovia's public trial would further polarize Spain and create even more hatred.

McKenna didn't mind the delay, because he had put the time to good use. Picard had been apprehensive about telling Carmen all the steps he had taken to gain her freedom, and he wanted McKenna there for moral support when he did. They spoon-fed her the story a piece at a time, taking a break whenever a point came up that upset her. However, a few aspects of the account actually pleased her, particularly the proposal to relocate the ETA prisoners and their families to the Canary Islands. She strongly believed the families of the prisoners had suffered enough through the years, and she wanted the best housing and the best schools money could buy for them in the Canary Islands, along with ample job opportunities—and she was eager to make it happen.

Still, Picard told McKenna, Carmen was annoyed with him as a result of some of his actions, but McKenna thought he was overstating the case. He saw not the slightest difference in her attitude toward Picard, and he knew she loved that loyal, crafty old man, and would rely on his judgment always. If she were indeed displeased with him in any way, she would get over it.

McKenna and Cisco were having breakfast in the hotel's restaurant at 10 A.M. the next day when the security chief came over to give them the message they had been waiting for: Segovia was finally checking out, and he had ordered a taxi. The security chief estimated he would be out in ten minutes, but the chief would delay his departure with some nonsense billing discrepancy.

Uranga had been briefed and was ready at the police station, and Ibarretxe had arranged to have the minister of the interior on twenty-four-hour standby in La Línea, so McKenna made the calls that set the plan in motion. Rollins also had a constable assigned, and five minutes later he was driving McKenna, Cisco, and Uranga to the border. There wasn't much of a line there, and they were in position on the La Línea side minutes later. McKenna, Cisco, and Uranga had a window table in a restaurant across the street from the border, and they took their seats.

A minute later a Guardia Civil car pulled up in front of the restaurant with two cops in the front and two passengers in the back. The two passengers got out, came into the restaurant, and the minister of the interior introduced Uranga to his arresting officer. "The colonel did just as you said he would," the minister then told McKenna while his detective front-cuffed Uranga. "Called the desk officer at the La Línea barracks and ordered him to have a car here to take him to the airport."

"Is that the car?" Cisco asked, nodding at the Guardia Civil car parked outside.

"Yes. I figured I might as well use them to get a ride here myself."

"Tough guys inside?"

"They'll do. They're the biggest I could get on such short notice."

"And your other units?" McKenna asked.

"In place, a block away on either side of the border. I hope you don't mind, but I also have a news crew from Channel One on the way."

McKenna had expected that move. If the minister wanted to personally supervise Segovia's arrest, why wouldn't he also want to do it in front of the cameras of the national news station? "Don't mind at all," he replied.

"Good. I'll be waiting in the car."

The minister left and got back into the rear seat of the car outside. McKenna then spent a few minutes reexamining the plan for flaws, and found none. As soon as Segovia crossed the border he would see his car waiting across the street. As he walked toward it, the backup units would race in, block his escape, and since Segovia was probably armed, they would cover the minister and the arrest team while the cameras rolled. Then, as an added touch of cruelty meant to totally demoralize Segovia, the minister would show him Uranga.

It should all make for good viewing, McKenna decided, and he planned to catch the Channel One broadcast that night.

It was another ten minutes before Segovia's taxi arrived at the border. He got out, carrying his suitcase and his briefcase. He wasn't stopped by the British border guards, and the Spanish border guards saluted him as he passed. Segovia acknowledged the salutes with a bare nod.

"He shoulda stopped to enjoy those salutes, because we just witnessed the last time anybody's ever gonna be saluting him," Cisco noted.

That was when McKenna's plan started to go awry, because Cisco had a plan of his own. Segovia had spotted the Guardia Civil car parked across the wide street, and he had just stepped off the curb when Cisco got up, ran to the door, and went outside. McKenna feared the worst and ran after him, leaving Uranga and the startled detective sitting at the table.

Segovia saw Cisco at once, and stopped. Then McKenna reached Cisco, but Segovia didn't seem to notice him. He was totally focused on Cisco as Cisco slowly took his gun from his holster. Segovia dropped his briefcase and his suitcase, then looked up and down the street and saw the Guardia Civil cars approaching from both sides. He also saw the Channel One news van following the Guardia Civil car approaching from the left.

The Guardia Civil car with the minister in the backseat was parked between Cisco and Segovia, and the minister was so focused on Segovia's actions that he hadn't yet seen Cisco.

McKenna feared a repeat of Cisco's Tannersville shooting, and he didn't want that. "Don't shoot him, Cisco," he pleaded. "Let him surrender."

"Don't worry, Brian, I know this guy. It's not in his script," Cisco replied as he trained his pistol on Segovia. "He's not gonna surrender, but I'm not gonna shoot him."

As the Guardia Civil cars screeched to a halt fifty feet on both sides of Segovia, Segovia slowly took his own pistol out and put it to his head. He stayed focused on Cisco, smiling his sardonic smile, and the cops in the minister's car exited with their guns drawn. By then, the cops in the backup units were also out of their cars, with their guns drawn and aimed at Segovia. "Colonel Segovia! Drop your gun or we'll shoot!" one of them shouted, and the command was repeated by a cop on the other side of Segovia.

"Under the circumstances, wasn't that the stupidest thing you've ever heard?" Cisco whispered to McKenna, and it was then that the minister finally saw Cisco standing next to his car. He rolled down his window to ask the big question: "Detective Sanchez, what are you doing out here?"

"Backing up your men, Señor Minister, and it's a good thing I did. I knew he was armed and dangerous, and I thought he was about to go for his gun when he saw you in the car," Cisco replied innocently, but he kept his pistol aimed at Segovia. "Did I do anything wrong?"

"I don't know yet, but please go back inside," the minister replied. "We don't want you getting hurt out here."

"Whatever you say, but I think he might kill himself. I know him, so can I have a try at talking him out of it?"

"Do you have any experience in this type of thing?"

"Plenty. I'm a trained hostage negotiator."

"All right. Give it a try," the minister replied, and McKenna dreaded that decision. McKenna knew it was true that Cisco was a trained hostage negotiator, but the only experience he had was the time he shot a bank robber holding hostages while he was negotiating with him. His skills were never called on again.

"Thank you, sir. I'll give it my best," Cisco told the minister with innocent enthusiasm in his voice. "Colonel Segovia! Please don't shoot yourself. We have Ignacio Uranga inside, and he's been saying very bad things about you," Cisco shouted. "Please give yourself a chance to refute his lies and clear your good name in open court."

Segovia heard, but he wasn't paying attention to Cisco.

His attention was on the Channel One camera crew setting up behind the Guardia Civil car.

"Oh, I get it, Colonel," Cisco yelled. "You want to say a few words to the press condemning this situation before you put down your gun and surrender. Well, there's no need to wait. The cameras are rolling, and they should have sound running soon."

Segovia glanced toward the Channel One crew. The cameraman was filming Segovia, and his soundman was behind him with a mike on a pole. "Are you able to hear me?" Segovia yelled.

"No need to shout, Colonel," the soundman replied. "We're picking you up perfectly."

Segovia then faced Cisco with his pistol still held to his head. "People of Spain! Our great nation is threatened by terrorists seeking to tear it into pieces and reduce it to a small, impoverished Third World nation. This godless collection of Marxist murderers, assassins, kidnappers, robbers, and cowardly bombers are succeeding and will ultimately prevail because our spineless politicians lack the courage necessary to deal with the threat. Our justice system has failed us, so to preserve the nation, terror must be met with righteous retribution. That is what myself and a small band of courageous patriots have tried to do. The Spanish people might now harshly judge our actions to be wrong, but I will not accept that judgment because history will prove us right. Viva España!"

"Very nice speech, Colonel, and it will be heard all over the world," Cisco shouted. "Now please put the gun down and surrender so you can explain your e-mail to Uranga."

McKenna knew what was coming next, and he braced himself. Segovia pulled the trigger, and the high-velocity 9 mm bullet passed through his skull. He had made himself into a very messy sight, and McKenna judged at once that his wake wouldn't feature an open casket.

McKenna looked at the minister. He appeared to be in shock, but he recovered quickly. He got out of the car and ran to join all the cops gathered around Segovia's body while the cameraman continued filming the scene.

"Ready to go, partner?" Cisco asked McKenna. "Our work is done here."

"Go where?"

"Back to the hotel to get our stuff, and then straight to the Gibraltar Airport. I think we should get out of this country while the getting's good."

What kind of business am I in, and who is this man I'm working with? McKenna wondered.

Cisco read his mind. "Now it's case closed, and he won't be writing his memoirs from jail to stir people up even more."

"Cisco! You just talked him into committing suicide!"

"Naw, he was ready to do it anyway. Probably been rehearsing that speech in his room for the past three days. I just showed him that the logic behind his decision was correct."

"Don't we even try to be the good guys anymore?" McKenna asked, even though he followed Cisco's logic, to a point.

"We always try, and we always succeed, but remember this, Brian: 'Good guy' is a relative term. Sometimes, to be called the good guys, you just have to be much better people than the bad guys. Not very hard in Segovia's case. Think about it."

Which is exactly what McKenna did as he stared at Segovia's body, stood there thinking for a full minute without reaching a firm judgment.

Finally, Cisco had enough. "Let's go, Sissypants, or does Cisco have to change his partner's diaper before we can get out of here?"

"Not necessary, Cisco. My diaper's still dry at the moment. Let's go."

MONDAY, JULY 14   QUEENS, NEW YORK

Gaston awoke suddenly, feeling nervous, and he automatically reached for the pistol under his pillow. Without knowing how he knew, he still knew: There was someone in the house, someone who didn't belong there. He checked the clock on the nightstand at the side of the bed. 3:06 A.M., an hour when criminals were up and about. He listened intently, trying to detect any sound. Then he heard it, a faint tapping downstairs that lasted only seconds.

Gaston placed his hand gently on his wife's back. Lela was sleeping soundly in her usual position, rolled up into a ball with her back to him and her hands clasped between her knees, breathing rhythmically. She purred at his touch, and he felt the muscles in her strong back tighten beneath the silk nightgown, then relax again.

Gaston considered waking her, but decided against it. It was man's work that had to be done. Someone foolish was trying to prey on a predator, and that wasn't allowed. He sat up, swung his feet off the edge of the bed, and stood up in one fluid motion, with his pistol extended in front of him and aimed at the bedroom door. He was wearing cotton pajamas that didn't hide his physical attributes; he was a compact, muscular man who moved slowly and gracefully. The house was dark, but he could see well enough as he silently headed for the door in his bare feet. He had grown up in the jungles of Colombia, and was used to hunting at night.

Gaston's first thought was his children, so he checked their bedrooms first. His six-year-old son, Gaston Jr., was asleep in his bed with his covers thrown off. The central air conditioning was turned on high, and Gaston thought the room too chilly. He covered his son, then checked his daughter's bedroom.

Three-year-old Alicia was also sleeping, sucking her thumb as usual. Her young nanny, Linda, was asleep in her bed across the room from Alicia's, and Gaston took a moment to admire her form under her sheet. Linda meant pretty in Spanish, and she was just that, seventeen, pretty, and always smiling, especially when he was around. A distraction, Gaston thought, especially since Lela had noticed and commented on it. Just once, but that was enough. Gaston was a man of few virtues, but marital fidelity was one of them. He considered Linda a test of that virtue, a test he wasn't sure he would always pass if she remained, so he decided just then that he would pay her a year's wages, and send her back to Colombia.

Gaston returned his attention to Alicia, and eased her thumb from her mouth. She stirred, but didn't wake up, and he smiled when she put her thumb back in. He left the bedroom, intending to take the back stairway, but something on the landing five steps down stopped him. His German shepherd, Peligra, was lying there, apparently asleep. He whistled soft and low, just once, but the dog didn't stir.

Drugged or dead, Gaston thought, and he cautiously descended to the landing. The dog didn't move as he stood over her, but her eyes were open and she was panting. He moved her head with his foot, and found what he expected. The dog had vomited, he felt the slime on his bare feet. Peligra wasn't let out at night, so her presence there told Gaston that he was right: There was an intruder.

Gaston considered going back upstairs and calling the police, but quickly rejected that idea. He didn't want inquisitive cops running around his house again, and he preferred to deal with the intruder in his own way. Once he did, the cops would have a puzzle to worry them, a tortured body found far from his house with sensitive parts missing.

There was a window at the landing, and Gaston opened it without making a sound. He felt the warm, moist night air rush in, then stuck his head out the window and looked around. The house was set on half an acre in the fashionable Malba neighborhood, and completely surrounded by a brick wall. The property was tastefully illuminated by dim lights designed to show off the house and the grounds, but security had been foremost on Gaston's mind when he had them installed. He could see both the four-foot wall in front of the house and the eight-foot wall in the rear. The electric driveway gate was closed, and nothing he could see appeared suspicious. Both the front and rear yards were crisscrossed by hidden infra-red motion detectors that should have alerted his bodyguard Carlos to the presence of any intruder. He saw no sign of Carlos outside, so he focused on the garage. It was twenty feet from his window, and the side door was slightly ajar. He couldn't be sure, but Gaston thought he saw a dim source of illumination coming from inside the garage.

Gaston opened the landing window wider, and slid out feet first. It was a fifteen-foot drop, and the ground stung his feet when he landed, but he ignored the pain as he rolled once, then sprang to his feet in a crouch with his pistol aimed at the garage door as he advanced toward it. He pressed himself flat against the garage wall, and took a quick look to his left and right. He had a better view of the front and rear yards from his new position, but still saw no sign of the intruder. Then he detected a faint odor, and knew at once what it was. Burning flesh, inside the garage. He lowered himself flat on the ground, and peered around the door jamb.

Carlos was the source of the odor. He was lying on his back on the hood of Gaston's BMW, and his shirt was the fuel for a smoldering fire that went out as Gaston watched. He strained his eyes as he searched the dark recesses of the garage. He saw no one but Carlos, but thought someone else inside might be lying in wait for him behind either the BMW or the Mercedes.

Gaston would have preferred a more cautious approach, but he didn't have the time. He stood up and entered, hugging the wall with his pistol held ready. It took him another minute to determine there was no longer a threat, and then he examined Carlos's body with anger welling up inside him. People would pay dearly for this, he promised himself.

Carlos had been more than just a trusted, faithful bodyguard, he was the closest thing to a friend Gaston had ever had. They were from the same village, and had come to the United States together to pursue Gaston's business interests.

Carlos had been killed by a single shot to his right eye, but death had not caught him by surprise. Gaston figured Carlos had begged for the bullet to end his suffering. He had also been shot in both kneecaps, his hands were handcuffed behind him, his mouth was stuffed with a roll of gauze, and he had been tortured with a blowtorch.

It was an interrogation technique Gaston knew well, because he had seen Carlos himself perform it. His face was burned, and there was nothing left of his eyebrows and mustache. That was where the flame had been applied first, Gaston figured, because that was the way Carlos used to do it. First the face, to get the victim's total attention and show him that the interrogation was to be a serious affair, and next the armpits. Carlos's shirt was burned away at both armpits, and that was probably when he had been offered a chance to talk. Carlos hadn't, and the procedure had continued, starting at his navel and working down to his groin. His shirt and pants were burned away in a straight line from his fourth button to the bottom of his fly, his flesh was charred black, and all his pubic hair had been burned away. That was when Carlos had talked, Gaston knew, because the next step in the procedure hadn't been applied to him. Carlos's shoes hadn't been burned.

Carlos was a big man, strong and tough, so even though he had been shot in both kneecaps, Gaston figured it still took two men to hold him down during that painful session. That meant two or more opponents, with at least one of them in the house. Tough odds, Gaston realized, but he would have the element of surprise on his side.

Or would he? In a near panic, Gaston rolled Carlos's body off the car, and saw at once that the situation was even worse. Carlos always wore an electronic wristband while guarding the house, and the device was keyed to the motion detectors. An LED display told him when a beam had been crossed, and which beam had picked up the motion. The wristband was gone, and Gaston realized that he had crossed a beam when he went from the house to the garage. If his opponents knew how the device operated, then they knew they had trouble brewing near or in the garage.

Carlos had told them everything they wanted to know, Gaston decided, so they knew he was there. Worse, Carlos's pistol and cell phone were also missing. The hunter had become the hunted, and he needed a little time to think in a more secure place. His opponents would know every move he made, so the alarm system meant to protect him had to be disabled before he could go back on the offensive—and he had a way to do that. A remote control device in each car activated or deactivated the alarm system, and Gaston used the one in the glove compartment of the BMW to shut the system down. He then put the remote control in the pocket of his pajamas.

Leaving the garage in a running crouch, Gaston zigzagged across his rear yard to the safety offered by a stand of pine trees planted along his west wall. He surveyed his house from the rear, and saw nothing out of place. There wasn't a light on in the house, the back door seemed to be intact, and every window he could see was closed. Then Gaston realized there would be no need to break a door or window to get in. The house locks were accessed by means of a code, and Carlos had surely given them the correct numbers to punch in.

But for what other reason did they torture Carlos? What information did Carlos have that they so desperately wanted to know? Carlos ordinarily wasn't included in the planning stages of any of Gaston's deals. Of course, Carlos had possessed enough incriminating information to send Gaston to prison for life, but Gaston was sure that whoever had tortured Carlos had nothing to do with the law. Even in Colombia the cops would never use such advanced and painful interrogation techniques.

Then who was he up against? He hadn't heard the shots that had wounded and killed Carlos, and he was sure that the sound of a shot would have awakened him instantly. They're using silenced pistols, Gaston reasoned, but how had they gotten the jump on Carlos? Carlos was like a watchdog, suspicious of everything, and alert to every sound and movement.

Then Gaston saw a flashlight shine for an instant in his dining room, and he knew what Carlos had told them. The safe was in the dining room, so carefully hidden beneath the floorboards that the police had failed to find it on the search warrant they had executed on Gaston's house—but Carlos had known where it was. The safe didn't contain much at the time, maybe four or five hundred thousand, but Gaston was sure that was what his opponents were after—and knowing their target placed them square in the bull's eye of his target.

Gaston crawled along the wall until he reached a point near the corner of the house. He was just about to dash for the house when he saw it, a pinprick of red light on the hand that held his pistol. He knew what it meant, and dropped to the ground—but not fast enough. He heard the dining room window break, and felt the sting in his hand at the same time. It took him a second to realize that he had been shot, and that he no longer held his gun. He searched the lawn in front of him, looking for it, but he couldn't see it.

His opponents showed him where it was with another pinprick of red light focused on the butt of his pistol, ten feet to Gaston's left in the pachysandras bordering the lawn. Gaston crawled for the pistol, and was just about to grab it by the barrel when another pinprick of red light focused on the offending hand. Gaston froze, staring in fascination at the two pinpricks of red light, inches apart. Then he looked up at the window, but in the darkened dining room he couldn't see anyone inside. Two of them, at least, he realized. Two men in my dining room at the window, and they're armed with laser-sighted, silenced pistols. Options?

Surrender was the only one that came to mind, and he slowly withdrew his hand. The red dot stayed on it, and Gaston was surprised to see himself get shot again. The bullet passed through his hand, and buried itself in the ground underneath. Although he was aware of the pain in both his hands, Gaston was still able to think clearly. "Don't shoot me again," he said. "I give up, and I'll give you anything you want."

There was no reply, so Gaston decided that if he was going to die, it wouldn't be while he was on his hands and knees. A painful effort pushed him up onto his elbows, then stood and waited.

Gaston finally got his reply, but it wasn't what he expected. One red dot remained on the butt of the pistol, but the other moved up Gaston's left arm until he could no longer see it—but he knew where it was because he could finally see the source of the laser beam. One of his opponents had sighted on the point directly between Gaston's eyes, and Gaston could see the laser sight mounted on top of the pistol. He raised his hands, and felt the blood running down his wrists. "Don't shoot, and I'll give you the combination for the safe," Gaston tried.

"Quiet, you idiot! If you wake up your wife and kids, I'll have to kill them, too," was the low reply from inside.

That simple statement gave Gaston a few pieces of information. One was that the man inside intended to kill him, no matter what. And, since he said *I'll* have to kill them, not *we'll* have to kill them, he was probably acting alone. But *what makes me an idiot?* The answer hit him at once. After I turned the alarm system off, Gaston realized, he turned it back on with the wrist control. He always knew where I was.

The news was all bad, but Gaston still felt a sense of relief. He would die, but his wife and kids would live. That relief ended a second later when Gaston was able to see the second laser sight on the pistol his opponent held in his other hand. Both pistols were sighted on the bridge of his nose.

Gaston involuntarily closed his eyes and waited for death to claim him. When that didn't happen, he opened his eyes again and found he could no longer see the source of the laser beam. Then he looked down: There was a red dot on each of his knees, and then his kneecaps exploded. Gaston's legs buckled, and he hit the ground hard. The pain was intense, but he didn't move and he didn't scream. He wasn't thinking clearly, but he was still trying to assess his situation when he lost consciousness.

When Gaston came to, he kept his eyes closed. He knew he was lying on his back, he knew he was handcuffed from the rear with his hands under him, and he felt the air-conditioning, so he knew he was in the house. He suddenly became aware of the pain in his hands and knees, and the pain intensified until it became almost unbearable. Gaston steeled his mind and bore the pain without moving. He then opened one eye a fraction for a second, and was momentarily blinded by the light. He realized that he was on his dining room table, and the chandelier overhead was on. A big hand slapped him across the face, hard, and he opened his eyes to face his attacker.

It was a black man who stared back at Gaston impassively. He wore rubber gloves and two shoulder holsters, with a large laser-sighted pistol in each holster. The man had almost no neck, just a head perched on top of broad shoulders. His face didn't show age, and although he was balding at the sides, Gaston couldn't tell if he was forty or sixty. There was something about the man that seemed familiar, but Gaston couldn't remember ever meeting him. "Do I know you?" he asked.

"If you were smart, you would. But you're not, so you don't," the man replied, and Gaston was struck by how deep his voice was.

"Why should I know you?" he asked.

"Because you've made yourself into my enemy, and smart men always take the time to know their enemies."

"What have I ever done to you?"

"Figure it out."

Gaston tried, but it didn't come to him. "Can you help me out with a name, at least?"

"Sure. You can call me Don."

"Don? Is that your real name?"

"Donald, actually, but Don will do."

The name meant nothing to Gaston, but Don didn't give him time to think about it. He grabbed the edge of the dining room table and lifted it, rolling Gaston off the table and onto the floor. Gaston landed hard, and broke his nose when his face hit the floor. He found himself lying next to the floorboards Don had removed to expose the safe. In order to remove the floorboards, the pegs holding the finished wood strips to the supporting cross beams underneath had been tapped down.

Don had gained that information from Carlos, and Gaston recognized his tools. Lying next to the opening in the floor was the rubber mallet and the dowel Gaston always used to gain access to the safe, along with a large duffel bag that appeared to be empty.

Don then used his foot to push Gaston's head to the opening, and Gaston could see some additional work he had done. Gaston's circular safe was embedded in the house's foundation, and Don had packed the space around the door with plastic explosives. A blasting cap with a radio detonator attached was imbedded in the explosives.

"Are you going to give me the combination, or am I going to have to blow it?" Don asked calmly, with no menace in his voice.

"You're going to have to blow it," Gaston replied.

"Fine, but do you know what's directly overhead?"

It took Gaston a confused moment to run the layout of the house through his mind, and then it came to him. "My daughter's bedroom."

"More precisely, your daughter's bed. What do you think is going to happen to the heavy door of that safe when I blow it off?"

"I don't know."

"I do. The way I have the charge rigged, that door will be propelled upward at an approximate speed of a thousand feet a second. It will go right through the ceiling above us, right through the floor upstairs, probably right through your daughter's mattress, and maybe right through her."

Gaston didn't know if that was true, but he wasn't going to take a chance. "Spin the dial right past zero twice and stop at nine. Then spin left to twenty, right to thirty-seven."

"Good decision." Don grabbed Gaston's legs, and pulled him away from the opening with ease. Then he got down on his hands and knees, bent over the safe, worked the combination, and opened the door. He reached into the deep safe and pulled out forty-three stacks of wrapped hundred-dollar bills and three computer disks.

It seemed to Gaston that the money didn't interest Don much, but he appeared elated to find the disks under the cash in the safe. "Those disks won't help you much. Everything on them is in code," Gaston commented.

"That's all right. I have the code."

"Impossible," Gaston countered. "I devised it myself, and I'm the only one who knows it."

"Liar. Jorge Rodriguez knew it," Don replied with a smile that told Gaston that he and Carlos weren't the first victims that night. Jorge was Gaston's wholesale distribution manager, and they shared the code to keep a record of transactions that included accounts of product imported and product delivered. "What are you going to do with that information?"

"Everybody that works for you or deals your stuff is going out of business the hard way."

"You're going to turn it over to the police?"

"No, that would be the easy way. I said it would be the hard way."

"You think you can kill them all?"

"Don't know, but I'm going to find out."

"Why?"

"It hasn't come to you yet?"

"No."

"Too bad, but if you love your daughter, you have a few more minutes to figure it out."

"What do you mean by that?"

"Watch." Don removed the plastic explosive, blasting cap, and detonator from around the edges of the safe, and placed it all inside. Then he opened the duffel bag, and Gaston saw that it hadn't been empty after all. It contained pounds and pounds of six-penny nails, and Don poured them into the safe on top of the explosives. He left the safe door open, then packed the money and the disks into the duffel bag.

Gaston got the plan at once. For some reason, Don was going to kill his daughter after all; the safe would serve as a cannon, and he was going to set off the charge and send the nails through his daughter's body upstairs.

Don pulled a roll of gauze from his pocket. He bent over, stuffed the gauze into Gaston's mouth, and stepped back to admire his handiwork. "I think you need a little more work," he announced. He took a switchblade from his pocket, opened it up with the push of a button, and he bent over Gaston again.

Gaston couldn't see what Don did to him, but he felt the cuts—four of them, two on each bicep. Finally satisfied, Don took the radio detonator from his pocket and showed it to Gaston. It was a small device that resembled an electronic garage door opener. "Once I'm away, I'm going to push this button and set off my bomb," he said. "You know what you have to do to give your daughter any chance for survival."

Don picked up the duffel bag and left. Gaston heard the front door open and close. In order for his daughter to survive when the bomb went off and blew all the nails toward the ceiling, a large part of the force of the explosion would have to be absorbed by a buffer. Gaston put it in place without a second thought. It was a short, painful crawl, but he ignored the pain as he used his shattered legs to push himself forward on the floor until his body completely covered the opening that contained the safe. Then he closed his eyes, and prayed for the first time in thirty years as he waited for his loud and messy death.

Maybe it was the prayer, or maybe it was just his sub-conscious working overtime, but Don's face suddenly popped into Gaston's mind, and he remembered where he had seen it before. On a TV news show, he was sure, but he couldn't remember if Don was a reporter or part of a story.

It didn't make much difference to Gaston, but Don's face was the last conscious image on his mind.

THERE'S A SECRET WAR ON
THE STREETS OF THE CITY.
ONLY A NEW YORK COP CAN WIN IT.

His claim to fame is finding the guns on the bad guys, and
Detective Second Grade Brian McKenna has just spotted
the beard carrying a piece. What he doesn't know is that
he's about to shoot his way into a war with a highly disciplined, well-armed enemy so treacherous, not even the
NYPD knows they exist.

Exiled from the bright lights of Manhattan for breaking
one too many rules, pressured by his girlfriend to quit the
job, this is McKenna's last chance to win back his reputation and make the coveted rank of Detective First Grade.
But if his moves aren't swift and right, a new breed of
criminal—who has found a leader in an exotically beautiful and ruthless woman—will own his city....

DAN MAHONEY
DETECTIVE FIRST GRADE

"First-rate...explosive...a winner."
—William Caunitz

AVAILABLE WHEREVER BOOKS ARE SOLD
FROM ST. MARTIN'S PAPERBACKS

A TERRORIST ATTACK IS AIMED AT
NEW YORK CITY, AND ONLY ONE MAN
CAN STOP IT OR DIE TRYING.

ONCE IN, NEVER OUT
Dan Mahoney

A girl missing in New York. A political bombing in Iceland. No ordinary cop would see a connection. But Detective First Grade Brian McKenna didn't earn his reputation by being ordinary. In ONCE IN, NEVER OUT, McKenna travels the globe in pursuit of his darkest foe yet: a terrorist bomber whose next target could be New York's St. Patrick's Day Parade. Along the way he finds a good friend and cunning ally in Thor Erikson, Iceland's sole homicide detective. This is a case that brings McKenna to the edge of his abilities, and puts both his detecting and survival skills to the ultimate test.

AVAILABLE WHEREVER BOOKS ARE SOLD
FROM ST. MARTIN'S PAPERBACKS